The Birth of a King

Volume One: Legends of Kinthoria

by
Deborah Marsh
and
Carol Marsh

Copyright © 2010 by Deborah Marsh and Carol Marsh

The Birth of a King
by Deborah Marsh and Carol Marsh

Printed in the United States of America

ISBN 9781615799459

All rights reserved solely by the author. The author guarantees all contents are original and do not infringe upon the legal rights of any other person or work. This is a work of fiction. Names, characters, places, and incidents are fictitious. Any resemblance to actual persons, events, or locations is entirely coincidental. No part of this book may be reproduced in any form or by any means without the permission of the author. The views expressed in this book are not necessarily those of the publisher.

www.xulonpress.com

This book is lovingly dedicated to the memories of
Gregory Dyc, our precious Daddy/Granddaddy,
who taught us by example that our only
limitations in life are self-imposed;
and
Beverlee Azalea Dyc, our Mom/Grandma,
who taught us how to love, and to treasure the living of life
by living it for others.

I would like to give a very special thank you to my mom who helped give birth to this story more than anyone else. She typed my scrawled long hand notes into the computer, and edited my descriptions to add much more flavor than I ever thought could be. She believed in me and gave me a purpose. This entire process has brought us closer to each other and to God, and I will forever be grateful for her nudging me to get this into print. I would also like to thank my dad for his many insightful suggestions and computer help throughout the years. Without his assistance, we never would have completed this story. I would like to thank my brother for giving me the basis for the main character, although he won't know that until he sees the cover of the book and reads the story.

I would also like to thank Dominic Catalano at Bowling Green State University for the creation and design of the artwork on the cover of the book. Thanks also to Amy B. for all your help with my map, and Ritney J. for putting the final cover together for me.

Auntie BJ, you did an absolutely fantastic job of editing the beginning of this book, and I thank you for your efforts in this.

I would also like to thank Cindy R. and Diana B. for their editing endeavors on this book. You both are true friends and true professionals in every sense of the word.

A special "thank you" to Xulon Press for giving people like me an outlet for publishing our stories. You guys are fantastic, and may God truly bless all of you.

The Prophecy given to Nuallain: Dragon rider
*as narrated to Bevan of Stonehaven, Ravenscraig,
Scribe to the service of Duke Diamhin Bradig MacCauley.
In the year 2358 S.M.**

*Weep for a time yet to come,
When the beauty you see before you is done away.
Events beyond the imagination of men
Will turn the earth to ash and dust.
Many thousands will perish in an agony of
Fire and pestilence and savagery.
Freedom will turn to slavery,
Gladness and hope, trust and love will be forgotten.
For the people of Kinthoria have begun once again
To put aside their love and kinship with
Their Creator, the True God.
They have put aside their acknowledgement
And adoration of Elyon.
Though they have read in Elyon's Book
The consequences of such choices in the
Histories of men, they shout,
"No! It is not true.
The Book is but tales to amuse the weak,
And to frighten children who misbehave."
They have chosen to seek once more
After the ways of darkness:
Believing that their pleasant existence
Comes from the earth and from themselves.
See…they grow more arrogant and self-adoring
With each passing generation.
From this day nine score years shall not pass before
Their descendants come under bondage to Lucia
Spurning the love which Elyon offers with
all his heart.
And so He will wait in silence once more until
They have had their fill at the
Table of the false god;*

The Birth of a King

He will wait until the scorching bile of self-delusion
Sears their souls causing them to
Cry out in sorrow for the foolishness of their pride.
He will wait, listening with a Father's heart,
To hear the words, "Come, Elyon! Forgive and rescue us.
We have abandoned you,
We have spurned your love;
We have cast aside your blessing."
When Elyon hears their cries He will shout with joy
And He will say to His people,
"Look for one who is seen, but unseen:
One who will rise like a sun
From beneath the waters.
You will know him by the healing in his hands.
You will know he has come when
The dragons acknowledge their Sanda Aran!"

*Second Millennium

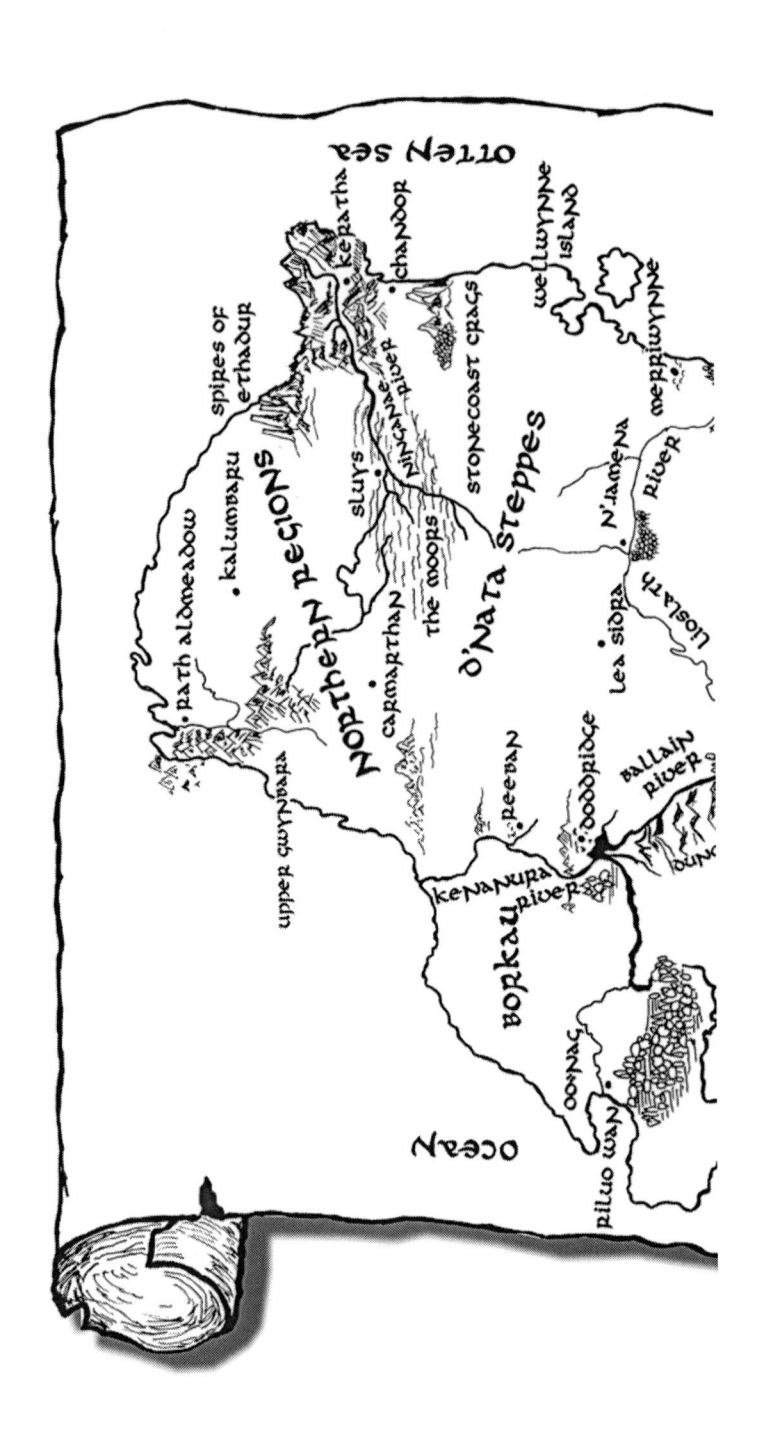

The Birth of a King

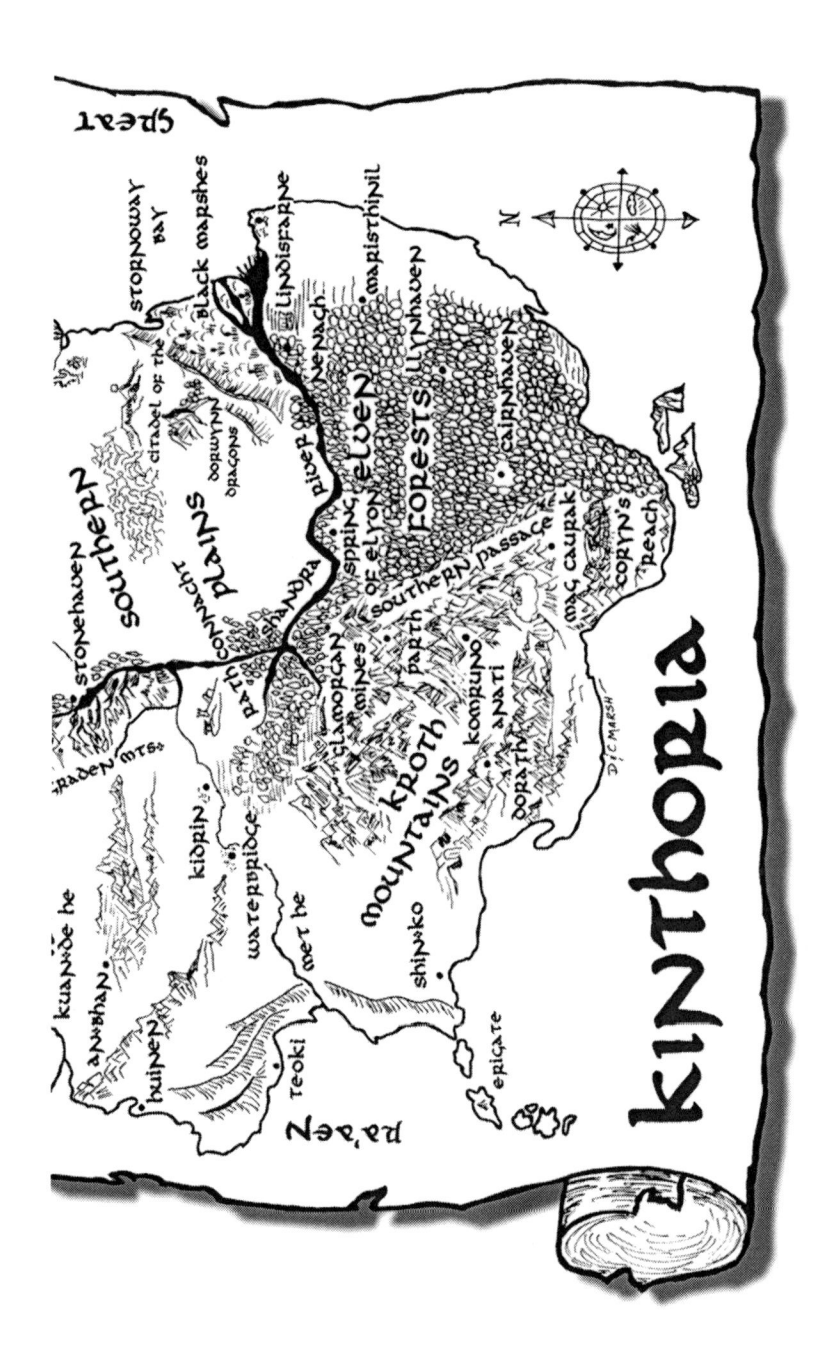

The Birth of a King

CHAPTER INDEX

1. The Scholars Hall 20
2. Eavesdropper 38
3. Dragonmasters 57
4. The Dark God 74
5. Tupper 86
6. Korthak's Tale 96
7. Choices and Consequences 102
8. Rites on the Spires of Ethadur 111
9. The Making of a Man 116
10. Doddridge 126
11. Thighern Mews 135
12. Waylaid 138
13. Dragonmaster Lies 143
14. Stonehaven 156
15. Rush to the South 166
16. Revelations 171
17. The Spring of Elyon 188
18. Chaos 209
19. Balgo 225
20. Questions and Answers 239
21. Elyon's Choice 249
22. Toll of Passage 256
23. Memories Shared 259
24. Fallen Friend 261
25. Scrying and Failing 267
26. A Healer-King 271
27. The Glamorgan Mines 281
28. Tanner's Dream 291

29. Fernaig 301
30. Prince of the An'ilden 314
31. Gifts..330
32. Rifts in Council..336
33. A Joke Reversed..340
34. Contemplation and Confrontation......................347
35. Cadan's Legacy..354
36. St. Ramsay's Abbey 374
37. Secrets Revealed 385
38. Duncan's Renewal 394
39. Fire and Ice 405
40. The Coronation 422

Chapter One

THE SCHOLARS HALL

Jaren jumped, startled by the scholar's firm hand upon his shoulder.

"Jaren, why must I always bring your attention back to my words? I do wish you would pay as much attention to your studies as you do to the out-of-doors, lad," the gray-haired Master scolded mildly.

"Yes, sir, I'm sorry, sir," Jaren murmured, flexing the arm he had been resting his head upon to stop its tingling. He stole a glance across the teaching hall and found Tanner shaking his head while coughing a chuckle behind his hand.

The scholar's voice faded once more to a distant drone in the back of Jaren's consciousness. He chanced another look out of the window. The fistfight on the street had ended, and the crowd had dispersed. He shook his head and sighed. He had witnessed many such brawls in the fifteen years since he had been brought to this hall as a toddling child.

More than seventeen years earlier the Dragonmasters began the war for the domination of Kinthoria. During the war they wrought widespread destruction throughout the land, and the oppression of their rule had since spread a heavy mantle of desperation and violence.

Produce mongers, tradesmen, and merchants inhabited the city of Reeban, located in the western half of the Northern Regions. The outlands surrounding the city were for the most part occupied by farmers whose lives were as barren and sterile as the contaminated soil from which they scratched a meager existence.

Jaren had never seen Reeban in its vigorous prime. When he had come here the havoc and ruin of two years of war had aged the once proud and prosperous city into near death. Streets that once bustled with lively activity and gaiety now heard only the laughter of very small children at play. Whispers and angry cursing had replaced shouts of friendly greeting. The majority of the population was destitute. Men and women plodded endlessly through long days of drudgery to gain the few coins necessary to keep families from starvation. Honest employment that paid a man a decent wage was scarce. Many driven by desperation, and those of dubious character dishonored themselves and their family names by becoming spies for the Dragonmasters. So it was that suspicion and cynicism passed from house to house like a dense, living shadow. Often, those whose treachery was discovered were shunned and treated with contempt by their countrymen. Some even died under "mysterious" circumstances, their lifeless bodies found in their own beds or along some deserted stretch of highway.

During the outset of the war the dragons burned most of the rich farmland and the lush, healthy crops ripening for harvest. In the following years many factions of the farming community continually feuded over the scarce fertile lands that had been left unburned and unclaimed by the Dragonmasters. Small fields of the damaged land had since been reworked for farming, restored enough by nature's healing to produce the quality of crops that in former times would have been considered fit only for livestock, but in these harsh days was sparingly shared between humans and animals.

The small Kenanura River ran around the southern outskirts of Reeban. Along its banks was stark evidence of some of the worst devastation. The rolling meadows that panned out into wide, flat plains had been a vast desert for nearly a decade; much of its rich, loamy topsoil had blown away for lack of vegetation. These meadows, considered useless after the war, had in the past few years produced a thin carpet of coarse, wild grasses, and hardy flowers. The farmers eyed them with hope for the future, but knew that they offered little help to people desperate for food in the present.

Most all of the woodlands in the Northern Region were gone, except for the occasional stand of thin, new trees.

The scholar's words broke into Jaren's thoughts once more. "It is time for midday meal. You are dismissed."

In the cookhall Jaren lowered himself to the wooden bench beside Tanner. He prepared to endure what he and his friend only half-jokingly referred to as a "your guess is as good as mine" meal. He steeled himself for the teasing he knew was coming, judging from the smug grin on Tanner's face.

"So dream boy, where were you today? Rescuing a beautiful princess in some far-off land?" Tanner teased.

Jaren's face flushed, but he did not answer his best friend. He was still musing on the brawl earlier in the morning, wondering if the desperation that prompted these basically good people to such anger would last forever. He wished for the hundredth time for help for his countrymen.

"Dols, Jaren, I was only kidding," Tanner nudged him in the ribs. "Besides, you probably know more about those star constellations than old Barnstable ever did, and he knows it. I almost fell asleep in there myself," he whispered.

Jaren finally looked up at his friend, a resigned smile on his face. He had always been at the top of his classes, and sometimes he wondered to himself how he knew so many things. Most of his studies bored him beyond reason; the lessons seeming more review than revelation.

He sighed, pushing nondescript gray-brown lumps from one side of his tray to another. "Tan, don't you ever think about running away? There must be some place in the world where people are happy and content. There just has to be," he whispered under his breath.

Tanner nearly choked. He glanced about, and seeing that none of the "house rats" was within earshot, he whispered angrily, "Are you coming down with the mind-plague? You know we don't dare speak of such things here. It's obvious that your constant daydreaming is getting out of hand. Have you forgotten that the scholars could report us to the Headmaster any time they even suspect such rebellion? And who knows what would come of that? Surely you haven't forgotten how poor Clive had to work in the scullery with the cook

The Birth of a King

maids for three solid weeks, just for saying that the scholar's lecture was boring...and what about Lothan having to scrub the entire meal hall floor with that tiny polish brush, just because he complained about the food?" Tanner shivered at the unwelcome memory of Lothan's raw and festered hands and knees.

He turned again to glare at Jaren. "You know what we have to do when we come of age. There are no choices for us. And as for *happiness*," he spat the word, "it's dead in Kinthoria. It's a thing of the past. The best we can hope for is a few moments of pleasure now and then. If you want to be happy, just be thankful that the two of us were considered eligible for a real education, instead of having to be like the majority here with just enough training to know their social place, to add sums, and to learn a useful trade; all of this and nothing but a life of slavery to look forward to."

Tanner finished his meal in angry silence, stabbing at his food and chewing it savagely, as much for Jaren's careless words as for the lack of hope in their lives. Jaren picked absently at his eating tray, his thoughts once again on the plight of his countrymen.

Tanner continued his silence as they walked to their afternoon lectures. Jaren knew that his friend had decided that life under the heel of the Dragonmasters was preferable to no life at all, but his own heart persistently rebelled against their fate. He was still several months from his eighteenth year; the age at which all children were removed from their homes or from the scholars halls to be sent away to learn a trade at which they would spend the remainder of their days working for the benefit of the Dragonmasters.

There were some who would be forced to join the Dragon Flights. Others, like Tanner, were eager though apprehensive to join. The dragon riders were the only free people in the land, though even they were not truly free, being under the iron fist of Volant, the Emperor of Kinthoria. Because of Tanner's excellent tactical capabilities and the natural talent he had displayed in the weapons yard, he had become the Weapons Master's favorite and protégé. The man was forever bragging to the Weapons Masters from rival halls that Tanner had the inborn qualities necessary to become a warrior of legendary stature. During the Aonghas, the war games held three

The Birth of a King

times yearly between the numerous halls, he had already won so many victories that he was known as The Foe Bane.

Jaren considered his friend's zest for competition. If Tanner thought he needed a new tunic or a sword, he simply had to arm-wrestle someone for it. At other times, his reputation being what it was, all he had to do was glare threateningly and his victim bowed to his will. These were the times that troubled Jaren, when it seemed that Tanner only entered these matches of strength and will to bolster his own pride. Jaren hoped he was wrong, and that his friend was sure enough of his capabilities that he did not need to prove his superiority by humiliating those less able than himself.

During an afternoon break, before being given his assignment for evening chores, Jaren sat contemplating once more the bleakness of his own future. He did not know where he would be placed for his apprenticeship when he turned eighteen. Tanner had always teased him about being sent to another scholars hall, since he could easily have taught most of the classes he endured each day.

His heart ached at the thought of being forever separated from this friend who was the closest thing to family that Jaren had ever known. Nearly a match in height, the two boys stood fully half a head taller than others their age. Jaren was only slightly leaner, and his complexion much fairer than that of his muscular, dark-haired friend. Yet, far more significant than these physical differences was the fact that Jaren had neither the will nor the enthusiasm for combat possessed by Tanner. Try though he might, he just could not change his benevolent character. The Weapons Master had told him incessantly during his drills that he was a worthy swordsman, and an excellent archer, but that his lack of aggression and his "nasty bent to trust th' entire breathin' world" would someday be his undoing. The man constantly shamed Jaren in front of the other boys, mocking him as "havin' the compassion of a woman."

"One of these days, lad, you're goin' to be givin' a hand up t' yer defeated foe and he's goin' to run ye through wi' his basilard! When ye've got 'im down then is the time to *strike*, lad!" Jaren could not count the times he had heard those words.

The Birth of a King

Two weeks had passed since the midday meal incident. Tanner seemed to have dismissed it since Jaren had not dared mention it again at the hall. This day, however, gave him the perfect opportunity to address the issue once more.

Both young men, sweaty and exhausted, were lying in a patch of new clover under an ancient, broad-limbed oak tree, one of the rare survivors of the dragon fire. The winter snow had melted and the surrounding vegetation hardy enough to take root was just turning the landscape to multi-hued greens that promised the emeralds and jades of summer. Tanner stripped off his tunic, to let the chill spring breeze cool his chest. All afternoon he had been attempting with no evident success to tutor Jaren on the finer points of cavalry battle maneuvers. Tanner could only shake his head and wince when he thought how sore and stiff his friend would be come the next morning, and sadly, with precious little to show for his efforts in the way of improved combat skills.

Jaren propped his head in his hand, while twisting some of the tangy clover grass in his teeth. Knowing there were no ears close by to overhear, he repeated the same question he had asked in the cookhall.

"Tanner, have you *honestly* never felt like trying to escape from the Dragonmasters to go somewhere to live your life the way you want?"

Tanner rolled his eyes, and groaned. "Aw, Jaren, why do you keep harping on these same ridiculous fantasies? There is no place in Kinthoria that the Dragonmasters wouldn't be able to find you."

He smiled at an evil thought. "Unless, of course you would like to move to the Kroth Mountains; or there is always the option of the Elven Forests?"

Jaren's face paled. "Never! I'd rather feed a dragon by hand. I will never be that desperate, no matter how bad my life gets."

He leaned back against the old tree and sighed in frustration. Perhaps Tanner was right. Perhaps he was just being a foolish daydreamer. Perhaps he truly was trying to avoid the issue of adulthood and its bleakness.

"Look, Jaren. I'll admit that Reeban isn't the place to live if you want excitement, and life here is tough, but no more so than anywhere else. Reeban has its good points. We've had all this open space to enjoy when we could, and there's always been enough small game to make hunting interesting."

Tanner noticed Jaren rubbing absently at his right shoulder. He wondered how many times he had seen Jaren unconsciously scratch at that odd birthmark. Tanner had seen the mark only a few times while swimming with his friend.

"Jaren, you should see this thing. It looks just like a dragon with a crown over its head," he had remarked one day.

Jaren turned crimson, and laughed uncomfortably. "Tanner, you fool," he retorted, "you've been thinking too much about your precious Dragon Flights."

Jaren was clearly embarrassed by the large mark, and had never spoken of it after that occasion, and unless he was alone with Tanner, he meticulously kept it covered. But Tanner had seen him lying awake at night, rubbing his shoulder, an irritated frown on his face. Lately, he seemed to be bothered by it much of the time.

The cool breeze blew through the budding branches overhead. Both of the boys were lost in their own thoughts: Jaren, unwillingly speculating about the Elven Forests and the dreaded Kroth Mountains. He shuddered, deliberately turning his mind to more familiar and far less threatening territory.

His thoughts landed on the scholars halls that were placed in the larger cities throughout Kinthoria. It was secretly rumored that in the days of the Cathain dynasty, the halls were used as apprentice schools for any trade a lad wished to choose. A boy could learn many skills from the Journeymen and Masters at each of the academies. Any girl who wished to do so could attend for an education in the arts, history, home management, and womanly deportment and enterprise.

Jaren could not know that such rumors were true; that not so long ago, during and after the war, all of the expensive and colorfully ornate trappings that had marked the individual prestige and successes of the Masters and Scholars at each academy had been part of the loot taken or destroyed by the victorious Dragonmasters.

Jaren's only experience was the dreary, dungeon-like halls used to hoard the youth of Kinthoria. The young people were little more than chattel from which the Dragonmasters replenished their slave and labor forces.

Without realizing it Jaren's thoughts eventually drifted once again to the Elven Forests. Legend had it that the forests and mountains far to the South were swarming with whole nations of vicious elves and dwarves, and other creatures too terrible to describe. He had never seen one of the creatures, though his dreams had provided a wide variety of terrifying possibilities, none of which he had any desire to meet in reality.

Jaren willed his body to relax, and tried to force his mind to other things. It was to no avail. He wondered why the dragon riders had not conquered the Southern Regions when they had conquered the rest of the land. It seemed to Jaren that it would have been a logical and prudent action to prevent the continual threat of war on Volant's doorstep. However, it was commonly and fearfully whispered that there existed in those lands an ancient and powerful magic of which even the dragons were afraid. It was said that they would go nowhere near those evil lands, no matter how hard pressed by their riders.

Jaren opened his eyes to escape his thoughts. "Tanner!" he yelled.

There was a man standing before them. The young men jumped to their feet, slipping their basilards from their boots. They slowly edged toward one another for protection. Jaren wondered absently why the horses had not stirred at the man's approach, while Tanner cursed himself for not having been more alert. *"And I want to be in the dragon flights. Hah!"* he raged at himself.

Jaren was confused at the kindly look about the man's tanned face. His bow and quiver were slung across his back, and his hunting knife was sheathed at his right thigh. He calmly stood before the two armed young men with apparent deliberate vulnerability.

Suddenly, the stranger laughed good-naturedly. "Put up your weapons, lads. If I had wanted to harm you, I could have done so long before you knew I was here."

Both of the boys knew this to be true, since neither had heard or sensed the slightest noise. The stranger seemed to have just appeared out of thin air, and then patiently waited until they noticed him before speaking.

The Birth of a King

He stepped slowly toward them, and Tanner, still smarting from the insult to his pride, raised his dagger. The stranger stopped, but not a trace of fear or anger crossed his face. He had seemed harmless enough to Jaren, but Tanner sensed something very powerful in the man, and it made him tense with suspicion. He was awed by the abilities of this very adept scout.

"*Who is he scouting for?*" thought Tanner. Suddenly, he recalled the traitorous discussion in which he and Jaren had been occupied. Had he overheard? Would he arrest them and drag them off to the Dragonmasters?

"Who are you, and why do you find it so humorous to sneak up on people like this?" he demanded, his trembling voice belying his bravado.

The man merely smiled and slowly rubbed his hand across his eyes. Jaren knew that even a green cadet would never deliberately blind himself as this veteran scout had just done. He instinctively suspected that this man's gesture had been intentional, to put them at ease. The stranger, as though reading Jaren's thoughts, suddenly sat down on the cool meadow grass just a few feet from the boys.

"My name is Llenyddiaeth aP Braethorn, but most people just call me Hawk. I didn't mean to startle you. I pray you, accept my sincere apologies."

Jaren studied the scout for some moments trying to determine if the man was attempting to disarm their caution with a pretense of ease and friendship. He could detect a sign of nothing save sincerity on the stranger's face.

He focused on the man's eyes, discovering that they were somewhat almond-shaped and of a striking emerald green color. He had never before seen such eyes.

His birthmark interrupted his scrutiny of the man. It was itching violently again, and he angrily reached up and began to scratch at it. He looked at Tanner and saw that he had relaxed very little, his dagger still trained on the scout.

Tanner had been keeping his eyes glued to the man's hands, just waiting for them to move. His Weapons Master had very effectively drilled into his head that it is an enemy's hands, not his eyes, that would be used to try to kill him.

"What kind of name is...uh...." Tanner could not even recall the stranger's name, much less try to pronounce it, "uh...Hawk?" he stammered, trying to cover his confusion.

The scout, still smiling, regarded both young men with a warmth that Jaren had seen only in the eyes of Tanner's good-natured mother. Those eyes seemed to hold Jaren's, and the boy fearfully waited for the wrenching sensation and painful violation that had always accompanied the mental probing of the Dragonmasters' mind readers as they made sure he was answering their interrogations truthfully. They wanted their subjects to fear their mental touch with the same fear that they held for the dragon's fiery breath.

This man's scrutiny was very strange. It seemed as though he was searching for answers to silent questions in a depth far beyond Jaren's ken; but he never touched the boy's mind. The boy was baffled. How did this man expect to learn anything by simply staring at him?

Jaren suddenly became aware that Hawk's scrutiny was completed, and his face flushed slightly.

"Are you a magician?" he blurted before Hawk had answered Tanner's question. He felt instantly foolish as it was obvious the man did not have the sinister look of a mage about him. Instead, Jaren intuitively sensed a highly complex nature behind those odd, green eyes, and he knew that the stranger was in deadly earnest regarding some unknown purpose. Yet, the soft, genuine smile never left his face. Jaren felt a pressing urgency, and oddly, at the same time, a remarkable peace issuing from the man.

Hawk laughed, "No son, I am no magician." Then he looked at Tanner and said, with a mischievous grin, "The name Hawk was given to me, because the giver was under the impression that I am a far-seeing fellow."

"Yes...your eyes," Jaren said, misinterpreting the man's statement. "I've never seen green eyes before, or the shape of them. And your clothes...where do you come from?"

Hawk chuckled, amused at the lad's naiveté at his use of the term *far-seeing*. He looked down at his worn leather breeches and soft leather jerkin with its rolled collar, sleeves with green insets, and scalloped hem. Under this was a soiled green tunic, which, even had they been new, would seem out of place to a youth who had more than likely never been a furlong away from Reeban. These clothes were made specifically for moving swiftly and unseen in most any terrain. His current mission had forced him far into the barren north and it was imperative that he be as invisible as possible.

Sadness momentarily touched his eyes as he recalled the fifteen years since the Dragonmasters had wrenched control of Kinthoria from the royal line of the Cathains. The races of the South had been banned from coming north of the river, and if they did venture across and were discovered, they were immediately sent to the mind readers for excruciating interrogation; those that survived were executed. Much could be said for their courage and skill, in that less than a dozen out of hundreds was ever caught.

Jaren slowly sat down in front of Hawk, curiosity finally overcoming his apprehension. As he leaned forward to sheathe his boot dagger, his muscles bunched up in rebellion against Tanner's earlier bruising lessons.

Tanner remained standing, tense and alert, wishing that he could inconspicuously gather the horses in case something went amiss and they needed to quickly flee.

Gesturing toward Tanner, Hawk said to Jaren, "Your friend here does not trust too easily, does he?"

Jaren looked at Tanner. "No, he doesn't. We've learned to trust only one another. We make a pretty good team. I use my brains and he uses his strength."

"Being cautious is a great asset to have these days," Hawk said, with noticeable regret. "You are fortunate to have such a companion."

Now that he had actually found Jaren, he had no idea as to how to approach the young man regarding the purpose for which he had come. All of his planned speeches and explanations seemed somehow inappropriate. Hawk sent up a quick, silent prayer. *"Elyon, please open his heart and his eyes. Provide him with strength to carry this difficult burden. And cause him to believe me and to trust me. I can't give him much to go on just yet, and I doubt he will comply without Your influence."*

Hawk had been scouring Kinthoria for two years in search of Jaren, hoping that he was yet alive. He had faced the dry and deadly heat of the Southern Plains, the savagery of the Trolls and Gundroths, and the murderous hatred of the Dragonmasters. Yet, he considered revealing to this boy the purpose of his mission to be the hardest obstacle he would face. He drew in a deep breath and looked at Jaren's young face. "Jaren, you asked about my eyes. Well, what about yours? They are certainly different than most, are they not?"

Jaren shifted uncomfortably and his face flushed crimson once more. The scout was right. He was the only one at the hall with gray eyes. Everyone else had eyes ranging from light amber to ebony in color. He had always been different, in so many ways, he angrily mused.

Suddenly, he looked at the stranger in astonishment. "How did you know my name?" he shouted, suspecting this man had lied about being a magician. Or worse, perhaps he was indeed one of the blood-chilling mind readers in the employ of the Dragonmasters. Could he have misjudged this stranger so greatly?

"I have been traveling for years looking for you, lad. It has taken longer than we expected." Hawk saw the questions beginning to form as the two boys exchanged glances. He continued quickly, "We have an advantage, though, because we are still a step ahead of the dragon riders. You see, we are fairly confident that they have...how shall I put this?" Hawk paused to choose his words, knowing that he had already alarmed the lad, "They have no knowledge of your existence yet, and we would like to keep it that way for as long as possible."

Jaren stared at the stranger, his mouth agape. The man seemed to be babbling insensibly. The only thing he had understood was that *he* had been searching for Jaren, and that it had taken longer than *they* had expected. He jumped up, suddenly feeling hunted and trapped. Flitting a quick glance to Tanner, he sent a signal to be ready to flee.

"What are you talking about? Of course the Dragonmasters know I'm alive. They make it their business to know about everyone who lives in Kinthoria. Why would they have any particular interest in me? And if you are not working for them, who are you working for and why were you sent in search of me?"

Hawk's face mirrored many things in the next instant: extreme weariness, uncertainty, and finally, courage and confidence.

"The Dragonmasters know about you, Jaren, but as yet they don't really *know* you. It would only have been a matter of time before they had discovered their oversight. That is why I was sent to find you and bring you back. I... No! Stay!" Hawk stood and held up his hand as though he would stop him, as the boys began their flight. "Wait, boy! Don't let your fears control you so. Please, hear me out!" he called after the youths, while making no move to hinder their flight.

Jaren had heard enough. The stranger was obviously a lunatic. *"They know about me, but they don't really* know *me? What kind of gibberish is that? He's come to take me with him? Not if I can help it."* His thoughts raced as he fled.

Then he felt an undeniable demand to stop, and to listen to what the scout had to say. He found himself slowing...stopping...turning, even as good sense demanded otherwise. He had every intention of making good his escape, yet he was keenly aware that the silent command had come from a source powerful enough to have compelled him to obey against his will.

Fearing an ambush, Tanner scanned the surrounding bushes and boulders for any signs of accomplices.

"It would be extremely unwise, at this time and in this place, to name those who sent me. Nor am I at liberty to reveal, at present, the reason why you *must* choose to accompany me. Yes, I did say *accompany*. You are certainly not going to be my prisoner. I am not planning to kidnap you. You will be my traveling companion."

Jaren opened his mouth to speak, but once more Hawk held up his hand for the boy to remain silent. "There is no time to explain. Nor is this the place to be revealing secrets long hidden. In a short time you will learn the answers to all of your questions. For the time being, though, I beg you to trust me."

Jaren stood dumbfounded. This was the craziest thing he had ever heard. This strange foreigner was asking him for absolute trust, and telling him that he *must* accompany him *somewhere*. The only reasons he would offer were unintelligible ravings about danger from the Dragonmasters and secrets long hidden. Jaren had no intention of remaining a second longer. He was sorry for the poor man's mental condition, but on the other hand, how many people had been killed by lunatics?

He turned once more toward his horse when he was fleetingly enveloped by a curious warmth. He staggered, momentarily weakened. Tanner was instantly by his side. "Jaren, what is it? Are you all right?" he asked fearfully, grabbing Jaren's arm and trying to keep him moving away from the stranger.

Jaren made no answer, but slowly pulled his arm from Tanner's grasp. Turning to look once more into the face of the stranger, he felt an overpowering compulsion to trust him. Incredibly, he heard his own voice whispering, "But what about the scholars, and my studies, and Tan...the day of Apprenticeship is just months away."

"Jaren, I know this is all very confusing and frightening for you," Hawk interrupted. "And I've said what little I may with the greatest incompetence. I know I am asking a significant amount of you far too quickly. But for now the less you know, the safer you will be."

Jaren's burst of anger seemed to break the hold of the Power that was so strongly influencing his mind. He was angry with the weakness in himself, with this stubbornly insistent stranger, with the absurdity of the whole situation. He was angry with whatever it was that was compelling him to believe this man when sensibility demanded otherwise. He wondered for the third time if Hawk was not a shape-changing mage, conjuring an aura of peace. Perhaps he was using his powers to force Jaren to believe him against his will.

"Safer?" he shouted. "What do you mean *safer*? I'm already *safe* at the Hall. Are you telling me that if I follow you I'll be in danger? Look, Hawk, or whatever your name really is, I may be young, but I'm no fool."

Hawk's reaction to this outburst of rage was not the loud, threatening command of a dragon rider to which Jaren had become accustomed. The man simply stood there, silent, unthreatening, yet unrelenting in the face of Jaren's accusations.

Jaren was shaken more by Hawk's stillness than if he had struck him across the face with a crop, as a dragon rider surely would have done. He knew it was not possible for a magician to alter what could be seen behind the shape and color of his eyes, and Jaren saw absolute integrity and honor in this man, though he did not know the source of his gift to so discern.

His anger abated as quickly as it had flared and his manner softened slightly. He saw that there was no question in Hawk's face but that he must and therefore would go with him. He sensed once more, that, for some unknown reason he had no choice in the matter: He must follow this stranger into whatever awaited, whether peril or pleasure.

His mind rebelled one last time. "I'll not leave Tanner," he said as a last attempt at defiance. "He's all the family I have."

Hawk momentarily closed his eyes. *"Elyon, help me,"* he silently prayed. After several moments he sighed with resignation.

"Tanner may accompany us. He appears to have skills that may be of help. Besides, Jaren, as I believe you have already guessed, you do not truly have a choice whether or not to come with me. I swore an oath on my life that I would return with you."

This sounded too much like a threat to Tanner's confused mind. He tensed every muscle and prepared to fight for his friend's freedom. He intended to show this Hawk fellow a few of the 'skills' he had just mentioned. He stepped between Jaren and the scout, his knife at the ready.

Hawk held out his hands in the sign of peace, and laughed. "Please, my intentions are absolutely honorable. I did swear an oath on my life. But since I am far too young to die, I would rather try to reason with you than to fight the pair of you. Please. Please, let us all remain calm, and Jaren, consider your decision with all prudence."

It was dusk by the time he had finished speaking with the boys. Hawk knew of the strict curfews the halls placed on their young charges and so he did not allow Tanner or Jaren time to probe for more answers.

He spoke quickly, "Meet me back here an hour before dawn if you wish to make things easy for all of us. If not, I will have to find you again. Though," he frowned with distress, "time is growing short."

"Bring a little food, one change of clothes and a bedroll for yourselves, but leave everything else. We want to make it appear that you've taken a short leave of absence as is done on occasion by

The Birth of a King

brave young men who are about to become apprenticed. If our plan works, it should buy us a month or so."

Jaren and Tanner watched as Hawk silently vanished among the boulders.

Tanner walked over to the horses and, gathering their reins, led them back to Jaren. "Come on, Jaren. The sooner we are away from here the better. We'll go to Sorley himself and report this as soon as we get back. Someone needs to see that this Hawk fellow is locked up somewhere far away from sane people."

Jaren spun around. "No. We shall speak of this to no one," he said with an authority that astonished his friend. As he mounted his horse, he rubbed at his birthmark again. He did not know which troubled him more, his sore, cramping muscles, his irritating birthmark, or his aching head.

They rode in silence back to the hall, and stabled their horses. Tanner knew that Jaren had already made up his mind on the matter. He had seen the weight of that decision settle upon his friend. Not another word was spoken of Hawk.

Later that evening, with chores completed and lessons read, Jaren fell into his bedrack exhausted. He did not fall asleep immediately as he had hoped, but lay on his back, his mind wrestling with many conflicting and frightening thoughts. He knew what he must do. He sensed this was his one chance to flee the oppression of the Dragonmasters. Hawk's strangely ominous invitation had appealed to the young man's longing for adventure. On the other hand, this was the only life Jaren had ever known. He had been raised in this Hall and had never ventured any distance from Reeban.

The population of the hall at Reeban was no different than in every other in Northern Kinthoria. The majority of the children had been sent here by parents or relatives as a last resort. Their privation simply would not allow them to feed another mouth. However, some of the children were sent to the halls with the hope that they would be chosen to receive a good education. Their parents secretly hoped that the leaders of a future rebellion would be fostered and trained at the Dragonmasters' own expense. Many children were sent through the secret channels of the underground rebellion to receive a true education and to learn how to fight to regain freedom for Kinthoria.

Jaren had never been accepted by his peers, presumably due to the dubious circumstances surrounding his arrival at the hall. The scholars had found Jaren, crying and abandoned on the doorstep when he was thought to be around his second year. They had assigned him a Birthing Day, because no one knew when or to whom he had been born. Thus, because illegitimacy was suspected, Jaren was never offered the hand of friendship by the other children. The name 'Alley Cat' echoed painfully in his ears.

Their animosity was also, in part, fostered by Jaren's obvious intellectual superiority. He always received the highest marks in every class, despite his frequent daydreaming. Often jealousy and bitterness had surfaced among his classmates in the form of cruel pranks. Many times arguments had become so heated they would have developed into fist fights had it not been for Tanner's physical presence and flashing black eyes.

Tanner had secretly hoped that a good portion of the stigma of Jaren's questionable parentage would lessen once he was transferred away from Reeban, and as he became confident in his own abilities, and gained worth for his name through honest labor.

Jaren recalled how Tanner's mother, alone of all the parents, had welcomed him as one of her own. In her beggary she could offer him nothing more than the mother's affection that he so desperately needed, and this she had given freely from a generous and loving nature.

His thoughts turned to Tanner. They had grown up together at the hall. Tanner had come a year after Jaren's arrival. His father had recently died and his mother was ill and weak, one of the few survivors of the dust-plague. She was very near her time with her unborn child, and she still had a baby at the breast. She just could not care for the three-year-old child any longer. She had tearfully turned him over to the hall, hoping they could give him a chance at survival, and that she would be allowed enough contact with the boy to help mold his character and, just perhaps, instill within her son the desire to join the rebellion when he came of age.

Jaren sighed and frowned. The question of whom or what Hawk was troubled him greatly. The doubts that had plagued his mind were eased only as he reminded himself of the honor and integrity, and the benevolent character which he had sensed in this unusual man.

As the night wore on, Jaren's aching body won the battle for much needed rest. His mind gave up the fight and his eyes closed in a not so peaceful sleep.

Chapter Two

EAVESDROPPER

Hawk spent the night huddled on the damp ground in a clover thicket, praying earnestly to the true God, Elyon. He had been revamping his return plans to include Tanner, since Jaren was reluctant to leave him behind. He sensed, too, that Tanner was somehow an integral part in the unfolding of Elyon's plan.

"Elyon, please help me," he whispered. "My resolve is so weak at times, but all strength is found in You. You brought me here through Your will and against incredible odds. Gracious One, You have kept this young man safely in Your care all these years, right in the center of his greatest danger. I am asking, as Your humble servant, that You grant all of us that same miracle of safety as we travel through the perils of the road ahead."

He paused, smiling, as he looked at the star-filled sky and sensed the peace of the true God's presence then released himself to a deep sleep just short hours before dawn.

It was the darkest hour of morning when Jaren awoke. He peered out of the narrow window above his bed and could see the red-hued moon, Lunisk, in its waning. But the sliver of the brighter and larger, white moon, Solisk, was still high in the early morning sky. He had slept fitfully and his aching muscles felt as though he had been through a real battle instead of Tanner's training session the previous afternoon. He wanted desperately to roll over and go back to sleep. He wanted in earnest to forget about Hawk. But Hawk's words, "I'll have to find you again," echoed ominously in his mind.

The Birth of a King

He listened for Tanner's rhythmic breathing as he quietly crept from his bedrack. He pulled on his heavy breeches and a warm tunic for protection against the chill dampness of early morning in mid-spring. He searched about in the darkness for his slate board and writing stick. Using the faint moonlight filtering through the window, he scrawled a note for Tanner to read when he would arise a few hours later. Leaving this one behind who was more brother than friend was a heavy blow to his heart. But he could not foresee what perils he would encounter on this uncertain journey, and he could not bring himself to put Tanner's life in jeopardy.

"Good-bye, my brother. You know that I must follow this adventure. I sense grave danger ahead and I cannot ask you to share in it. I shall miss you. Perhaps all will turn out well and we may meet again. Your friend, Jaren."

He carefully slipped the slate onto the floor near Tanner's cot, then, quickly gathering his bedroll, he silently crept from the dormitory. He earnestly hoped that Tanner would understand his reasons for leaving him behind.

With a heavy heart he hurried down the nearly pitch black corridor leading to the kitchens. He was grateful that most of the torchlights were allowed to burn down throughout the night. It would be easy for him to slip past the watchstanders both inside and outside the hall. Most of the children learned early on to slip undetected past the guards. It was a standing joke that you could not be a watchstander unless you were blind, or at the very least grossly nearsighted. Jaren made his way into the kitchen, groping in the darkness.

He chanced upon some cheese, meat sticks, and hard biscuits to throw into his food sack. Hawk had not told him how long it would take to reach their destination, but he had warned not to take so much that it would be missed. He knew some theft from the pantry was expected almost daily, indeed was provided for by the more kindly of the cookmaids, but he decided that in this case prudence was far better than a satisfied stomach. Tanner occasionally pilfered some of the sticky, sweet buns made just for Sorely, the obese headmaster of the scholar's hall, and for the other hall masters. Jaren wished that he could chance lighting a candle to find them.

The Birth of a King

Suddenly, he froze as he heard someone enter the kitchen. He crouched in the shadows by the massive hearth at the end of the large room. He strained his ears, listening for the slightest noise. His heart beat so loudly in his ears that he was sure the sound would wake the entire academy. Despite the cool morning air, he felt beads of perspiration forming on his brow and upper lip.

"Surely the cookmaids don't arise this early in the morning," he thought with sullen humor. *"At least their food certainly doesn't taste like they put much time into it."*

"Jaren, are you still in here?" a harsh, familiar whisper came through the darkness.

Jaren bowed his head and let the air explode from his lungs in relief. "Tanner," he whispered, "you nearly scared me to death. I thought you were sleeping."

Tanner snickered and put his arm across his friend's shoulders. "I slept in my clothes and waited for you to get up. I figured you'd try something stupid like this, and I couldn't let my *brother* go off on an adventure without me."

Even in the darkness, Jaren could sense Tanner's crooked smile, and caught the emphasis on the word "brother." He punched Tanner playfully in the ribs and smiled.

"Come on then, my friend. We must hurry."

They filled another food sack for Tanner, hoping that the cookmaids would prove as blind as the watchstanders. To Jaren's delight, Tanner knew exactly where the sticky buns were hidden and went straight to them in the inky darkness of the pantry. They slipped out of the cookhall into the deep shadows and chill air of early morning.

They moved from doorway to doorway as much as possible. On only one occasion did they see another living soul. One of the watchstanders, whom every boy in the hall had come to hate because of his bestial character, was lying in his own vomit, asleep in a drunken stupor. Tanner would have stepped on him had Jaren not yanked him back by his cloak at the last instant.

"Watch where you're walking, Tan. I know its dark, but you should at least have been able to smell him. Ughh," Jaren whispered, wrinkling his nose in disgust.

The Birth of a King

Tanner looked down at the man and grinned. "Looks real natural lying there, don't he? Just the sort of bed you'd expect for ol' Krin, eh?"

They walked briskly past the darkened merchants' shops, and down the unlit streets of Reeban. Jaren glanced around at the sleeping city he had known all his life. Just a hint of melancholy touched his eyes as he turned down the last side street. They slipped into an alley that led out of the city and into the meadows, and far beyond into a future full of the unknown.

Hawk stretched broadly once more, breathing deeply of the brisk morning air. He smiled that a man his age could feel so rested with so little sleep on cold, damp ground. His thoughts turned to Jaren once again. He was amazed how much the boy resembled his father in temperament and character. The lad was cautious, though wanting to trust; quick tempered, though equally as quick to regain his composure. He was honest, direct, and compassionate. Each of these characteristics would serve Jaren immeasurably as protection throughout the long and uncertain journey that awaited them. They were also attributes that Jaren would need for the rest of his life as...

Hawk caught himself, *"Best not to even think these things just yet - not here - not in the middle of enemy territory, with the Dragonmaster's spies and mind readers prowling about."*

Hawk wondered if Jaren would look like his father. It was impossible to tell while he was still protected by the miracle that the true God had performed for him as a toddling child. His true features had been miraculously hidden at that time so that no trace of ancestral blood could be seen about the child.

But the concealment was only illusion, and Hawk had readily seen his old friend in Jaren yesterday as he had watched Tanner trying in exasperation to teach him fighting skills. Hawk remembered himself being utterly frustrated during Jaren's father's lengthy and seemingly fruitless drills.

He laughed softly at his thoughts, and then turned silently to look for the boys. He was not troubled that they had not yet arrived. He was trusting Elyon to work His will.

The young men returned to the gnarled oak tree where they had met Hawk the previous afternoon.

"Well, so far so good, Tan," said Jaren, still breathing hard from their quick dash into the countryside. "No alarm bells yet." He did not know whether to be scared senseless or to give in to the excitement of the flight. This was the first time he could ever remember actually trusting someone other than Tanner. He wondered to himself if trusting Hawk would prove to be the biggest mistake of his young life.

"Well, I don't think anyone heard us leave," said Tanner softly. He was entirely alert now, the trained warrior in him watching for anything that moved. "Where is that stupid magician, anyway?" he asked. *"He's probably right under our noses,"* he thought to himself with a shiver.

The two young men scanned the area intently for any sign of the mysterious stranger, anticipation increasing their tension with each silent, passing moment.

"I'm glad you made things easy for all of us," a soft voice came from close behind their ears. Even spoken softly, Hawk's words had sounded loud as a clarion call to the young watchers. The lads nearly bolted and much could be said for the excellence of their military training that neither yelled out in fright.

"Dols, man, why do you do that?" Tanner whispered hoarsely in angry disapproval. "Better yet, *how* do you do that?" The youth was enraged by this unnatural ability of Hawk's to appear as silently and suddenly as though he were a specter. Tanner could track just about anything, and yet he honestly had to admit that as far as he was concerned, if Hawk was not within nose length, he was invisible.

"I was hoping you would come, despite our parting yesterday." Hawk smiled, choosing to ignore Tanner's queries.

Jaren, still trying to control his shaking body and to slow down his breathing, was now even less convinced that he should trust this stranger, honest smile or no. Hawk seemed to be thoroughly enjoying scaring the flesh off the both of them. He wondered how many of these little surprises awaited them along the way, and if Hawk's game would become seriously dangerous the farther they got from Reeban.

The Birth of a King

Yet, he still sensed no evil in the man. He felt strangely drawn to explore the awareness of an unaccountable ease he felt when he was with Hawk - once he knew where he was - a puzzling pleasure that made him feel as though he had just met an old friend.

"We have a lot of ground to cover today, so we had better get to it. We need to be quick about getting as far from here as possible," Hawk said as he strode away.

"Hawk, I...uh...that is, we were just wondering where we are going." Jaren stammered, as he stumbled through the darkness trying to keep up.

"We are going south to the Kroth Mountains," he said matter-of-factly. He pretended not to notice that the boys had suddenly stopped walking. He knew what the Dragonmasters had been teaching about his homeland, and he waited for their reply. He continued walking, but slowed his pace and shortened his stride.

If he had turned around, he would have seen two pale young men, mouths agape and bodies ready to bolt back to the safety of the hall. Finally, driven by fear, Jaren raced to catch up to Hawk and grabbed his arm, spinning him around.

"You can't be serious. There are vile and deadly races down there!" Jaren screamed in a voice raspy with fright, all thought of stealth torn from his panicked mind.

"Quiet," Hawk warned softly, placing his hands on Jaren's shoulders, hoping to will calm into the boy. "I've heard such rumors, lad. But you will find soon enough that not all you have been taught is truth." He caught and held Jaren's eyes. "You must trust me, Jaren. I swear this...in time things will become clearer to you than you may now wish, but you must be patient and wait for the proper time. I will not allow any harm to come to you or Tanner as long as I have life to protect you."

Once again, Jaren saw truth in this man's eyes. To his amazement, and beyond his best judgment, he found himself trusting Hawk.

Seeing that Jaren had made his decision, however reluctantly, Hawk smiled in reassurance and gently slapped the young man on the back. He turned and set a steady, loping pace for this early stage of their flight.

They traveled through thin, newly forming woods filled with spindly young beech and poplars, small oaks and firs. Charred, decaying trunks blasted by dragon fire littered the floor of the woods. In other areas, the dead trees stood like ghostly sentinels, calling travelers to remember the beauty that had once graced much of Kinthoria, and yielding a grim reminder of the penalty for open rebellion against the Dragonmasters. They crossed wide, breezy meadows thinly carpeted with short coarse grasses and dotted with small beds of crocus, daffodil, and hyacinth.

At first, the land had been familiar to Jaren and Tanner. However, it was not long before they found themselves traveling through entirely unknown territory. It was then that they realized how restricted and inadequate their experiences had been to fit them for such a journey. They also came to understand just how heavy would be their reliance upon Hawk and his knowledge of this country.

Once they passed through a forest that had remained untouched by the destructive war with the Dragonmasters. It was vast, and filled with ancient, gnarled oaks, and rank upon rank of firs a hundred feet tall and more. The undergrowth was thick with budding gorse, long, naked, blood-red berry vines, and ferns whose blades were just beginning to uncurl in the warmth of the spring sun. Rotting trunks of fallen trees and a thick mat of decaying leaves littered the forest floor.

Jaren found the pungent odors delicious. This first experience with an undamaged, ancient forest awoke something primal within him that seemed somehow as ancient as this land. It seemed to sing with an urgent call and a desperate longing. It was overwhelming in its sorrow and in the power of its beauty. Jaren's eyes filled with tears and he hurriedly wiped them away, lest either of his companions mistake them as a sign of fear. However, Hawk's quick eyes had seen, and he knew the source of Jaren's tears. He smiled and sighed in satisfaction, nodding his head in quiet approval.

Hawk allowed only a few short rests with cold meals. He wheedled a sticky bun from the boys, savoring its homey flavor. By late evening of the second day, they had covered many leagues and had come to a small village. Hawk whispered for them to stay under cover in the shadow of an outcrop of boulders cloaked with wild rose vines.

"I must meet with our traveling companion at that inn on the eastern edge of town." He pointed to a dimly lit structure that appeared to Jaren like a renovated cattle barn.

Hawk had reservations about lodging at an inn this far north. However, he knew the boys, being unused to the rigors of such travel, would need rest before they began their journey in earnest. For weeks to come their beds would be nothing more than the hard ground under the cover of cave or thicket. He would continue to trust Elyon for their safety, and he would do his part by trying to make their small company as invisible as possible.

"If all is well I will signal for you to come inside." The young men nodded and Hawk moved out toward the village.

"Jaren, do you think he was joking about taking us to the Kroth Mountains?" Tanner sullenly asked after Hawk's disappearance into the darkness. Jaren seemed to have come to some sort of understanding with the man, and Tanner could sense that he trusted him implicitly. But Tanner had spent the days recalling all of the tales that the scholars had so skillfully and often dramatically instilled in his mind. He shivered once again at the unwelcome pictures of the torture and cannibalism of humans by the southern races; even the Trolls and Gundroths of The Moors in the heart of the North marched in endless succession through his thoughts. He was understandably terrified of the unknown northern country to the east of Reeban, and of the Kroth Mountain ranges south of the Shandra River. But he could not share his fear, even with his best friend, and especially not with Hawk.

Jaren shook his head, without looking at Tanner. "It's all right, Tanner. I trust him. I know this sounds crazy, but leaving the hall has somehow started a change in me." He thought about what he had been feeling as they followed Hawk farther and farther from the only life he had ever known. He looked into Tanner's eyes. "I can't explain it. I just trust him."

Tanner sat down against a large rock and retreated into his own thoughts as they awaited Hawk's signal.

The Birth of a King

The night air was unusually cool, and Jaren pulled his cloak more tightly about his shoulders. He saw Lunisk, a sliver now, riding high in the clear, starry sky. But he did not feel the comfort this old friend usually brought. He suddenly felt the need to be inside, away from even the dim light of the red moon.

His eyes searched the shadows surrounding their hiding place. Then, as his uneasiness increased, he looked once more toward the sky. As his gaze returned to Lunisk, he saw a dark shape momentarily blot out his vision of the moon. He sucked in his breath and held it, as the silhouette of a dragon and its rider raced through the sky overhead, and flew off toward the northeast. It was all Jaren could do to stop himself from making a run for the inn without waiting for Hawk's signal. The only things which held him in place were his knowledge that it was too soon for the dragon riders to have discovered their absence, and Tanner's firm grip upon his shoulder.

It seemed as though an eternity passed before Jaren finally caught the signal from Hawk.

As soon as they passed through the door of the inn, the senses of both young men were assaulted by the noxious, sour odor of ale soaked straw left to rot along the walls and in the corners of the low ceilinged room. Jaren was hard put to keep his stomach under control. He slowly scanned the dimly lit room. Cobwebs hung from the corners of dust-covered windows, the tables were soiled and sticky, as though they had not been scrubbed in weeks. He watched something scurry across the floor under the straw, and shuddered.

Only a handful of people were left in this common room at this late hour. These were the homeless and the drunkards, passed out on benches and tables, sleeping in the only comfort they would receive before being tossed out onto the street when the inn closed its doors for the night.

"*Of course,*" Jaren thought, eyeing the room with disgust, "*it's possible that these are the only people who ever enter this gutter in the first place.*"

Tanner nudged him. "Why don't we order some ale? I haven't had any since drinking that little we found in the watchstander's mug last Michaelmas."

The Birth of a King

Jaren just wanted a bed and a warm fire to ease his aching body. He could have sworn they had walked the whole of Kinthoria and back. His hand lifted in habit toward his shoulder to rub at *The Bane*, as he disdainfully called his birthmark. "Not on your life. I don't have a death wish, or haven't you looked at this place? I just wonder if these people are sleeping, or if they've all died from tainted ale or rotten food. Besides, how are you planning to pay for it?" he mumbled over the edge of a yawn.

Hawk led them to a room at the top of a stairway of questionable stability. He scanned the hallway, closed and bolted the door, and then turned to introduce the man comfortably seated by the fire, drinking contentedly from a mug of hot mead.

"Korthak, this is Jaren and his friend Tanner." He gestured toward the two boys as he unclasped his cloak and tossed it onto a narrow bedrack. "Lads, this is my truest friend, Korthak. You will not find an abler or more entertaining traveling companion in all of Kinthoria."

The man stood and faced the lads. He was tall and heavily built with a shock of thick, sandy hair streaked with gray; a bushy, red beard covered his lined face. Both hair and beard needed a great deal of attention before either would again be considered reputable assets.

Korthak looked at Tanner and then stared long and hard at Jaren with unblinking, deep-set amber eyes. Finally, as though satisfied, he said simply, "Pleased to meet you both." He had the same friendly warmth in his eyes that Jaren had found so compelling in Hawk. He knew immediately that he could trust this man even as he had trusted Hawk.

Tanner stared at the burly man's tankard, licking his lips and thinking he would surely die of thirst at any moment.

Korthak, amused at Tanner's flagrant entreaty, held his mug out to the lad. "Here boy, you look like you're about to die of thirst. I'll share a wee dram of this with you. Mind you, leave some for me, though. I've only just started on it, myself."

Tanner's face broke into a huge grin as he eagerly took the mug from Korthak's enormous hand. "Thanks," he said as he put the cup to his mouth. He took two lengthy pulls at the warm brew, and long-

The Birth of a King

ingly eyed the remainder before reluctantly handing the mug back to Korthak. Tanner decided then and there that he was going to like this fellow immensely.

Seeing the fatigue on the lads' faces, Hawk pointed to two rough beds along the wall. "Now that the introductions are over, you two should get some sleep. We have another long day ahead of us, and we will be leaving before Solance rises.

Korthak, may I have a word with you while you finish your tankard?" Hawk asked with a crooked smile, as he lowered himself to a small stool in front of the fire.

"Why certainly, my lord, and thanks to this young lad, I should have it finished in a trice," Korthak winked at Hawk.

The older man looked long at the two young men who appeared to have fallen asleep even as their heads approached their pillows. His eyes searched Hawk's face. He pointed with his thumb and said softly, "He doesn't look a'tall familiar to me, Hawk. Are you sure that's him? I mean, his eyes are lighter than most, but, dols, man, what makes you so sure you've the right one?"

Hawk rubbed his weary eyes and sighed. "It's him, my friend. You will see for yourself by watching his manners on the morrow. Besides, I have seen him scratching and rubbing at his right shoulder countless times. You know what that could mean."

Korthak grunted. "Hmmm, that he was bit by a stinging fly?"

Hawk chuckled as Korthak continued, "He still doesn't look like any one I remember, if you follow my meaning."

Hawk gazed into the flames softly flickering in the fireplace and said, "That is a good sign, though. Don't you see? If you, Cadan's most trusted Captain, can't see the similarity, then we know that the Dragonmasters surely will never have suspected anything."

Hawk chuckled quietly. "It's unbelievable...under their noses so many years and they never once suspected. What a brilliant strategy Elyon planned. And praise be to Him for keeping Jaren's true identity hidden," he slapped Korthak on the knee, smiling in satisfaction.

Then, turning serious once again, he whispered. "The lad has no idea who he is, even with his birthmark."

Korthak saw the familiar pain in his friend's eyes and gently said, "He must be told soon, my friend. We will need his power as quickly as possible. The people will laugh us out of Saint Ramsay's if we bring him before them in this condition."

Hawk nodded his head, "I'm assuming they'll know him on sight. It's just my guess, but I'm thinking Elyon will reveal his true features to the world once we've been to the Spring. I could be wrong...I don't know. I don't pretend to understand the ancient prophecy." He leaned forward with a weary sigh and propped his elbows on his knees. He rubbed his eyes with the balls of his hands, and wished it was all over and done.

Korthak continued. "The Spring of Elyon is more than three months ride, and once he has the Power, the Dragonmasters will probably know he's alive. Even they shouldn't have too much trouble making the link to the missing boy. It won't be long, my friend, before the dragon flights will be scouring every inch of Kinthoria looking for these two. This time they won't stop at the Shandra River."

"Mmmm...but how will they manage getting the dragons to cross, I wonder?" Hawk mused. "Besides, young boys go missing all the time, so it will take them a while to discover which boys are with us."

The two men sat quietly for some minutes, once again considering the monumental task before them.

Suddenly Korthak broke into a fit of quiet laughter as he pictured the enraged, half-mad Dragonmasters screaming epithets at one another for having been too blind to see the truth about Jaren for more than fifteen years. *"Dols,"* he thought, *"the Dragonmasters might even start roasting each other with dragon flame, and make it unnecessary for any innocent blood to be spilled. Wouldn't that be a stroke in our favor?"* Korthak continued to chuckle as he stared into the fire, imagining confused and angry dragons spewing flames at one another, lighting the sky all over northern Kinthoria.

Hawk stared at him, humorously suspecting that perhaps his friend had a touch of the mind-plague. "What could possibly be so amusing about this situation?"

Korthak wiped the tears of laughter from his eyes with the ball of his hand and snuffled his nose. "I'm sorry, Hawk," he said, chuckling once more in spite of himself. "It's just that I do so wish I could be there to see Volant's ugly face when he realizes what's happened."

Hawk thought of what this would do to Volant's notorious pride, and began to quietly laugh. The two old friends, in a much-needed moment of rest and relative safety, talked and laughed for an hour or more.

"It has been a brilliant plan, indeed, my lord. Who would have suspected he would have been within Volant's grasp all this time?" Korthak snorted. "It's a good thing Elyon stepped in and took over. Looking back on it, our original plan would never have worked."

Tanner turned over in his bedrack and moaned, and the two men realized they were being far too free with their tongues. The realization of what lay ahead for all of them brought a somber tone to their conversation.

"It will take us months to reach Saint Ramsay's," murmured Korthak, "and that's if everything goes as planned." He sighed, "Ah, well. It'll do no good brooding about it. I'm going to turn in." He rose wearily from his chair and lay on his bedrack. Soon he was snoring softly.

Hawk watched the last of the flames die to embers before going to bed. He was uneasy being in the North, and it took him a long time to give in to sleep.

Jaren lay awake long after the two men's breathing had become slow and regular. The muscles in his body were a mass of coiled springs. *"Volant, the king of the Dragonmasters, angry about me? Why?"* His mind was racing from one inconceivable thought to the next. If he was not whom he had always known himself to be, who was he? Everything was in confusion…nothing made sense to him. His whole world had been upended and his life put in terrible jeopardy since meeting this man three days ago. Had it really been only three days? In his terrified state, it seemed that all he had ever known was fear. He was further away from his hall than he had ever been. He was following two strangers, heading for a place in which he could quite possibly end up being the main course on some fiend's table. But the most incredible thought to Jaren, was that he had done all of this voluntarily.

The Birth of a King

He felt a rage building inside his mind; rage at his naiveté, and at Hawk's unwillingness to give him any real information. He swore to himself that tomorrow, before he left the room, he would have some answers. *"Dols, Hawk can't keep me in the dark forever. He has no right. I've trusted him, now it's time for him to trust me."*

When Hawk shook him awake a few hours later, Jaren's mind refused to believe it was time to rise. The night could not possibly have passed so quickly.

Korthak had left the room to ready the horses. Since Hawk had decided to bring along the second lad, they would have to get by with only three mounts until they could reach the market at Doddridge. This meant a full three-week journey, with the lads riding double.

Tanner had slept quite well, which put him into his more normal frame of mind. He decided to start the day with his usual prickling banter with Jaren. He could see, by the sour look on his friend's face, that he was already ripe for the picking. He walked over to the fireplace and stretched out in the chair, his fingers locked behind his shaggy head.

"Ah, yes," he sighed smugly, "today will be most enjoyable." He glanced furtively at Jaren, hoping he would take the bait. Jaren remained ominously silent.

Hawk had also noticed Jaren's dark mood. He watched him yank his bedroll into shape. Thinking that perhaps the lad was angry with himself for being fearful, Hawk thought he might try to turn his mind from the dangers ahead and lighten his mood. An angry, brooding companion was an unwelcome burden on any journey.

Hawk moved to the center of the room and traced the widest, most regal bow Tanner had ever seen. "M'lord was not pleased with these most exquisite accommodations so painstakingly obtained for his pleasure this past evening?" Hawk asked in a playfully mocking tone.

Tanner laughed heartily and immediately made plans to take lessons in needling from this man when they had the time.

Jaren looked directly into Hawk's emerald eyes and glared at him. *"Don't* call me M'lord. And I do not see any humor whatever in your ridiculous posturing," Jaren growled. "Furthermore, until I

The Birth of a King

get some explanations from you, you may consider Tanner's and my participation in this journey at an end."

Tanner instantly stopped laughing and decided he would postpone asking for those lessons. Hawk was too good at this. Tanner wanted to have fun, not risk death. He decided to see if Korthak needed any help with the horses. Carefully and quietly sliding his body out of the chair and inching his way to the door, he silently slipped into the hallway with a cautious sigh of relief. He descended the stairs, casually glancing at the few patrons who were up at this early hour. He covertly inspected their bowls of gruel for any accidental additions of the furry or multi-legged variety.

Hawk turned toward the fireplace. "Jaren, I'm sorry," he said firmly, "but the fact is that we must travel much farther south before taking the risk of telling you more than the little I have. If something should go awry and you were captured and questioned, the only thing that would save you from the mind readers and certain death would be your ignorance of our plan."

"I heard you last night," Jaren mumbled angrily under his breath. He felt ashamed for having pretended sleep while eavesdropping on the conversation of the two older men. After hearing everything, he had cursed himself for having resisted the forceful call of sleep.

Hawk whirled round to face him. "What did you say?"

Jaren could not bring himself to look into his piercing eyes. "I heard what you and your friend were talking about last night."

Hawk slowly turned back toward the fire, and clenching his fists, berated himself for not having been more careful with this young man. "So...you know," he said quietly.

"No, that's just it, I *don't* know." Jaren said heatedly. "I am entirely at a loss about *all* of this. If I'm not me, then who am I? Who were my parents? If I don't look like this, what do I look like? Why are we sneaking around like common thieves? Why would the Dragonmasters have such an interest in me? And who is this mastermind, Elyon? Why has he done all of this to me?" Jaren sat on the bedrack and held his head, trying to stop its pounding, and struggling against tears of fear and frustration. "Hawk, I'm scared to death."

Hawk turned and went to sit beside the boy. "Look, Jaren. You have just asked me a lot of questions, each of which deserves an answer. Believe me when I tell you that I am just as frustrated at not being free to give you those answers as you are in needing to know them. I want to answer you, Jaren, to relieve your fears and to actually bring you happiness, but I simply can't risk our quest by giving in to your needs or mine." Hawk carefully selected his next remark. "Right now, you must understand only this, the rest you will learn as we travel; we are all in very grave danger the longer we stay in the Northern Regions. We must move south with all speed. I know I've said this before, but you must trust me, lad, at least a little while longer. I promise I will teach you as we go and when it is time, I will answer all of your questions, freely and most gladly."

After some moments, Jaren looked into Hawk's face. The now familiar sincere honesty was plainly seen. He knew that if he made good his threat to return to Reeban, Hawk would tell him everything right then. However, something inside warned him that this venture was far too important to risk its failure out of stubbornness. Whatever all of this meant, whatever it was for, Jaren wanted to prove himself worthy of the effort these people had already given.

"Alright, but you must promise to keep true to your word to tell me as soon as may be. I need to know."

Hawk smiled, and slapped Jaren on the back in approval. "You have my promise," he said. "Now, let's go find Tanner and Korthak and see if there's any decent food in this rat hole of a place. I think from now on, I'm going to choose our accommodations instead of that wild weasel Korthak."

As they gathered their belongings Hawk silently thanked the true God that He had carried them through this ordeal. He also made a mental note to be much more attentive to studying Jaren. He vowed to himself that in the future he would hold his private conversations with Korthak well out of the lad's hearing.

"By the way, Jaren," he said as they left the room, "don't worry, you won't be turning into some hairy, half-human monster when your true appearance is revealed."

Jaren stopped short and stared at him in surprise.

The Birth of a King

Hawk laughed, "I rather suspected that was one of your major concerns. I see that I was right. No, I think you'll be quite pleased with the Jaren you'll see in a few months."

They made their way down to the com-mon room and found Tanner and Korthak waiting for them at a table. Korthak's eyes immediately questioned Hawk. Hawk's answer was an almost imperceptible shake of his head.

"Well, the innkeeper has graciously agreed to bring us some hot gruel before we leave," Korthak said with a smug smile.

"I hope it's of better quality than the room. I was expecting to wake up to a rat gnawing at my ear," Tanner said, only half-jokingly.

Korthak's face took on an expression of pained insult. "What do you mean, sir?" He glanced around the table at his three companions. "Did you not appreciate this most splendid hostelry? Was there not the warmth of a fire to take the chill from your bones? Were there not soft, downy cots on which to lay your weary bodies?"

"Please, Korthak," Hawk interrupted teasingly, "restrain yourself. It is much too early in the morning for such extravagant stretches of the imagination, especially on empty stomachs."

Korthak looked at Tanner and frowned. "And as for you, my lad, who was it that had a nice, welcomin' draft of hot mead last night? And who was it that was asleep before his head hit the pillow? Awake to a rat eatin' your ear, y'say? Bah! A whole pack o' rats could have eaten you clean away and you wouldn't have awakened to take notice."

The innkeeper, his hair hanging in oily strings across his forehead and his leather apron slick with weeks of unwashed use, approached the table bearing four steaming bowls of gruel and four cups of dark, bitter cafla.

"Ahhh," sighed Korthak, as he smelled the rich aroma of the breakfast brew favored most in all Kinthoria. "At least this worthy innkeeper knows how to brew a cup of cafla that will get a traveler up and on the road in good speed and light spirits."

After breaking their fast, the four companions took to the road heading southeast. All through the bright, sunlit morning, Jaren dozed behind Tanner, who bantered back and forth with Korthak and Hawk.

The Birth of a King

Korthak was roaring with laughter as he gave in to Hawk's urging and began to relate one of the tales for which he was so famous.

"Ah, yes," he chuckled, wiping the tears from his eyes. "Let me see. I seem t' recall a sword fight. Yes, that was it, you'll remember this, Hawk, I'm certain," he said, inviting his friend to aid and abet in the telling of his outrageous tale. "She was a beautiful young thing and I was smitten." He clutched at his heart in a tragically comic pose.

Hawk laughed. "Aye, my friend, she was beautiful, indeed, but I don't know as I'd have gone to arms for her. Come now, she was merely an inn maid," he looked at Tanner and winked.

"Merely an inn maid?" Korthak snorted, playing on Hawk's words. "I ask you, Tanner, is such inequity just…is it fair? I tell you, lad, her beauty belied noble blood, and that buffoon had insulted her honor. I, of course, had no other choice but to come to her aid in defense."

"Of course," Hawk said, drolly, rolling his eyes heavenward.

Korthak fell silent and Hawk followed his lead. The story seemed for all purposes to have come to an abrupt halt.

Tanner was ready to burst. "So, what happened?" he pressed.

Korthak's face flushed and he cleared his throat. "Well…um… you see, we all went outside to the front of the inn…and, well…," he looked imploringly at Hawk.

"And I had to step in to save the fair lady's honor…and Korthak's worthless hide," Hawk finally said.

Korthak winced and shifted in his saddle, clearly uncomfortable with the way this story always ended. Tanner looked at him, questioningly.

"Oh all right," he glared defiantly at Hawk. "The bloated-faced, oily pig who had insulted the fair beauty turned out to be her husband."

Hawk burst into laughter at his friend's obvious discomfort.

"Well, dols, Tanner," Korthak whined, "what was I to do? A man is allowed to say what he wishes to his wife, is he not?"

Tanner began laughing at Korthak's incredible misfortune as Hawk finished the tale. He related how he had apologized profusely to the incensed husband, and had ended up handing over a rather substantial settlement to salve the much-maligned honor of the greedy oaf.

"You see, Tanner, he was young way back then, and thought it was his duty to take on the whole of Kinthoria for the sake of honor and justice. Take a lesson from this, lad," Hawk ended in mock severity.

Tanner nodded as somberly as possible, attempting to crush the smile on his face.

Chapter Three

DRAGONMASTERS

"An excellent batch of eggs, by the look of them, sir," said the Lieutenant Colonel, as they walked out of the sweltering heat of the egg chamber. As was his habit, he had removed his light tunic upon entering the enormous cavern, tucking it into the waist at the back of his breeches. He pulled it out now, and found it damp with the perspiration that ran unchecked from his glistening, dark hair, and down his bare, muscular torso. The young man wiped his hair, face, and neck with the garment and pulled it on as he fell into step with Volant.

Volant nodded to him. "Yes, Bendor, I should think we will have our best hatching yet." His steely, black eyes glinted with the prospect of strengthening his dragon flights.

Volant was extremely glad that he had chosen not to wear the standard heavy leather uniform of a dragon rider to this inspection. From the appearance of the Red Flight leader walking beside him, he could tell that he would easily have lost fully half a stone weight had he worn the heavy leathers in this oppressive heat. Volant had no wish to lose an ounce from a body that he considered the ideal masculine form.

The leader of the feared Dragonmasters was fanatic about maintaining excellent physical condition. Though he had just recently passed his fortieth Birthing Day, he did not look a day above twenty-five years. His body was compact and muscular, his hands thick and very strong. Unlike most of his troops, he kept his black hair

The Birth of a King

cropped short, and wore no facial hair, save for a thin mustache. He strode with that arrogance and confidence of a man who is fully aware of his abilities and of the power of his high position.

As they continued down the corridor, Volant considered once again his wisdom in placing the egg chamber in this huge cavern; located just above a natural hot spring, the extreme heat remained constant in all seasons. The floor was covered with the soft, silty sand of the Great Otten Sea that stretched out before his capital fortress to the distant horizon. Hundreds of slaves had been brought in to fill the vast chamber with a deep bed of sand. Scores had died, as Volant had driven them beyond human endurance in his haste to have the work completed by the next dragon mating season. The soft cushion provided an excellent conduit for the heat of the springs, making it the perfect place for the incubation of the leathery dragon eggs and the healthy growth of the small hatchlings.

Volant had selected Keratha, on the eastern side of Kinthoria, for the headquarters of the Dragonmasters; its vast caverns might have been carved out by ancient ocean currents specifically for the purpose of housing his dragons. It was the ideal place to build an impregnable military empire. Sheer cliffs soared along the coastline for many miles, turning inland at both ends to join the Ragani mountain range miles inland, a range considered the backbone of northeast Kinthoria. High within this ring of mountains stretched a vast, lush plain, broad and fertile enough to accommodate many future generations of dragons and riders. Its meadows and dells wound for hundreds of leagues among the long arms of the mountain heights. The snowmelt and subterranean springs supplied creeks and streams that fed into the Ninganae River as it roared and spilled in scores of waterfalls over the western rim of the mountains and into the moors far below. No one could approach this high place without being seen for leagues in any direction. Yes, Volant's empire had begun well in this place.

He turned to Bendor, "We still need more riders to train, if we are ever to crush the Southern Regions." He slammed his fist against the wall of the corridor. "We must rid the kingdom of the filth of the elves, dwarves and An'ilden if we are ever to gain complete control of Kinthoria. Unless my guess is wrong, a sizeable portion of the An'ilden race is hiding south of the Shandra River since we still have not been able to eradicate them, despite all of our raids. Their influence is felt all over the land, even after all these years of separation. We must find where they have hidden their women so that we can stop the vermin from breeding like flies. I want them wiped from the face of the earth," Volant ranted as frustration and rage washed over him.

Bendor decided to risk offering his opinion, even though he knew the Southern Regions were a dangerous topic, especially when Volant was in such a state.

"I think, sir, that they just do not understand what you are offering them. Remember, the southern races are simple folk, who tend the forests and work the mines. They trusted the dragons, until we turned them for use against the northern people during the war. They have seen the destruction that occurred up here, and they want to avoid such devastation in their own land."

Volant's eyes were alive with raw hatred. "Yes, but that is ancient history. They have had close to a score of years to adjust to our use of the dragons. Even a fool would know that there is nothing to fear if they would only capitulate. I feel that I have been more than patient with their stubborn rebellion."

Bendor had been a lad of just sixteen years when he first joined Volant's service. The Cathain line was nearing obliteration and the war was raging at its height. The old-line members of the Dragon Army and those who had been loyal to the Crown fought desperately against a host of military insurrectionists led by an ambitious and extraordinarily intelligent young man named Volant.

Bendor had been soured by the hypocritical ways of the so-called "followers of Elyon." He had seen no difference between these people and the ones they condemned, whom they branded as "evil-doers and pagans." They were just as full of greed, violence, and lust as the unbelievers. Yet these supposedly righteous people scorned and shunned their neighbors if they did not go to the assemblies on Holy Day, or if they refused to adhere to the thousand and one laws of their religion.

Longing to break free of the bonds of rules and regulations imposed by these religious tyrants during his childhood, Bendor had

The Birth of a King

decided to join Volant's swelling ranks. He was drawn by the offer of a life free of restrictions of any kind, with no pious judgments. Even more compelling had been his life-long dream of flying a dragon. He was constantly amazed at the beauty and the graceful agility of these creatures of such vast size and incredible strength.

The young Lieutenant Colonel agreed with his leader regarding the need to subjugate the Southern Regions once and for all. However, he also recognized the fact that killing simple, unarmed peasants with fire-breathing dragons was something not easily forgotten. In the years since the war, the lethal capabilities of the beasts had been used chiefly against the An'ilden as Volant's insatiable hatred of that race threatened their obliteration. The charred and barren evidences of these atrocities, along with the frequent ravening of livestock by the dragons, had resulted in almost daily reminders of the deadly threat of the winged beasts. It was common knowledge that despite Volant's interdiction against the Southern Regions, communication was freely exchanged across the Shandra River. The races of the South received daily reports of the savagery of the dragon riders.

Bendor ran his fingers through his dark brown hair, attempting to brush the sweaty strands from his face. He decided it was best to keep these thoughts concealed, and instead, try to fend off Volant's growing impatience.

"Sir, be patient a while longer, and let's keep breeding the dragons and training our flights until the size of your army proves invincible. Perhaps, too, we might have more speed and success building our flights if we were to take the boys when they are much smaller, say, six or seven years. We could begin training them in schools near our military posts. That way they could see the dragons flying and become used to them. As things stand now, by the time we get the youths at apprentice age, the fear of the dragons is already instilled in them. And, as you have said before, it is desirable for the rest of the population to fear the dragons somewhat. It makes the job of containment much easier for the troops. I believe if we started the boys earlier it would speed up the process and hasten our success in crushing those religious fools in the Southern Region. Then they will have to bow to your power, and acknowledge you as Emperor of Kinthoria."

The Birth of a King

Volant smiled broadly at the Flight Leader. Ever since he had met Bendor, he had been drawn to respect the wisdom of the young man. Less than a handful of others could boast such a position of honor. Somehow, Bendor even had the added ability to persuade Volant to see both sides of an issue, without resentment or anger, even when the young man's counsel ran contrary to Volant's opinions. At this particular time, however, he was especially pleased by Bendor's optimistic words, since they had amply fed his ego as well.

"Yes, I think you may be right again, Bendor." He clasped his companion's shoulder. "I shall give it strong consideration, although I am now of the firm conviction that our conclusions regarding the tenacity and character of the Southern Races was in error. We have been hoping that they would recognize our superiority, especially with the power of the dragons at our disposal, and that they would unite with us. We have made the mistake of thinking they would desire such power, or that they would capitulate out of trepidation at our winged friends. I don't believe any of us foresaw the possibility of such strong resistance for such an extended period of time."

He sighed as they entered the cookhall. "I still maintain that it is crucial to crush their spirits first, to make them malleable enough for complete domination. It is imperative that we find the means of bringing them to their knees. They must become so weak and dependent upon us that they will obey without question...or die."

Bendor shook his head in agreement, while silently recalling the disconcerting reports coming in from the southern scouts. These caused him to fear privately that perhaps Volant's plans would never be accomplished entirely, unless, of course, the Dragonleader was willing to annihilate entire races of people in his desire for domination. He found himself suddenly deeply troubled by the possibility that his emperor would order the genocide of thousands in order to become the absolute ruler of Kinthoria. He shook the thoughts quickly from his head and forced himself into a lighter mood.

"After that steam bath, I'm in dire need of some refreshment. Would you like some ale, sir?" Bendor glanced at his leader.

Volant shook his head. "I must decline this time. I have some other business awaiting me that promises to lift my spirits even more effectively than ale," he said with a menacing leer. He turned on his heel and strode away, leaving the younger man's interest suddenly piqued.

Bendor was about to ask if he might join him, when he saw Mavi coming in his direction with a tankard of frothy ale. Oh, how this slave girl attracted his interest. He found himself constantly scanning the cookhall for the long, black hair that had a way of falling alluringly over her shoulders. Those large, brown eyes and that delicate oval face were almost enough to move his cynical, young spirit. He shook his head sharply and inhaled deeply to calm his heart which had a curious tendency to beat erratically every time he was in her presence.

Bendor knew he could take her if he had a mind to, and with the full approval of his superiors. But, there was something about Mavi that compelled him toward fierce protection. He cringed mentally at his gentle thoughts as he envisioned the relentless ridicule he had endured through the years by the troops when it was discovered that he held women in honor, even to so worthless a class as the common cookhall slaves.

He sat at the long, wooden table and took the chilled mug offered by the girl, making sure to brush his hands along her small, delicate fingers.

She smiled shyly, "M'lord." She curtsied, and turned to busy herself with other tasks. Bendor caught her by the arm, and gently turned her around to face him. Mavi flushed deep crimson. Her long, dark eyelashes rested on her cheeks as she lowered her eyes.

"Where are you off to so quickly, little one?" he asked softly.

Mavi would not bring her eyes to meet his, and when she spoke, her voice could barely be heard above the din in the huge hall. "I must be getting back to the cookpots, m'lord."

Bendor smiled, and said teasingly, "Ah. The cookpots are now more important than the Red Flight leader, are they?"

Mavi shifted uncomfortably on her feet, and stammered as she looked to see if anyone was watching. "N-no, m'lord," she finally raised her dark eyes to meet his gaze; then looked away quickly in embarrassment.

Bendor released her arm. He allowed a few seconds to pass, then shooed her away with a smile. "Run along, Mavi, I would hate to cause you any trouble with the mistress of the kitchen."

She made a quick curtsy, and scurried off toward the great cookpots simmering over the fire pits.

Bendor sat watching her a while longer. There was something in his character that recoiled from the very idea of men so misusing their strength as to take women by force. He would have nothing to do with so heinous an act that not only hurt and damaged women, but that to his mind also showed an entire corruption of true manhood. He knew that in this one area, he was unlike the majority of the younger dragon riders. He had never participated in the ravaging that went on during most of their raids, nor would he allow such atrocities from any man in his flight. In his eleven years as Flight Leader, close to three dozen men had requested transfer into the Blue Flight for this single objection alone. They had suggested in their requests that perhaps their illustrious leader had a major problem with his masculinity.

Bendor was aware that he had been contemptuously nicknamed "The Eunuch," and his Red Flight unit was called "The Harem." He was always rather surprised, therefore, when a man from the Purple or Green training flights requested to join his unit because of his unyielding stance on this one matter of conduct. Volant had never questioned him on it, so he assumed he was free to operate his flight in any manner he chose. It was his ambition to lead the finest, most capable, and most respected unit in Volant's empire.

Bendor swallowed the rest of his ale in one quick draught, and walked across the hall toward his own chamber. Mavi's eyes followed him until he turned the corner. She vowed to continue praying for this man who showed so much promise.

Volant entered the dimly lit room where his two advisors awaited him. A young man was lying prostrate on the floor in unbearable pain.

The Dragonleader looked at Sirtar, his Force Commander, as he stood over the man. He was continually amazed at the size of this giant who virtually filled any room with his immense body. His arms, which were at present twisting one of the legs of the man into an impossible angle, were as thick as some men's thighs. His mere presence brought fear into most men's hearts, and they cowered before him. With his black, shoulder-length hair, and his full dark beard, he resembled not so much a man as an enormous black bear.

Volant glanced at the third man in the room and could barely see the gleam in the eyes beneath the bushy gray brows of his elder advisor. Beland, the ancient, former Red Flight leader was smiling at him with a near toothless grin. He was almost into his seventieth year, and his hair was a solid ash gray. His aged face was wrinkled and weathered like that of an old mariner. The dark eyes that shone from under those enormous brows were alert and bright, evidence that even at this age the old man's brilliant mind was still as sharp as ever. This was the sole reason he had been included in Volant's council. His once powerful body was unfit for further flying, now flaccid and weak through years of debauchery. He was the principle reason that Volant took such great care to keep his own body fine-tuned. The Dragonleader did not intend ever to be put out to pasture. He would die flying his dragon. Indeed, Beland's own heart and mind rebelled against his weakness and begged to be airborne once again.

The old warrior had withstood everything life had offered him, the good and the bad. He could tolerate just about anything...anything that is, except a thief.

"Good morning, sir. Sorry we had to bother you, but we knew you would not want to miss the opportunity of dealing with this filth." Beland nodded toward the man on the floor, who was groaning loudly. Even in his semi-conscious state, the pain inflicted by Sirtar's mighty arms assaulted every part of his being.

Volant gave the slightest motion for the giant to ease up enough so that the slave would not lapse into insensibility. He wanted the miscreant to be entirely aware of what was taking place. He picked up a pitcher, moved to the young man's side and flung water onto his bloodied face. The slave gasped and opened his eyes.

"This worthless trash was caught inside the meat house, trying to steal a piece of oxen meant for the yearling dragons," Beland reported.

The Birth of a King

Terror filled the young mans eyes. Volant was half-angry with his two advisors for obviously having started the entertainment before his arrival. He casually inspected the man's broken nose and the deep gash above his eye. The rags which hung from his gaunt frame marked him as a drudge.

"Please m'lord," the slave cried through his pain, "my wife and baby girl are starving...."

"Kill him," Volant said quietly, without emotion. "I will not allow thieves in my kingdom."

Sirtar's sinister smile broadened. Crossing the room, Volant spoke casually, looking the young man directly in the eye. "Bring his woman to me that I may console her in her sorrow," he grinned maliciously. "The thief's brat may be left to fend for itself. I don't need a kingdom full of thieving whelps sapping away at my wealth."

The doomed man glared back at him in hateful defiance. "You filthy...aaahhh!" He screamed as Sirtar twisted his leg until the knee snapped and gave way.

"Now, no one gave you permission to speak, laddie-boy," he purred as he unsheathed his dagger. "Besides, is that the proper way to thank your Emperor for caring for your little wife after your death? It's not every monarch who would do so much for a poor, grieving slave woman. Tch, Tch, such ingratitude." He smiled and deftly ended the young man's life.

The huge man wiped the blood from his dagger on the dead man's breeches, and called for three of his slaves. "Clean up this trash at once. Move, unless you want to join him!" He barked, as the slaves stood in shock at the sight on the floor.

"Sorry for the mess, sir," Sirtar said, his ebony eyes shining with pleasure at Volant's smile of approval.

Beland filled three goblets with wine as Volant sat down, stretching his legs out before him. He looked at his two counselors as he sighed in satisfaction. "This is turning out to be an excellent morning. Bendor and I have just inspected a fine batch of eggs that will be ready for hatching on the Day of Apprenticeship. I expressed my doubts that there will be enough new lads fit to bond with them, and I believe he has come up with a very good plan for future hatchings. And now," he smiled at the corpse being carried out of the chamber, "the empire is infested with one less thief."

Volant regarded Sirtar as he oversaw the slaves at their grizzly work. They had removed the body of the slave, who in desperate concern for his starving family had become a thief. At least one of them determined to send word to the man's wife to disappear with her daughter. Others, with scrub brushes and wooden buckets, removed the dark stain from the floor, and spread fresh, new rushes.

The Blue Flight Leader's dark eyes glistened at the sight of his kill. Volant recalled watching Sirtar many times with the Dragon Army, during the grueling war games known as the Solurko Tolgo. The dark giant was in his mid-thirties, and despite his fast-paced living, his body was stone hard. He was invincible with any weapon. Volant was forced on many occasions to intervene in the games to remind Sirtar that they were trying to build an army, not maim or kill everyone in it.

The Colonel demanded the same unrelenting fierceness from each of his own men. His Blue Flight was notorious for its combat expertise, but it was also known for the bestial cruelty of every one of its troops. Privately, most of the troops in the other flights, while envying the success of Sirtar's flight in the battle arena, disdained their use of dishonorable and unprofessional tactics. It was widely felt that no respectable knight would think of participating in such conduct. Sirtar selected for his flight only those men disencumbered with conscience or moral principle. These had been the banes of their scholars, the disreputable, angry, troublemakers at each of their halls. Most were nothing more than swaggering, perverted brawlers. In Sirtar's twisted opinion, these were the characteristics of real men. He would tolerate nothing less in his troops.

The only cadet he had never been able to break was Bendor, the Red Flight leader. Volant had abruptly promoted the young man to Flight Leader directly out of his cadet training in the Purple Flight. Sirtar had been stunned and outraged. For three years he had waited to call Bendor into his own flight. Planning the torment and final destruction of the younger man had been Sirtar's most compelling purpose during that time. Suddenly, with Beland's forced retirement, the talented and intelligent nineteen-year-old Bendor was a Flight Leader, and Sirtar's plans had turned to dust.

Bendor had been well aware of Sirtar's animosity. The two men hated one another because of their diametrically opposed philosophies on the proper character and conduct of a dragon rider. Sirtar was incensed that someone seven years his junior should presume to instruct a seasoned dragon rider on the conduct of military personnel. More than once Beland had taken action to keep the two from shredding each other to pieces during their frequent disputes. Sirtar would most likely have murdered the young man in secret, had he not been told by Volant to see to it that no harm came to him, on pain of dismissal should he fail. This served well for the preservation of Bendor's life, but it served also to fuel Sirtar's jealous hatred of the younger man.

Captains Tulak and Tomas were in command of the Purple and Green Flights. These flights were for the training of new riders, and were used by Volant on missions that did not require the expertise of seasoned troops. The younger cadets served chiefly as messengers. The older ones flew monthly tours of duty to the outlying scholars halls. There they monitored the progress of the young boys who showed promise for the dragon flights. It was also their duty to gather up the youth for each year's Day of Apprenticeship.

Beland handed his leader a goblet of wine, as Volant thought about his selection of Sirtar as Force Commander of the Dragon Army. He was not entirely satisfied with his choice, but the man was the best qualified to accomplish Volant's present goals. He was ruthless and ambitious. His physical presence secured the fear and obedience that Volant demanded to maintain undiminished control of his forces.

He took a draught of wine, and looked at his older advisor with disdain. "So, how many young *squires* have you been able to locate for the hatching this year, Beland? I trust you have left no stone unturned?"

Beland cleared his throat, and gazed out of the window, casting about for the right words to deliver his unfavorable report. This was always an uncomfortable subject for him, especially as it seemed that year after year the number of eligible apprentices was never

The Birth of a King

enough to satisfy his ambitious leader. Each year saw fewer and fewer young men of apprenticeship age. Granted, many had died of the dust-plague or during the massive starvation after the war. However, Beland secretly suspected that the accounts of the Birthing Days of Kinthoria's male youths were being tampered with, if not obliterated altogether. He suspected, and rightly so, that many people were keeping their boys hidden, and were not sending them to the scholars halls.

"I think not enough to please you, sir. There are approximately forty-five boys in over four hundred coming of age this year who are considered eligible to stand in the egg chamber. Although it is impossible to calculate how many of those will turn tail and run. Dhragh!" he cursed, as he kicked the wooden bench beside the table. "Why do they have to be so bloody afraid of such beautiful beasts?"

Even this minimal exertion threw him into another fit of coughing, further increasing his anger and frustration. Beland would have given anything to be atop Caecr again. The unreasoning fear of these young idiots who would not allow even the small, new hatchlings to approach them was beyond his understanding. Did they not see the power they would have atop the mighty beasts once they were grown? In the meantime, what satisfaction they would have in the bond of absolute trust and friendship with their dragons. He absently rubbed his beard as his fit of coughing subsided. He turned his eyes back to Volant, silently pleading once more, for permission to fly his aging dragon.

Volant put up his hand, and shook his head. "No, you old fool, don't even attempt to gain permission to remount. Your mind is needed for my service now, not your tired body. You have nothing of which to be ashamed. You have served Kinthoria with excellence and distinction as a dragon rider. Now it is time to serve her just as singularly with the wisdom you have gained in all those years."

The Day of Apprenticeship was the only thing in Beland's life that was dear to him, as it brought back so many prized memories of his dragon. Many of the children brought into Keratha on that day were sent to indentured service under the often harsh training of overworked journeymen and crofters, to become nothing more than nameless drudges. The few who showed an active interest in the

The Birth of a King

black priesthood were sent to the Lucian temples to offer their souls, service, and lives to the dark god. Only the elite of the Weapons Masters trainees were chosen to enter the cavernous egg chamber to be placed before the eggs.

In the month after the Day of Apprenticeship, the lads were briefly trained in encouraging the friendship of the dragons, and in establishing the life long bond between human and beast. Then, at the appointed time, each boy was placed before an egg. Once the tiny dragon had poked a hole in its shell, the lad was directed to assist the hatchling by encouraging its escape from confinement. After emerging from the tough, leathery shell, the baggy little hatchling was bathed by the lad as he spoke gentle reassurances to his new charge.

Most of the boys, upon seeing the sparkling eyes, and hearing the delightful chirping of friendship from the miniature dragons, fell instantly in love with the creatures. A handful saw only gargoyle-like little beasts with their large eyes, oversized heads, and taloned joints on leathery wings groping the air for support. These boys turned and raced from the chamber, screaming in terror. In fear, they had mistaken the nudge of friendship from the hideous little beasts for the desire for flesh and blood.

Beland did not know how many more times Volant would merely place the terrified boys in training for the Knights army. Each year the Dragonmaster's anger became more intense as he saw his dreams of a vast army of dragon riders diminish with each fleeing youth. Beland knew it was only a matter of time before his leader would begin slaughtering the young men on the spot.

Sirtar returned to his seat, satisfied that the slaves had removed all traces of their recent amusement with the young slave-thief. He laughed at the absurdity of Beland's foolish delusion that he was fit to ride. "I thought I told you to see the herbalist or one of the Lucian priests about that cough. Whatever is ailing you seems to have affected your mind, also, old man." He jeered maliciously.

Beland shot him a look of murderous anger. "So you have, young Sirtar. But as you can see, I have not heeded your unsolicited advice. It is equally apparent that you have not thought to heed mine about your overbearing mouth," he snapped back.

Sirtar chuckled derisively as he finished off his second flagon of wine. He glanced at the older man with evil hunger in his eyes. *"How easy and entertaining it would be to slice open his bloated, useless body,"* he mused.

"Enough!" barked Volant. His eyes bored into Beland. "Are you telling me that in the whole of Kinthoria there are less than fifty boys considered eligible? That's impossible. The dust-plague and starvation didn't kill off a whole generation of children. I should have been in complete power by now, and instead I'm struggling year after year just to fill my flights."

He took a deep breath, willing his rage to subside. Bendor's words from earlier that morning echoed in his mind. He hoped that the young Flight Leader had been right, and that he would soon be the unquestionable Emperor of all Kinthoria.

Much to the surprise and infinite relief of Beland and Sirtar, Volant said, more in disgust than anger, "Both of you leave my sight. Apparently, I have misjudged your mental and military capabilities. It would seem that neither of you is capable of any substantial effort to establish my empire. Fifty-seven eggs. Fifty-seven! And the two of you, with four flights, are unable to find enough boys in the entire land to stand for the hatching. I swear by Lucia, my enemies could do me no less disservice than you. Truly, I should banish the both of you to Gundroth territory. Now get out!"

A week later Volant was roused from his sleep by a knock on his bedchamber door.

"What is it?" He barked in annoyance.

"Sir, I have a message from Reeban, something about two eligible lads missing from their scholars hall," said a muffled voice from the corridor.

Volant stared into the darkness in disbelief. "You woke me in the middle of the night to tell me that two more boys are missing? What am I, the nanny of Kinthoria?" He screeched. "If you value your worthless hide, you'd better never let me discover your identity. Give the message to Sirtar, you fool. He'll know if they're worth the time to spend looking for them."

His wife Vanessi stirred in her sleep beside him. *"Probably just two miscreants out having some fun before we bring them in for apprenticeship,"* he thought. He felt Vanessi's warm breath on his neck, and smelled the flowery fragrance of her dark red hair on the pillow next to his face. The courier and his message were quickly forgotten.

The exhausted young man sketched an angry bow outside the door, and returned hastily to the cookhall. He was extremely grateful that Volant had not recognized his voice for he had no misgivings about the man making good the threats upon his life.

He had been flying most of the day, and felt in need of some ale to soothe his throat. He sat down opposite a slumped figure at one of the long tables in the cookhall. He took a lengthy pull from his mug, and wiped the foam from his mouth with the back of his hand.

The other man raised his head and stared at him with two fiery red eyes. Sirtar blinked several times, squinting and peering through swollen eyelids as though trying to recall the identity of his own Green Flight leader.

"Ah, Tomashhh, you're bacckkk." He slurred loudly, his breath blasting the young Captain with a noxious reek.

The young flight leader nodded. He eyed his commander with disdain. The man had obviously been deep into the keg for much of the night.

"Yes. I have just now returned from Reeban," he answered, consciously drinking his own mug with more moderation than usual.

"Rheeebbaahhhn?" Sirtar drawled, swaying a little on the bench. "Wha' were you doin'...all the whay ofer there for?"

Tomas pushed a leather pouch across the table to Sirtar. "Sir, you will recall that it was time for the monthly visits to the scholars halls to tally the number of new boarders. While I was in Reeban the Headmaster gave me this. It's a message for Volant, but he refused to be disturbed. Said it could wait, and that I should give it to you."

After much cursing, and nearly destroying the leather pouch to withdraw the parchment, Sirtar finally managed to pull the message loose. The Colonel broke the seal, and unrolled the sheet. Although his bloodshot eyes could barely focus, he was able to recognize the evenness of a scholar's script on the page. He turned to Tomas, and said groggily, "I'll take care of thish."

Tomas rose immediately, leaving his ale unfinished. He had been flying for close to a fortnight. The Headmaster at the scholars hall in Reeban had been highly unnerved that one of his prize pupils was missing, and had apparently taken his lackey with him. Sorely was distraught at the possible loss of a lad with Tanner's brilliant potential, and the prestige that his undoubted success would have brought to his hall. The man had understandably pressed Tomas to get this "urgent" message to Volant himself, with all due haste. The Flight Leader had complied, only to be abruptly turned away by his Emperor. Now, the necessity of having to endure the presence of this drunken buffoon was quickly threatening to undo the tenuous control of his temper. "Very well, sir. I'll take my leave then, with your permission."

Sirtar gave a quiet grunt and slightly waved his finger in dismissal, and the young Captain walked away. The Colonel's brow formed a deep vee, as he doggedly attempted to read the message. Even in his semi-conscious state, he was somewhat disturbed by the letter, though he could not have given a reason.

Two boys were missing from the scholars hall in Reeban. One of them, a youth named Tanner, was rumored to be a very promising young warrior. Sirtar vaguely remembered wanting to meet the young man who had already made such a name for himself at the Aonghas. The message said they had been missing for at least two days. "Hmph. Th're pro'bly back by now. Ish been a for'nigh sinz then." Sirtar knew that many boys disappeared for a day or two, to do a last bit of carousing before coming of age. They always returned with rather severe hangovers, assorted wounds, and bruises from a brawl or two. However, even in his inebriated state, Sirtar recalled that The Day of Apprenticeship was still a few months away. He rubbed his beard and stared at the parchment in foggy bewilderment.

"Cowards!" He slammed his heavy fist down on the table, the noise echoing through the empty cookhall. Taking no notice that he was talking to himself, he continued, "Runningh away when they could be knihgss."

The Birth of a King

He stared blankly at the paper in his hand; then slowly turned his gaze to the dying fire in the hearth. "Lethem run for a while. When I fine themm, I'll perzonally crush them to dus," he muttered quietly, grinding his boot heel into the stony floor just as the room turned black, and his head hit the table with a loud thud.

Chapter Four

THE DARK GOD

Volant stared at the stone walls of his war chamber, his hands folded on the table. Loose parchments and charts littered the table and the floor about him. He loved to sit in this dark, windowless place. Often he would blow out the one tallow candle burning on the table and sit quietly, deeply inhaling the heavy, dank atmosphere. During these times, the chamber mirrored the depth of the blackness of his heart. A malevolent smile rested unconsciously upon his face. He sat, stone still, and basked in the evil that flowed in and out of his soul, like an oily tide on the shore of a diseased, long forgotten land. His ability to tap into the abundant, raw power of his master filled him with a colossal confidence that bordered on self-worship. Tonight he would implore his master's presence, as he had done countless times through the past years.

His power had been gradually drained by the constant threat from the Southern Regions and the accursed An'ilden, his unsuccessful attempts to fill his dragon flights, and overseeing the training of his army. The many petty cares accompanying his chosen title as Emperor of Kinthoria, all served to heighten his awareness of his incessant need of the comforting confirmation of his incomparable value to Lucia and his plans for Kinthoria. He craved the sensation of Lucia's power rushing in once again to slake his thirst for absolute control.

Volant picked up a large chunk of incense and held it in the flame of the candle. He turned it slowly, until a portion the size of his fingertip glowed red. He placed it carefully onto the golden image of his lord, staring at it for several minutes. His unblinking eyes reflected the red glow of the incense, causing his face to take on a demonic aspect.

Staring as though entranced, he picked up the stiletto from the table. As the metal caught the light of the candle's flame, he ran the razor-sharp edge slowly across the palm of his hand. Blood beaded up along the cut and pooled into his palm. Lifting his hand above the golden image of Lucia, he let the blood drip onto the brightly burning incense. Each drop hissed as it touched the ember. The smoke wafted in fretful curls to the top of the war chamber.

He waited with that curious mixture of dread and exhilaration, for the now familiar sound of howling wind filled with maniacal shrieks and half-human screams. Volant shivered when his body arched, as the ever-present icy cold that surrounded his lord invaded his body; for Lucia had somehow absorbed all of the cold of countless millennia of death into his being. There was not one hint of warmth, no love, and no light present in this ancient creature. Lucia was the "dark god" who knew only pain and death. He was bloated with the filth of eons of hatred for light and beauty, and for every other living thing except himself.

Lucia, at one time, in ages long past, had been a glorious being, full of light and adorned with unparalleled beauty. Precious jewels of every kind had been set with gold and were woven into his hair and brilliantly white robes. The fire of his inner being illuminated every facet of the jewels and turned the gold settings to small suns. His beauty was indescribable. He had been pure and good, living in a paradise of absolute perfection and glory. The highest of all created beings, he alone bore the privilege and responsibility of having been created for the sole purpose of guarding the glory of the one true God, Elyon. However, at some time during the infinite space of an eternity past, he began to desire the place of Elyon for himself. He had deceived himself into believing that his beauty and power were self-produced instead of gifts from the hand of Elyon. He became gorged with love for himself and for his extraordinary magnificence. So great was his vanity and jealousy that it poisoned his being. His once glorious inner fire consumed him, destroying the perfection of his beauty. Inwardly he became a dark, evil, loathsome being, full of hatred and envy. So poisonous did his nature become that millions of other once perfect beings were contaminated with the darkness of his essence. It was truly a day of ineffable sorrow and tragedy, when this once, most beautiful of all created beings, and all of his followers were cast away from Elyon. They fell from the presence of the loving Father who had created them, and were forced into the confining atmosphere surrounding one small planet. Lucia alone was allowed entry to speak before his Maker, as an enemy is tolerated in the presence of the High King.

Lucia's desires had been granted him, but with the same measure of perversion with which he himself was perverted. He was now a ruler, but his kingdom was a small, beautiful planet and the atmosphere surrounding it. His evil nature hated this dominion, and he planned to demonstrate his displeasure to Elyon by making it a kingdom of darkness filled with the stench of everything vile and loathsome. He had retained power, knowledge, and some freedom, but never had his power been so impotent, so lacking in authoritative strength. Never had his knowledge been so useless or his freedom so confined. Worst of all, his greatest desire was forever out of reach. He would never know the total domination of all of creation, and of the only true God.

After his banishment, Lucia had resolved to begin on a smaller scale. He would use the creation on this planet against the Creator. The inhabitants were weak and malleable, easily deceived and contaminated. His greatest advantage was their terror of the evil violence of his power that caused them to hold him in awe. He plotted to enthrall as many of them as possible and through them to devastate the lands of Kinthoria and all other worlds, one at a time, until he became ruler of the universe. In the unending darkness of his perverted nature, he centered all of his thoughts, all of his existence, on this one single design. He would see that all of the pain, the anger, the disappointment and defeat that he had endured would be heaped upon Elyon in triplicate. He, the master deceiver, had deceived even his own mind into believing that he could eventually dethrone Elyon and place himself as the Supreme Power. All of his

The Birth of a King

darkest plots and intents had but this one goal - Elyon *would* bow to him. He would see himself seated in majesty, or Lucia would destroy himself and everything else that Elyon had created in the trying.

As centuries passed, he had momentarily tasted the sweetness of victory when he held Elyon's Son, Yesha, in the grips of death. He had even been able to confine the Son in his dark realm, or so he thought. However, even in all of this, he was deceived, for the Son was not killed by Lucia, but momentarily shed his mortal body in sacrifice for the inhabitants of this planet. He was not a captive in the realm of death, but was on a mission unknown to Lucia.

In the midst of Lucia's ecstasy and celebration at his supposed triumph in this crucial battle, the unimaginable happened. His eternal foe had simply walked out of the prison of death. Not only had the enemy walked free, but he had taken Lucia's prized possessions with him: the most powerful weapons with which he had threatened humanity since the beginning of their creation. This Yesha had snatched the Keys to Lucia's domain and his rule over Death. He no longer had the power to hold the souls of his prisoners in a living death forever. The Son would now give those who believed in Him and in His sacrifice the ability to live again with immortal bodies. Lucia had been devastated. Many of his evil minions had suffered unspeakably as he unleashed the full force of his hatred and wrath against the true God and His Son.

Volant's thoughts turned back many years. He was but into his twentieth year, and had just been raised to knighthood. This was a tremendous honor that almost every youth in Kinthoria coveted. All through Kinthorian history, the dragon riders had been the peacekeepers. When danger came in the form of marauding alien bands from across the seas or from the unruly Trolls or their distant, miniature cousins, the Gundroths, the dragon riders were always there to protect and to help.

To be a dragon rider was to hold a position of highest respect. This appealed to Volant's rather large ego. He had been reprimanded many times for his tyrannical behavior toward his countrymen. His superiors had demanded that he atone for his overly proud manner by taking on extra patrols or doing tasks that he felt were considerably below his status as a Kinthorian knight. He executed these penances quietly, to appease his Captain, and for the satisfaction that knighthood brought him. But inwardly he seethed and vowed vengeance on every officer who had offended him.

In those days, everyone in Kinthoria loved the beautiful dragons, cheering and waving as they flew overhead. They trusted the creatures without question. There had never been an incident of a dragon harming any of the races in Kinthoria. Not even the Trolls or Gundroths had been harmed during the frequent skirmishes to keep them under control. It merely took the presence of the immense beasts in the vicinity and a few arrows shot over their heads to cause these slow-witted, though vicious races, to turn tail and run.

That time was long past and, Volant wished, long forgotten. He shifted unconsciously in his chair and continued, in his possessed state to stare at the candle flame. He mind moved ahead several years, revisiting the day he had started his long, dark journey in the service of his lord.

He had been riding his horse through a meadow when he caught a glimpse of a man dressed in a black robe, standing at the edge of a large wood. He recognized at once that this was a Lucian priest and dismounted. His body trembled with apprehension as many thoughts raced through his mind. He did not know if he should be ecstatic that this day had finally come, or outraged at the man for risking their capture by openly revealing his presence.

The priest merely stood silently eyeing Volant. Finally, the young knight began to wonder if the man was unaware of his identity. If not, Volant could be in deadly peril. The now familiar, bone-chilling air surrounded him, and he knew he could no longer flee, even if he chose to. The priest's mere presence seemed to suffocate Volant's mind and press in upon his soul. The man was speaking to him with barely a movement of his lips. He saw now that it was Dreag, one of the priests with whom he had observed the criminal and vile rites of the Lucian religion.

Dreag croaked into Volant's mind. *"Our Master has summoned you."*

The young man shivered involuntarily as the dark memories of the past years raced through his mind. He saw many black-robed

The Birth of a King

men swaying to and fro around an altar in a macabre dance. He recalled the pigeons and doves and other animals confined in cages. The odor of burning flesh and the dripping blood moved across his consciousness. As he watched with a detached dismay, he witnessed those around him chanting the words of dark incantations.

He had visited one of the outlawed temples many times since he had first discovered it by mere chance while he was out on patrol. His unit had been looking for roving bands of Trolls who were spreading fear and havoc in some of the villages bordering the Northern Moors.

He had smelled a faint whisper of smoke as he flew just over the top of a small wood near Carmarthan. Desperately wanting to make a good impression by single-handedly capturing the Trolls he circled back and landed his dragon, Lok, a few hundred paces from an outcrop of boulders. Volant drew his sword and walked cautiously into the wood. He searched the area for almost half an hour, finding not so much as one Troll footprint. He sat on a huge boulder, and sniffed the air again, trying to locate the scent once more. His shoulders slumped as nothing but cool, clean air filled his lungs.

"Capturing those filthy Trolls would have been more than enough proof that I am ready to enter the Knighthood," he thought to himself. He cursed loudly as he began walking back to his dragon. He had walked but a few paces, when he caught a movement in the trees up ahead. A black-robed figure slipped between two boulders and disappeared.

Volant stood frozen in shock for several moments before he realized what he had just seen. "It can't be," he whispered to himself, "Volant, get hold of your senses." An uneasy smile slowly spread across his face. He knew that the black priests had been purged from Kinthoria long ago. Practicing the dark arts of the fallen god Lucia had been forbidden for generations. Anyone caught doing so was immediately put to death; so dangerous and contaminating was the evil of their arts. Yet, he had just seen the shaven head and black robe that were the trademarks of the priesthood.

He took a step toward the two boulders. He saw and heard nothing. He advanced at an excruciatingly slow pace toward the spot where he had seen the priest disappear. By the time he had reached the boulders his heart was racing wildly and his sword hand was sweaty and trembling.

"This is insane," he said, gulping in deep breaths of air to calm himself. He had always been a risk taker, unconcerned whether or not harm came to him. In fact, he liked living life on the edge. However, this was something almost beyond even his recklessness.

Volant stepped between the boulders and almost fell head first into a darkened chasm. He caught himself and allowed his senses to adjust to the deep blackness. He felt for something solid under his foot and placed it down, slowly shifting his weight forward. To his surprise, he found that he was on a narrow stairway. He began a slow descent into the cool darkness, carefully placing one foot in front of the other. His tunic snagged on the rough stone wall as it raked across his shoulder. It was not long before he could discern a red glow at the bottom of the stairway and smelled the sweet odor of burning incense.

Curiosity overwhelmed and compelled him even as his courage would have failed. This was a mad adventure, and Volant reveled in the excitement coursing through his body.

He stepped onto the floor of a chamber, holding his sword at the ready in expectation of attack. Instead, almost to his disappointment, there was not a soul in sight. He slowly scanned the large, circular space. The stone walls were covered with paintings and carvings of demons, gargoyles, and creatures for which he knew no names. He stared at each one intently, trying to read the inscriptions carved in the stone beneath the grizzly scenes. The texts were written in a language unfamiliar to the highly educated Volant. Most of the scenes were hideous, filled with a violence and perversion which incited his interest, but which eventually made even his lust for perversion turn away in revulsion.

In the middle of the room was a circular, stone pit, in which red-hot embers glowed. They cast an eerie light about the chamber, causing shadows to shift in the carvings on the walls, as though giving life to the hideous creatures. He walked to the pit and noticed for the first time since entering the cavern, a huge face hanging from the stone roof above the red embers. He stared at it in fascination. One moment it appeared to be made of stone and the next, he would swear it was solid gold. The nameless face held his attention for the better part of an hour. He lowered himself to the sandy floor, and leaned back, resting his head against the wall. The features of this huge mask-like carving mesmerized him. All fear of being in a forbidden place was cast aside and replaced by the lure of that face.

Volant could not tell if the mask was grimacing or smiling. As with the paintings and carvings on the walls, the features changed with the light from the glowing embers.

His gaze went to the hollow eyes and remained there for quite some time. He sat motionless as something began to stir faintly within his soul. It grew with every heartbeat, until finally a feeling raced through him that was so terrifying and yet so exhilarating that it overwhelmed his senses. He found himself panting for breath, fearful of what had just happened. He did not realize it at the time, though he would begin to understand later, that the vile, dark god, called Lucia, had just begun bartering for his soul. In that one instant, Lucia had violated Volant's heart, soul, mind, and body. The god knew his deepest aspirations, his darkest secrets, his strengths and his weaknesses. That simple brush with the awesome, though heinous, power lying behind the deep, hollow eyes of the mask had planted the seed of an intense hunger in the young man's heart. That invisible presence had hinted that absolutely nothing could be done to stop Volant from gaining this new, raw power if he chose to take it. Volant, in his consuming lust for power, reveled in ecstasy as he imagined what it would be like to hold and wield such endless strength. He imagined himself finally breaking free of all of the rigid, intolerable ways of the religious fanatics at the castle. He would see his dream of being the greatest Knight in Kinthoria fulfilled at last.

The dark eyes peering out from under the hood of a black robe had watched the exchange between his master and this young renegade with intense interest and satisfaction. He would stay close to this insolent rebel. He would be his mentor, his guide, his teacher - perhaps his death if he proved false.

The dark priest slowly advanced toward Volant, waiting to see if he truly was deeply in trance. Satisfied that such was the case, he came forward and drew the sacred dagger from his sash. He held it

The Birth of a King

up to the mask-like face of his god, whispering evil incantations. He then knelt beside the young man, took his hand, and drew the blade across Volant's palm, catching the first six drops of blood in a tiny golden bowl. He kissed the bleeding gash with reverence. He repeated the ritual with the other hand, then slowly rose, smiling to himself with blood drenched lips. He lifted the golden bowl in offering to the image of his god, and then poured one drop of the blood on the glowing embers. An intense burst of flame and a deep roar shot out of the embers, and was gone in the space of a heartbeat. The priest then drank the rest of the blood and tossed the golden bowl into the now white-hot embers. He watched in fascination, as the vessel slowly melted away.

Looking up into the face of his god, he spoke softy, "The way is prepared, my master, even as you have instructed your servant." He turned silently, leaving Volant's hands bleeding in his lap.

The priest melted silently back into the shadows hoping against hope that they had chosen the right man. Once their lord's power was released, they would be able to spread their evil like a ravaging disease across the land.

"Lucia's power must be freed. We will never succeed without greater access to it," he thought.

Surely, this young man was the right one. Who else was so defiant against the teachings of Elyon, so egotistical in his thinking, so perfect a vessel for the filling of the dark god?

Volant jerked out of the trance. He wanted to stay and drink more deeply from the cup of power he had just tasted. But he would have to wait until another time. He sensed he had been here too long already, and he did not wish to raise any suspicions. Not now, not when he had finally found the power that would make all of his dreams come true.

Suddenly he noticed the pain in his hands. He looked down at his lap and saw them covered in blood, and saw the pool of blood on the front of his breeches. He cried out and jumped to his feet, his eyes darting about the cavern to discover his assailant. As before, he found it silent and empty. He looked at his hands once more; then checked the rest of his body for other possible wounds. To his relief he found that his hands had been his assailant's only target.

The Birth of a King

He bounded for the stairs and taking them by twos reached the top and burst out into the blinding sunlight, gasping for fresh air. He instinctively raised his hand to shield his eyes from the light. To his amazement, he saw no blood on it whatever. He looked at his other hand - no blood. Both wounds were no more than hairline scars across his palms. He looked at his breeches and found no trace of the blood that had covered them. Volant spun around to face the cave, eyes wide and mouth agape, and stared in terror down into the dark hole from which he had come. He was suddenly so filled with fear that he fell against the boulder and retched violently.

He knew that his fear would pass, and was grateful that such things never affected him for long, for he knew with certainty that he would come to this cave often in the coming months, to meet with the source of such overwhelming power. He would give anything to share in that power...anything. He would tell no one of his discovery.

Energy was surging through his body as he raced out of the woods. He marked the terrain in his memory for his return, wishing the time for revisiting this place to come with haste. He smiled to himself as he ran back to his dragon. His mind reveled in the imagined revenge he would take upon all of the people and institutions that had tried to control and mold him.

As he broke through the edge of the forest, he could see Lok dozing in the afternoon sun. "Dhragh!" He shouted to the dragon as he patted his flank, "I could have been killed in those woods, and you're out here napping. Some protector you are, old friend." Lok rolled his sparkling eyes toward him and nuzzled him with his huge snout. The huge beast suddenly pulled his head back with a snort that sounded for all the world like a question. His eyes shone brighter than Volant had ever seen, as he seemed to be inspecting the young man in deep confusion. Volant laughed, "Hey, what's the matter, Lok? Did the sun bake your brain inside that huge skull? It's me, old friend," he said with reassurance as he held out his hand to the creature.

When Lok smelled his hand, he became even more agitated. Volant was not able to mount him until he had spent quite some time speaking softly and coaxing him gently with his voice. He found

The Birth of a King

that the dragon would not abide the touch of his hands unless he first put on his riding gloves. It was so from that day forward.

Volant rubbed the dragon's chin. The familiarity of Volant's voice and his rough caresses seemed to calm Lok's strange agitation.

Volant jumped on his back. "Let's go!" He shouted. "We need to see if anyone has found those Trolls yet."

But that was three years past. Now he was standing in this meadow, facing a priest who was quietly calling him to obey the summons of his master.

He obediently, if not happily, followed the dark priest on foot as he disappeared into the woods. He was hoping that, over the past few years, he had proved he was worthy of being accepted into the outlawed religious sect. He had memorized many of the rites and had been tutored in the ways of the priesthood of the dark god by one of the black-robed priests who had appeared in the cavern during his second visit to the forbidden place. He had come to the temple whenever he could get away, lying and making excuses for his absence when need arose. He had been careful to keep the scars of the ritual cuttings hidden from view. Each time he had gone to visit with his new god, he had been given just a taste more of that vast cup of power. So great was Volant's ego that he never once suspected he was only a pawn in a much larger game. He never understood that he was being lured like an animal into a trap. His eagerness to consume or be consumed by all that power blinded him to the possibility that it was all an immense deception.

They had walked a few hundred paces deeper into the woods when the black-robed figure came to a sudden halt. Volant clutched his horse's halter, and immediately drew his sword. He did not know who or what had startled the priest, but his mind was racing with possibilities. What if it was another dragon rider, or his Captain? Perhaps it was that spy of King Cadan's, that sneaking Hawk fellow.

He could still get out of this predicament if the need arose. He could say that he had just stumbled onto this priest, and he was just about to arrest him, and.... These thoughts melted away, however, as he saw another black robe step from behind a tree, and then another, and another. Soon, he stood alone in the middle of a circle of priests. He was desperately trying to calm his racing heart. He did not understand what was happening. Had he misread the priest's intention? He had seen enough sacrifices to know that this was beginning to have all the required elements - including the sacrifice in the center of their unholy circle. Just as he had decided to attempt to break out of the control of the priest and to flee, he saw Galchobar. Relief flooded through his body at the sight of his mentor and teacher.

Galchobar stepped off the paces between them as though he were floating on air. The ancient priest smiled as warmly as his face would allow, but years of serving the dark god had removed any beneficence from him, and his face resembled more an icy sneer than a friendly smile. He held out an old, gnarled hand. "It is time, young Volant, for you to make the commitment."

Volant swallowed hard as sweat ran freely down his back. "You must either join us, or be banished from us forever. Choose now."

He leaned against his horse as his head began to reel. What was wrong with him? Was this not what he had ached so long to hear? What was holding him back now, at this final moment? Certainly, it was not his conscience. He had surrendered that long ago. He stood, staring at Galchobar's outstretched hand. Finally, he took a deep breath, knelt on one knee, took the priest's hand and kissed the fiery stone on his ring.

With that one simple act, Volant would involuntarily change an entire land of people. He would change the balance between light and darkness, between good and evil. It was an irretrievable gesture for himself, and one that would start a chain of events more horrible and devastating than anything ever seen in Kinthoria.

Chapter Five

TUPPER

Upon leaving the unsavory inn that would forever be jokingly referred to by Jaren and Tanner as "Stenchman's Pit," they had traveled through a day and a night. They made camp for the day behind a small hill overgrown with brush around two furlongs distant from the road. It was Hawk's plan that they travel at night and rest under cover through the day until they were nearer Doddridge.

Tanner had drawn the late afternoon watch, and was scanning the area from the top of the hill after checking the horses. He saw a dozen armed men on horseback heading south along the road toward them. He dropped to the ground behind the nearest bush and fervently hoped that their horses would remain silent.

Suddenly one of the riders jerked his horse to a halt, looked in Tanner's direction and pointed to the ground. Three men slid from their mounts, and drawing their bows slowly began to walk forward, searching the ground.

Tanner decided it was time to wake the others. As he ducked his head behind the hilltop, a hand suddenly clamped his shoulder. He turned in an instant, dagger in hand. Hawk grabbed his wrist and whispered hoarsely, "Hold. Watch."

The three men suddenly pulled back their bows and shot into a stand of gorse. They leaned down, and shouting in triumph, raised what appeared to be three rather large coneys. Their companions laughed and hooted as they tied their kill to their horses and rode off down the road at a brisk trot.

Hawk and Tanner watched until the men had disappeared from sight.

"I don't know what their business is, but I don't like being this close to men that well-armed. Come, we must wake the others. We will ride well away from the road tonight," Hawk said. "You did well Tanner," he said, gripping the young man's shoulder.

As the days passed, Hawk and Korthak observed much resemblance in Jaren to his father: the way he carried himself, the inflection in his speech, his facial movements as he pondered a question, his intuitive wisdom. Many of his mother's traits were there, also: his ready smile and easy laughter, his love for nature, his pleasant, warm personality, and his enthusiasm for learning. No one who had known Cadan and Alanna could possibly deny Jaren as their offspring. The spirits of the two older men were somewhat lifted, being in such close company with this youth who was a living, breathing replica of their friends. They felt that somehow the memories of past years had suddenly put on physical form.

Late one afternoon a light fog gathered, giving the countryside a soft, indistinct aspect. The four were riding across a meadow, having just begun the evening's travel. A darker shadow flitted over their company. Hawk knew without looking that it was his worst fear. A dragon rider! His mind instantly reacted as he saw a flock of sheep just ahead. "Everyone spread out around the sheep and behave as though we belong here," he said under his breath. He saw the stark look of terror on the faces of his two young charges, and sent up a quick prayer to Elyon for help.

Korthak shifted uncomfortably in his saddle, sweat beginning to roll down his back even in the coolness of evening. He tried to ease some of the tension by humming a tuneless melody.

"Just hold it steady, lads," Hawk spoke softly. He was thankful he was wearing clothing more suited to hiding his true identity. He slid off his horse, and greeted the shepherd with a warm smile and handshake, as though he and the man were well acquainted.

The dragon rider flew past, and then circled back toward them. Hawk's heart froze, and Korthak tripped over the notes of his tune.

Tanner and Jaren were just barely restraining themselves from kicking their horse into a full gallop to attempt escape.

The Birth of a King

"Blasted beasts!" screamed the angry shepherd, shaking his fist at the dragon and his rider. "Always hungry! Stealing my sheep until a man is so poor he cannot keep his family fed."

The man with tanned, leathery skin looked pleadingly at Hawk. "Do you have any weapons to use against this beast? I do not want to lose another sheep. My flock is only a feeble remnant of what it once was. These cursed Dragonmasters have made a poor man out of me."

Hawk spread his hands in helplessness. "I'm afraid we're no match for a dragon and its rider, my friend. They would burn us to a crisp the moment our weapons were drawn."

The shepherd eyed Hawk suspiciously, and then glanced beyond him to his companions, as though just becoming aware of them. No one had called him "friend" in years. He was very uneasy that a stranger with three unsavory looking companions should use the word in addressing him. Hawk's casual manner and warm handshake only increased his discomfiture; no one could be trusted these days. He began to suspect that their intentions could be deadly. He knew he would be no match for four obviously travel-hardened men, especially as it was clear that at least two of them were battle trained. *"Those two young ones look very capable of taking care of themselves, too, even if they do look terrified of the dragon,"* the old shepherd thought. *"It would seem that I must choose between them or the dragon rider."*

His shoulders sagged. "No, I guess you are right. There is nothing anyone can do. I will just have to watch them continue to devour my flock until I have nothing left."

The group on the ground watched as the dragon made an arching dive straight for the middle of the flock. It drove its talons into a large, plump sheep, and flew off to devour its prey. The shepherd did indeed watch helplessly as the rest of his flock scattered in panic in all directions.

He threw up his arms, tears of anger and frustration flowing down his cheeks. He looked at the four riders with a silence that bespoke a spirit that was slowly being driven to the limit of despair.

Jaren's blood was boiling. Gone was his fear of the dragon, and in its place was an unrelenting anger - anger at himself, because of his

The Birth of a King

fear of the Dragonmasters which always reduced him to a senseless fool, and anger for the arrogance displayed by these winged beasts and their riders. He was enraged at the injustice of the many things Hawk had told him since leaving Reeban. His mind was made up that if there was ever anything he could do to change this hopelessly desperate situation he would do it no matter the cost to himself.

Hawk watched for several moments to see if the dragon rider had been flying alone. He watched the sheep scattering wildly across the meadow. He turned and eyed his two weary young charges. He realized that the time had finally come for a solid rest for the lads.

Looking at the shepherd he said, "I will make you an offer, Goodman...?" Hawk waited for the man to give his name.

"Tupper. Folks call me Tupper," he responded with hesitation.

Hawk nodded and smiled. "Well then, Goodman Tupper, it seems your sheep are widely scattered, which means it will be well into the night before you are able to gather them all again."

"No thanks to that filthy beast flying around out there," Tupper interrupted.

Hawk nodded his agreement. "If my friends and I were to use our mounts to round up your sheep it would take only the passing of perhaps an hour. Would you be willing to trade a place for us to sleep tonight for our assistance with your sheep? We have been on the road nigh on two weeks now, and our only rest has been taken in the wild, and much of it spent in vigilance."

Tupper eyed him cautiously, trying once more to decide if these were trustworthy men. He stared at each of them in turn. *"Dols,"* he thought, *"they are a dirty, scraggly bunch. But I expect I have looked as bad to strangers after days of driving my sheep to market. Besides, this one speaks in the fashion of the gentle-born."* Tupper nodded his head, "I suppose a little company would not hurt a man." He gestured toward his sheep. "You get them back in their pen and I will find some place suitable for you and your companions to sleep."

Hawk remounted his horse. "Thank you, Goodman Tupper. You are very kind to four unsavory looking strangers."

The shepherd smiled and waved over his shoulder as he headed for his hut. He began preparing a hearty meal for the travelers, and laid soft grass and straw for makeshift beds along the walls of his small hut.

Korthak and Hawk circled the meadow, slowly gathering the skittish animals into a tight knot and driving them toward Jaren and Tanner, who herded them through the open gate of the pen. As promised, they had retrieved even the shyest stragglers in a little over an hour.

Hawk dismounted and handed his reins to Korthak as he approached the open door of the hut and called the shepherd's name. He caught the aroma of a savory stew and freshly baked bread as Tupper stepped to the door.

"Ah," said Tupper, "your meal is almost ready. There is a spring out back. You will find soap and linen on a tree stump next to it. When you are finished refreshing yourselves, just come inside."

Tanner and Jaren had removed all the gear from the horses and had picketed them inside a lean-to beside the shepherd's hut to conceal their presence. Hawk and Korthak quickly gathered up the young men and led them to the back of the small house. "Did you smell that food?" Hawk asked Korthak enthusiastically.

"Yes, indeed, I did," replied the older man rubbing his hands together in expectation. "Come on, you two lazy lobs," he called to the boys as he walked quickly down the hill to the spring. "You'd better hurry and clean up or Hawk and I are going to get to that food and have it gone by the time you get your ears washed. If you think my fish were good the other day, just wait until you get a whiff of this shepherd's...." He had not finished speaking before the two young men had raced passed him to the spring. "...stewpot."

The foursome stripped and jumped into the cool water. They scrubbed layers of dirt from their bodies. Korthak set about trying to trim up his unruly beard with his knife as Tanner looked on in admiration and envy. Jaren caught him rubbing thoughtfully at the peach fuzz on his chin, and laughed. "Go ahead and shave it, Tan. After I see what kind of a bloody mess you make of yourself, I may try it, too."

Tanner was thoroughly embarrassed, and immediately paid back his friend by dunking his head under the water. Jaren came up sputtering and laughing. Korthak added to Tanner's embarrassment by

The Birth of a King

stoically offering, "Come ahead, Tanner. I'd be honored to show you how to shave your beard before it gets completely out o' hand."

Hawk wisely kept a burst of laughter to himself. He had taken this opportunity to quickly glance at Jaren's birthmark, while the young man's attention was diverted. He was pleased at what he saw.

As it turned out, Tanner did not do too badly for his first shave. He had a small cut under his nose and another under his chin, but he was very proud to have accomplished this amazing rite of passage with such apparent ease. The smooth-faced Jaren, however, mindful of Korthak's comments about Tupper's stewpot, decided to forego his introduction to shaving for the time being.

As they were dressing, Jaren happened to look at Korthak's back and was stunned to see an angry, red scar that reached from his left shoulder to just below his right arm. He wondered how he had got the awful wound but did not think it was the time to ask his huge friend about it.

All things considered, a more rapid, albeit complete, bath had never been achieved by any of them. They finished cinching belts and tucking in clean shirts as they raced back up the hill and into the hut.

Tupper, concluding that these were, after all, reputable men, welcomed them to his table. He was highly pleased with their comments about the savory aroma.

Hawk and Korthak offered up quick, silent prayers in thankfulness for this meal, and for the shepherd's kindness. The man placed a piping hot skillet of dense, hardy, oat bread on the table. "Eat all you want, I have not ever cooked a really large meal before. I guess I overdid it just a little."

Hawk glanced at Korthak, who only winked at him while he shoved a huge piece of honey-and-butter covered bread into his mouth. Indeed, there was enough vittles for ten or more. Tupper had also laid out some apples and wild strawberries and a saucer of cream.

"This is truly the best rabbit stew I have ever tasted," Hawk said around a mouthful of the savory stuff.

Tupper beamed with appreciation, as he swallowed down a bite of the spicy stew. "Thank you. It is my family's own recipe and it

The Birth of a King

has sustained many generations of Tuppers. Of course, it used to be made with lamb instead of coneys. But I can't afford to use my stock for eating anymore. There are just too few animals left to me."

They all made a grand attempt to eat everything put before them, but discovered that, after all, a man's stomach is only so large and will hold only so much. Finally, Korthak pushed himself away from the table and patted his over-full stomach with both hands. "Ahhh, I feel like a stuffed gamin' hen," he groaned contentedly.

Jaren agreed that he definitely looked as though he would burst. He glanced across the table at Tanner, who was trying to get one last bite of bread into his mouth. It was a disgusting sight and Jaren chuckled to himself as he watched the half-sick look on Tanner's face.

He glanced at the shepherd. "Thank you, Tupper. You have been very generous to four strangers."

"You are quite welcome, lad. I have to say that the solitude of my occupation oftentimes wears on me. I am truly glad of your company," he said.

Tupper disappeared from the table for a few moments, and then returned with four mugs of a cool, pale yellow beverage. Tanner's eyes lit up with expectation, thinking that, at last, he was going to have a mug of ale that he did not have to share with anyone. He anticipated enjoying it immensely, even if it was as weak as it looked.

As he took a large gulp from the mug, his eyes popped wide, and his mouth puckered. Tanner choked as the biting liquid hit the back of his throat with an acrid bitterness.

"This is a beverage made from lemons, son." Tupper smiled as he watched Tanner's reaction. "It will quench your thirst even better than water...or ale," he added with a chuckle. "I take it you have never tasted such nectar before, heh?"

Despite his crushing disappointment, Tanner admitted, "No, sir, but it's real good." This magic elixir did indeed seem to wash away all of the dust that had been in Tanner's mouth and throat for the past weeks. It was delicious, and he drank slowly, savoring every drop.

"I hope this repays you somewhat for your help with my sheep," Tupper said with a smile. "I would still be out looking for them if you had not aided me."

"Nay, Goodman, you have repaid us ten times over. We are glad we were here to help you," Hawk said. "But tell me, how is it that you are out here unaided? You should at least have a dog for help with the flock and for companionship, even if you can't support a boy for help."

A look of sadness crossed the shepherd's eyes. "How true your words are, my friend. Before the Dragonmasters came, I was one of three brothers, all heirs to our father's vast sheep holdings. Our house was no mean hut like this, nor even a comfortable cottage. We lived in a greathouse, established by my great-great-grandsire more than one hundred years ago. We were taught to care for our sheep in every possible way. But our sheep were always to be held of lesser importance to us than our shepherds and their families. As my grandsire used to say, 'The sheep are our income, but our shepherds and their families are the reason for our income.' We looked after them, treating them as our own family. We gave each new family a young bitch sheepdog, so that they would always have help with the sheep and playmates for their children. We were very prosperous, and everyone was content and happy."

He sighed and was silent for a moment. Then he continued with a look of longing in his eyes. "I will probably be the last shepherd of my line. The Dragonmasters came to our home while I was away in the high country with the sheep. They completely razed the greathouse, and all of the shepherds' dwellings. They killed every living thing within three leagues of the place. My first wife and four children, my brothers and their families, my parents and my grandparents were among them. When we returned, laughing and happy from a successful lambing, we were met with the total destruction of everything we held dear.

The Dragonmasters have returned periodically. They eventually killed three of the six men who were with me. The other three pleaded to stay, but I could not bear the sacrifice they were willing to give and I sent them away. I could not take the chance of anyone else being butchered. The sheep you gathered up for me are all that

The Birth of a King

is left of the flock we brought down from the mountains that year. Even though we have several lambs a season, the flock gets smaller and smaller because of the travesty that you saw take place today. The dragon riders have destroyed my family and my livelihood. My small son lives with his mother in a village two day's walk from here. By the time he is old enough to come shepherding with me the flock will be completely gone. He will never learn to love the sheep, nor how to tend them, as did all of his forebears. If the dragon riders find out about him, he will be taken away to become someone's slave laborer, or worse yet, a dragon rider." The man pressed his hands to his eyes to stop the tears from coming.

Tanner's face reddened as the words, "or worse yet, a dragon rider," pierced his conscience. Was this truly how people felt about the dragon riders? His dream of becoming a dragon rider suddenly began to diminish in light of Tupper's story. He had only seen the supposed freedom in such a career. He had mistaken the people's deference of the riders as esteem, and natural fear of the dragons. He had never before considered the fact that he would be expected to engage in the type of destruction he had visualized from Tupper's words.

Jaren was amazed at this gentle man. He had been so gracious, his demeanor so quiet and peaceful, his smile so ready. How was it that he could have suffered so much and not come away bitter and hateful toward the world? Jaren felt his own hatred for the Dragonmasters growing with every new proof of their brutality.

It was mid-evening; Lunisk had just risen, when the four companions and their host left the cottage. The fog had moved on and settled into a glen below. Tupper checked on his sheep and Korthak and Tanner fed and watered the horses.

For some time the men talked quietly as they sat near the cottage, looking up at the myriad stars circling overhead. Tupper had been suppressing yawns for some time. Finally, despite his obvious enjoyment of their companionship, he excused himself.

"Grass and straw are not much for beds," he apologized before entering the cottage. "But it is under a roof and you will not need anyone to stand watch for the night. From the look in all of your

The Birth of a King

eyes I think your beds could be made of stone and you would still sleep like babes," he chuckled.

"Goodman Tupper," Jaren said out of the blue. "Would you by any chance have a numbing salve for an itch?" he asked, reaching over his shoulder to scratch. Though he had not spoken of it to his companions, he was nearly beside himself now with frustration over the incessant irritation.

"Doesn't every shepherd have itching salve?" Tupper smiled. "Come. I'll apply it for you; looks like it might be a little awkward for your reach."

Jaren followed Tupper. "Thanks, Tupper. I'll take care of the application. You get some sleep. I have a notion that you will be up long before this troop of sluggards rises," he said lightly, masking his aversion to having his birthmark seen by others.

One by one in the next hour, the four exhausted travelers entered the hut and fell easily into a deep, peaceful slumber. Outside, a full, bright Lunisk slowly moved across the sky, illuminating the landscape into shades of crimson against a backdrop of deep, black shadow.

Chapter Six

KORTHAK'S TALE

Jaren gazed up at the clouds drifting across the late afternoon sky, arching his back to stretch the cramped muscles along his spine. They had left Tupper's cottage behind three days hence, and their pace had been grueling. Many times in the past days, the old shepherd's words had echoed in Jaren's mind. *"I will probably be the last shepherd of my line."* He knew that this man's desperate story could be told by hundreds of other "Tuppers," whose families, livelihoods and spirits were being destroyed. Jaren cringed at the blatant deceitfulness of everything he had been taught to believe. For the first time in his young life, he was beginning to fully understand the extent of the methodic, predatory, destruction of Kinthoria by the Dragonmasters. The gaining of the full knowledge of the heinous activities of the Dragonmasters would be a long and painful process, involving months of revelation and experience. This particular day however would mark the beginning of more than just an anger that demanded revenge upon the Dragonmasters. This day would be the first of many in which Jaren would give serious thought to what his own part might be in the restoration of this land that he loved so well.

The aroma of cafla and the loud crackling of the cook fire brought Jaren out of his reverie. He rubbed his eyes and rolled his aching body toward the fire. He had never imagined that he would ever wish to stop riding a horse. He had always loved the beautiful creatures and, although the boys at the scholars hall were allowed

The Birth of a King

only to ride the old and worn horses in the stables, he had treasured the hours in which he and Tanner had spent riding the countryside near Reeban.

He lay on his bedroll watching the flames dance along the logs; dreading the hour when necessity would drag his rebelling body back into the saddle. He smiled, thinking he should have asked Tupper for a cure for aching muscles. The shepherd had insisted that Jaren take a small jar of the numbing salve for his journey. Each morning and evening Jaren thought gratefully of the kind man and wished, as he applied the salve, that he could help return the favor in some way.

Glancing at Tanner, he winced with envy. Of course, his sturdy friend was still deeply asleep with probably not a sore bone in his body.

Jaren noted that Hawk was gone, as usual. He heard Korthak humming quietly to himself as he stirred the food simmering in his cookpot.

"Looks like another beautiful evening, master Jaren." Korthak gazed up at the darkening blue above the eastern horizon in which Lunisk and a few of the brighter stars could already be seen.

"We should be in Doddridge in less than a week." A large smile, barely seen under the bristly red hair, covered his face. "Your unfortunate mount will enjoy a lighter load, I'll wager."

The older man never said as much, but he was especially proud of his two young companions. They had never complained about sharing the horse for three weeks of steady, hard riding, and he knew they had to be saddle sore.

Almost in confirmation of Korthak's thoughts, Jaren again arched his back and turned his neck to relieve some of the tension in his muscles. He rubbed his face with his hands as though the mere act of wiping his skin would cleanse away the pain in his body.

"Where does Hawk disappear to every day, Korthak?" Jaren broke into the man's thoughts, as he absently rubbed his aching backside.

Korthak handed him a steaming cup of cafla before answering.

"He goes to talk with his Master, Jaren. He receives his strength and guidance from Him." Again, Jaren noticed the warmth in

Korthak's eyes inviting his friendship and offering his willingness for conversation.

"His Master...is Hawk a slave then?" The young man asked incredulously. "We are not being followed, are we?"

Korthak shook his head, "Ah, no, my young friend. There's no one followin' us, yet. But if you're so interested in the Master, why don't you ask Hawk about it. We have another long ride tonight and I'm sure you will find plenty of time to talk with him," he offered. He picked up his traveling pack and pulled out some cheese and hard bread to complement his soup. He handed the cheese to the young man.

Jaren broke off a chunk of the milky white stuff and handed it back to Korthak. He nibbled at the pungent morsel while Korthak ladled the steaming soup into two large mugs.

"How long have you known Hawk?" Jaren asked between bites.

"Dols, this boy never lacks for questions," thought Korthak, as he rested the ladle on a stone in the fire ring.

"A long time, lad," Korthak smiled. "Sometimes it seems like forever." He sat back on his haunches and began the narration of his first meeting with his friend.

"I was a boy close t'half yer age." He took a sip of his cafla, and settled back by the fire. "I was out huntin' in the woods just north o' the Shandra River. It was safe back in those days for a lad my age to be out by himself, and I was always out chasin' rabbits or squirrels. Dols, how I used to love runnin' through those woods." Korthak closed his eyes, and chuckled softly as he enjoyed the comfort of his boyhood memories. Jaren watched him intently, half forgetting the bread in his mouth.

"It was a bright sunny day, and I had just sat down in the heather after catchin' my first coney. I was gutting it to take home to me ma for supper. All of a sudden, I hears a tremendous huffing and smashin' comin' through the brush, right behind me. I was so scared I could only sit there paralyzed with fear. I turned around, and found m'self face to face with the biggest pair of tusks I ever clapped my eyes on! I'm tellin' you boy they weren't but mere inches from my

The Birth of a King

scrawny throat. I was lookin' into the beady, blood-red eyes of a raging giant boar.

I didn't know what to do, I tell ye! I knew if I so much as flinched a muscle, that ol' boar would charge me, and gore me clean through in a heartbeat. But, if I sat right where I was, he could just grind me into the ground and never miss a step. I kept thinkin' to myself that whatever had spooked the beast had done a real fine job of it. I mean, there was foam flying out of his mouth, and he was huffing hard enough to stoke a blacksmiths' fire. I sat there undecided as to what to do in my predicament. Just as I was sayin' a prayer to let me die quickly, with little or no pain, I hears a whizzin' sound, and then...thud! I slammed my eyes shut, 'cause I just knew that boar had made up his mind before I had. All that was goin' through my mind was 'Please, just let it be over quick.'"

Jaren was completely absorbed in the story, his breathing quick and shallow, as he imagined the young Korthak's horror.

"Anyways, I squints open my one eye, like so," Korthak demonstrated by screwing his face up into a tight mass of wrinkles and hair. "I didn't know what to look for first: Myself hanging from a giant tusk, or angels walking up to greet me."

Jaren cocked his head quizzically toward Korthak. He had never heard of angels, but he figured they must be another one of those horrible creatures lurking around the Kroth Mountains.

"Now, listen up, cause this is the best part of the story, lad. I opens my t'other eye, and sees that big ol' boar with an arrow sticking right into his heart. He was layin' there twitchin' on the ground, and lookin' right at me, like he couldn't believe he was dyin'. I turned and saw a bunch of men come racin' up on horses. I'm thinking to myself, 'What else is goin' to happen to me? First, I almost have the biggest boar in Kinthoria run me down, and now I'm gonna be trampled by stampeding horsemen.' But they pulled up right in front of me, and one jumped off his horse, and ran to my side. He asked if I was all right. I was so frightened, I couldn't even get my tongue to work, so I did what I thought was the proper thing to do, and just stared at him, like this." Korthak gave Jaren a look of dazed terror, but it looked to Korthak as if the boy already had the look down pat for himself. He chuckled inwardly and continued his tale.

The Birth of a King

"One of the other riders jumps off his horse, and walks over to stand b'side the boar. 'I think we must have got to him too late, Hawk. The beast has obviously taken the lad's tongue.'

Hearin' him say such a thing made me immediately check to see if my tongue was truly missin'. It wasn't, thank heavens.

"'No,' said the man squattin' next to me, 'He's just had the wits scared out of him, that's all.'" I looked at that man's face, Jaren, and saw the most odd, green eyes. I'd never seen the like before."

Jaren supposed he was talking about Hawk for he had experienced that same feeling only a few weeks past.

"He pulls me up to a stand, and called for a skin of water from one of the riders. 'Make him drink something, Merrick,' he says.

Well, I don't know how I ever choked that water down, but it seemed to help me find the ability to speak again. The tall, fair-haired man standin' over the boar looked at me with his deep blue eyes, and said, 'Are you able to speak now, lad?'

'Yessir,' was all I could croak out.

'Good. I am glad you were not hurt.' He smiled at me, then turned to the rest of the hunting party and shouted, 'Let's get our prize ready to take home. The cookmaids will love us for this one.' The men had a good laugh, and began to truss up that magnificent boar.

The one they called Hawk yanked his arrow from the huge beast, and took me a little ways off, to sit under the shade of a big hickory tree. When I had finally drunk enough water, without shaking half of it out onto myself, I thanked him for savin' my life.

'How did you learn to shoot like that?' I asks him. He was real kind and not at'all boastful. He just smiles at me, and says, 'I've been practicing for a good many years, lad.'

I thought that I needed to offer him somethin' in return for my life, but all I had was my coney and my spear. I offered the coney to him along with my thanks, but he kindly refused. 'No son. We have won our prize for the day.' He nodded towards the big boar. 'It is only an extra reward that we were able to save you in the bargain.' He patted me on the head, and told me I'd better be off for home.

'By the way, son. What's your name, in case we ever meet again?'

I was still stammerin' over words, but I says, 'Korthak, sir.'

The Birth of a King

I began walkin' towards home, when I turned back to him, and I says, 'That man called you Hawk. Is that your real name?'

'It sure is, son,' he says."

Korthak took a swallow of his cafla and scowled at the now cold brew. He glanced over the rim of his mug to see Hawk leaning against a tree a short distance away from the firelight. Korthak choked and spit his cafla into the fire, causing it to hiss and steam.

"Dols, Hawk, why do you have to sneak around like that? I'm getting too old for your antics!" he accused.

Jaren glanced over his shoulder to see Hawk with his arms folded across his chest and a smile on his face. The man chuckled to himself, as he walked toward the firepit. Korthak stood, stretched out his long legs, and moved away, tossing the rest of his cold cafla onto the soil. He began leading the horses to water, muttering under his breath along the way.

Jaren silently wondered how Korthak could have been just a small lad when Hawk had rescued him from the boar, yet now looked much older than his friend. He intended to ask Korthak if he had finished his tale. Perhaps Hawk had been named for his father. He would also ask Hawk about his Master when they had the time for a talk.

CHAPTER SEVEN

CHOICES & CONSEQUENCES

Hawk called an unusual four-hour rest a few hours before dawn, announcing that they would risk riding through daylight hours until they reached Doddridge.

As Solance broke the horizon, he led them onto the road for the first time on their journey.

Jaren nudged his horse abreast of Hawk's. "Would it be all right for Tanner to ride with Korthak a while? I think we are riding this poor beast into the ground with me and this big buffoon on his back every day."

Tanner shot a threatening look at Jaren. "At least I have a healthy amount of meat on my bones you sorry little runt."

Jaren laughed and gave him a hard shove, "Get off, you overgrown boy!"

Tanner slid off the horse, and ran to catch Korthak. "One of these days, I'll show you who the boy is around here," he yelled back at Jaren as Korthak offered his huge arm to swing Tanner up behind his saddle.

Hawk had been scanning the sky and surrounding countryside since the first faint light had tinged the horizon. He explained that the increasing number of carts and caravans gathering on this main southward supply route would provide them with excellent cover against detection by the dragon riders. They passed carts groaning under the weight of furs, carpets, trinkets, silver and pewter items, and many other goods destined for market in the large city of Doddridge.

Jaren rode next to Hawk for quite some time before deciding to ask some of the questions that had been nagging him.

"Hawk, Korthak told me you talk to your Master every day, but he said we are not being followed. Where is your Master? I must say that you do not have the bearing of a slave."

Hawk threw back his head and laughed heartily. "Your question is a very good one. I keep forgetting what a bright young man you are." He glanced at Jaren with open frankness in his eyes. "I am a slave to my Master by choice."

The young man was genuinely stunned. Now he was even more confused. "Choice? Why would you choose to become a slave?"

"Jaren, it's not really an issue of Master and slave. My people live for only one thing and that is to worship and obey Someone far greater than ourselves."

Jaren started to interrupt but Hawk raised his hand. "Let me answer your questions one at a time, son. The spiritual teachings you have received so far in your life have been nearly negligible, or at best severely one sided in favor of the worship of Lucia. That is the teaching of the Dragonmasters, is it not?"

Jaren nodded his head, thinking of the dreaded Lucian priests and their dark temples. Worshipping in the temples was encouraged, but had not been forced at the scholars halls. He had heard of their grotesque rituals and sacrifices, but had never been inclined to participate in them. He shuddered, recalling rumors of priests actually performing human sacrifices. He had decided long ago that dabbling around in spiritual things and worshipping unseen deities was something he would leave for others with weaker minds and stronger stomachs.

Hawk looked at him intently. "You need to keep your thoughts on what I am saying, Jaren, or you will miss the truth and your questions will be in vain. Do you understand?" Jaren nodded, remembering his scholars' constant reproofs for his mental wandering.

"Good. Now, the reason you have never heard what I am going to tell you is because the Dragonmasters no longer allow such things to be taught or even discussed on penalty of death. For the past fifteen years, Volant's cadre of scholars has taught a curriculum designed to replace Kinthoria's true history with nothing more than falsehood. They have taught that anyone who contradicts their word is not to be trusted. I can assure you that the legends and so-called histories taught in the academies are nothing more than fantasies created by Volant to keep the truth hidden. He has three very obvious motives behind his suppression of truth: He intends in the next few years to use a misinformed, fearful generation to exterminate the An'ilden. You know who they are, yes?"

Jaren nodded.

"He also wants to subjugate the peoples of the Southern Regions and lure the naïve younger generations into slavery to Lucia. His greatest fear is that somehow they will learn the truth and begin walking in the Light."

Jaren was listening closely, but was not very sure he understood much of what Hawk was saying.

"Jaren, my people and I serve the one true God. He is the Creator of everything that has been created. His name is Elyon. You're a smart lad. Use your mind to think about the incredible power it would take to create from absolutely nothing this world and the rest of the stars and moons out in the sky and far beyond."

Jaren was given ample time to consider Hawk's weighty assignment, as they rode on in silence. They had come upon another trading caravan, and could not risk being overheard in their conversation.

They passed a wagon laden with heavy iron and pewter wares. Everything from enormous black cooking vessels to shiny eating trays filled the large wooden cart. A sturdy team of oxen pulled it along at a lazy pace. The driver was a balding man who had obviously become wealthy through his trade. He wore many rings on his fat fingers, and his enormous belly pushed against his expensive belt and voluminous robes. Jaren considered the contrast between this merchant and the poor, starving merchants and farmers of Reeban. Then he hit upon a precise double for this man. "He looks just like Sorely," he mumbled to himself, recalling the obesity of the Headmaster at the scholars hall.

Hawk watched Tanner and Korthak bantering back and forth and he thanked his Master once more for his old friend. Korthak was aware of Jaren's need to hear and understand many things before they reached the Spring of Elyon. The old bear would see to it that Hawk was provided all the time he needed to teach the lad, even if it meant keeping his young friend occupied for hours at a time.

Hawk smiled to himself, as they passed the ironmonger's wagon. He breathed a silent prayer, before continuing his conversation with Jaren. *"Father, this young man is so eager for truth. Guide my speech toward something that will touch his young heart. Send your Spirit to open the door to his understanding."*

Jaren was riding in silence, reflecting upon the things that Hawk had told him.

"Look at me, lad." Hawk's voice came through his musing.

Jaren gazed into the man's eyes.

"You see something different in my eyes, do you not, more than just the shape and color?"

Jaren nodded.

"And do you not also see that same something in Korthak's eyes?"

Again, Jaren nodded.

"What do you suppose that something might be, Jaren?"

Jaren answered slowly, attempting to piece together all that he had been observing in the two older men. "I see...a peace, inside of you. I mean, it's calm, but it is full of energy. No. Energy isn't the right word. Power. Yes, that's it. You are both full of a calm power. Does that make any sense?" He floundered, rubbing his forehead.

Hawk nodded, encouraging him to continue.

"I don't understand it, but you both seem to be so strong inside, yet you do not use your strength to do harm or to cause fear. You show only patience and consideration."

Hawk squeezed Jaren's shoulder. "That is very well put, lad." He was gaining more admiration for the boy each time they talked. Jaren's perceptions were astonishing for one his age.

"Korthak and I have given our lives to a Master whom we firmly believe is the one true God. He is the source of our peace and strength, Jaren. He is very strong, strong enough to have made the universes. Yet He is a very gentle Father to His children. He loves each one of us beyond anything we can imagine. He is always present for us. He never abandons those who belong to Him. This is why we have such peace inside. We know that we have our Father's power working for us, and residing in us as a gift of His love. Korthak and I have asked the one true God to control our lives; to give us wisdom beyond ourselves in order to live our lives honorably before Him. That is why He is called our Master." Hawk paused for a moment. "Do you understand me so far, son?"

Jaren nodded his head. "I think so. But Hawk, if this true God is so great, and loving, why is there so much unhappiness and trouble in our land? Why has He allowed so many inhumane crimes to occur? Why must good people like Tupper suffer so greatly?" He asked in angry confusion. "And, if He is so powerful, why has He allowed the Dragonmasters to outlaw the teaching about Him?"

Hawk's fingers tightened around the reins in his hand. This was one question that was almost too painful to answer. "Well, Jaren, as I said, Elyon, that's the true God's name, is very loving, and when his children disobey Him, it truly breaks His heart. It breaks His heart because justice and purity are just as much parts of His nature as love and gentleness and strength, and because He knows that disobedience will lead to pain, disorder and unhappiness for those who choose that path.

"In the long ages past, the people of Kinthoria always remained true to Elyon alone. They were happy, prosperous, and content. Then, many centuries ago, they began to listen to the whisperings of Lucia and they slowly grew unconcerned about acknowledging the Master as the source of everything they had, and so they ceased thanking Him. They stopped praying for guidance in their lives. I guess their lives were so ideal that they simply forgot the source of their very existence and took Elyon's blessings as their due. These indifferent people neglected to train their children in the knowledge of the true God and in worship of Him. In just a few generations, their descendants had become very callous toward the Father; they believed that they no longer needed His help and they did not desire His companionship. Nor did they wish to be indebted to Him for His care. Many even doubted His existence."

Hawk held Jaren's eyes with his own. "Never forget, Jaren that it is *always* human nature to try to live without being accountable to

Elyon." He allowed Jaren some time to contemplate this statement as they passed another long stretch of wagons.

Hawk continued when they were well past of the group. "As Elyon observed the indifference of mankind it became clear that they had replaced their trust in Him with a trust in the lies of Lucia. They had turned their allegiance over to Elyon's greatest enemy. The Father grieved at the loss of His children and for the generations to follow. He saw what lay ahead for these ones whom He loved with such great love. However, the part of His nature that demanded justice caused Him to partially remove His protective hand from mankind in order to demonstrate to all of creation the truth about the depth of His love and care, and, as Creator God, His right to sovereignty and honor. He would prove that humanity's ideal existence was not due to man's perfect nature, nor to his ability to care for himself, but was due to His loving care in the form of blessing and grace. He would thereby justify to every created being His rightful claim to obedience and worship because there is no other being wise enough to declare what will be done, and strong enough to see that it is done. To Elyon's infinite sorrow, mankind was now to reap the results of their cold and heartless dealings with Him and their dishonorable treatment of one another. They would 'sow the wind and reap the whirlwind' in their misuse of Elyon's creation, because to reject the Creator means that one chooses Lucia, and in the end the dark god always repays his followers with pain and death."

"But I thought you said that Elyon would never abandon His people," Jaren interrupted. "It sounds to me like this true God created the world and then got angry and walked away from it, leaving everyone pretty much to their own designs. Since He doesn't have anything to do with it anymore isn't it up to us to do the best we can? What other option is there?"

"I did not say that Elyon turned His back on mankind. I said that He *partially* lifted His protective hand for the purpose of proving to the rest of His created beings His right in demanding that justice be done. If He had abandoned the world entirely, Lucia would have caused mankind to annihilate itself ages ago and he would have destroyed the Earth. No, Jaren. Elyon is ever observing His creation, and is at work in its preservation. It is His tender heart that has caused

Him to show mercy to mankind by reining in Lucia's vicious acts all through our history. That dark menace would cause far worse than the injustices to the world's Tuppers if he had a free hand in this world, as you have yet to learn. No. Elyon has not abandoned the world - He is continually watching over and defending it.

When Lucia realized that he had been given more freedom, he immediately increased the spread of his evil and dark deeds across the land. Those who fell under his influence became as depraved and corrupted in spirit as he. There was chaos and destruction, murder and atrocities of every description all across Kinthoria. Many are of the opinion that it was during this time that the races of the Trolls and Gundroths were spawned into the world - terrible mutants of demon kind brought forth through unthinkable acts.

Finally, the An'ilden, who alone had remained true to Elyon, could no longer abide the works of Lucia and his priests. They rose up against them and began ridding the land of Lucia's disciples and their despicable places of worship. Eventually they made the practice of their heinous religion a crime. The people of Kinthoria were as ones wakened from a nightmare; they heard and once again believed the Words of Elyon, and could see with their own eyes the world of difference between life with Elyon and life with Lucia. For several centuries, Kinthoria had been a peaceful, pleasant place in which to live, until the people once again pushed Elyon out of their lives and so their children became ignorant of man's elementary need for the Father.

So it is that history has now repeated itself. Only this time Lucia has powerful help in the Dragonmasters. Those from races other than the An'ilden, who volunteered as dragon riders, became increasingly weak in their belief in Elyon through the past hundred years. Eventually, when Volant was building his army of dragon riders, these new generations who didn't know Elyon were easily seduced into his service by promises of freedom and power. Volant and his dragon army decimated the An'ilden dragon riders. Now, the greatest danger for Kinthoria is in the Dragonmasters' control of the scholars halls. The slow but effective teaching of their new history of Kinthoria is remaking the minds of a whole generation of children. Your generation knows only a Kinthorian history devoid of

The Birth of a King

the courage and honor of people of all the races - a new history that fosters hopelessness and makes slaves of all races: a history without the truth of the true God. The Dragonmasters are using the scholars halls to create a new world populated with people of no conscience, who are full of suspicion and hatred – people who will automatically follow the Lucian way, whether or not they even realize they have made the choice to do so.

But, to get back to the point: The Lucian priests came out of hiding and began whispering lies about the royal family, and King Cadan. The Cathains had always been careful to tutor their children in the written Word of Elyon, passing on the knowledge and the love of the true God to their heirs. Their strong faith in Elyon touched every aspect of their lives and of their rule. They were benevolent, just, generous, brave, and wise. Their devotion to Him meant that they would become a prime target for destruction by the Lucians. The Lucian cult gained more and more acceptance, especially with the power of Volant after his successful takeover of the dragon army. They promised to create prosperity for the people unlike anything ever seen upon Kinthoria. They promised the abolition of the rules and restrictions enforced by a deity they would not acknowledge. The people would be free to follow Lucia or to have no religion at all. They made many promises, Jaren, but they were all lies, every one of them. They were greedy, and ruthless. Their sole purpose has been to gain undiminished power for themselves and to enslave people under the iron fist of their god.

When the worship of Lucia was once again made the official religion, the Dragonmasters began ridiculing and persecuting those who worshipped the one true God. Volant eventually turned the tables and outlawed the worship of Elyon everywhere on Kinthoria. They were hunted down and slaughtered outright wherever they were found.

"Now look at the poor souls living in our land. Can you see what happens when Elyon is cast aside by His own creation, and when people do not follow His ways?" Hawk fell into a thoughtful silence.

Jaren considered all that Hawk had just revealed to him. He was stunned at the revelation of this true God, who was Hawk's Master.

He had never heard of Elyon before. Yet Hawk's words, while new and somewhat overpowering, had made sense to the young man's heart and mind. His instruction had an indisputable ring of truth about it. Jaren could easily envision how wonderful a world could be, if the One who had created it and knew its purpose was honored and obeyed by those He had created. Jaren could understand how, if the Creator was given complete control, everything would be balanced and harmonious. It was only logical. He unconsciously shook his head as he thought how Kinthoria was just the opposite of these things. He was amazed that people would throw themselves and all of nature into chaos, with such apparent abandon. They seemed to prefer death and calamity over simple accountability and submission to this God. *"How foolish,"* he thought. *"Which is the better life, to love the Creator and to be loved by Him, and to allow Him to give you an ideal life, or to reject Him and to have your world fall apart?"* If Hawk's story were the truth, Jaren found it incredible that anyone would reject the one true God.

Many things started to fall into place now, but it seemed with each new piece that fit into the puzzle, ten more pieces would be laid out on the table in his mind. Somehow, he knew he would find the answers to all of his questions and the picture would be completed. He knew at that moment, riding south under the warm, watchful eye of Solance, that he had decided rightly to trust Hawk and to follow him. Where this journey would take them and how much time would pass as they traveled on, he had not the slightest idea. However, a new contentment began to infuse him as he became certain of his own place somewhere in this giant puzzle. He was now positive that the fit would be perfect when he was placed into his own particular space.

Chapter Eight

RITES ON THE SPIRES OF ETHADUR

It was already late afternoon when Bendor crossed the weapons yard, and waved to the head Weapons Master. "Ho, there, Keb. How goes the training?"

Keb wiped his brow with the back of his hand. "I think the lads are gaining, but it's like throwing a pebble against a fortress."

Bendor chuckled, "Aye, sometimes it's a slow process, eh?"

Keb snorted, "Like cold honey." The muscular man hurried back to a cluster of young men sparring with their swords, "No, no no! How many times must I tell you...."

Bendor watched as the swordplay became ever more frenzied, and the wooden blades cracked against each other, echoing off the walls of the surrounding yard. Some of these boys would have bruises on all their limbs tomorrow, but others he would have to remember when it was time for the Solurko Tolgo to take place. He could add some fine weight to his coin purse with some well-placed wagers on a few of these lads.

He continued walking toward the temple. He would be accompanying a score and a half of young riders and their dragons to the Naming Rites tonight. He bounded up the black marble steps that led to the portico of the temple. The black onyx columns held carved images of gargoyles, demons, and frightful creatures for which there was no name. It was said that the priest who designed the columns screamed long in terror while in a trance, and when he awoke, his hands trembled as he sketched their images. Bendor stood outside

The Birth of a King

and waited for the thick wooden doors of the temple to open, signaling an end to the gruesome labor taking place behind them. He did not have to wait long, and sensed the evil emanating from within the place of macabre worship, as the massive doors opened like the maw of some ravenous fiend.

The Lucian priests handed the pale and sickly looking young riders the satchels as they slowly shuffled past them. Inside were the herbs, chalices, and other assorted items necessary for the ceremony each of them would perform this night. The riders had fulfilled the ritual sacrifices in the temple and would now fly to the Spires of Ethadur to complete the naming of their dragons individually.

Bendor watched as the young men slung the bags over their shoulders and mounted their powerful dragons. He would be joined by Tomas and Tulak, to keep vigil for the young men and their charges. This was a long and solemn ritual, but one that most riders looked forward to, as this was when they would gain near absolute control of their dragons by receiving their names from Lucia through their ceremonial services.

This particular practice was never required prior to Volant ousting the Cathain heirs and asserting himself Emperor of Kinthoria. But given that Volant was now demanding the dragons to perform acts that were highly offensive to the very nature of the beasts, there were certain measures that must be taken to ensure the dragon's compliance while the riders carried out their duties. The ancient creatures were created to be protectors of the land and all the races who lived in Kinthoria. They were the very essence of justice, power, compassion, kindness, and decency. When Volant seized control of the throne and the dragon riders, he also had to establish a binding dominance over the dragons in order to continue his dream of becoming the Emperor of all Kinthoria.

"Are you ready, Sir?" Tulak questioned as the last of the dragons leaped into the air. Bendor had been gazing at the riders' departure, and nodded his head.

"Yes. It should be a clear night at the Spires," he mused as he jumped up on Kekn's foreleg and swung himself into the saddle. "Let's ride." Kekn shot into the air with two powerful strokes of his wings, and the phalanx soared out of Keratha to the northwest.

The Spires of Ethadur were a cluster of lofty buttes on the western end of the Ragani mountain range; each of them soaring up out of the valley floor to dizzying heights. They rose like giant sentinels standing watch over Keratha, and were reached only by dragon back. Bendor was relieved to see that the young men were eager to accomplish the task at hand, as they settled on the elevated peaks. The three Flight Leaders circled their dragons above the Spires and kept a sharp eye out for any riders who might need help. Bendor watched as several young men yanked open their satchels and plucked out the items stowed in each bag. The dragon bone athamé, the black obsidian bowls, the chalice wrapped inside a dragon's claw, the pulverized lodestone, the small carafe of wine, and lastly, the mandrake oil and herbs.

Each boy stripped himself to the waist, and began drawing pagan runes upon his chest. They each found true North and drew a circle in the earth with a demonic symbol inside. They aligned their dragons to be directly across from this point, and began chanting the ritual words to call the *Watchtowers*. Bendor watched a group of young men begin the ritual by mixing herbs into the obsidian bowls then cutting their left palms. Flying on to survey another group, he could hear the boys calling Lucia's demons to give to each the name of his dragon. Much later, on another butte, a rider had just embraced his dragon. The young man lifted his eyes to Bendor and screamed, "Her name is Aeri!"

Bendor smiled, thrusting up his fist in approval, and then flew on. He saw another young man on his knees in front of his dragon, holding both sides of the beasts' jaws in his hands, a huge smile splitting his face. "Well, Kekn, I wonder what that one will be called." Bendor felt the dragon growl beneath him.

He continued flying in huge circles, watching as the young men offered the wine to Lucia, gave thanks, took one sip, and poured the remaining contents of the chalices into the circles. The ritual took the whole of four hours to complete, and he was impressed that none of the young men had encountered any difficulty with their dragons, or the spirits they had summoned, as was sometimes the case.

There were no overt changes in the dragons, but Bendor knew that their ability to disobey their riders was now all but entirely obstructed, and their recoil when encountering any grievance against their nature would be minimal at best. Bendor had no idea how this overriding of the innate sense of right and wrong within the very fiber of the dragons would result, either in danger to dragons or riders, whether short or long-term. But Volant had judged that the necessity for control and dominance far outweighed any possible negative consequences. Bendor had seen what had happened to the dragons that refused to comply with the expectations of the riders under Volant's control. It was a horrific sight that he hoped would some day vanish from his mind. The dreadful clamor and the horrendous impressions unexpectedly filled his thoughts if he allowed even the smallest mental touch on the memories of that day. Painfully clear images and emotions ran unchecked through his mind and body. The riders lined up along the wall on their knees, hands bound tightly behind their backs, heads hung low; his own dread at what he knew would come next; the line of Lucian priests who stood in front of them, mouthing words of dark magic. The dragon and knight's armies were standing at attention to witness the consequences of disobedience and insubordination, whether from dragon or rider. The bone-chilling screams of horror and fear from the dragons assaulted the senses as one by one the riders were killed by the black-robed priests. Immediately after the slaughter, the dragons keened and wailed loudly as one by one they died along with their bond-mates. Bendor, even at the memory, struggled to keep down the bile that rose in his throat. Many more than just Bendor's unit had shared the sense of helplessness at witnessing such cold-blooded carnage.

    When Kekn sensed Bendor's emotions and saw his memories, he rumbled deeply and acrid smoke rose from his nostrils and flew back into his bond-mate's face. Bendor shook his head to cast away the revulsion of that day and roughly patted the dragon's vibrating body. "I'm so sorry, Kekn," he said with tenderness. "Certainly there must come a day when we will undo this heinous deed and return to our former bond of equality." He smiled, "In the meantime, I'll do my best not to press you on things against your nature."

    Kekn began the soft thrum that signaled his affection, and Bendor turned the dragon toward Keratha, willing himself to be happy for the young men who had just gained lifelong bonds, even if on the dragon's part there had been no true consent.

It was better this way…at present.

Chapter Nine

THE MAKING OF A MAN

Two days before reaching Doddridge, they had met with a spice trader on the road north of the city. The trader had mistakenly taken the four dust-coated companions for mercenaries.

While they were eating their supper around a small fire, the man approached Korthak, assuming from his size and appearance that he was the leader of the small company.

"You, sir, I'm in need of protection for my caravan for two nights and a day. You appear unemployed at present. Perhaps we may each benefit from the other," he said brusquely.

When Korthak remained seated, wide-eyed and silent before him, the trader assumed he was curious to hear his proposal.

"I'll give you five silvers for the services of you and your three men here if you'll join my caravan and give us protection along the road to Doddridge. Seems these days there's more thieves than ever, just waiting for honest traders such as myself to come along, and to steal everything they can lay their filthy hands on."

When Korthak showed no sign of stirring from his seat, but continued staring at him, the man began to wonder if the reason these men were obviously unemployed was because they were a band of simpletons.

"Come, come, man. What say you?" he inquired sternly.

A deep red began to creep up Korthak's neck and face, the veins at his temples swelled, and his eyes narrowed. He stood slowly, feet apart, clenching and unclenching his massive hands.

"Protect your caravan, you say? Five *whole* silvers for the four of us for two nights and a day, eh?" Korthak's voice was as low and threatening as a distant thunderstorm.

When the trader saw this huge man's reaction to his offer, he was shaken, and did not know if Korthak was just eager for the employment or if he had somehow offended the giant. The merchant prudently stepped back out of harm's way.

Hawk stepped between the two. "Excuse my friend 'ere, yer worthiness," he said, taking on the crude speech of the unschooled. He tapped his forehead with his finger, and whispered confidentially to the man. "Just a mite slow up 'ere."

Upon hearing a strangled noise behind him, he rushed on. "We been on the road fer a good many days, an' would be mighty glad of a few coins' weight in our purses. Yer offer is more'n fair and I promise you'll get no better protection anywheres…sir," Hawk said, sketching a quick bow and touching his fist to his forehead.

The trader, somewhat suspicious, and half-angry with Korthak's surly glare, reluctantly tossed a tiny bag of coins into Hawk's hand while scowling ominously in Korthak's direction. It was obvious that if the trader could have found another band hungry enough to hire themselves out for so paltry a sum, he would have told Korthak rather plainly what he could do with his pompous attitude and kept his purse for someone who would appreciate it.

"I will decide for myself if you have given me your best protection," he growled. "If I am satisfied with your work, I will give you the rest of your wages when we reach the gates of the city." He shot one last glowering look at Korthak as he turned on his heel toward his wagons.

Korthak returned the man's dark scowl, but said nothing until he was well out of hearing.

"Have you gone mad?" He screeched in a whisper to Hawk, who was tucking the little bag of coins into his belt. "You can't be serious to hire Jaren out as a mercenary. Especially to protect the wagons of a charlatan like that. The man's offer was laughable. I wouldn't be at all surprised if, when dawn comes tomorrow, we'll find the man dead, eaten clean away by his own avarice during the night."

Hawk looked over his shoulder and saw that Jaren and Tanner had begun loading the horses once again, in preparation for joining the caravan. Seeing that they were well out of earshot, he looked at Korthak sternly.

"Listen, *nothing* we have to do to protect Jaren's identity is beneath us. I don't care if we have to become swineherds in order to get him safely back to our people. We'll do whatever it takes. We both know that far worse than this will be required of us on this quest." Hawk whispered.

Korthak knew that Hawk's anger was fueled by the desperation of their circumstances, and not by his own foolish behavior. Still, it was the darkest look Korthak could remember ever having received from his closest friend, and it stung far more than Hawk's harsh words.

When Hawk saw the shock and remorse on Korthak's face, his anger immediately abated. He smiled and slapped the man on the back.

"It's fortunate that the merchant merely thought we were mercenaries and not brigands. Just look at us, covered in dust and stubble from ear to ear."

Then, pretending to scrutinize Korthak's disreputable beard with a near military thoroughness, he cleared his throat. "Well, some of us have stubble...others of us have filthy haymows hanging from our chins."

Hawk chuckled as Korthak's hand immediately shot up to touch his beard, his face an odd mixture of indignation and doubt.

"Now tell me honestly, Korthak. Would you think we were reputable men at first glance? The merchant made an understandable mistake, that's all." He smiled again at his friend and shook his head as he turned to join Jaren and Tanner.

Korthak looked at Hawk's retreating back and wondered how he could possibly have made a bigger fool of himself. He had acted like a green cadet fresh out of the Weapons Master's yard. He was embarrassed by his actions, and truly distraught by yet another display of his quick temper.

"Father, will I never learn? Forgive this servant of Yours. Forgive my pride and my temper. Teach me instead the strength that

lies in humility and the power of knowledge that comes from our Yesha," he prayed softly.

He joined the others as they were kicking out the fire. Tanner handed him the reins with a smile, and they silently followed Hawk toward the trader's camp. As a means of self-imposed penance for his previous behavior, Korthak offered to take the third watch, during the first hours after midnight.

Hawk, understanding his reasoning, smiled and gave him a hearty slap on the back. "Right," he said softly as he gathered his saddle and bedroll.

On the second night of their employment, they camped just outside the city, having arrived after the gates were closed. Korthak drew first watch that night. He looked out over the wide expanse of fields dotted with many other campfires. It had been a long winter, and now that spring had come, there were many caravans and travelers on the road, eager to sell their wares or to visit relatives from whom they had been cut off because of heavy snows.

As he watched, late into the night, he heard raucous laughter from a distant camp, as some played at games of chance or told ribald stories, each trying to outdo the other with the tallest tale. At another camp, someone was strumming a harp with such tenderness that it made his heart ache. A few times during his watch, he heard a baby cry, then its mother's soft, soothing voice.

He circled their camp several times during his watch, stopping to check the horses at their picket line, and examining the wagons. When he returned to the fire, he glanced at his three companions before pulling the tin of cafla off its hook and pouring the hot, steamy liquid into a mug. He sat down against a boulder and watched into the darkness. Slowly, one by one, the watch fires from other camps died down and blinked out.

He had been sitting against a boulder about three quarters of an hour when Tanner walked up with a mug and poured himself some cafla.

"What are you doing up, lad?" Korthak asked, genuinely surprised.

"Thought you might like some company. Besides, I couldn't sleep." Tanner poured some of the hot, strong brew into Korthak's mug. "Whew. That's been steeping for a good long time, hasn't it? If I drink this stuff during my watch I could probably have a full beard by morning," he said with a crooked smile. He stepped back to the fire and slowly added more wood.

Korthak watched as Tanner busied himself with this mundane task and wondered what was on the lad's mind. *"Couldn't sleep, eh?"* he thought to himself. *"That boy could sleep anywhere and anytime. Why, a whole flight of dragons could fly an arm span over his bed and he'd miss it."*

Sitting down next to Korthak, Tanner stretched out his long legs and looked at the velvet sky with its thick blanket of stars. Lunisk stood night watch at her zenith and Solisk sat at the edge of the eastern horizon. Both were mere slices of light, and so the night was very dark and the stars very brilliant. He sat in silence, drinking his cafla for a long while.

Korthak waited patiently, not pressing the boy into conversation. It was quite some time before Tanner spoke. In fact, Korthak had just about decided that the lad had finally fallen asleep with his eyes open.

"Korthak, have you ever lost anyone who was very close to you?" It was barely audible, even on this quiet night.

The older man nodded and scratched his boot heel into the dirt. "Yes, I have, son. Why do you ask?" He looked at Tanner's face and could see the pain in his eyes.

Tanner looked away quickly. "Well, I don't know how to put this the right way, without sounding like a spoiled child. But...it just seems that since Jaren met Hawk, even though it's just been a few weeks ago, he doesn't seem to really want me around anymore. He's always finding excuses for me to be pushed off with you."

Tanner caught himself and instantly flushed. "Korthak," he stammered, "I didn't mean that the way it sounded. I'm not known for being very good with words." He stared down at the mug in his hand, wishing earnestly that he had never left his bedroll.

Korthak chuckled. "Go on, boy... I'm not exactly a first rate orator or a renowned bhaird, myself," he said modestly.

Tanner took a deep breath and rushed on. "Well, anyways, Jaren said he wanted me along on this journey, but so far it's like I'm just extra weight on the back of his horse." The boy turned his anguished eyes toward Korthak. His next words came tumbling out before he could stop them.

"He's my family, and it hurts almost as bad as...when I lost my father." Suddenly, by speaking out his pain, he had released the memories of the deepest wound of his young heart, a wound he had thought healed by time. The anger and sorrow of his father's death came rushing over him, and he realized that he had simply buried the memory and its pain very deep within himself. As the emotions overtook him, all unexpected, he jumped up and fled into the darkness, away from the camp and the light of the fire.

Korthak was instantly on his feet and would have pursued him, but felt a strong presence throughout his body holding him back. *"Stay! I will be with him, but he must face this by himself,"* a voice within him said. His Master had touched Korthak in this way on rare occasions in the past. He would make no other choice but to obey. But he could not force himself just to sit idly and wait for Tanner's return. He made another circuit of the camp, and replenished the wood by the fire. Throughout the remainder of his watch, he strained to hear anything of the young man who was out there in the darkness, going through one of life's hardest struggles alone.

He thought back on the losses in his own life, as he had been forced to say good-bye to people he loved. He thought he could have been of some help to Tanner, and the urge to leave his watch and to find the youth was nearly overpowering, but for the memory of the explicit instructions against it.

He decided, instead, to make a fresh pot of cafla for when the boy finally returned. He chuckled to himself, "It wouldn't do to have the lad grow a finer beard than mine all in one night. This stuff is strong enough to grow a beard and put hair on his chest to boot."

He watched as bits of dry sap caught fire and burst apart, sending sparks of burning embers flying in the fire pit, then he returned to the quiet musings that Tanner's question of personal loss had evoked. He smiled sadly to himself as he envisioned sparkling green eyes, and cascading hair the color of chestnuts, shot with flaming reds and golds. He saw lips the color of ripe peaches as they had smiled so many thousands of times. He saw the young mother as she held a plump baby close to her breast. Oh yes, he had lost someone he loved and the pain was still there, acute as ever. Only now he had come to think of the pain as the friend that accompanied precious memories of his beautiful Megen and their infant son, Shayn.

His watchful anticipation of Tanner's return had seemed endless when he heard footsteps approaching. He did not look at Tanner directly as the youth quietly sat down beside him.

"Feel like talking?" he asked cautiously after several minutes.

The young man's tear-streaked face and swollen eyes were sign enough of the struggle through which he had just come. Tanner shook his head and breathed in a ragged sigh.

He told of how his father had fallen ill with the dust plague, as everyone had come to call it. After the war, the ashes of everything the dragons had burned were tinged with a deadly toxin. The powdery substance settled into the soil, and as the farmers worked their land to try to raise a new crop, the acrid dust filled the air and was breathed in. It collected in the lungs of the unsuspecting laborers. Soon, they began to experience slight fevers, and then persistent coughs developed. In a few months' time, their lungs filled with a thick, black fluid, and the people died horribly of suffocation. There was nothing that could be done for them. The usual cough remedies, the plasters, and the herbal teas and steams proved useless. Families had been forced to watch member after member succumb to the plague, for after the fathers fell ill the oldest children and the wives took their places in the fields.

Many thousands of people had died, not only from the plague, but from starvation as well. There was nothing left in the fields to eat, since the dragons had destroyed everything just as the crops were reaching the peak of their growth. The people began eating the fodder set aside for the livestock, and so they lost the animals they could not eat in time, as one by one the livestock had starved for lack of forage.

Tanner had been too young to help in the fields and so had not breathed in the deadly dust. His mother was heavy with child, so his older sister had taken on their father's duties as best she could. He had watched his father die the slow and agonizing death, as each breath became a frightening and excruciating struggle. His sister died of starvation, even as the plague was running its course in her emaciated body.

When Tanner had finished telling his story, there was resignation in his voice, but there were no tears in his eyes. Korthak knew that this night the boy had indeed become a young man. Tanner had been challenged, and had gone out willingly and alone to meet that challenge, and because he had come through changed, but not broken, he would be the better man for it.

Korthak spoke quietly to his young friend. "Tanner, I'm very sorry about the death of your father and your sister. I'm sorrier still that you had to suffer this pain when you were such a small child and were unable to understand what was happening. But I'm glad you consider me friend enough to have told me about it, even though it is still so painful for you. I want you to know how highly honored I am to be your friend."

Tanner looked at him doubtfully.

"There is no loss of manhood in the shedding of tears, son. You did not run from the pain of your memories, but faced them alone, without even the thought of asking for help. In showing such mettle you have proved tonight that you are a true man, a man of fine mental strength and determination. There are not many such men living in Northern Kinthoria these days.

"As to the question of Jaren that you asked me earlier, I think you need to allow him the same opportunity to prove his mettle by dealing in his own way with the burden of his own past. He has had to hear and think through many strange and new things in the past few weeks, and he's going to need some time to take it all in and adjust to it and come to his own conclusions. Then, he's going to have to make some very thorny decisions. I would imagine he's feeling a whole lot like a fish out of water, and he's reaching for the strongest anchor he can find. Right now, that anchor is Hawk. But I can guarantee you, once he has thought things through, once he has found who he truly is and has made his choices, you will be his closest friend in the years ahead. You will be a much stronger support to him because of what you have gone through tonight."

Tanner hung his head in embarrassment, first at the unexpected praise from Korthak, and then at the pettiness of feeling sorry for

The Birth of a King

himself when his best friend, no, his brother, had been facing his own fears and apprehension.

"Look at me, son," Korthak said gently. "Tonight you have left the road of your childhood behind and have entered well onto the road of manhood."

He chuckled at Tanner's injured expression. "Ah, it is just as I thought; you assumed that you had become a man a few years ago when you were allowed to enter the Weapons Master's yard."

Tanner smiled, and flushed hotly that Korthak could read his thoughts so easily.

"Don't be embarrassed, lad. It is a misconception held by every budding young warrior. You will find, however, that manhood has little to do with brute strength and arms. If traveled correctly you will find that manhood is an often difficult and confusing road, not easily walked upon with true success. You have a double burden to bear on your road, since you need not only to learn quickly for your own sake, but for Jaren's as well. He will need a man of very strong character and high worth to stand beside him for the rest of his life. You will be the one who will fill that need. You will be there through all of it with him."

Korthak looked intently at the young man. "If I am not mistaken that is what has been worrying you since the beginning of this journey, is it not?"

Tanner looked down at his breeches and tugged at a loose thread. "Yes, sir."

Korthak smiled and prayed silently to Elyon. *"Thank you, Father, for stopping me when I wanted to go after him. I can see how harmful that would have been to Your plan for Tanner. As usual, Your ways are always best. He never would have come through this as strongly as he did if I had followed him and offered to help carry his load."*

He looked up into the early morning sky and saw the sliver of Solisk just settling on the western horizon and suddenly realized that his watch, as well as Tanner's was over.

He stood, offering his hand to Tanner and pulling him to his feet. He squeezed his shoulder and said, "Let's get some sleep. I'll rouse Hawk for last watch, since he likes to spend the hours just before dawn in conversation with the Master. Tomorrow we'll have some fun at the market in Doddridge," he laughed and gave Tanner a conspiratorial wink. "And don't worry. Men are allowed to act like boys any time they please."

Tanner laughed at the thought of this huge man romping and capering through a marketplace like a child. He stopped by the fire and poured Hawk a mug of cafla, handing it to Korthak.

Tanner looked at the face of his sleeping friend on the way to his bedroll. He knew that Korthak's words had been the truth. Jaren had been carrying an incredible load in silence. *"As a man!"* he thought with wonder. Suddenly, Tanner understood that within the space of just a few weeks both Jaren and he had been unalterably changed. They were, indeed, becoming men. He also realized that in manhood, his love and allegiance to this *brother* would have behind them the strength of a maturity born of experiences, both pleasant and painful. He eagerly looked forward to a future of growing into the man that Korthak had described him to be. He looked forward to being by Jaren's side as his strong arm in the years to come.

As though Tanner's thoughts had touched Jaren's mind, his friend jerked awake. He focused his eyes on Tanner and smiled, stretching and yawning broadly. "All right, I'm up."

"No, no. It's just the beginning of Hawk's watch," Tanner whispered. "Go back to sleep."

Jaren mumbled something and pulled his blanket up under his chin. Tanner wearily crawled into his bedroll and was deep asleep within minutes.

"Amazing," Korthak chuckled to himself, as he yanked off his boots. "And this is the lad who said he couldn't sleep."

Chapter Ten

DODDRIDGE

Dawn arrived long before either Korthak or Tanner were ready for it, and Hawk spent the better part of an hour rousting them from their sacks. Jaren had already watered the horses and was tying his bedroll behind his saddle.

"Good morning, gentlemen...for the fifth time," Hawk said sternly as he handed each of them a steaming mug. "Nice to see you both so eager to join the living this morning. May I remind you that we are hired men with a schedule to keep?"

Tanner was still trying valiantly to open his eyes.

Hawk sat down by the fire. "By the look of you two, I think I should go back to our merchant friend and tell him he owes us a few more coins for our protection. Surely, 'you both must have fended off an army of bandits while we all slept like babes. No? You chased away a pack of starving wolves, then?" He needled with a wry smile.

Korthak scowled at him and then looked at Tanner. "You see what kind of mistreatment I've had to put up with most of my life? Do I need this at my age?" He waited for someone, anyone to answer. Failing that, he finally sat up in his bedroll, and rubbed his large rough hands over his face.

He looked up at his friend. "Why are we getting started so early? I expected that we could take it a little slower today. Dols, I feel like a bear wakened in mid-winter."

Hawk laughed at him. "Well, you look like a bear, too. Now roll out of that thing and do something with that bristle on your face. I'd like to look at least somewhat respectable when we go to market. And don't worry, you'll have plenty of time for some fun, *lad*. I may even give you and the other boys the coins that our employer reluctantly parted with this morning. Just imagine all the amazing things you can purchase. Maybe a tiny stiletto to pick your teeth, or half a dozen sticky buns," Hawk chuckled. "But, seriously, we need to get another horse and be on our way to soil I feel more comfortable having under my feet."

Hawk's use of the word "lad" was not lost on Korthak as he finally hauled his bulk from the ground. The others were hard put not to add to his foul mood by laughing outright as he yanked a comb through his hair and washed his bearded face, grumbling none too softly. "Fancied up like a dandy," he mumbled, "probably make me trim my beard, too."

Suddenly, he seemed to remember something and quickly walked over to Tanner. He stood squinting just inches from the lad's face, to the total confusion of his three companions. He then turned on his heel and walked abruptly away.

"Huh," he grunted with satisfaction. "Knew he couldn't do it."

Tanner looked about at the others, waiting for some explanation. Then his eyes lit up with understanding as he recalled his remark about the burnt cafla the night before. He laughed and rubbed his chin.

That left just Hawk and Jaren looking dumbly at one another for answers. Since none seemed to be forthcoming, Hawk stood, signaling that it was time for all of this foolishness to end and for everyone to mount up.

When they crested the hill and Jaren saw the lake city in the brilliant light of the morning sun, he was stunned. The walls of Doddridge were thirty feet high and shone like white marble as they reflected back the morning light. Parapets were placed every fifty yards around the city. Colorful flags danced and snapped in the brisk morning breeze. Domes and spires rose above the walls throughout this city that appeared as a shining jewel set on the silver band of the Kenanura River as it flowed from the north along the western edge of the city, and emptied into Lake Aerandir before joining the Ballain River to the south.

As the four made their way nearer the gates of Doddridge, the look of amazement and wonder steadily increased on the faces of the two lads. Never had they seen so many people gathered in one place. Jaren thought to himself that surely every race on Kinthoria must be gathered in this city. Races he had learned of in the scholars hall suddenly became real, living beings, instead of words and descriptions and facts to be remembered on examination days. Jaren's heart and mind were racing as his eyes eagerly studied this mass of humanity, trying to quickly call up from memory the identities of the people swarming about him. Each one was so blatantly unique in speech, dress, and mannerisms.

He saw the short, solidly built Athdarags, dressed in drab brown robes, short conical hats and those odd sandals that looked as though two blocks of wood had been nailed to the bottoms. These slight people were expert wood workers. The carts behind their donkeys were filled with beautifully crafted and carved pieces: everything from vases and plates, to tables, chairs, and intricately carved screens.

He stood open-mouthed at the gigantic Thigherns with their tanned skin drawn tightly over bulging muscles, dressed only in black, baggy breeches and brown leather vests. Each man wore knee-high stockings and a matching sash tied around his waist. These were brightly woven with colors and design to signify each family and house. Each was mounted on one of the famous Thighern stallions, beautiful with their chestnut bodies and long, black manes and tails. The thick necks of the steeds arched proudly above massive shoulders, nostrils flared, and hooves were lifted high with each step.

Bagpipes wailed and trilled as two lines of proud Murdocks walked in step through the crowds, their ruddy faces clearly proving the strength and pride of their race and their love for the sea. Behind them rolled wagons laden with dried and fresh fish, decorative driftwood, and fancy items of carved bone, including pipes of outlandish design and stunningly intricate and elegant jewelry.

Jaren was jostled from his observations by Tanner's hard nudge.

The Birth of a King

While Jaren had been struck by the human factor of Doddridge, Tanner had been in raptures, eyeing the goods being carted into the city. Everything from the back of a child to wagons the size of a small house and drawn by two pairs of oxen, was used to transport an unimaginable variety of wares through the city gates.

It seemed that everyone had thought to get an early start. Although the four companions had camped within half a league of the city, it took them the better part of an hour to get through the gate.

The marketplace took up every available foot of ground along the main thoroughfare and spilled down into the shorter side streets. Tanner's nostrils were assailed by hundreds of aromas. Some called like insistent sirens to his empty, protesting stomach. Others were so noxious and fetid that he felt waves of nausea rise in his throat.

They rode past booths filled with linens and silks, past tents crammed with anything that could be molded or hammered out of bronze, copper, pewter or silver. Bales of wool and bundles of furs were strewn throughout the marketplace. The clamor of merchants calling to potential customers, and the ensuing haggling over quality and price, the discord of fractured harmonies from roving balladeers and the sounds of livestock of every sort, all combined into an ear-splitting din.

The tables that most caught Tanner's attention were ones filled with foodstuffs. Aisle upon aisle of tables was filled with fresh, dripping honeycomb, sticky sweets of all kinds, fruits, and vegetables, many of types and quality that defied description. He fleetingly wondered where these things had come from, but then his eyes spotted more tables filled with moist, brown cakes, cheeses, meat pies, and assortments of nuts. More varieties of food than Tanner could ever have imagined were right there under his eager young nose.

"Jaren!" He yelled into his friend's ear. "I asked if you want to buy some of that hard stuff over there."

Jaren reluctantly drew his eyes away from the human tapestry and looked to where Tanner was pointing. Instantly all memory of studies and races was gone as his empty stomach screamed in protest. "You bet, Tan!" he shouted.

The Birth of a King

The sweet food was a wonder and a delight to the two young men, as neither had ever seen or tasted candies before. Tanner said it tasted just like the drink that Tupper had given them in his cottage. Hawk gave them money to purchase a few extra pieces to take on their journey. Korthak began to seriously doubt his recent judgment of Tanner. This person, whom he had called a 'man' just a few short hours ago, was rushing from one table to the next in wide-eyed wonder, fingering, smelling, and prattling as excitedly as a child in its sixth year. Jaren was right at his side all the while, behaving just as curiously.

Korthak looked at Hawk, and was pleased to notice that he, too, seemed somewhat nonplussed at their behavior. He whispered mockingly into Hawk's ear, "Hail, the King."

Hawk's look of shocked dismay pleased Korthak tremendously. He felt that he might just have pulled even with him for all of the times that Hawk had scared the life out of him with his sudden, silent appearances. Both men burst into fits of laughter.

Overhearing their friends' laughter, even above the din of the marketplace, Jaren and Tanner rejoined the two older men.

Tanner asked, "What's got the two of you so merry?"

"Just a little scorekeeping, that's all," Korthak replied with his chest swelled, thumbs hooked into his belt, rocking from heels to toes, and a look of enormous satisfaction on his face. Then he slapped both young men on the back. "Come on. If I have to wait much longer to break my fast you're going to have to drag my rail-thin body to the inn, prop it up in a chair, and try to figure out how to feed a corpse."

Hawk led the way to a large, white, two storied building. It boasted a long covered porch, and numerous windows in both levels. The large, freshly painted sign, swinging from two new iron hooks announced that this was the Golden Eagle Inn, Devyn Brewster, Esq., Proprietor. Jaren thought it far too grand a place for them to enter and expected Hawk to lead them right past it in search of another disgusting sty like *Stenchman's Pit*. He was very pleasantly surprised, then, when Hawk headed straight for the door of the elegant looking establishment.

Because of the abundance of windows, this inn was very light, and the air was full of the odors of roasting meats and freshly baked breads. There were tapestries hanging on various walls, with scenes of hunters standing over their fallen prey, of an eagle flying above a wide valley, and of a woman and her lover picnicking by the edge of a stream. All of the unoccupied tables and chairs were clean and neatly arranged around an open hearth.

Jaren spied a table by a window and asked if they might sit there so that he and Tanner could watch the marketplace as they ate. Korthak accompanied them and Hawk went in search of the innkeeper.

"Korthak, I've never seen anything like this city," Jaren said.

Korthak smiled at the excitement of the two young men. He had enjoyed coming to Doddridge whenever their business brought them over the Shandra River and into the North of Kinthoria. They were in constant peril from the moment they stepped onto this forbidden soil, but Doddridge was always such a vibrant city, so full of the zest of living, that it seemed to magically give them respite from danger while they were within its walls. Korthak, even at his age, enjoyed the noise and bustle swarming about the streets. He always looked forward to seeing the street jugglers and roving musicians and mimes.

"Well, the kind innkeeper has graciously offered us a bowl of his best gruel and what he described as 'the best cafla in all Kinthoria,'" Hawk reported with a look of satisfaction as he joined them. "We shall eat and then look to finding an inexpensive mount for Tanner."

His smug look melted away, however, when he saw the faces of his three companions as they stared blankly back at him.

"What?" he asked, as disappointment registered on all their faces. "What?"

Tanner was the first to voice their objections. "But Hawk, we've been on the road for weeks eating gruel. I was hoping...I mean, I think we all were hoping for something a little more appetizing."

"A whole lot more appetizing," Jaren affirmed.

"Ahem," Korthak grunted, "I do my best. If anyone else would care to turn his hand to the onerous task of cooking, I shall be more than happy to stay in my bedroll longer each morning," he said in mock injury.

"Here, hold on. That's not what we meant," Tanner hurriedly replied, trying to mollify the only excuse they had for a cook.

"It doesn't matter what any of you *mean*, my friends. It's either a large 'appetizing' meal or a horse for Tanner. The prices in this city of thieves are just too high. Our funds are far too meager to be squandering them about on frivolousness," admonished Hawk.

When all three were sufficiently downcast, he threw up his hands. "Oh all right. But if we end up with a mount that is lame, half-blind, and so starved that his ribs rub your backside, Tanner, just remember that you had an appetizing meal. I can see that I'm the only one around here thinking with his head instead of his stomach."

He had no sooner finished speaking than the innkeeper and a maid approached their table with huge platters of stack cakes and spiced meat patties, bowls of steaming hot gravy, and boiled potatoes. Saucers of sweet, white butter and small pitchers of fruit syrup and golden honey were placed about the large board. There were plates of dark brown muffins, bursting with apple chunks and nuts, and cafla that did indeed smell as though it would prove worthy of the innkeeper's boast. Best of all, not one bowl of gruel was to be found.

"There's enough here to feed the whole scholars hall," Jaren exclaimed.

"You should have seen the looks on your faces," Hawk laughed. "You looked like cats that have been tossed out in the rain."

Tanner was busily stuffing his second meat patty into his mouth, and Korthak was not far behind. The older man looked at Hawk as he placed one of the muffins on top of the four stack cakes already on his plate. "You know, my cruel friend, one of these days your joking ways are going to get you into a mess. And I won't be there to get you out." He pushed an enormous bite of the cakes into his mouth and mumbled around them to Hawk as a second thought. "In fact, now that I think of it, I might take great pleasure in being the one to put you into that mess."

The Birth of a King

An hour and many trenchers of food later they left the inn in search of a horse. Hawk noticed that he was the only one who did not have a miserable look on his face. He grinned evilly.

"You see? I should have ordered only gruel for the lot of you. I should think you would be embarrassed with yourselves, eating everything in sight, like starving swine."

He allowed his eyes to linger briefly on each of their bulging midsections as he glanced around the group frowning critically.

"Perhaps we'd better walk our mounts to the mews. We wouldn't want to break their backs." He grabbed his horse's reins and walked away laughing to himself. His three miserable companions looked daggers into his back and slowly followed him into the crowds.

The man's eyes narrowed as he watched the four strangers walk from the inn. Something about them made the hair stand up on the back of his neck. His instincts about such things were usually spot-on, and were the reason Volant paid him exorbitant sums for the information he supplied. He would follow the group and see what business they were about. Who knows, they might be the means to markedly increase his wealth.

They had walked only a short distance when Hawk suddenly turned to them and whispered hoarsely, "Quick, everyone move to the left of your horses! Keep your eyes down. Korthak, you and Tanner head toward that stall," he ordered, pointing to a leather monger's tent. "Move!" he hissed to Tanner who seemed frozen with fright.

Jaren had never seen Hawk in such a state before, and it frightened him greatly. He followed Hawk, keeping his head lowered and hoping that his horse would stop them from walking into someone's tent or table. He saw Hawk stop and pretend to be looking at some wares. So he followed his example, pausing before a table of trinkets.

"Somethin' you wanted, boy?" A gruff voice said above his head.

Jaren was afraid to lift his eyes, so he spoke to the oversized mid-section on the other side of the table. "Uh, no, sir. Just looking," he mumbled.

The Birth of a King

The merchant grunted. "Make sure yer just lookin' and not thinkin' of takin', or I'll hail that 'er dragon rider over there t' come and cart you off right short, y' hear?"

Dragon rider! The word caused Jaren to turn rigid with fright. Was the dragon rider sent here to search for them? Were they in danger so soon? He had not thought the headmaster would seriously have considered Tanner and himself worth reporting to the Dragonmasters.

He waited for a signal from Hawk. He anxiously looked for a way to escape, should the dragon rider spot him and try to capture him. It seemed as though hours passed before Hawk came up beside him.

"Come, son. We must find your mother." He said quietly, leading the trembling lad away from the increasingly suspicious merchant.

Jaren turned reluctantly, expecting to see the dragon rider looking straight at him. But the man had already melted into the surge of people moving through the marketplace. As Jaren cautiously followed Hawk, he tried to calm his racing heart and absently wiped the perspiration from his forehead and neck.

They found their two companions, still at the leather monger's tent. Korthak was heatedly, although quietly, haggling over the cost of a harness and a light saddle for Tanner. When he saw Hawk and Jaren approaching he pretended defeat and purchased the gear, grumbling and complaining sufficiently to make the merchant feel that he had finally won the contest of wills.

As the four walked away, Hawk quietly said. "Let's get that horse and be on our way. Even one dragon rider is too many in this city."

"Do you think he was searching for the boys?" Korthak whispered.

"I doubt it, but I'm not going to wait around here to find out. Let's move."

Chapter Eleven

THIGHERN MEWS

Hawk led them to the southwest corner of the city, to the section known simply as Thighern Mews. He headed for a corral that had perhaps the fewest, but by far the finest looking horses of any they had yet seen. A giant of a man saw Hawk's approach and smiled broadly, holding out his hand in welcome.

"Salamut D'Jamen, it's been a long time, my friend. How do you fare?" Hawk said, as each grasped the other's forearm.

"Very well, indeed, sir. Fortunately, I have few customers with as tight purse strings as yours. My Melfi and the children would be paupers begging in the streets, if everyone who came to my pens were as shrewd a businessman as yourself. Please, don't tell me you have come to deal. I can't afford it," he laughed.

"No, I still have the excellent steed you sold me eight years ago," he said, patting his horse's neck. "I have brought someone else, though, who has long since tired of riding double." Hawk motioned for Tanner to step forward. "This young man is looking for an intelligent horse with a good heart, strong legs and long wind." As an afterthought, he added. "And he can't afford to pay a thief half a year's wages for it."

Salamut frowned good-naturedly at his friend and said quietly. "Still on the run, eh? When will you ever learn?" Then more loudly, "Who are you calling a thief? For that, I should run you and your scraggly bunch out of my stables. Luckily for you though, I'm in a generous mood. I think I can match this lad up with just the horse he's looking for."

With this, he turned on his heel and followed Tanner around the enclosure, until the young man spotted a horse. He inspected the animal thoroughly, all the while talking quietly with the trader.

Korthak was once again nonplussed at this seeming paradox in human form. Gone was the wide-eyed, breathless youth of this morning. Before him moved a young man with obvious excellent discretion and thoughtfulness as he selected a beautiful black stallion.

Hawk had decided to allow Tanner to choose his own mount, since he knew his own abilities and preferences. He was looking forward to the friendly bantering with D'Jamen over the cost of the beast, and was therefore surprised as he heard Salamut's pained voice.

"Done and done!" the trader wailed. "Sir, I do believe that you really are out to make a poor man of me. Where did you pick up this skinny weasel of a bandit? He's taking one of my finest stallions and giving me tuppence in return," the man said in weary resignation.

Hawk laughed as much at Salamut's mock misery as to cover his own amazement.

"If I know you, I'll be handing over a sight more than tuppence for this animal. And the lad is no bandit. He's just an excellent businessman...I hope," said Hawk.

His hopes were more than realized upon learning that Tanner had bartered with the Thighern so shrewdly that even Hawk considered the price more than fair. He counted the coins into the trader's hand.

He looked at a beaming Tanner. "I am very impressed, young man. And thanks to your choice, I'm also now very poor."

As it turned out, Hawk did indeed pay a 'sight more than tuppence' for the stallion, but that was to be expected. The steed was of the famous Thighern stock, and perhaps one of the stronger of the breed. However, because its coloring was solid black and not the desired chestnut with black mane and tail, for which the breed was known, Salamut had been willing to let the magnificent beast

The Birth of a King

go for a lesser price. The knowledge of Hawk's mission also bore a large influence on D'Jamen's generosity.

The three older men held a quiet conversation for several minutes as Jaren helped Tanner saddle the enormous animal. Bidding Salamut farewell they continued to walk their mounts to the southern gate, not wishing to have their faces seen above the crowd. At the gate of the city, they mounted up and began a brisk trot down the road southward. They rode hard most of that day, following the Ballain River, the northernmost tributary of the great Shandra River.

Tanner was delighted with his horse, and in the days that followed both beast and human soon developed a deep respect and love for one another. The lad felt free for the first time since leaving Reeban. He no longer felt like the odd-man-out and suddenly sensed the return of his former self-confidence.

Hawk smiled to himself as he saw the change in the young man's demeanor, and was once more amazed at the great potential he saw in the man that Tanner was becoming.

None of the companions had observed the man whose eyes and ears had taken in all their movements that day. The man had engaged five men, former and reliable agents, to shadow the travelers. Their reports had provided him with much interesting information, much more than Hawk or Korthak would have thought possible to gather from such an uneventful day at market. The spy would soon know if there was a price on any of their heads.

As the four travelers left the southern gates of Doddridge, they were followed by six riders who had hidden themselves among the traders heading south to the smaller towns that sparsely dotted the banks of Ballain River. Neither Hawk nor Korthak were aware they were being followed.

Chapter Twelve

WAYLAID

It was four hours to dawn when Hawk found a small thicket in which to make camp. While Korthak busied himself with the fire, Tanner and Jaren went to wash the horses down, for Tanner would not allow his new treasure to remain coated with the dust of the road. When they returned to camp, they found Korthak had laid out a hasty, cold meal. Hawk had once more disappeared to speak with his Master and had not yet returned. Weary with the long ride from Doddridge, the younger men turned to their bedrolls.

As they lay by the fire waiting for sleep to come, Tanner asked Jaren. "Do you miss Reeban?"

Jaren was silent for some time. Tanner's question immediately brought to mind the taunts he had endured daily from the other boys at the scholars hall. "Hey, gray eyes!" They shouted across the yard, "Watch it! Don't touch him! Nobody knows where the mongrel came from." These and other, far worse insinuations regarding his parentage always caused fits of laughter among his peers. At other times, they would gather around and push him from one boy to another, shouting, "Scholar's bootlick! Scholar's toady!" The memories brought with them a pain that clearly showed in Jaren's eyes as he answered Tanner.

"Not really. I'm sort of enjoying not getting teased and pushed around every day. Hawk and Korthak treat me as an equal, just the way you always have."

Tanner was fully aware of the churlish boys who had delighted in taking advantage of Jaren's peaceful nature by seeing how far they could push him every day. He had himself come to Jaren's aid on many occasions. It was not that Jaren could not have taken care of himself; after all, he was tall and sturdy enough. He could easily have sent most of his oppressors away with their tails between their legs. But Jaren was for the most part a serious, gentle young man, who was always willing to see the best in people. His heart and mind were always searching for a better way, a better life, not just for himself, but for everyone.

Tanner sighed. He was glad that they had met Hawk and Korthak and that they had decided to accompany them. Maybe they would be able to teach Jaren that he needed to use his strength to protect himself, even if others were hurt as a result.

He settled down into his bedroll further and smiled. He enjoyed the feeling of self-confidence at being in the company of these two men who had accepted Jaren and himself just as they were. Yet, they had made it clear that they were able and willing to help them become even more than either young man had ever imagined possible.

"Yeah, I know what you mean. This is the kind of school I like - learning about real life by living it." Tanner had abhorred sitting for hours day after day in the scholars halls, listening to them prattle on endlessly about things that had happened in the past, or about things of which he felt he would never make use, although he was, to his amazement, beginning to understand the importance of history and its effects on the present. Yes. He was glad he had followed Jaren out of the scholars hall on that dark morning that seemed years past.

Korthak sat by the fire and watched as the two young lads drifted into sleep. He was amused at how the natures of these two were evident on their faces, even in slumber. Jaren's face was sober, yet full of peace. Tanner had a slight smile on his face, as though he was preparing, even in sleep, to greet the next day with a laugh. Korthak chuckled to himself and shook his head.

He was concerned about Hawk's long overdue return. It was not like Hawk to stay away so long without forewarning his friend. As he stirred the embers of the fire, he heard a noise. Then one of the

The Birth of a King

horses snickered. He jumped to his feet, turned around and saw a group of men spreading around the edge of the camp.

"Jaren! Tanner!" he shouted, as he kicked dirt onto the fire. Tanner and Jaren came out of their bedrolls with swords at the ready.

"Whoa there," said one of the strangers. "We're not here for a fight. We just want to have a little chat with you."

Tanner and Jaren had joined Korthak and were standing back to back with one another. They could make out six figures in the darkness.

"Oh, well then, if its just friendly company you're after, come and join us around the fire," Korthak said with mock affability.

"There's one missing," said another of the men.

"Where's the other man?" questioned the first man in anger.

"Oh, he's off somewhere, don't know exactly; it's nothing to get yourself upset over," said Korthak, "we don't need him to have a nice chat. Now, would you like some cafla? Oops, I guess I kicked dirt into it. Hmmm, now what else can I offer...."

"Don't get smart, old man," said the stranger. "I'll ask you one more time, where is your leader?"

"See now, I don't understand this. Why would you think he's the leader? I'm older and wiser, and better built than him. Probably smarter, too, now that I come to think...."

The man jumped at Korthak and back-handed him across the mouth, splitting his lip. "I'll have an answer out of you one way or another," he threatened. He motioned for his men to close in. They drew their weapons and began to advance.

"Hold, if you want to leave this place alive!" Hawk's voice came from the darkness.

The leader of the band immediately attacked Korthak. As Jaren spun to help his friend a strong arm clamped about his neck and fetid breath accompanied the gritty whisper in his ear. "Don't even think it, laddie." Jaren lowered his eyes and saw the glint of steel aimed at his heart.

Jaren knew Tanner was fighting to get through to Korthak when he heard his friend's scream of rage in the struggle with his attacker. He heard cries of pain and knew that the man was paying dearly for standing between Tanner and his giant friend.

Jaren was surprised when his captor's body suddenly went limp and the arm around his neck fell away as the man slid silently to the ground without so much as a word. He turned and saw an arrow piercing the man's back. He spun and saw Tanner shrug off the body of his assailant and then rush to Korthak's side. Jaren unsheathed his basilard and crouched to attack at the sound of footsteps coming toward him.

"Jaren! Are you alright?" Hawk slid to a stop, his bow in hand. Jaren could hear the fear and alarm in the scout's voice, and quickly took stock of himself.

"I'm fine," he panted. He heard the sound of hoof beats racing away from the edge of the camp. "One of them got away!" he shouted.

"It's no matter, he won't get far," Hawk said. "The adrastai will have him in seconds."

"Who are the adras…" Jaren broke off his question when he saw Tanner easing Korthak to a nearby log. He ran to see if he had been injured, and in the darkness, he nearly tripped over three bodies lying where Korthak had been fighting. His eyes were wide with concern.

"Dols," growled the old bear. "I'm not hurt. I just twisted my ankle a tad. I don't need the help of a nurse maid," he said hotly to Tanner between clenched teeth.

Hawk uncorked his water skin and handed it to Korthak as he quickly inspected his friend for any injuries. Seeing none, he said, "Well old man, it looks like you didn't lose your edge along with your youth. What happened here?"

Korthak took a long pull on the water skin and wiped his bleeding lip on his sleeve. "I dunno. I was waiting for you to return when I heard noises and that bunch moved in on us." He took another pull on the water skin. "Any idea who these mongrels were?" he asked.

Hawk shook his head. "No, we knew they were here, but we don't know who they are or what their intent was. I do know that we need to move on quickly. Pack up the gear and be ready to leave when I return." He dissolved into the darkness once again.

When Hawk returned some time later, he was very much agitated. The adrastai, scouts who were covertly protecting the four travelers, had been observing the band of attackers throughout the day. When the scouts had seen them make camp half a league north they had supposed them to be harmless. However, they had just received information that one of the group was a favored spy of Volant's, and were en route to Hawk with the news when they saw one of the men escaping and had easily captured him. Hawk had questioned him at length; the man's actions appeared to be merely fostered by greed, and his motive came from seeing four strange men in the city purchasing a grand stallion for an older boy. The man had sworn that he had not sent a courier to Volant as yet, since he had not garnered enough information to make any judgments as to whether knowledge of the strangers was worth selling. Hawk, however, did not trust the man's word, and instructed two of the scouts to imprison him at their base and to place extra guards with him.

"We don't know whether or not the man sent a message to Volant to let him know he was tailing us." Hawk took the reins of his horse from Korthak and said, "Let's be away from here. I will not feel at ease until we are well away from Doddridge."

He headed off at a canter into the darkness. They all were in much need of rest, but tonight's events reminded them of the unexpected dangers that lay on all sides. They were playing a perilous game, and Hawk knew that he had to deliver Jaren alive to the Spring of Elyon at any cost.

Chapter Thirteen

DRAGONMASTER LIES

Solance rose an angry red ball spilling an omen of crimson across the horizon of the Southern Plains, while to the North dark clouds roiled ominously, threatening fierce weather before day's end. They were four days south of Doddridge. The incident with the spy and his brigands had left them wary and alert. Hawk had pushed them hard from one shelter to the next and their constant vigilance was beginning to take its toll on the younger men. Hawk asked one the adrastai with whom he took counsel each evening to stand watch around camp. It was the first time since visiting Tupper that all of them were able to sleep soundly and without tension.

"We'd better keep riding through the day as far as we are able." Korthak said to Hawk. "That sky is going to break wide open in a few hours."

Hawk nodded his head in agreement. "I feared as much."

Korthak tossed Jaren and Tanner each a chunk of cheese and chewy bread. "No time for rest and hot food today, lads. Tighten your cinches and your belts. It's going to be a long day."

He walked past Hawk toward the horses. "Any good news last night?" He asked quietly regarding Hawk's two-hour absence during their night ride.

Hawk finished tying the thongs of his boots and nodded to his friend. "Yes. They still have not raised an alarm. The Elders were right in believing that the Dragonmasters are momentarily so arrogant and confident in their own power that they assume the boys have merely run off on holiday because the Day of Apprenticeship is approaching."

Korthak nodded, smiling at this welcomed news. "Things are still in our favor then."

Hawk agreed, and then added soberly, "Mmm, before we become too satisfied with our success, though, we must remember what will be taking place a few months from now."

The thought of the wide spread results of the events that would occur at the Spring of Elyon was never far from the minds of the two men. After their plans had been executed, and the Dragonmasters suddenly realized the threat to their power, the reaction of the enemy would be swift and deadly. Korthak mourned for the innocents upon whom the Dragonmasters' rage would be directed when they found that the greatest threat to their empire had not been crushed and obliterated years ago as they had believed, but was instead alive, and full of that ageless Power. Korthak shook his head to banish the scenes of violence from his mind. His heart was heavy with the thought that so many lives would yet be ruined and lost, so much land destroyed once again, before help could possibly arrive.

The four companions mounted and continued their southward tack at a steady canter. Their path was sandwiched between the Ballain River to the west and the beginning of the Southern Plains to the east. The Ballain River rolled steadily along the base of the Dungraden Mountains, whose northernmost slopes had seen dragon fire for the timber they offered the northern races. Now, stands of strong, young trees rose a few feet above the undergrowth along its slopes. They could see the land ahead rolling away into the distance, and far ahead, a small purple-hued mound rising above the horizon.

Hawk had told Jaren and Tanner about the adrastai posted at intervals along their route. The young men felt relieved to know that the scouts were there as added protection; however, it was a bit unnerving sensing the possibility that enemies could just as easily be as invisible as their allies.

Saddle weary though he was, Jaren felt thankful to be riding in the warm sunlight today instead of under the light of the two moons. He felt an excitement building within as he beheld the beauty of

Kinthoria being remade, and began to understand the promise she held for the future of her people.

He spent much of his time drinking in the beauty of this northern edge of the Southern Plains. The plains had escaped the dragon fire, as they were for the most part uninhabitable. He nudged his horse forward to ride by Hawk's side.

"Hawk, I've studied enough geography to know that these are the Southern Plains," he pointed off to the east, "but what is that small purple mound up ahead on the horizon?"

Hawk smiled at Jaren, "You are correct, Jaren, those are the Southern Plains. They're incredible, aren't they, even in their barrenness? Every hour of the day brings change in the beauty of all the vast leagues of that desert. But it's an unforgiving place, lad. It will test a man to his limits, and beyond. When you travel into its heart, it will try to burn the soul out of you during the day. Solance seems to take an eternity to cross the sky in there, as it turns the sand and hills of granite into an inferno. Only those who have come to know that land well, and have come to respect it, are allowed to find the secret watering places. The plains hide the water like a jealous husband hides his bride."

Hawk gestured toward the southern horizon, "That 'small purple mound', as you put it, is the Kroth Mountains."

Jaren turned to face him, wide-eyed in amazement. "But how can that be? I was taught that the Kroth Mountains are the tallest in all of Kinthoria?"

Hawk laughed. "And so they are, Jaren. What you are seeing up ahead is near a three-month ride or more distant."

Jaren was speechless. How could any mountain be so enormous that it could be seen from such a distance? But this fact paled in his mind as he suddenly realized how swiftly they were approaching the haunts of all of the dangerous creatures about whom he had been taught during his young life: creatures that had given him such terrifying nightmares as a child. He hoped one more time that Hawk's remarkable and appealing teachings were indeed genuine truth.

Tanner had been listening to the exchange, and as he looked toward the mountains, he wished he had been able to purchase a new sword in Doddridge. This was no place for a man to be headed armed with nothing more than a boot dagger and hunting sword. He was not encouraged by his thoughts of their old training regarding the South. He suddenly gasped for air and realized that he had been holding his breath as he watched the ghastly visions in his mind. He looked quickly at his companions to see if anyone had noticed, and found Jaren looking at him with a crooked smile, his right eyebrow lifted in question. Tanner smiled back sheepishly and shook his head.

Jaren leaned down and patted his horse's neck. He was very grateful to be riding single. He knew that Tanner had truly drawn a bargain in Doddridge. Cadeyrn was an impressive animal, and Jaren could not remember having seen a horse quite as wide and muscular. Every movement of the beast caused countless ripples in the muscles beneath his ebony coat. He truly was the finest horse in their company, and he was fit for a prince.

Jaren smiled and breathed in the fresh, cool air of the late spring day, trying to calm his own apprehension at actually being in sight of the Kroths. He determinedly turned his mind once again to the land. The ruggedness of the Southern Plains was, as Hawk had said, exquisitely beautiful. As the sun rode across the wild and irregular terrain, it caused a continual movement of light and shadow, of color and hue. It was as though the very land itself was a living, breathing entity.

Around mid-morning Hawk increased their pace dramatically. Korthak had been right about the weather. Just after noon, the dark clouds they had seen to the north had overtaken them, bringing with them an unusually violent storm. Once it hit the plains, it seemed to grow in intensity. As the leading edge passed overhead, lightning broke the sky with incredible frequency, many times sending a crackling bolt sideways from one stone outcropping to another. The continuous roar of thunder struck through their chests and beat at their ears.

Hawk had been leading them through the concealment of brush and trees just off the main road, but the danger of uprooted trees and soft ground was too great to risk any real speed, and so they returned to the road, hoping that others would not be out in such weather. For two days, he drove them soaked to the skin, in torrential rain and high winds, until he located a dry cave just across the now rapid and swollen Ballain.

As Korthak prepared a small supper, Jaren and Tanner stripped off their sodden boots and clothes, laying them out to dry beside the fire. They donned fresh tunics and sat down a short distance from Hawk and Korthak so that they could speak privately, each of them wrapped in a heavy blanket against the damp chill that had invaded their bones.

Jaren sneezed for what seemed like the hundredth time, as he rubbed his hands briskly through his hair, trying to shake the water from it. Tanner looked at his friend and spoke softly. "Jaren, this is really starting to get to me."

"What do you mean, Tan?" Jaren sniffed his nose and pulled his blanket around his shoulders more tightly.

"I mean this constant riding, hiding out in the dark, getting soaked like rats in a well. It's crazy. If the Dragonmasters were really looking for us, or even cared that we were gone, don't you think they would have at least tried to take us at Tupper's or even in Doddridge?" Tanner began reasoning with Jaren under his breath, asking him for one good reason why they should not head back to Reeban, far away from those menacing Kroth Mountains and the mysterious Shandra River.

He was startled as Hawk squatted beside them, his presence not even sensed until he made himself known. "I want you both to drink some of this. We don't dare risk having any sickness slowing us down." He stood up and walked back to the fire.

Tanner scowled at Jaren with a 'Thank you very much' look on his face, half angry that his friend had been the cause of having to drink down some vile tasting physic.

"What?" asked the innocent-faced Jaren. "What is that look for?"

Tanner looked down at his steaming cup with distaste, but after inhaling its fragrant, inviting aroma, he looked back at Jaren. "Forget it."

Both lads sat in silence, sipping their mint-flavored cups, which turned out to be the best medicine either had ever tasted. Tanner turned

The Birth of a King

his body just enough to be able to keep an eye on Hawk, wondering silently if the man had overheard any of their conversation.

Jaren finally broke the silence. "Tan, I'm not going to apologize for my decision. Nor am I going to have any regrets about it. We can waste this entire adventure looking backward and dragging our feet, or we can look ahead and face whatever comes, like men. I prefer the latter. I know these men only as well as you do. I will admit I've had my doubts a couple of times, but I can only tell you that in my heart I know they will protect us with their lives."

"I just don't understand how you can be so positive that we aren't being lied to again." Tanner shook his head. "Dols, I don't know what to believe anymore. Sometimes I feel closer to Korthak than I think I would have even with my own father, and other times I look at him and see a complete stranger." Tanner gazed across the cave at the older man humming at his work by the fire.

Jaren followed Tanner's eyes and said very softly, "Believe what's in your heart, Tan." Then he added with a hard-edged voice that Tanner had never before heard from his friend, "And remember Tupper."

Korthak looked up and smiled, as though he knew his name was being used. "You two wet puppies ready to eat?"

Both lads, still wrapped tightly in their blankets, moved closer to the fire, and accepted the bowls Korthak offered.

"This is the finest watercress and wild onion soup north of the Shandra," he said with confidence. He ladled some into their bowls as Hawk joined them around the small firepit.

"Yessir, I boil it with a little bit of salt and add a few herbs, and...." Korthak watched as both of the young men cradled the spoons up to their mouths. "Then I add just the right amount of hemlock for flavor."

Spoons froze in mid-air, as the lads' bulging eyes dropped to the steaming broth just under their noses.

Korthak roared with delight, handing Hawk a bowl of the steaming broth.

"Oh, come now," Hawk said, snickering. "Korthak was only having a little jest with the two of you. That soup really is the best watercress soup north of the Shandra. No one can make it like Korthak. Go ahead and eat it. It will warm your bones, believe me."

"Very funny, Korthak," said Tanner, not at all amused. Then, in an effort to prove that he had not been the least fearful, he proceeded to stuff himself with three bowls of the tasty treat.

Some time later, Hawk said, "We're ten weeks from the Spring of Elyon, depending on weather conditions." When he saw the fear in their eyes, he smiled. "I think it's about time you two told me everything the Dragonmasters have been pouring into the heads of Kinthoria's youth. That way I'll know what I'm up against here. I can't have you two jumping at shadows all the time, and cowering at mere words."

This led to a very colorful and imaginative narration by Jaren and Tanner. They recited the many legends which the Dragonmasters had forced the scholars to teach the children: legends of monstrous beings and ghouls prowling the forests of the Kroth Mountains. And elves that kill and eat humans and their horses if they dare to venture too close to their forests.

The longer Hawk listened to these tales the more enraged he became. Finally, Korthak leaned to whisper in his ear, "Easy there, friend. It's just more lies. It's only words, and that makes them easy to prove wrong with visible, tangible truth."

The lads continued their narration, relating how extremely vicious the Dwarves were in those mountains, even worse than the Elves, and more animalistic than the savage Gundroths up in the Northern Moors. And how one had to be cautious from which stream one drank, because these evil races poisoned some of them with hemlock and pigwort, and if one drank more than a few drops he could die a quick and agonizing death. They told of the southern race of Trolls who were shape-changers and far more dangerous than their northern cousins.

By the time the two had finished recalling many of the stories they had been taught, Korthak was hard put to control his laughter. Hawk, on the other hand, despite Korthak's previous reminder, was thoroughly enraged.

Talking about the legends had caused the two young men to become increasingly tense. Tanner, with an oddly morbid detachment, wondered if one of the huge boulders in the cave would suddenly turn into a Troll, and hoped beyond hope that they were not yet near enough to seriously have to worry about an encounter with them. He considered whether or not the trolls would eat them all alive or just tear them apart and leave them for dead; worse yet, would they cook them alive?

Hawk, sensing the rising discomfiture of his two young companions, forced his rage to calm and started whistling a tune that had been taught to the people of his race for centuries. It was at once full of mischief and delight, and yet woven through with the deepest of sorrow mingled with an unending hope. It was like light dancing on water. It was bird song and summer storms and rainbows. Its melody seemed to surround the four travelers and cast away all darkness and fear.

"What is that song, Hawk? Its melody sounds faintly familiar, but I know I've never heard it before." Jaren spoke softly, so as not to break the spell of peaceful serenity.

"It's Truth, my young friend. Truth. I learned it from some of my acquaintances." He paused to make certain that the young men were paying full attention to his words.

"They live in the Kroth Mountains." When he saw their look of astonishment, Hawk was satisfied that his musical diversion had accomplished his intention.

He continued, "I told you on the day we started that not everything you have been taught is the truth. The Dragonmasters say that races of monsters live in the south. Judge for yourself, would monsters be capable of creating music like this? That song is but one of thousands, all created through the centuries by the races that inhabit the lands south of the Shandra. Really lads...ghouls and monsters? A southern race of Trolls? Come now, it is time for you to begin opening your eyes to see truth. Don't keep the truth at bay out of fear fostered by the lies you've been taught."

Hawk entertained them for a time with music and tales that he had learned as a lad growing up in the South. He taught them games that children of the southern races play around the fire on winter evenings. Korthak told some of his outrageous stories, making everyone laugh until their sides hurt. The evening was peaceful and entertaining, unlike any the two young men had ever experienced.

Hours later Hawk was awakened by a deep sense of danger. He sent up a quick prayer for Elyon's protection and slowly picked his way around his sleeping companions. He searched the entry inside and out, but found nothing out of the ordinary. He even went so far as to seek out one of the adrastai for information, but there had been no movement observed in the area. Still, Hawk could not shake the sense of impending danger. He was soon joined by Korthak at the opening of the cave.

"What is that smell?" Korthak said quietly.

"I don't know," said Hawk, "But it reeks of evil. The adrastai are unusually alert as well," he added grimly.

Tanner rolled over and grabbed his sword. All in a moment, he peered into the dim light, saw Jaren tossing in his sleep, and noticed the absence of Hawk and Korthak. His stomach rebelled against the suffocating stench in the cave, and he sensed a powerful threat nearby. He forced down the bile rising in his throat, as he fought to control the dread surging in his chest. Suddenly, he noticed a dark, insubstantial shape gliding toward Jaren. An immediate sense of rage overpowered his thoughts and turned his vision red with battle fever.

Korthak and Hawk reentered the cave, and saw Tanner lunging toward the apparition. When Hawk recognized the being and understood Tanner's purpose he shouted, "Tanner, hold!" intending to interpose himself between the youth and the evil spirit. But the air was so thick with the power surrounding this malevolent presence that it seemed he was pushing against an invisible wall and he could only inch forward.

Tanner did not hear Hawk's shout. He raised his sword over his head and swung it down in an arching blow, as if to cleave the dark shape in two. Suddenly, a powerful presence rushed into his body, and he shouted, *"Aut, rauko senta, mi e esse Elyon!"*

As Tanner's blade struck the image, a screeching, inhuman howl of fury burst from the evil spirit as it spiraled into a racing whirlwind of oily smoke, writhing and twisting in apparent agony. It sent out a bone-wrenching wail of despair, and then tattered into nothingness.

Tanner stumbled with weakness, sinking to one knee beside Jaren, as his friend gasped for breath and grabbed the front of Tanner's tunic. "What happened? I couldn't move…I couldn't breathe! There was something…dark and foul, and freezing cold."

"I don't know what it was, Jaren," said Tanner with a voice that trembled. He helped his friend to sit. "But it's gone now, and you're safe."

Hawk and Korthak, able now to move, rushed to their two young companions.

"Jaren, are you hurt?" Hawk asked while eyeing Tanner with a probing gaze.

Jaren nodded. "No. I'm just shaken a bit. That was terrifying. Do you know what that was?"

"It was a demon of some sort, most likely sent by a Lucian priest to ascertain your location."

Jaren's face paled, "A demon? They can do that? I mean, they can make demons do their bidding? Great! Now I've got the spirit world after me, too."

Hawk grinned, "Hopefully that will be the last we see of the accursed creatures."

He turned to Tanner with a serious look. "Now, young man, you've got some explaining to do. Where did you learn that language, and what did you do to destroy the spirit?"

Tanner, still kneeling beside Jaren, looked up into Hawk's eyes. "I dunno. I just saw that thing going for Jaren and I got really mad, then everything turned red and I raised my sword to strike it and I felt this really strong tingling surge inside me, and the words just blurted out of my mouth. Do you know what they mean?"

Hawk placed his hands on his hips and roared with laughter. "My dear, bold, young friend, you have just been anointed by Elyon's Spirit. He did through you what was impossible for any of the rest of us to do. He sent the evil one into imprisonment. That's one that will not be bothering anyone ever again. The meaning of the words you spoke with such authority and power seems quite clear. You told the thing to go away…and it obeyed. That's how we can be certain that the surge inside you was the Spirit of Elyon."

The Birth of a King

Tanner was speechless. So this was the kind of power that Elyon held. And even Lucia and his angels of darkness were subject to the true God's word. "But why did Elyon chose me instead of you or Korthak?" he asked. "I am not one of His followers."

"Simply because you were the closest, and Jaren needed immediate help," Hawk answered. *"So, the lad begins to show his part in this path. He has the mark of an outstanding warrior stamped upon him,"* he thought.

The sun had risen and was filling the cave with shafts of soft light by the time everyone had related their part in the ordeal. Hawk left to inform the adrastai of the night's events. The two young men hovered over a crackling fire with Korthak, appreciating the ample heat. Their clothes were still somewhat damp from riding in the rain, but the sun would soon dry and warm them. Hawk's minty physic of the previous night had apparently done its job as Jaren's sneezing and constant sniffling were gone.

They spent the day in leisure, roaming the woods, sitting beside a clear, fast running stream, and taking their lunch on a wide patch of thick moss. Then, the warm sunlight, the sound of buzzing insects mingled with water splashing in rills down a rocky streambed, and bird song lulled them each into a lazy slumber. It would be long before they again enjoyed such a time of peace.

That night they started out just as Solance dipped to the horizon, and just as the wind began to pick up once more. They rode for days, continuing their southward direction. The weather remained unusually cold and wet, so that Jaren and Tanner, much to their delight, were often dosed with Hawk's "Miracle Medic," as they began calling the delicious physic.

They had reached the end of the worst forest devastation this side of the Shandra River, which made riding off the open road more difficult as they were forced to press on through the underbrush, ducking the lower limbs of the trees, and watching for fallen timber in the near total blackness of each heavily overcast night. They slept only briefly during the day, while Hawk disappeared to speak with his Master and to gather information from the scouts.

Finally, Hawk announced that they were far enough to the South to begin cautiously riding in the daylight hours. And so, this day,

The Birth of a King

they rode in the welcomed warmth of the sun, during a brief respite from the rain.

The irrepressible Korthak began another of his tales. This time, he told of a tournament that was held for all of the King's knights. It had been assembled just to the northeast of Doddridge.

"I wish you two could have seen one o' those tourneys," Korthak looked at the two young men in earnest. "They make the Dragonmasters' war games look like school boy scuffles." He chuckled to himself at the memories. "The Archbishop didn't like the idea of the tourney, and kept preachin' about low morals, and how ridiculous it was to purposely injure good soldiers and cavalrymen. All that sort of rot, you know. The man just didn't understand how a soldier thinks. So..." he cleared his throat, "we came up with the idea of wrapping our swords with cloth, and tying wheat sacks, filled with linen onto the ends of our lances." Korthak smiled at his young audience. "That way no one would really get hurt, so the Bishop gave us his blessing and we went to it. We had jousting, and hand-to-hand competitions, wrestling, sword games, knife and axe throwing contests, all the usual kind of things. We had nigh on a regular fair at our tournaments."

Hawk covered his mouth and coughed quietly, and Korthak, catching the gesture, stopped his narrative long enough to notice the puzzled looks on the faces of his listeners.

"What's a fair?" Tanner asked.

The old man furrowed his bushy eyebrows. *"Dols,"* he thought, *"near to eighteen years old and never even heard of a fair. That's downright criminal."*

He glanced at Hawk and then back to the boys. "Hmmm. Well, a fair...well...I guess you could say it would be like Doddridge. Only with a lot more space so that you don't feel all crowded and piled up on one another. And you don't need as big a money pouch, either. It's not full of greedy, thieving vendors. Everyone is there to have a good time."

Hawk added. "There are games of chance and skill that you can play to win prizes. And there is always lots of food everywhere. People used to come from all over Kinthoria to go to the Fair. It was the most exciting time of the year."

The Birth of a King

Tanner was excited now, especially when food and games were mentioned. "When can we go to one of these fairs?" he asked enthusiastically.

Korthak looked at him with regret in his eyes. "Son, they don't have fairs, anymore. They haven't since King Cadan's time. Seems no one has a reason to celebrate these days, and it's for sure that no one has even two shillings to line his pockets with, much less to spend at the booths." He regretted having even begun this story at the look of disappointment on the faces of the two younger men.

"I'm sorry, lads. I keep forgetting how young you are, and what you have missed since the Dragonmasters took control. He glanced at Jaren and smiled. A far-off musing shone on his face for several moments. "Maybe, someday soon, you both will get to see a fair."

Hawk prayed fervently that it would be so, while Korthak finished his tale of the days of honor and bravery, and the finest examples of knighthood evidenced throughout the tournaments.

Chapter Fourteen

STONEHAVEN

Hawk knew that the Dragonmasters would now be aware of the two missing boys, though he knew they would have no idea of the significance of their disappearance. Always at the edge of his consciousness were the events that had preceded the beginning of this quest. He could not count the times they had revised their plans, seeking and heeding the advice of the Elders and the Council of Seven, as they attempted to prepare for every contingency. Through all the years of waiting for the heir to come of age, they had exercised extreme caution and self-control. They reined in their natural instincts to fight against the Dragonmasters and their army and to deliver Kinthoria from their deadly evil.

Hawk's thoughts turned to the hundreds of people of many races: Elves, Dwarves, and Humans, especially the heroic An'ilden. All had sacrificed homes, fortunes, and even precious lives to ensure that this desperate undertaking would succeed.

At mid-morning, they passed through one of many breaches in a long, stone wall, and on through a field that appeared as though it had once been tilled and used for farming. It had been ravaged by dragon fire and, like so much of Kinthoria, had been left to fallow ground to heal itself. Now hardy tansy, yarrow, and fuller's herb were opening their leaves in clusters here and there, and millions of dandelions covered the area. Puffy spikes of purple meadow clover bloomed among the trillium whose flowers boasted a brilliant white to celebrate the warmth of mid-spring.

Soon they came upon the charred remains of what once had been a magnificent manor. The high walls were half crumbled and fallen down, still blackened from the fire that had raged through the immense structure. There was no roof to speak of, it having burned and collapsed into the rooms below. Yet the two or three remaining buttresses and arches still bore the faint remains of intricate carving, giving proud witness to the height of splendor that once had graced this place. Mists curled softly in the corners as the morning sun touched the cold, damp stone. Grass and moss grew between the broken marble slabs of the floor. Ivy, reviving from its black-green winter shades, and tangled, budding honeysuckle vines clung to the walls and hung down in graceful cascades of green and brown.

As they passed closer to the ruins, they could see that room after room had been utterly sacked and maliciously destroyed before the torch had been set.

Jaren noted the somber expression on the faces of Korthak and Hawk, and that persistent melancholy that crept so often into their eyes.

"Hawk, what is this place?" Jaren asked quietly.

Hawk turned his eyes from the ruin and looked at Jaren darkly. "This was Stonehaven, Jaren. It was the centerpiece of one of the most beautiful and prosperous duchies in all of Kinthoria."

Jaren stared as they slowly rode past the broken giant. He could see many other buildings placed around the estate. Each had been just as viciously razed as the main house. Jaren thought they looked like old skeletons that were receiving a long overdue burial by nature and time. The absence of the life that should have been bursting noisily all through this manor and its grounds was eerie and oppressive to the young man.

"Who did it belong to? And why was it so brutally destroyed?" he asked.

Hawk was reluctant to talk about the obscenities that had occurred here. However, he wanted the young man to be fully aware of the inhumanities for which their enemy was so despised by those who knew the truth.

The Birth of a King

"It belonged to a man named Cavan MacAulay. He was the Duke of Ravenscraig. We have been on his land for the past four days, and will be for two more. Everything you see belonged to the MacAulay clan." Hawk stretched out his arms to the vast landscape, as he forced down the lump in his throat.

Jaren gazed around in every direction, taking in the rugged beauty of the young forests dotting rolling hills that abutted the Dungraden Mountains to the west and the long, wide meadows to the east. He even caught a glimpse of the shimmering waters of Loch Hembrow, where the Lioslath River joined the Ballain on its journey south. He could not imagine anyone possessing so much land, except perhaps a king. The granting or holding of estates was a luxury no longer allowed, even for the titled. Even those awarded scant tracts of land for their treason against the Cathain crown paid a heavy tribute to the Dragonmasters.

"But where is he, and what happened to all of this? Where are all of the people?"

"Dead, Jaren...all of them. Just like Tupper's home." Hawk's gaze fell to the ground.

Korthak knew his friend could not continue, so he fell back beside the boys and motioned for Hawk to take the lead.

"Y'see, lad, Cavan MacAulay was completely against the Dragonmasters takin' over Kinthoria. He could see what was coming if they won the war." Korthak sighed, and added under his breath. "You were right, too, my friend." He told how Cavan had used his wealth to supply King Cadan and his loyal supporters with food and arms. He had used this manor as an armory and a hiding place for spies and for the protection of anyone loyal to the Crown.

Jaren interrupted him.

"But why was this beautiful place not saved? Why was it necessary to destroy the land? Was there no one to come to the aid of all of the innocent people who lived here?" he asked angrily.

"These people were of An'ilden blood, lad. As you are fully aware, they are not high on the list of favorites with the Dragonmasters, unless you're listin' raiding targets. I believe they despise that race more than they despised King Cadan and all of the Southern races put together."

Jaren could only stare in disbelief at the evidence of the carnage everywhere as he and Tanner took in both the total devastation of their surroundings and the facts that Korthak had related to them.

"I wouldn't think that a race, even as traitorous as the An'ilden, would justify this kind of brutal punishment." Jaren observed.

Korthak yanked his horse to a halt and glared at Jaren with barely controlled anger flashing in his eyes.

Hawk shouted, "Korthak! Remember who has been teaching these two. They are just now learning the truth. Jaren is speaking from the years of lies poured into his head. Give him time to let the truth settle and become real to him."

Korthak trembled violently as he struggled to bring his rage under control. He looked long into Jaren's eyes. Then, seeing only questioning innocence and fear, the huge man pulled his own eyes away. He slowly dismounted and walked his horse toward the remains of the home in which he had once found such welcome friendship and joy.

"Let's stop here for a while." Hawk said. "We'll give Korthak some time to gather himself, and I'll give you two another lesson. This is too important to put off, and I think that it is well past time for both of you to hear the entire truth about the An'ilden."

Hawk dismounted and led the lads to what had once been a private garden. He motioned for Jaren and Tanner to sit on a weathered marble bench under the twisted remains of a grape arbor.

"Let me explain Korthak's reaction to your words, Jaren. What you just said back there is one of the most offensive and hated teachings of the Dragonmasters. It's particularly detestable to those of us who know the truth. The An'ilden have long been held to be the noblest of all races on Kinthoria. They trace their lineage back for thousands of years. They are highly respected and honored by all but the Dragonmasters. They are venerated because of the antiquity of their race and because they have ever been the powerful protectors of the weak. The An'ilden kept the land peaceful by their unquestioned military superiority long centuries before they established the brotherhood of the true Dragonmasters, in which men of other races were included to fly the dragons. They are still trusted implicitly by all of our countrymen, though the Northern races may not speak such treason for fear of the spies of the Dragonmasters. The An'ilden have always been very astute with the use of their power, using force, justice, and mercy in carefully determined measure so as to mirror the character of Elyon, whom they love and honor above all else. The An'ilden were the only ones to remain entirely true to Elyon when all other races turned from Him. They kept the Cathain line under their spiritual protection and mentored them in the teachings of Yesha and His Father, Elyon.

They are the people most feared and hated by the Dragonmasters because they pose the biggest threat to Volant's dreams of the complete domination of Kinthoria. The Dragonmasters are enraged because the An'ilden have never been bowed or intimidated or conquered. For no other reason than their noble strength, they have become the prime target for destruction and brutality with no other purpose than to obliterate them from the face of the earth. The obscenities you see here are not just an event from history, lads. Atrocities like these are taking place even as we speak. The An'ilden suffer daily. Their race is slowly being decimated by the Dragonmasters, all because of the valor and unflinching allegiance of these people to the one true God and to the royal line of Kinthoria."

Hawk's words had visibly shaken the two young men. This raid had been just as savage as it was hateful. They knew instinctively that there had been few if any survivors from the manor area. It was a known fact that the Dragonmasters would not take An'ilden captives because of their obsessive hatred of the race, and because even their children could not be broken to slavery.

Jaren began to understand why they were so feared by the Dragonmasters, for he believed all that Hawk had just told them.

"But why would the An'ilden hang on to a lost cause like this, to the destruction of their race? There is no royal line left on Kinthoria. Don't they know they are sacrificing themselves for nothing? It just doesn't make any sense, Hawk. If they are so intelligent why can't they see the hopelessness of their cause and give in to the Dragonmasters in order to preserve their race?" Tanner asked, wondering at such blind dedication to a cause long lost.

"Well, that's a subject for another day. You have much to learn here today. Let's just say that not everyone believes that all hope is lost. How much would you value your life, Tanner, if you had no hope?" Hawk posed. "Besides, you must understand that above all else the An'ilden would never reject Elyon and embrace Lucia. The cause of the truth of the one true God will never be lost or hopeless."

Jaren considered Hawk's question to his friend through the following days and weeks, always coming to the same conclusion. His hope for a deliverer for Kinthoria was what had made his own life bearable.

They spent the day at Stonehaven, walking through its ruins. Hawk and Korthak related stories of the An'ilden as a race and the McAuley clan in particular. They described the ballroom where ladies adorned in their finest gowns and jewels and danced the night away with men of strength and honor. Hawk showed them the balcony where Korthak had first met his beautiful Megen and had been hopelessly lost in her eyes. Korthak could not bring himself to enter there. He did, however, take them below the ballroom through a hidden stair, and showed them where the scores of true patriots had been hidden away during the dragon riders' raids. The room was choked with charred bones that spoke volumes to the boys regarding the fate of those trapped here in the final assault. Many of the skulls were cracked and arm and leg bones deeply scored or fractured.

The more the two young men saw, the more their old beliefs were shaken and shown for blatant lies.

Tanner looked at Jaren and said with incredulity, "How easily the truth has been concealed and replaced by the lies of the Dragonmasters. It doesn't seem possible that all of this could be unknown to people our age. We have to do something. We have to tell what we've seen. This has to be avenged and made right!"

Jaren and Tanner had been moved by the depth of their friends' affection and honor toward these people, and they felt that they had through the narratives come to know some of them personally.

"Yes, Tan. You're right," said Jaren. "We *will* do something about it. I'm not certain what just yet, but after knowing the truth, we can't allow the Dragonmasters to continue as they have. I believe Hawk and Korthak will show us what we can do. Perhaps we'll be able to fight with them against all of this. They found us and brought us with them for just such a purpose, I'm certain."

"No, Jaren," Tanner countered. "They found *you*, because *you* are somehow related to all of this. I'm merely an accidental body here, despite what Korthak and Hawk have said. I'm here because you wouldn't come without me, remember?"

Jaren smiled. "According to Hawk there are no 'accidents' where his God has made a plan. So be assured, my friend. You are *deeply* related to all of this."

Tanner was shaken by Jaren's words. Korthak had been tutoring him somewhat about Elyon, but he had not paid much attention, considering his older friend's belief to be fine for him if it was something he needed to make him feel better about life. But, he had not gone beyond the fact that Korthak's *belief* was a true thing, to the possibility that *what* he believed was truer still. To think that a being far greater than anything in creation had made plans that involved his own participation was sobering, and very unsettling. He was not at all certain that he liked the idea.

As the four companions walked away from the manor in silence, they rounded a large outcropping of twisted and blasted trees that had once been an orchard. The sight, known to the two men, jolted Jaren and Tanner to the core. They stood stone still, staring at row upon row of empty stakes - mute testimony to the final agony of well over one hundred and fifty souls. The scene was undeniable proof of the senseless brutality of the Dragonmasters. Jaren shuddered in horror at the unthinkable torture of these people for whom Hawk and Korthak's recent words had kindled such compassion. He felt the sight burn into his soul and vowed that somehow he would help others to avenge these people and break the power of the Dragonmasters. He would see Stonehaven once again a place of beauty and splendor, to bring long overdue honor to these heroic people.

The sight similarly affected Tanner; however, he experienced a deep shame at his former eager expectation of joining the Dragon Flights. He now understood that he had allowed his desire for the limited freedom and the excitement available to dragon riders to override what he had always known in his heart to be an occupation that fed off of cruelty and the death of others of his countrymen. The revelation of his selfishness nearly overpowered him. He was crushed by the weight of his self-imposed blindness and repulsed by the thought of how close he had actually come to realizing his former dream. But for Hawk's intervention at the oak tree in Reeban, he felt that he would have been lost forever in a world of lies and death.

They gathered their horses and moved on silently, as though not to disturb the atmosphere of that place made sacred by innocent blood.

Several hours later Hawk stopped the company deep in a copse by a wide, sparkling brook. "We'll camp here for the night," he announced.

Korthak attempted to draw their minds from the sights of Stonehaven, and to create an atmosphere as near normal as possible after the unnerving experience. He drew his line and hook from his saddlebag and meandered to the edge of the brook. Selecting a pliant branch from a nearby tree, he sat down on one of the large stones lining its bank and tied his line in a notch at its end. He began singing one of his spontaneous melodies as he tossed his hook into the water to angle for fish. He was tired of the monotonous fare of meatsticks and cheese. He felt the need for some relaxation to clear his mind of the traces of anger that could so easily fester if ignored. Nothing would accomplish this so quickly for him as fishing. And there was no better time for prayer than while waiting for a tug on the line.

Tanner sat down beside the huge man and prepared his own line to cast into the clear water. "Korthak," he said softly, intending to relate his earlier soul-searching to his now trusted friend.

"Hmmm?" The older man replied with contentment.

Tanner's line suddenly jerked. He quickly pulled a fat, squirming fish up onto the bank and took the hook out of its gaping mouth. The creature was so large, and flopping about so wildly that it took extra care on Tanner's part not to hook himself. He took the fish to Jaren to clean and returned to the side of the still crooning Korthak. Tossing his line back out into the water he said, "Korthak, I was about to say..." Before he could finish his sentence, his line was pulled taut once more. He landed another good-sized fish, and took it to Jaren.

Korthak's song had noticeably diminished as he avidly concentrated on yet his first catch. This time the young man prudently sat down a few paces on the other side of his huge friend. He hesitantly cast in his line while flicking a cautious glance at the man. "Korthak...Dols!" He shouted, landing an even larger fish than the previous two.

"Korthak," he blurted in frustration, "I've been trying to tell you to quit baying like a sick moose! But I'm beginning to think you make a better bhaird than a fisherman," Tanner laughed, snatching up his fish, and springing away before Korthak could grab him. Jaren and Hawk, having observed the whole affair, sat laughing as the old man sulkily threw his line into the water once more, while adding just a touch of resentment to his prayer list.

Korthak eventually became resigned to his bad luck and returned empty-handed to the fire. He scowled deeply at Tanner. "You need to learn how to bring in a fish without scaring all the others away," he accused. However, he could not hold the sour look on his face as he laughed at his own joke. He took great care in preparing the fish, sprinkling them with dried bitter herbs from his bag, and adding some small, wild onions he had found growing on a sandy knoll near the brook. He wrapped them in leaves and baked them near the coals of the fire.

A short time later three sated men were soundly asleep under the trees as Hawk took the first watch. He was concerned that the rigors of the past few days and the emotional strain of this day had begun to give evidence to a growing weariness in his two charges. He had been waiting for weeks to have Jaren experience Stonehaven, so that he could finally reveal the truth about the An'ilden to the young man. He knew that no argument against the Dragonmasters' lies would be as effective with Jaren as seeing the truth with his own eyes.

"Elyon," he prayed quietly, "thank you for allowing these two young men to see and believe the truth that Stonehaven speaks with such force. Thank You, also, my Father, for receiving the souls of your people who lived there into your Kingdom of Light. I confess, my Lord, that I still harbor a longing for vengeance toward the Dragonmasters for what they have done to Kinthoria. I understand that many of the younger ones are just as deceived by lies as were

Jaren and Tanner. I lay down before you right now my hatred of these deceivers and murderers. I pray that they may see truth and receive it, as these two young men have done today. Work a miracle in their hearts as well, Yesha, by your Spirit's power."

Hawk spoke with Elyon long into his watch. By the time he woke Tanner for second watch he was renewed in the vision and purpose of his mission, and in his unwavering assurance that they would safely make it to the Spring of Elyon.

Chapter Fifteen

RUSH TO THE SOUTH

Steadily, the small purplish mound that Jaren had seen on the horizon days after leaving Doddridge turned into a mixture of greens, browns, black, and white. Slowly the horizon had been swallowed up with rank upon rank of increasingly higher hills, which served as the footstool of the majestic, impossibly vast Kroth Mountains. Many of the peaks of that endless range were still capped with pristine snow that shot back the sunlight with bright white fierceness. Deep in the southernmost arm of the range soared Coryn's Reach. Jaren had heard of this ageless and silent giant, but no description had been adequate to prepare him for the awesome beauty and sheer size of this breathtaking wonder of nature. A quarter of its height was shrouded by thick, radiant clouds.

"Magnificent, isn't it?" Hawk said quietly, on this rare, clear day of bright sunshine.

Jaren, riding next to him could only nod in silent awe. He recalled a day when the sky was heavily overcast, and damp fog filled their vision on all sides. He thought he occasionally caught the scent of pine. At those times, he would draw in a deep breath, and found himself surprisingly revitalized. He and Tanner were still reticent as they neared the mountains and the endless forests climbing their slopes. Yet, he felt a curious anticipation course through his body with the passing of each league. Something inside seemed to whisper to him that it was right for him to enter the Kroths, for what reason, he could not begin to imagine, but it was of little import to the lad at that moment of wonder.

Now, on this bright day he sensed that each of his companions was falling under the same spell of fresh air and incredible beauty. It was near overwhelming at times.

"This air smells wonderful. It's...it's..." he breathed deeply once again, "it's so clean," he said, at a loss for words.

Hawk turned in his saddle and smiled at the youth. "I know, Jaren. That's because no dragons have been here to burn and foul everything."

Jaren gazed up at Coryn's Reach again, and then asked Hawk in a voice, barely above a whisper. "I'll bet that mountain is so high, you could sit beside your God and talk to Him face to face."

Hawk chuckled. "No, lad. It's not quite that high. But then again, why would I want to waste my time and energy climbing that huge rock, when I can talk just as easily to Him right here?"

Jaren nodded his head bashfully. "I keep forgetting what you've said about Him being all around us. That must be nice."

Hawk looked at him, "It is, Jaren. It truly is."

Three days of blinding sheets of rain driven by gale force winds had climaxed the last weeks of near steady rain, turning the country into a morass of turbid lakes, rushing streams and thick mud, all of which had slowed their progress considerably. There had been frequent long detours around flooded plains and areas where the road had become a rushing offshoot of the Ballain. Hawk knew well the capabilities of the dark god, Lucia. He suspected the work of Lucia in the violent weather, more characteristic of a turbulent autumn than of early summer. Lucia would most certainly be aware of their plans and of what the fulfillment of those plans would mean to himself and his control of Kinthoria.

It was just before dawn when Hawk roused them from their bedrolls, hurried them through a quick meal and into their saddles. The challenge and probable delay of crossing the swollen and angry Shandra River lay ahead of them today.

Hawk was determined that they should reach their destination well before evening, as there was much to be accomplished before dawn, and none of it could be hurried. Indeed, great care would have to be taken not to force any of the events of the coming hours. Therefore, Hawk would not even consider the possibility of any obstacle that might delay their arrival, and cause his plans for tomorrow to be postponed. They rode under roiling skies and through a howling wind, as Hawk pushed them on relentlessly, eventually infusing them with his own sense of urgency.

They had been riding for several hours, and it was well into the middle of the afternoon, when Hawk dismounted and led the way along the northern bank of the Shandra. He shielded his eyes from the wind-driven sheets of rain. An eager, concerned look clouded his face as he scanned the water's edge, just as he had numerous times in the last two hours. His three companions followed closely behind. When Hawk found the sandbar for which he had been searching, he stopped so abruptly that Jaren had to rein in quickly to prevent his horse from plodding over the top of him. The weary young man flushed. "I'm sorry, Hawk. I wasn't paying attention."

Hawk did not acknowledge Jaren's statement, but instead shouted back to Korthak, over the roar of the swollen river, "The flooding is even worse than I had expected!"

Korthak rode up beside him. "Might be a little tricky getting the horses across."

Hawk peered out into the middle of the raging torrent, trying to discern the strength of the current. "I think we'll be all right as long as we all stay right on the ridge of the sandbar!" he shouted. "We can't risk any further delay, the next ford is six leagues down river and there's no guarantee that it would be any better than this one. If we did get across down there, we'd have to back track on the other side all the way back here."

"You lead the way," Korthak replied. "Jaren can follow you and I'll have Tanner in front of me. I'll keep everyone in line with you."

Hawk nodded, grabbed his horse's mane, and leaped into his saddle. "Stay together!" Then as an afterthought, he turned and looked at Jaren. "You might want to keep a tad more alert than you were a moment ago. I really don't think I'd like the permanent shape of a horse's hoof on my backside." Jaren flushed a deep red as Hawk

The Birth of a King

smiled at him, turned, and cautiously urged his nervous mount out into the roiling water.

Tanner laughed, and looking at Korthak said, "Jaren's always off in his own world. I swear the boy has a touch of the mind-plague."

Jaren would have turned and thrown a biting retort at Tanner, but his horse was already in the water, and he was struggling to keep the agitated beast following Hawk's lead.

The four made their way along the sandbar with agonizing slowness. The white foamed water was surging with such force that it threatened to drag the horses off balance. More than once Hawk and Korthak could be heard shouting, "Keep it steady!"

They were nearly three-quarters of the way across, when a large tree limb came sweeping, unseen, upon them. It hit the hip of Hawk's mount, nearly sweeping it off its feet. The stallion screamed in pain and terror, his nostrils flared, and his eyes rolled. He reared up, almost throwing Hawk into the raging waters.

Jaren and Tanner were terrified. Korthak screamed over the roar of the river. "Keep your horses' heads! Don't let them break!"

Hawk's mount was still thrashing about wildly in fear and pain. Hawk twisted and turned with him for what seemed an interminable time before he was finally able to bring the panicked and wounded animal under control. The other three had been forced to stand and watch, using all their wits to keep their own skittish mounts on the ridge of the sandbar. Had Hawk been thrown off, he surely would have been swept away and drowned by the water's undertow as it churned past massive boulders. Hawk took just a moment to soothe and calm his horse, before slowly starting once again. The other three followed along in silence, as they willed their hearts to beat slower, and at least one thanked his God for the protective mercy He had just shown them all.

When they reached the south bank, Hawk dismounted and checked his horse's hip. Korthak slid out of his saddle and went to stand beside him. "How does it look?"

Hawk was stroking the beast's heaving belly, while pressing gently on his tightly swollen hip and bleeding flank. "He'll be sore and stiff for a while; his muscle isn't torn, but it sure took a beating. The flank wound seems to be only superficial; I doubt it will need stitching. Thank the Lord we arrived before anything worse happened. Let's set up camp for the night, and I'll pack a poultice on this hip. I'll have to ask you and Tanner to walk him a bit this evening, so that he doesn't tighten up on me. I'll have our other business to attend to, as you well know."

He gave the horse a strong, affectionate pat. "You're a steady one, aren't you, Deakin." He turned to Korthak, "He should be fit enough to continue after a few hours of rest. I believe the Father will assist in his recovery a good deal."

Korthak looked into his eyes. "You gave us quite a scare back there. I've never seen even you handle a spooked horse so well before."

Hawk glanced around to see where Jaren and Tanner were and smiled. He gathered his horse's reins, and patted Korthak on the shoulder. "Just remember," he said, speaking into Korthak's ear. "I'm one of those man-eating, shape-changing, monster elves, Korthak. We have a way with animals...at least the ones we don't butcher and eat." He walked away chuckling devilishly.

Korthak stared at his friend's lean back and shivered. "I wish he wouldn't do that," he mumbled, "it makes my flesh crawl."

Chapter Sixteen

REVELATIONS

Leading their horses on foot along the rock and pebble strewn shore, they soon came upon a copse fronted with a thick undergrowth of gooseberry and gorse. They followed the edge of the thicket to where it grew tightly against a large mound of boulders perhaps thirteen feet in height.

"Well, what do we do now? This is a dead end!" Tanner shouted above the wind and the roar of the river.

"Just keep following Hawk!" Korthak shouted from the rear.

As Tanner turned to follow Korthak's instructions, he saw the tail of Jaren's horse as it disappeared behind the pile of boulders. Quickly following, he found himself instantly out of the raging wind and standing at the edge of a large clearing inside the copse.

Jaren was studying the clearing with some interest. He was puzzled at the calm that so permeated this place, like the lull in the middle of a hurricane. He heard birds singing in the surrounding trees, and only the faintest breeze stirred the leaves and grass.

He unsaddled his horse, and tied him to a small bush, leaving him to browse in the thick carpet of grass and clover. Then suddenly he reached up again and scratched at his birthmark. He could not for the life of him understand why it had become so bothersome these past few months, and it seemed to be getting worse daily. He wished he had not used Tupper's numbing salve quite so liberally. The jar in his saddlebag had been empty for a week. He half decided to swallow his pride and to ask Hawk to take a look at it, fearing it had become infected. But when he saw his friend smearing a dark green poultice on his horse's hip, he decided his birthmark could wait.

A short time later, as they were setting up camp for the night, Jaren finally became consciously aware of a warmth and a peace which he had been feeling since entering the copse. He noticed that his three companions seemed to be similarly affected. They stood, quietly watching, as Solance broke through the gray clouds, spreading golden bars of late afternoon sunshine through the forest canopy and creating a quiet cathedral. Everything was hushed and serene, except for the bird song and the muted roar of the swollen river. Yet, the atmosphere seemed alive and expectant, unlike anything Jaren had ever experienced. The very air was pulsating with a stronger force even than the peace that had settled over them when Hawk had whistled his haunting melody a few weeks ago. This was something far more than just peace. It was enormous, throbbing with life and its presence filled the entire clearing. Jaren had never experienced such a sensation. It was almost…too much. Jaren wanted to laugh and cry at the same time. His emotions were so strong and heady that he had a hard time not giggling like a silly scullery maid. On the one hand, he felt he could stay here forever, but on the other hand, he sensed that emotionally it would be too overwhelming. He wondered if this was what love felt like. He had strong affection for Tanner and Tanner's mother; that was the closest reference he had to what might be called love, having known neither father nor mother, brothers, or sisters.

Each member of the company had been moved by the force that pervaded the glen, and in an effort not to romp about the clearing like a bunch of yearling colts, they busied themselves with the mundane tasks of camp life. Each of their faces was split by an impossibly large grin. Jaren began to gather wood for the fire, while Tanner began digging a firepit and placing stones around it. Hawk checked and picketed the horses, and slowly walked his stallion around the perimeter of the clearing for the third time. Korthak unpacked his cooking utensils and went for water.

Surprisingly, with this small task of gathering wood Jaren sensed a deep weariness just under the surge of energy he was experiencing from this 'Presence', as he seemed to want to call the source of his emotional rampage. They had been making their way steadily south from Doddridge for close to two months. The nearly constant rain, especially during the past weeks, and the harshness of life on the run had drained even his youthful resources, and his body was beginning to demand a rest. He wondered how much longer any of them could go on at this pace. He was to find out in the weeks that followed, that the human body and spirit can endure much more than he had ever imagined possible.

"How about a swim in that pool before supper?" Tanner asked. Always eager for fun, he raced Jaren to the pool, flinging off his clothes along the way. He bellowed in surprise as his body hit the iciness of water not yet warmed by the sun of summer.

As they were swimming, Tanner smiled mischievously and asked, "How do you like swimming in water from the "evil" Shandra River, Jaren?"

Jaren stopped swimming in mid-stroke, shocked that he had not thought of it himself. Then he smiled. "Oh, I don't know, Tan," he said off-handedly. "I mean, I haven't felt even a small nip from one of those fanged fish yet. I have to admit, I'm sort of disappointed." They both roared with laughter, and proceeded to attempt to drown one another. After a while, Tanner fell silent, and allowed his body to just float on the water.

"But was everything they told us a lie, Jaren? Nothing seems to be the way they taught us, you know?"

Jaren did not answer for some time, and both young men merely relaxed, listening to the loud croaking of bullfrogs in the reeds at the far end of the pond.

Finally, after Tanner had forgotten his question, Jaren said, "Hawk says that the Dragonmasters have told us all of the lies to keep us from ever coming to the Elven forests and the Kroth Mountains. I guess they just don't want anyone to know the truth and find out whatever it is that they're trying so hard to keep secret."

Tanner dunked his head under the water and came up spewing a fountain from his mouth. "It would be interesting to know just what's so important that they work so hard to keep it from whole nations." He started to wade toward the shore to begin gathering up his clothes. "It's going to have to wait for a while, though, before

I go off trying to find the answers. I'm starving. Come on, let's see what kind of feast Korthak has prepared for us."

Korthak had returned with a pot of water, and had done his own style of bathing for a short time, while absently feeding the fire. When the boys returned, he was just taking a food sack from behind his saddle. He rubbed his hands together in dramatic anticipation and said, "Now, let's see what I can rummage up." He pulled out a thick meat stick, a cake of soft, white cheese and some hardbread. "Hmm. Not quite spiced meat patties and stackcakes, but it's something to chew on, and it will keep body and soul together." He threw a couple of handfuls of cafla into the pot of water and set it into the burning coals. Within minutes, the aroma of the brew filled the campsite and drew them back around the fire to eat.

They ate in comparative silence, as the exhaustion of their bodies gave way to the peaceful atmosphere pervading the copse. After their meal, they sat staring into the fire for a long while, each deep in thought. Finally, Hawk got to his feet. Jaren, thinking he was going off for his nightly reconnaissance, stretched out by the fire to doze.

Hawk looked at Korthak and Tanner and said softly, "You two get some rest, but don't forget to walk Deakin now and then. Jaren and I need to talk." He gestured for Jaren to follow and he quickly obeyed, thinking he was finally going to find out who Hawk talked to every time he disappeared. He ran to catch up with him, fearful that he would disappear into the woods.

"Well, he doesn't have to tell me twice," Tanner yawned, stretching out his long legs. "Wake me up in a while and I'll take a couple of rounds with Hawk's horse," he said. A moment later, he was fast asleep.

The older man just smiled and shook his head as he poured more cafla into his mug. "Never saw the like in my entire life." He looked in the direction that Hawk and Jaren had gone and was surprised to see that they had not entered the woods, but were sitting on a log at the far edge of the clearing. Korthak knew what Hawk was going to tell the young man, and he knew it would not be an easy task. He began to pray silently for his friend to receive wisdom with his

The Birth of a King

words, and that Jaren would have an open heart and strong enough mind to receive all that would be revealed to him.

"Jaren, the time has come to give you the answers to the questions you have been wanting to ask for so long," Hawk began. "What I am going to tell you is of the utmost importance, not only for your life, but for the whole of Kinthoria, and when I am finished you will understand why I have kept this from you until this moment." Hawk paused, casting about for the right words. "You and I have been talking about the strength and power of my God for quite a long time. I would like to invite you to talk to Him with me now, if you think you're up to it."

Jaren was hesitant. *"Talk to a god? How does one talk to a god?"* he thought to himself. He considered the possibility of dire consequences if one did not say what a god wanted to hear. But then he remembered what Hawk had said about his God being a Father who is the source of all love.

"Is it the presence of your God that we have been feeling in this camp?" he asked, hope shining in his eyes.

Hawk beamed a smile at him. "Yes, it is. He's been with us all along, but sometimes He lets us actually sense His presence in an almost tangible way."

Jaren shook his head. "Then I do want to talk to Him. I need all the help I can get, I think."

To Jaren's amazement, Hawk simply bowed his head. "Father, tomorrow will bring a tremendous change to our world. I'm asking, as Your humble servant, for You to give each of us courage, and strength to stand against Your enemies, and the enemies of Your good will in Kinthoria. Please give us the understanding of Your will, and the wisdom to do it. Elyon, I ask now that You help Jaren to overcome any fear that he may have of You, and that You will shine the light of Your truth into his heart, and ease the pain in his soul. He will need your comfort, Lord, and Your strong, protective hand. In the authority of our Master's holy name I lift up my petitions."

Hawk lifted his head and found Jaren staring incredulously at him. "That's all you have to do to talk to your God? No sacrifices? No incense? You don't need a priest or anything? I mean, you sounded like you were just talking to a regular friend, or just some

The Birth of a King

other person. Doesn't it offend gods if people are just casual about them? Don't they want everyone to fear and respect them because of all their power?"

Hawk laughed softly. "There is only one *real* God, Jaren. There are other beings, like Lucia, that like to pretend that they are gods. They have a lot of power, and they enjoy using it to intimidate people because it makes them feel more important. But they are nothing compared to the only true God. Do you remember what I have told you about Elyon being as close to you as any breath you take? If He is that close, by His own choice, do you really think He wants a priest or anyone else stepping in between you and Him? No, He listens to every word you say, because He is a very personal Friend - a very loving Father. Better than any father in Kinthoria could ever hope to be. He wants all of His children to speak with Him in love and confidence, and to be familiar with Him. Elyon is not angered by our friendship; He has asked for it. As for incense, the Words He has left written down for us tell us that every time we give praise to Him it is like sweet incense to Him. People used to sacrifice to Him for centuries, but He sent our Master, Yesha, to live among us a long time ago, so that He could become the final sacrifice. After that sacrifice was made, no one ever had to kill another animal to appease Him. Our Master is Elyon's Son. Can you imagine how much He must love us and want us for His children? He sacrificed His own Son so that there would never be anything that could stop us from knowing Him and experiencing His love. You don't ever need to be afraid, Jaren, with Elyon as your Father. He is always there for you."

Jaren nodded thoughtfully. "I understand...at least most of what you have said. I can see that it's going to take a lot more teaching for me to understand everything about Elyon and your Master. Do you think I could be His friend? Would He be my God, too?"

Hawk laughed, slapping Jaren on the back. "Yes, Jaren, He is more than willing to be your God, and your Friend, and your Father."

"You said that your Master is Elyon's Son, and that He was sacrificed for us. If He died centuries ago, how can He be your Master now, Hawk? I don't understand."

"He is not dead, Jaren. He did every last thing that was required to be the perfect, ultimate sacrifice, even surrendering Himself into the hands of those who opposed Him, undergoing the cruelest torture. Elyon's Word says that He 'dismissed' His spirit when all was accomplished. That means He allowed His life to leave and His body died. But He didn't stay dead. Elyon's Spirit brought Him back to life again. Hundreds of people saw Him walking and talking, eating and drinking for many days after He came back to life. Then they saw Him rise up into heaven and that's where He lives now with Elyon."

"Then how is it that you can talk with Him, and hear Him talk to you, if He lives in heaven?" Jaren asked, as he tried to make sense of Hawk's words.

"He speaks to us through the words that He left written down for us. He also speaks to us and we speak to Him through His Spirit, whom He has placed inside everyone who believes in Him. It's hard to explain, Jaren, but Elyon and Yesha and the Spirit are all parts of the same Being known as the only true God. They have the same mind, the same Life, and the same power. Elyon speaks to our minds by His Spirit talking to our spirits. You see Elyon made people to be like Himself – to have three parts: body, soul, and spirit. He gave us each a spirit for the purpose of communication, so we could know Him by His Spirit telling our spirits about Him."

Korthak glanced at the two as he slowly walked Hawk's horse. He saw the eagerness of an avid young scholar in Jaren's face, and because he had been in Hawk's boots before, as teacher, he knew what joy Hawk was experiencing in being the one to pour truth into this thirsty mind and heart. Soon, he saw them both kneel on the ground before the log. His eyes misted, as he knew that Hawk was helping Jaren to say the few words that would ask Elyon to be his God, Yesha to be his sacrifice, and the Spirit to live within him. He knew that all of the angels in heaven were rejoicing at that moment, and he was again amazed and saddened that human ears no longer had the ability to hear angelic song. He knew instinctively that when a soul was brought before the heavenly throne of Elyon the Most High, it was always a moment that caused jubilant celebration and one that would never be forgotten throughout eternity.

The Birth of a King

Hawk glanced at Jaren when he had finished praying. He smiled. "It's done. How do you feel, son?"

Jaren looked at him in wonder. He felt some indefinable difference inside, as though some enormous weight had been lifted from his soul.

"I feel...*new*...somehow," he said, pressing his hand on his chest.

Hawk pulled Jaren into a bear hug. "Welcome to Elyon's kingdom... brother," he said hoarsely.

Jaren was still awestruck by the sense of freedom that had come over him. A silly grin began to spread across his face.

"Remember, Jaren. You may speak to the Father at any time. He has promised that He will always hear. You can share all of your happiness and joy with Him, too. The Holy Word says that He will sing and rejoice over you with joy! Every day He wants to celebrate your relationship with Him."

After some moments, Hawk looked intently into the young man's eyes, searching for the words he had been rehearsing in his mind for months. *"How to begin?"* he thought. He sat back down on the log, motioning for Jaren to do the same. "Elyon wants you to come to Him for help in your hard times, too. He wants you to know that He is strong enough to take care of you, no matter how terrible the situation, or how evil your adversaries may be. Any time you feel about to be overwhelmed with this life, He wants you to run to Him as you would a father. I know that you never have had a father to run to and to trust. But, can you understand what I'm saying, Jaren?"

Jaren nodded. He sensed that Hawk was not yet finished with him this night and that Hawk's reference to being "overwhelmed with this life" was not just an off-hand remark. The hair on the back of his neck began to bristle in anticipation.

Then, as though reading Jaren's thoughts, Hawk slowly put his hand on the young man's shoulder. "Jaren, I've noticed that you've been rubbing your shoulder quite often."

Jaren quickly pulled his shoulder from Hawk's touch, his face turning scarlet as he lowered his eyes in embarrassment. He had tried to be so careful not to let anyone see him scratching at the irri-

The Birth of a King

tating birthmark, but it had become such a nuisance, that he found himself just absently rubbing at it.

"There is no reason for you to be embarrassed, Jaren," Hawk said firmly. "Don't ever think of it as a nuisance."

Jaren's head shot up and he stared at Hawk in wonder. "How did you know what I was thinking?"

Hawk chuckled. "Well, let me give you three clues: One, your constant scratching; two, that frown on your face while you're scratching; three, your frequent sighs of resignation as though having to put up with a burden when you find that scratching doesn't help."

Jaren smiled sheepishly. "Guess I haven't been as careful about hiding it as I thought, huh?"

"Not quite," Hawk chuckled, and then sat in silence for a moment.

"What is it, Hawk? Why are you suddenly so quiet and tense?"

"Jaren," he hesitated once more, and then rushed on, eager to be done with this assignment from Elyon. "Jaren, that mark on your shoulder is your birthright."

Seeing the non-plussed look in the young man's eyes, he asked, "Do you know what the mark looks like?"

Jaren shook his head. "Tanner says it looks like a dragon with a crown on its head. But I've never been able to see it that well. It's too far back on my shoulder. All I know is that I've always been ashamed of having a birthmark, so I've kept it hidden as best I could. The thing has always been a..." he caught himself and laughed, "a nuisance."

Hawk spoke his next words very slowly and deliberately, "Tanner described it perfectly, Jaren. That mark is called 'The Dragon Lord Stigmata.' It is given only to the King's first-born son as a gift. It is placed on the shoulder of the King's son shortly after birth in a very secret and holy ritual, involving four participants. Those participants are Elyon, the Archbishop, the Chancellor of War and the King.

From each participant, the infant is infused with a certain power, through that birthmark. From Elyon, wisdom, power and peace. From the Archbishop, the mercy of Elyon to desire holiness, though under normal circumstances, the child is taught the meaning of holiness and how to receive it throughout his childhood in the King's palace. From the Chancellor of War comes a blessing for understanding of military strategies and the ability to command. Finally, the King fuses into the mark the blessing of strong love for family, for people and for the earth, and the strong desire to serve them with all of his heart. He imparts the desire to rule with wisdom, and justice tempered with compassion."

Hawk paused for just a moment, looking for a reaction from Jaren, and then continued. "Jaren, *you* have been given all of this... and more."

Jaren felt a rising sense of panic begin to seize him. He felt as though the world he had always known had just disappeared in the flash of a moment, and he was frightened more than he had ever thought possible. He had heard Hawk's words, but they had all become jumbled in his suddenly throbbing head. *"Birthright...King's first born...Archbishop...compassion...childhood in the palace...military strategies. What was Hawk rambling about? Why was he telling him all of this? What did it have to do with him? He, Jaren of Reeban, had been given all of this and more?"*

Once again, the questions came at a rapid pace. "What are you talking about, Hawk? How would I come by this 'gift?' My father certainly was no king. What does 'Dragon Lord Stigmata' mean? Why would I have this thing? I'm just a plain, orphaned peasant boy. You've confused me with someone else."

Jaren forced his eyes to focus on Hawk's face, trying to find something solid and substantial to hang onto as his world shifted and changed. He was struggling desperately to bring his racing mind under control. "What do you mean, I have been given this? I don't understand...how could I...." He stopped in mid-sentence, his eyes going wide, as Hawk's words found their mark and understanding exploded into his resisting mind.

"No! No, it can't be!" he yelled, jumping to his feet. "All of the royal family was killed, executed for being traitors and thieves of the kingdom's wealth. Everyone knows this. The Dragonmasters made sure they found every last one of the treacherous lot!"

Hawk shot to his feet and retorted hotly. "Jaren, the King and his family were not traitors and thieves any more than the An'ilden are. It's nothing but more lies." He was trembling with anger as he heard the reprehensible teachings of the Dragonmasters spewing like poison from Jaren's mouth after months of the truth being poured into him.

Both stood glaring at each other with flaming eyes, panting with the fierceness of the emotions that threatened to overwhelm them. Finally, Hawk forced his hand over his eyes and willed his anger to abate.

He said softly, "*Think*, Jaren. Think of all of the lies the Dragonmasters have spouted as truth. The hateful and poisonous words you have just spoken so easily about your own family are more of those lies."

"I *am* thinking, Hawk…about all the lies. How do I know that what you are telling me is the truth or merely a mistake in identity on your part? How do you *know* I am the one? Why are you telling me this now? There is just no way that I can be who you think I am!" Jaren shouted.

Hawk began again, "Jaren, I was there at the placement of your birthmark. I was the King's Chancellor of War. When your father knew he was going to be defeated by the Dragonmasters, he commanded me to escape with you to a safe place, and to save you from the slaughter that obliterated your family. He made me swear an oath on my life to see to it that the royal line would one day be restored to the throne."

He paused briefly to give Jaren a chance to take in his words. "I have been waiting for over seventeen years to honor that oath. My people, and all of the rest who are loyal to the crown, have been preparing long and hard for your return."

Jaren was terrified. Everything he had known about himself was untrue. He could find no solid ground to stand on; he was thoroughly disoriented. Was he really a King? Dols! He was only seventeen years old. Where were all the blessings Hawk had just promised when he surrendered his life to Elyon? A thousand questions were running through his mind.

Watching the exchange from beside the fire, Korthak sighed, and stretched broadly. He watched as Solance finally slipped below the

The Birth of a King

horizon and the copse darkened. He knew it would be a long night. His heart went out to both of his friends, knowing how painfully hard this evening was likely to be for both of them.

He gently prodded Tanner awake. "Time to take a turn with Hawk's horse, you young sleep hound. Just don't go near Hawk and Jaren."

Hawk saw fear and turmoil in the lad's eyes, when Jaren asked, "But why did you send me away, then? If you had been commanded to protect me, why did you not keep me with you?" he asked in pained accusation.

Hawk looked past him, into the darkened woods beyond, as though trying to find the words to answer such painful questions. Finally, he said more to himself than to Jaren, "That was a decision that still haunts me," and then louder, so that Jaren could hear, "but I had to do it. The Dragonmasters have never questioned that they were entirely successful in wiping out the Cathain line. For three years they kept me under surveillance. They would have spotted you immediately had I suddenly shown up with a babe in my personal care. I dared not try to take you to my people. As things turned out, the Dragonmasters never even had reason to suspect that an heir could be alive, and especially that he would be living right under their noses."

Jaren interrupted him. "Why not? They must have known I was missing. Weren't they suspicious when they couldn't find the body of a dead child? They aren't that stupid, Hawk. They would have been searching everywhere for the heir until they found him and killed him."

Hawk stood silently with his head bowed for so long that Jaren thought he would refuse to answer.

"Hawk, please, tell me! I need an answer, now!" Jaren pleaded.

Hawk nodded his head. "Yes, you need to know." He gestured to the burly figure sitting by the fire. "Our good friend Korthak has a lot more to do with this than you could ever imagine."

"What do you mean?"

"When the Dragonmasters raided the palace in the middle of the night, Korthak's wife and infant son were killed in the first wave of

The Birth of a King

the attack. Korthak knew of my oath to your father, so he took his dead child into the palace nursery and laid him in your cradle. In doing so, he was almost burned alive, with you, inside the palace. But he found a hidden passageway behind a tapestry in your mother's dressing chamber, and escaped the flames with you wrapped inside his cloak. Then, as he was crossing the courtyard wall, his back was slashed deeply by a Dragonmaster's sword. As he leaped from the wall to the outside of the compound, he was trying to protect you in the fall, and landed wrong, breaking his ankle. I found him, dragging his bleeding, badly-burned body and a little bundle into a creek almost a thousand paces from the castle. I thought all was lost, because I had not been able to fight through to the King in time to save him or to rescue you. But then Korthak handed me his bundle just before he lost consciousness, and there you were, sooty and frightened, but alive. It was a miracle from Elyon that you never once cried out or made any sound. And that's why they didn't think there was a need to search for you. They did find the body of a child in the Prince's nursery."

Jaren stared across the clearing to the man by the fire, and remembering the long scar he had seen on Korthak's back. He was stunned by the horrors of the senseless savagery in Hawk's story, and by Korthak's selfless bravery. How was it possible that this good-natured bear of a man could have gone through such pain for him? And he had never known, would never have known, if Hawk had not told him, because he knew it was a sacrifice of such magnitude that Korthak would never have been able to tell of it. He wondered to himself, *"How many others? How many have suffered so greatly for me?"* The burden of their pain was almost more than the young man was able to bear. He choked down a sob, and dropped to his knees, burying his face in his hands. He felt in that moment as though the weight of the world had been set upon his shoulders - so much loss and sorrow, so many heroic sacrifices, and for what: the belief that he, an orphaned boy from Reeban could overthrow the Dragonmasters? It was madness. Fear rose in the back of his throat and he felt he would retch.

Hawk rubbed his weary eyes and continued. "I gave you into the care of a preacher, far in the north, whom your father had loved as a brother. Because of their friendship, I knew the man would care for you as he would have his own son. One of the most devout women in his parish was still suckling a child, and so he left you to become a part of her family. She kept you until you were old enough to wean, even after she had lost her husband to the dust-plague and had become destitute. After your second birthing day, they agreed to send you to the scholars hall. It was unthinkable to place you in a monastery, since the persecution of the church had already begun, and churches, cathedrals, and monasteries were being put to the torch all across the land. Believers were being impaled, burned at the stake as heretics to the Lucian church, or herded into the Gundroth territory and left there. Had I known of their plan, I would not have allowed it, but as it turned out, it was the best thing that could have happened, and it was surely our Master's plan. You have lived the life of hardship that the Dragonmasters have imposed upon your people. You have experienced and lived through their pain and fear. It has been an invaluable education. You will know how to help your people because you know their need first hand."

He smiled. "You will find all through your life many similar events. Something happens that you think should be otherwise, and Elyon says, 'No, everything is proceeding precisely according to My plan'. Always try to remember, Jaren, that Elyon's ways are always the best, even when we don't understand them, even when they include extreme pain of all sorts, even when they appear full of injustice, and even when they seem to suggest that Elyon has forgotten you and left you all alone. Trust, always, that His plan *will* be revealed in the end."

Jaren, still not willing to believe this incredible story of his royalty, despite Hawk's explanations and assurances, and still not wanting this unlooked for honor and responsibility, asked, "How is it that I don't have any of the features of the royal race, save for this birthmark that no one has ever heard of? Tanner's mother said that they all had hair golden as the sun, and deep blue eyes."

Hawk had been expecting this question. "When your father found out that they were plotting to murder the entire royal line, instead of exiling or imprisoning them, he knew that I could not successfully escape with you without some type of concealment. So he petitioned the Archbishop to fast and pray that your true identity would be hidden from the eyes of the world, much the same as happened to Yesha while He was talking to some of His friends after He came back to life. He didn't want them to know His identity yet, and so they could not see Him for who He truly was until He allowed it.

The Archbishop said that Elyon had revealed to him that no one would be permitted to see you as you truly are until you immerse yourself in the Spring of Elyon. And it was true. From that day forward we would not have known you, save that you had been in our arms when our sight was altered toward you."

Jaren paled. He respected Hawk very much. He longed to trust what he was saying. He wanted to do everything in his power to please the man. But years of indoctrination were very difficult to overcome simply because one wanted to believe differently. The old lies had instilled such fear. He was uncertain that he could force himself to touch the waters of the Spring of Elyon.

Before Jaren ever formed the words to admit his reticence, Hawk misread his thoughts and said with heated exasperation, "More lies, Jaren. I've heard about all of them that I can stomach on this journey. I assure you that I have not lived the past seventeen years of my life waiting for this day, nor spent the past two years parted from my family and scouring the whole of Kinthoria just to ask you to kill yourself. How could you think me such a savage fiend? How could I just tell you about Korthak's sacrifice, and your father's, and the wonderful miracle which Elyon has done to protect you all of these years and then send you off to die? Would a brother in the family of Elyon send another brother to his death? I promised you before that I would not let any danger come to you. Dols, boy, you've trusted me ever since we left Reeban. Why are you being so hardheaded and frightened now? Why can't you just believe what I've said and trust me?"

Jaren glared at him, and silently rose and stalked into the woods. He was furious at Hawk's accusations, whether they were true or not. What did the man expect from him? He had just been told he was the sole heir to the throne of Kinthoria, that his parents had been brutally slaughtered, that people had suffered untold agony just for him, and that the Dragonmasters wanted him dead! Now he was asking him to glibly disregard years of teaching about the lethal water of the Spring of Elyon, and just walk up to it and jump right in. How did Hawk think he would react?

He heard a footfall behind him and spun around. Hawk stood there in the darkness, a shadow in the shadows. "Jaren, I'm sorry. I shouldn't have been so hard on you. I know we're all exhausted, and I've just put an enormous burden on your young shoulders. Please, forgive me. All of these lies that the Dragonmasters have packed your head with are just a bit too much for me to handle. They are defiling the names and memories of people I have loved and respected, and are blaspheming the God I have worshipped my whole life. Many good people wait eagerly to know their sacrifices were not in vain, to see you sitting on the throne. It just makes my blood boil to hear the way the Dragonmasters have deceived the people. I'm not angry with you, son, only with the words you spoke, and as our burly friend back there reminded me some time ago, they are only words, and that makes them easy to prove wrong with visible, tangible truth. Again, I beg your forgiveness."

Jaren's anger ebbed away as he looked into the shadowy face of his friend. He ran his fingers through his hair, pressing his palms to his throbbing temples. "You're forgiven. But you have to ease up on me, Hawk. Did you think I would be happy about this? I didn't just wake up this morning and think, 'Dols, I'd sure like to become a king.' You may have saved my life by taking me out of Reeban, but tonight you have just taken my life away from me by telling me who I really am. A good king is bound hand and foot in service to his people. I've *never* been free, Hawk, just to do what I wanted to do. You've just told me that I never will be. I'm sorry, but I'm not going to accept this just off hand. You need to give me some room here to think."

"Jaren, I confess that I did think you would be happy to know your parentage, and to know that you will soon have the power to begin righting the wrongs done to your people. I had not thought about it from your point of view. I would like to tell you to take the time you need to consider all of this, but I'm sorry to say that I have one more revelation with which to burden you. You must make your

The Birth of a King

decision by tomorrow morning, because our task at the Spring of Elyon must be accomplished on your true birthing day."

Jaren stared at Hawk. "Tomorrow is my birthing day?"

"Yes. You have come of age."

Jaren walked toward the camp in a haze, his mind churning like a whirlwind. Hawk followed him with his eyes and then headed deeper into the woods to speak with Yesha for a while. He felt in great need of the calming influence of his Master's wisdom and peace at that moment.

When Jaren got back to the dying campfire, he found Korthak, with his back against a tree, snoring loudly. He stared at this man whom he had thought he knew. He had thought him to be a simple, solid, good man. He had never suspected the bravery and complexity of this hero of Kinthoria. He was profoundly honored to know him, and felt incredibly indebted to him. He firmly resolved that if he ever did truly become a king, he would reward this great old bear, and try to make up for some of his pain.

He walked over to Tanner and nudged him. "Get up and get into your bedroll. Somehow I think that before tomorrow is over, you're going to be thankful for getting a good night's sleep." Then he covered Korthak with a blanket, and slid into his own bedroll, yawning widely. He laced his fingers together behind his head, staring up at the blackness of the forest canopy against the darkened sky. How long he lay there thinking about Hawk's revelations, he did not know. Some time during that quiet night, he heard Hawk slip back into the camp. His last conscious thought was how incredible it was that he was King Cadan's son.

Chapter Seventeen

THE SPRING OF ELYON

Jaren pulled Hawk aside, ostensibly to ask a question about his saddle. "We're going to the Spring of Elyon this morning, aren't we?" he asked with resignation.

Hawk looked at Jaren with surprise while giving the cinch strap a strong tug. "You've made up your mind, then?" he asked.

"Yes, I have," Jaren replied. "Knowing all that I do now, I wouldn't be able to live with myself if I denied my birth and my family. I'm certain this is what Elyon desires of me."

"Then, yes, we are going to the Spring of Elyon," Hawk said with obvious delight. He gestured over his shoulder, "It's only a few minutes walk through those trees." He looked at Jaren, and seeing the concern on his face, he gestured toward the saddle in the lad's hands. "Why don't you set that down and go talk it over with Elyon for a few minutes, son. I'll keep these two jesters busy for a while."

Jaren thanked him, and walked a few strides into the forest. He sat on a large rock, and let the sun beat down on his face. The young man poured his heart out to this new Father. He cried freely over the loss of a family he would never know. He thanked Elyon for placing him under Hawk's care, recalling the depth of the man's strength and compassion. He especially thanked Him for Korthak, and the terrible sacrifice the man had already made for him. He opened his soul to Elyon, and all of his fears came rushing to the surface: The fear of losing Tanner's friendship when he would take on his true identity, both in appearance and status; the fear of inadequacy for the awesome responsibility of kingship; the latent fears in his mind, caused by the lies of the Dragonmasters; and understanding that acknowledgment of his royal title and his bloodlines was his death warrant. He spent a long time giving over to Elyon, every emotion, including the intense anger and hatred for the Dragonmasters that had been building at every new proof of their savagery. Finally, he asked the true God to give him some place within himself that was solid, as he tried to grasp that elusive "something" which would pull everything together. He rubbed at his birthmark, and it sent a tingle through his body, reminding him that Elyon, through his bloodlines, had already determined the destiny of which he was so afraid. He confessed to Him that on several occasions he had wished Hawk had never found him, and that he had stayed in the safety of his old life at the scholars hall. He felt like a child who had wanted so desperately to leave his father and mother, and live his own life, only to discover after the fact, that he had been much more content and happy at home than he had ever imagined. He mourned once more the family whose love and companionship was lost to him.

Very quietly, so quietly that Jaren almost missed it, sounds came into his mind. He strained to listen, until he was certain he was hearing words. *"I am your peace,"* a voice whispered. *"I am your reason for being. Put your trust in Me, and be amazed as I bring all things together, and cause My will to be done throughout this land. You have no place within yourself in which to find calm, for within the human breast there is only a poor reproduction of My peace, given by the enemy for the deception of mankind. Behind his peace is the chaos and terror of a life without Me. But you are now in Me and I am in you, therefore you have My authentic, perpetual peace as close as your next breath. I am always the firm ground upon which you may stand."*

Jaren's heart was racing. Had his new Father spoken to him? To his amazement, he began to sense a powerful new peace seeping into his heart, until his mind and soul became filled with a wonderful, soothing calm. Jaren sat on the rock for some time, basking in the new wonder of this true God who willingly walked at all times with His people. No wonder Hawk would never allow anything to hinder

The Birth of a King

his nightly visits with his Master. Having an affinity with the Master provided a limitless source of peace and refreshment. His soul soared at the knowledge that for the rest of his life he would have a safe haven to run to when he needed to find renewal.

When he had finished talking with Elyon, he took a deep breath and stretched expansively. He rose and walked back to the clearing.

Korthak and Hawk both noticed with a sense of satisfaction, the firm set of the young man's shoulders, and his confident stride. They also noted the determination burning in Jaren's eyes, and knew that he was ready to accept any task placed before him. And there, for all the world to see, was the mirror-image of the two men's unique, warm smile upon his face.

The four companions turned and began to walk the short distance to the spring. Jaren saw that Korthak was carrying a bundle under his arm, and that Hawk had left his ever-present bow and quiver by the fire. Almost as an afterthought, he remembered seeing Tanner's boot dagger lying alongside the other weapons. He glanced at Tanner in amazement, and wondered at the strength of Korthak's influence over his friend, for he rightly guessed that the huge man had asked Tanner to leave his dagger behind. He also saw Tanner looking at him with a strange expression in his eyes.

"He knows," Jaren thought to himself, but a soft, spongy sensation under his feet diverted his attention. He looked down and saw that the ground was carpeted with a thick mat of moss, covered with a myriad of tiny, white, star-shaped flowers. There were hundreds of different wildflowers blooming in the meadow that opened out before them. The delicious scent of the flora was heady, yet pleasant, and the sight was so beautiful that Jaren thought he must have stepped into a dream. He wondered if winter's icy fingers ever traced their mark upon this spacious glen. As he looked across the small pool in the center of this perfect garden, he could see no ripple on its quiet surface. No sound could be heard, save for the high-pitched notes of the wrens, the soft cooing of doves, and from across the pool the lone, sweet song of a meadowlark.

Enjoying the gift of this place of perfection, the four men walked in silence toward the pool. When they reached the edge of the spring, Korthak knelt and began untying the small leather pouch he had been carrying. Jaren felt his hair begin to rise on the back of his neck as he stared at the mirror-like surface of the Spring of Elyon, reflecting back the morning sunlight. He couldn't help but ask Hawk, "What will happen once I get into the water?"

Hawk knew his uneasiness and squeezed the young man's shoulder. "You will become your true self, Jaren." He smiled, adding with a quieting calm, "You were born for this very hour, son. It is Elyon's perfect will for you, so don't be afraid."

Jaren stared into those deep emerald eyes, hesitant to ask the next question. "Who am I, Hawk? What is my real self?" He was trembling slightly as he waited for Hawk's reply.

The lean man's face took on a solemnity that Jaren had never seen before. "You are Prince Jaren Iain Renwyck Cathain, soon to be High King of the whole of Kinthoria, Prince of all Regions, Lord of the Seven Races, and *Sanda Aran* of the Dragons."

Jaren paled at the final title. "Dragons? What would I have to do with the dragons?" he shot the question to Hawk.

Hawk grinned. "I'm guessing that will be your favorite part of being King," he said, his eyes sparkling with mirth.

Jaren felt a small shudder in his resolve. Try though he may to remain strong, he knew himself, and he was no king. Dols, how inept he was at so many things. How could he possibly rule an entire continent of people?

Hawk watched the emotions moving across the lad's face, and he understood. He held the young man's gaze. "Jaren, I know you don't feel capable of such a task, but trust in the Father, son. Remember, too, that once the physical effects of Elyon's miracle are removed, you will receive, as your birthright, powers far beyond what you could believe possible. You will be instructed daily as to how to use many of your powers, others will be tapped into when the need arises. Sovereignty is an awesome responsibility, but you must remember the awesome Spirit of Elyon who lives inside you now. He will never desert you. He will assist you and supply what you are lacking, so that you may be the king that He has shaped you to be. Never forget this one thing: our Father never calls us to a task without equipping us fully to accomplish it.

The time has come for the rightful heir to be ruling over Kinthoria once again. Believe in the strengths Elyon has given you and in the strengths He has given to the ones standing here before you, and to those whom you have yet to meet. Believe me, Jaren, you will learn how to be a good ruler and leader for your people."

Jaren recalled Elyon's words to him and nodded with understanding. He took a deep breath and enjoyed once more the influx of Elyon's assurance.

Hawk turned, moving toward the water's edge. Korthak was kneeling, gently unfolding a beautiful white robe, and laying it out on the grass. Tanner was sitting on his heels, watching with little attention. Korthak had told him this morning of Jaren's true identity and what would be taking place at the Spring of Elyon. He had laughed, thinking that Korthak was playing another of his colossal jokes. He replied to the older man, "Yes, and when we're finished with this journey, I'm going to become a Lucian priest, too!" It was completely beyond his comprehension that his lifelong friend, the boy he had called 'brother' was the heir to the throne of Kinthoria. It had taken Korthak the better part of an hour to get the truth of the matter through the young man's thick skull.

He reminded him of their early morning conversation outside Doddridge. He pressed him to remember how much Jaren would need him, and assured him that they would always remain the closest of friends. Tanner became resigned to the unbelievable things that Korthak had told him only after being asked if he had ever seen Jaren's birthmark. However, he kept silent his misgivings about Jaren's need of him, or that a Prince would desire the friendship of the son of a simple farmer. The young man had been quiet and sad after the conversation. Korthak knew he could say nothing more to ease Tanner's anxiety, so he left it in Elyon's capable hands to prove to him through the coming days just how important his life would be to Jaren. Through all of their preparations, Tanner frequently looked at his friend, his eyes boring into the young man, as though straining to see with other eyes some unmarked sign of Jaren's true identity.

Hawk busied himself with preparing a protective space in which the transformation would occur. In the unlikely event of an attack in this holy place, whether by physical or spiritual forces, the young

Prince would be totally inaccessible to anyone who might decide to interfere with the process. He pulled out a small, soft leather bag, removed a pinch of green-tinted earth and sprinkled it in the form of a cross in the sand at the water's edge. Then he pulled out three similar bags in succession, sprinkling out red, blue, and yellow hued earth as he moved from one place to the next, forming a large square with the crosses. He tucked each small bag very carefully back into his belt pouch. The contents of these bags were very rare and ancient, having been gathered by the first 'Seven' who had been gifted with the knowledge of the location of the precise centers of the four corners of the earth when the planet was still quite young.

Hawk stood, and saw that Korthak and Tanner had helped Jaren into the soft white robe. Korthak produced a golden vial from his sack, along with an ornate golden cup, and brought them over to Hawk. "You think he's ready for this?" he asked grimly.

Hawk nodded, "Elyon has been working in him." He glanced over at Jaren, "I believe he can never feel truly ready for what he is about to undertake, but I do know he is very willing to proceed."

Jaren was speaking softly with Tanner. "I want you to know that no matter what this water does to me, Tan, you will always be my brother. I swear I'll not lose the only family I have ever known. Please, promise me that you will not let this destroy our friendship," he pleaded.

Tanner was completely taken by surprise. All along, he had thought that Jaren would no longer desire his friendship, and now Jaren was confessing to suffering from the very same uncertainty. Tanner beamed a huge smile at Jaren and yanked him into a crushing bear hug, which Jaren gratefully returned. Neither young man could speak, but each was touched deeply by the other's complete and unconditional affection.

Jaren saw that Hawk was waiting for him. He smiled and gripped Tanner's shoulder. "It's time to go," he whispered shakily. He inhaled a deep breath and slowly released it.

Hawk handed the golden cup to Jaren, "Go to the water's edge. Fill this and bring it back to me."

Jaren did as he was told, taking extreme care neither to touch the water, nor to allow it to drip onto his hands from the cup. As he handed the cup to Hawk, he was stunned and relieved that his friend had easily grasped the dripping cup without the least thought of danger. He noticed Tanner's face and prayed that he did not look half as frightened as his best friend at that moment.

Hawk took the golden vial from Korthak, and very carefully poured its contents into the cup. "Jaren, this is 'Lormin.' You must drink it before you step into the water. It will ease a good portion of the disorientation you will experience during the transformation. Only those with royal blood can drink this without fatal consequences." Jaren's eyes shot up to look at Hawk. The tall man smiled, "Now you will see that everything I have told you is the truth. Are you ready?"

Jaren took the cup from Hawk with trembling hands. He looked first into Tanner's eyes, then into Korthak's, and then returned his gaze to Hawk. He whispered, "Father, protect me," as he slowly put the cup to his lips, tipped his head back, and emptied the golden vessel.

Hawk removed the cup from his hands and placed him inside the square made by the placement of the crosses. He dipped some water from the Spring of Elyon, and poured three drops on the cross of green-hued earth and prayed, "Elyon, Yesha, Spirit, three are One. Our God is One God. It is He, Who at the beginning of time, established and firmly set the pillars for the four corners of the earth. Let all created things praise His Name, from Aquilonius to the universes beyond." He moved quickly to the next cross of red earth, pouring out three drops of water over it. "Elyon, Yesha, Spirit, three united in One. Our God is One God. It is He, Who at the beginning of time, established and firmly set the pillars for the four corners of the earth. Let all created things praise His Name, from Orientis to the universes beyond." Moving to the third and then the fourth crosses, he repeated the same prayer of praise, giving the names of the third corner of the earth 'Australis,' and the fourth 'Occidius.' Then he continued, "Our Holy Father, Maker of all the heavens and the earth, we pray now for Your divine protection against any evil or harm which could overtake your chosen King. Send now, we pray, your angels and your Spirit to guard and to protect him as he, with faith in Your protection, is obedient to Your will. Thank you, Lord Most High, the only true God, for hearing our prayer and supplication."

Suddenly, they heard a faint sound of wind, though there was not the slightest breeze moving across the meadow. As the sound of the wind grew almost immediately to a roaring gale, a faint iridescent shimmering traced the lines between the four stones. It could not be seen when viewed directly, but could just be made out on the periphery of one's vision. The shimmering aura shot up and arched over Jaren, completely enclosing him. Immediately the roar of the wind vanished from the hearing of the three standing outside the protective square.

Tanner lunged forward as he realized that any hope he had of coming to Jaren's aid was now an impossibility.

Jaren's mouth and throat began to burn. His head started swimming, and he felt as though he was strangling. He clutched at his throat and fell to the sand at the edge of the pool. His heart and mind were racing as he gasped for breath. He felt certain that Hawk had made a mistake in his preparations and that something had gone terribly wrong. He could not control the chaos of his thoughts and he was terrified. Then, suddenly, the all-consuming peace of Elyon enveloped his mind and body and the world slowly spun into darkness around him, and he knew no more.

Without the benefit of having Elyon's Truth in his heart, Tanner panicked as he stared at Jaren's twisted body as it lay motionless on the sand. Even after months on the road with Hawk and Korthak, building a bond of trust, and a son's love for his burly friend, he began conjuring up all sorts of reasons why these two men might have brought them to this strange and desolate place. Any second now, the two older men's flesh would slip to the ground, and he would be face to face with the most hideous creatures he could imagine. *"The Dragonmasters were right all along. I never should have allowed Jaren to listen to Hawk. We should not have left Reeban and crossed the cursed Shandra River,"* his thoughts became a blurred jumble of terror and self-accusation.

"Why did you have to kill him? He trusted you! You...murdering savage," he screamed and made a lunge for Hawk's throat.

The Birth of a King

Hawk wheeled around to see Tanner's wild eyes flashing with pure animal instinct, and he knew that the young man was too hysterical to listen to reason.

"What is wrong with you, boy?" he yelled, deftly avoiding Tanner's grasp.

Korthak rushed at him, but the young man quickly turned aside.

"Tanner, what are you doing?" Hawk yelled again.

Korthak moved in close to the insensible young man once again, and, speaking softly, tried to reason with him. "Son, we are not harming Jaren in any way. I promise you that he is perfectly safe."

It was to no avail, for Tanner's mind was convinced that these two men were his enemies, that they had foully murdered Jaren; and, that he was in deadly peril himself.

Hawk knew that his time was limited to accomplish the tasks needed to gain Jaren's transformation. He could not waste those precious moments on the hysterical lad. "Tanner, I need to tend to Jaren. Get yourself under control," he demanded in frustration as he started toward Jaren's protective shield.

Tanner jumped between the shimmering structure and Hawk, "You will not touch him again, you liar! You may kill me as you have him, but I swear you will not lay a hand on his body again as long as I have breath!"

The sand was warm on Jaren's fingers. It was very strange here. *"Where is here?"* he mused absently. He was grateful that his head had stopped spinning, and that he was capable of lucid thought once again. *"So this is death. Peaceful, warm...much noisier than I expected."* He noticed that his heart had quit racing, and...his heart? *"My heart! I'm not dead!"* He had reveled in the thought for only a moment, when he realized that he could not move so much as a finger, nor could he open his eyes. He was surrounded by complete roaring darkness. *"Hawk! What's happening? I...I can't move! I can't see!"* he screamed mentally.

Hawk suddenly reeled backward to the ground, crying out and clutching at his head. Korthak raced to his side. "What's wrong?" demanded Korthak. "Are you all right?"

Hawk caught his breath and tried to shake the stabbing pain from his mind. "I'm fine. And nothing is wrong; in fact, everything is going perfectly. It's his mind...he's screaming at me. I seem to have overlooked a small portion of his training." He smiled painfully at the oversight. "Dols," he shook his head again, "he almost sent my brain out through my ears."

Korthak helped Hawk to his feet. The tall man shook his head to focus his mind, and then he sent words to Jaren.

Jaren heard the words as they broke into his confusion and alarm. *"Jaren...Jaren, try to focus on my words."* He knew that voice. It made his brain tickle as it entered his mind. *"Jaren, from now on you will be able to communicate not only orally, but with your mind as well. If you can hear me, answer with your mind. Just think the thoughts, don't speak them and please try to control the 'loudness' of your thoughts."*

"Hawk, is that you? I thought I was dead, but I'm not...am I?" he thought in cautious relief.

"You're very much alive, Jaren. I'm afraid we've got a problem with your friend, out here. He won't allow us to continue. He thinks we've killed you, and he's panicked."

Hawk's collapse and outcry had held Tanner's attention just long enough that he missed Korthak's final lunge.

"And now, my young friend, I'll see that you take back every last one of your foolish words once we are finished with Jaren. Proceed, Hawk," Korthak said as he pinned a struggling Tanner's arms to his sides in the crushing circle of his arms. "I'll make sure this young wolf doesn't interfere again."

Hawk stood just outside the square that enclosed Jaren's still form. *"How are you feeling?"* Hawk sent.

Jaren concentrated on calming his mind and fed a quieter thought to Hawk. *"I'm feeling...very curious...like myself, but...not."*

This time Jaren's words came softly, and Hawk smiled. *"That was excellent, Jaren. Much better. I'm certainly glad you're such an apt student. Now, I want you to try to open your eyes."*

Jaren struggled for several minutes, willing his eyelids to open. Finally, he was successful and squinted at the bright sunlight. He did not know how long he had been lying on the shore, but his muscles felt cramped. He saw the beautiful colors swirling about him. *"What is this?"* he asked.

"It's all right, Jaren. The Lord has answered our prayers and has placed His angels and His Spirit around you for protection. What you see are traces of their presence. Can you try to stand?" he urged.

Tanner watched as Jaren attempted to stand. He was so excited to see his friend alive that he slipped right out of Korthak's hold and ran toward him.

"Do not touch the shield!" Hawk yelled in warning as he reached to stop the lad. Tanner came to an abrupt halt just inches away from the all but invisible aura.

"Jaren, you're alive! I thought for sure they had killed you!" he shouted with joy.

Jaren looked at him in bewilderment, and pointed anxiously at Hawk.

"He can't hear you, Tanner. I know it looks as though there is nothing solid between you and him, but I can assure you, the power around him is enough to kill all of Volant's armies were they here attempting to reach him. Jaren is untouchable by anyone right now, and all he can hear is the wind inside there, and my voice," Hawk said.

"Your voice? How can that be?" Tanner asked, thoroughly confused, "You haven't spoken a word to him yet."

Hawk tapped his head. "I'm speaking to him with my mind." He could see that Tanner was not grasping this in any way. "Here, watch this. I'll tell Jaren that you are glad to see he is all right, and that you want him to brush the sand off his robe, because it is not very becoming for a Prince to wear soiled clothing."

Tanner watched as Jaren appeared to be listening to something. He smiled at Tanner and then quickly brushed the sand from his robe.

"He says he's glad to see you, too. He says he's fine, except that his head feels a little strange."

"But how can you do that?" Tanner asked incredulously.

"I thought in my head what I wanted to say, and then directed it right into Jaren's mind. It's the same as carrying on a verbal conversation, only you don't use your voice."

Korthak cleared his throat loudly as he walked up behind them. "Might I suggest that we get the last part of this out of the way? We can learn how to use our new *toys* at a later time," he grunted in disapproval.

Hawk raised his eyebrow and looked at his old friend indignantly. "Toys? This is an important gift which will be of more value to us on this journey than any of us may suspect."

Korthak shook his head, and walked away, mumbling something about cheating and card games.

Tanner saw the twinkle in Hawk's eyes, and realized that the two men were joking again.

"He's right, Tanner. We do need to finish this," Hawk said with a smile.

Tanner turned slowly, and with much reluctance joined Korthak. He was mortified by his recent behavior and kept his eyes averted.

Hawk directed Jaren to step into the water. The moment his foot touched the water the walls of the shield extended into the water, parting it to both sides, so that a path formed between two walls of water.

Hawk, standing with his hands on his hips, looked toward his young charge. *"From this point on, Jaren, you must concentrate on my voice. Allow the transformation to happen, don't fight the changes that are occurring. Just focus on my voice in your mind. I will help to keep your mind settled as the changes occur inside you."*

Jaren's face suddenly took on a worried expression, "What do you mean inside *me*? I thought this was going to be a physical change."

"No, Jaren, you have always been as you truly are. It is the eyes of the world which will now be given the ability to see the truth of your image. The changes will take place in your mind, emotions, and spirit. None of us has been able to foresee everything that will happen. There has never been a need to do this in the history of the Cathain line. Under normal circumstances, water from the Spring *is used during the coronation of the King, and he receives his power and all that accompanies it at that time. The only thing we know for certain is that you are Elyon's chosen King and so we know you will be safe."*

Jaren nodded his head in understanding. As an afterthought, Hawk added, *"Remember to control your mind-voice, and* do not panic. *I will be here with you, lad."*

Hawk motioned for Korthak and Tanner to join him. He wanted them near for support, in the event that Jaren should accidentally weaken him by screaming in his mind once again.

He heard his name slip softly into his mind. *"Yes, Jaren?"* he replied.

"I want to do what's right for the people who have fought so long for this to happen. I'm not afraid anymore."

Hawk's face broke into a wide grin. *"You'll be fine, son. Remember, people all across Kinthoria are praying for you at this very moment."*

Jaren turned, and walked into the tunnel. His body began quivering for no apparent reason. Since the walls of protection had sprung up, he had been hearing the sound of a great wind tearing about him. However, he could see that the surface of the water outside the protection was perfectly still. He heard Hawk's voice softly enter his mind. *"Keep going, Jaren. You're doing fine."*

When Hawk told him to stop, Jaren had walked deep enough into the tunnel that the water was a few feet over his head.

"Reach your right hand out to touch the water, Jaren. Gather some in your hand and rub it onto your birthmark."

Jaren tentatively stretched his arm toward the protective shield. He squinted his eyes shut and touched the glimmering surface. Instantly a tingling energy shot up his arm and throughout his body with exhilarating power. He gasped at the joy of life that suddenly filled his senses as Elyon's Spirit surged through him. He shot his hand through to the other side. He had expected the water to be icy cold to his touch, like that which contained the Lormin. Instead, it was nearly as warm as a hot spring. He gathered the water in his hand as Hawk had instructed and then drew it back through the shield, splashing it over his birthmark, and rubbing it in as though

The Birth of a King

bathing. As soon as the water touched the mark, it began burning intensely as though the water had set it ablaze.

Hawk and Korthak sent up silent prayers for strength and protection once again, as their eyes searched the darkness of the submerged tunnel where they knew the young prince's ordeal was merely beginning.

Jaren took a deep breath against the pain in his shoulder. What happened next took less than an hour, but to Jaren, it seemed to last for age upon age.

Every muscle in his body tensed; the sound of the rushing wind in his ears became such a roar that it made his head pound. His mind was reeling and he felt himself losing control. He called out to Hawk, forcing aside his pain and fear so that his mind-voice would not cause Hawk more agony. *"Are you still there?"* he asked, panic lacing his tone.

Hawk, sensing Jaren's rising fear, said quietly, *"Yes, Jaren. The three of us are still here. But more importantly, Elyon and His angels are here."*

Reassured, Jaren forced his body to relax. Soon, strange pictures flitted through his mind with such rapidity that he could not grasp the meaning of one scene before another took its place.

"Keep calm and let the transformation do its complete work, Jaren," Hawk's voice pressed through the rising confusion in the young man's mind. *"Just allow your mind and spirit to take in whatever Elyon is allowing. He will reveal to you all of it's meaning as you are capable of making it a part of yourself in the weeks and months ahead. Use your mind only for communicating with me... otherwise, let it rest and become a vessel to be filled with the blessings of the Father."*

Jaren watched, mystified, as scenes of wars, beautiful dragons, armies, and palaces flashed into his mind and then raced away. Magnificent men and women, dances, rituals, people of all races, image after image filled his thoughts. The aroma of smoke, horses, sweet perfumes, wines, and incense accompanied each of the scenes. It was as though he was actually present in the exact place and time of each event as he stood watching.

The Birth of a King

Suddenly, he heard girlish laughter and saw golden hair, crowned with a wreath of fragrant flowers. Playful, coquettish blue eyes sparkled above an impishly smiling mouth. A young woman was dressed in a white gown that showed plainly the lines and curves of her youthful body. She was looking directly into his eyes, *"Cadan, come on. Everyone is waiting for us."* She laughed again, reaching out for him - and then she was gone.

His nostrils were suddenly assailed with the smell of horses and campfires. He heard the jingle of harnesses as he looked and saw a much younger, leaner Korthak mounted on an enormous dappled stallion. He was staring out over a vast camp of strange, tall creatures arrayed in full battle gear. *"My Lord, they outnumber us six to one. It should not prove to be much of a challenge. We should have them dispatched by noon."*

From inside his head, as though it were himself, Jaren heard a deep, resonant laugh. *"Ah, Korthak, my friend, we really must do something about this attitude of yours. Your lack of confidence and valor is truly appalling."*

Clouds spinning and changing in a blue sky - suddenly Hawk's face leaning over him with that same stern look that was so familiar to Jaren. He had seen that look often enough on the faces of his unhappy scholars when he had been caught daydreaming. *"Unasae, Ashan'rai, you will never learn to use a sword lying on your back."* Then a boyish voice, much like his own, panting with pain and exertion, *"I can't, Hawk. Please no more training today. Every muscle in my body is aching, and I'm sure you must have broken my wrist this time."*

Jaren broke through the stream of events rushing into his mind. *"Hawk, what are the strange words I just heard?"*

Hawk beamed and then said, *"Narwa!"*

Jaren gasped with fear, as he saw hills, forests, and a river hundreds of feet below. The wind was ripping through his hair and roaring in his ears. The thunderous trumpeting of a dragon broke through the sound of the wind. He saw a strong hand, bearing a sapphire signet ring, reach out in front of him to pat the scaly hide between his legs. *"Yes, my friend. I am enjoying this beauty as much as you. It's been too long since last we flew together. But, alas, ruling a kingdom is time consuming if done properly."*

All was quiet, but for the chanting voice somewhere to his left. He saw two small hands reaching in front of his face. He heard a small child's delighted giggle from within, and *"Da...da."* He saw a man with hair like the sun, and eyes blue as a clear evening sky looking directly at him, and felt him fold his hands around the child's. There was a look of urgency, sorrow, and adoration in those eyes. *"My son, Jaren Iain Renwyck Cathain, receive the love for family, the love for your people and your kingdom. Receive the desire to serve with every fiber of your being. Receive the desire to rule with justice and compassion, and with all of the combined knowledge and wisdom of your forebears. I, Cadan Brys Renwyck Cathain, place this Dragon Lord stigmata upon you."* A burning pain shot through Jaren's shoulder as he heard the child cry out.

Once again, Jaren became aware of the constant roar of the wind in his ears. He held his hand to his moist eyes, and whispered simply with his thought, *"Father."* For some time he stood motionless, overwhelmed by joy and sorrow.

He slowly realized that he had been carrying a minute portion of this knowledge in his mind for years. He shook his head and smiled ruefully, *"And here all along I thought I was intellectually superior to the others."* He laughed inwardly at the joke, trying to ease the melancholy that lay upon him after seeing his mother and father for the first time.

Jaren's mind seemed of its own accord, without any conscious effort on his part, to be sorting out and storing away all this knowledge for reference whenever the need might arise in the future. His mind had just been infused with much of the collective knowledge, wisdom, and experiences of past generations of his forebears. Such a treasure was beyond value. He knew that no one could ever receive a greater birthright. It would be as great a benefit to his future experiences as actually sitting down with his father, grandfather, and great-grandfather when council was needed for ruling well and for pleasing Elyon.

The Power that had been infused in him as an infant was now surging through his entire being. It was raw and exciting, as he sensed the existence of every muscle, every nerve. He actually felt the blood racing through his veins. He was keenly aware of every breath. His body didn't just tingle; every cell was vibrant, and throbbing with life and Power.

This new young Prince sensed that he was now a force to be reckoned with, by virtue of Elyon's gifts. He was increasingly grateful that Hawk had promised to teach him how to control and use this new Power. He instinctively knew that this gift was far too immense for him to try to use without instruction. Jaren could feel the nearness of Elyon, just as Hawk had said he would. He knew that his new Father was the source of all Power and that He would watch over Jaren and protect him far better than any other person ever could. He felt Elyon's love pouring through him, and realized with a shock that Love from Elyon was the ultimate Power.

As the pictures ceased rushing into his mind, Jaren remained still for many moments, his body calming to a normal pace. Finally, he sent a thought to Hawk. *"It is done, Hawk. This part is completed, but we have much more to accomplish."*

Hawk and Korthak exchanged nervous glances. They would all need the Power given to this young man now that the transformation was complete. The fact of the matter, however, was simple. This event had, without a doubt, alerted the Dragonmasters to the fact that an heir to the Cathain throne was alive somewhere in Kinthoria. That knowledge would certainly start a chain of events more horrifying than when the Dragonmasters had first wrested control of the land from the royal family. Years of evil rituals and murderous deeds done in the black temples had immensely pleased the malevolent god of the Lucian priests, and he had reciprocated by bestowing incredible powers upon many of them. Hawk and Korthak knew they would stop at absolutely nothing to find this new heir, and to kill him, even if it meant the carnage of the entire land to accomplish it.

Immediately, as the three watched from the shore, the iridescence which had been Jaren's shimmering protection broke through the water, swirled into a magnificent helix, shot into the sky, and disappeared.

Jaren sprang up out of the water, sputtering and coughing. As he turned to face his three friends, and waded from the water, he saw the astonishment on each of their faces. Seeing the true appearance of the young Prince was a tremendous shock, even to the two older men who had known what to expect. Before them stood a young man out of whom radiated an aura of strength born of his noble ancestry. His eyes were very deep blue, and they shone with a light of wisdom and intelligence that Hawk remembered so well. His hair was no longer straight and of a dark sandy hue, but was now wavy and shone as burnished gold in the sunlight; a replica of the manes which had crowned the heads of all of the royal family of Kinthoria.

Hawk and Korthak were beaming, their eyes moist with tears. All of their sacrifices and labors were rewarded in that one moment in time. They both knelt before him, and pledged their fealty to the new Prince. Hawk said, "My lord, your humble servant," and lifting the hem of Jaren's robe to his lips, he kissed it.

Tanner, not knowing what to do, and still in complete shock, just fell to his knees on the sand, and stared dumbly at this stranger, who had been his life-long friend.

Jaren touched the heads of Hawk and Korthak. "Please, don't do that," he said with consternation. "I want to earn the respect of my people. You have been my friends. There will be a time for such things all too soon, I fear. For the moment, allow me a short postponement of the inevitable." It was a very awkward moment for Jaren. "Let's get on with other more important things, please."

Hawk and Korthak both stood, and could not restrain themselves from embracing the young Prince. Korthak nearly crushed the breath from Jaren. His eyes misty with tears, he said, "Lad, you don't know how good it feels to see royal blood standing in full Power before these old eyes again."

Hawk agreed, "It's been too long, my friend, much too long."

Jaren pulled the saturated robe from his body, and quickly donned his traveling clothes. He was not quite swift enough, though, for Tanner's quick eyes had seen Jaren's birthmark. It had undergone as dramatic a transformation as the rest of his features. It was now almost radiating its own light, as though a piece of gold had been placed into the skin on his friend's shoulder and sunlight was glinting off its shining surface.

The Birth of a King

Tanner quickly looked away, feeling as though he had invaded something private and holy.

As Jaren cinched his belt around his waist, a look of alarm suddenly replaced his smile. *"The dragons know,"* he sent to Hawk's mind.

Darkness clouded Hawk's eyes, for he knew that the most dangerous part of this hopeless journey had begun. The Dragonmasters would be in a frenzy for blood and retribution until they could find and finally destroy their enemy.

"We must be on our way quickly, then, for it will not be long before Lucia is also aware; and I must speak with the Dwarf elders regarding at least one of our next steps," Hawk returned grimly to the young man's mind. He wondered how long it would take before Jaren would discover and understand his power as the true *Sanda Aran,* the Dragon Master, and to bring them under his control.

Jaren placed his hand on Tanner's shoulder. "Tan, are you all right? You don't look at all well," he teased. "Hey, c'mon, Tan, it's only me. Remember what I told you about always being my brother?"

He waited for Tanner to say something, but the young man just stood, staring in amazement at the face of this stranger. Jaren shook him playfully. "Look, I still need your instruction with my horse and sword. And you'll still end up knocking me to the ground every time we practice."

Hawk and Korthak exchanged concerned glances as they watched Jaren try to bring the young man around. Jaren shook his head and pleaded with him, "Tan, please don't do this. I need you of all people with me now."

Tanner finally found his voice. "You...you...look...you look so different. You are like a stranger to me."

Jaren looked at his friend with moist eyes and said in a husky voice, "It's me, Tan. I'm the same person inside, and I need to know that I still have my brother by my side. There is no way I can do this without you and your support."

Tanner looked at the ground, and was silent for a moment. Then he looked shyly at his friend and said, "I don't think it would look very good for me to knock you off your horse anymore."

Jaren slapped his arm and laughed. "Nonsense, I am not so different that we cannot still be ourselves with each other. Besides, unhorsing me will keep me humble."

Hawk walked past them and said, "Very well put, Jaren. Now, shall we be on our way?"

"In just a moment," Tanner said softly. He looked at Korthak and Hawk, remorse and shame turning his face to crimson. He did not know where to begin admitting his unforgivable behavior. "I'm sorry about the things I said and did to you both. I was just so scared - I mean, Jaren wasn't moving at all."

Korthak stopped him before he could say anything more. "No, lad. It was our fault for not telling you what would happen to Jaren after he drank the Lormin. From now on, though, you must understand how important it is for all of us to trust one another completely. Our lives may depend upon it some day."

Tanner nodded to him, and said, "I swear to you both, that from this day to the end of my life, I will never mistrust either of you again, no matter what the circumstances may be telling me to the contrary."

The two men smiled as they saw the honest determination written in the youth's eyes.

Jaren smiled and squared his shoulders with his father's air of confidence, so familiar to the two older men. "Come on, we have work to do." He led the way back through the woods to their camp. Jaren was amazed that it was only late morning. It seemed as though he had passed through a lifetime since leaving camp just a couple of hours before.

As Tanner was tightening the cinch around his stallion's wide body, Korthak walked silently up behind him. "Well, are you ready to shave your head and don the black robes, lad?" he whispered teasingly in his ear.

Tanner spun around in horror. "That's not one bit funny, Korthak!" the red-faced youth shouted past clenched teeth as Korthak roared with laughter. He knew that Korthak was only joking, but he was sorely embarrassed for ever having mentioned the possibility of becoming a Lucian priest.

Hawk and Jaren turned to look at the pair. Hawk raised one eyebrow. "Something you can let us in on?"

Tanner paled as Korthak began to speak. "Well..." he paused, allowing Tanner's emotions to rise just below the boiling point. "No, I don't think so. It was just a little joke between Tanner and me," he said as he mussed the young man's hair and walked away.

The air exploded from Tanner's lungs as he released his tension. *"With friends such as this man,"* he thought, *"I don't need Gundroths and Trolls around. He'll drive me to my grave soon enough."*

They mounted up and headed southwest toward Parth, the dwarven village high within the Kroth Mountains. The fears caused by the many legends that the Dragonmasters had so carefully taught were now completely gone from the minds of the two young men. Both of them had seen that the legends were nothing more than lies.

As they traveled south, both Jaren and Tanner were actually looking forward to seeing real live Dwarves and Elves face to face.

In the stronghold of Keratha, chaos reigned. The mountain caverns reverberated with the ear-splitting din of hundreds of dragons roaring and trumpeting; rider after rider was tossed from atop their own beasts.

"What the blazes is the matter with them?" Volant shouted in fury.

Chapter Eighteen

CHAOS

It was close to midday when Volant was suddenly awakened by the din of hundreds of dragons roaring and trumpeting. His head, already pounding from heavy drinking the night before, felt as though it was in a vise.

"Dhragh! Can't someone quiet those beasts? What the blazes is the matter with them?" he shouted. He immediately regretted his outburst as he pressed his hands against his temples. He carefully rolled out of his bedrack, and began pulling on his breeches. The stench of the ale-soaked garment was enough to cause his already rebelling stomach to lurch. He threw the breeches across the bedchamber with a curse, and began violently rummaging through his clothing chest.

As he was struggling with the clean breeches there began a loud, insistent knocking at his bedchamber door. Volant grabbed his aching head. "Stop that infernal pounding!" he screeched hoarsely toward the door. "The noise from those overgrown lizards is enough to have to endure without you adding to it."

Tulak, the leader of Volant's Green Flight, threw open the door, which abruptly slammed into a table, knocking a pewter mug onto the stone floor with a loud clang. The sound reverberated in Volant's head, causing searing pain to shoot through his brain like white-hot iron. He lifted his raging, blood-shot eyes to the ruddy-faced, stocky young man, "I'll have your hide for that, you imbecile!"

Tulak, apologizing profusely, retrieved the mug and set it back on the table. "I...I'm sorry, sir," he stammered, "but Sirtar told me to find you as quickly as I could. The dragons have all gone mad. No one is having any luck quieting them."

Volant downed half a flask of tonic to alleviate the pain in his head, and turned to his Captain. "Hmpf...typical of my Force Commander's mental superiority to send someone to tell me the obvious. I swear, if there was anyone else with enough experience.... Where is the fool?"

Tulak asked with feigned innocence, "Sir?"

"Sirtar, man. Where is Sirtar?"

Tulak pointed out the window. "He's down in the courtyard, sir."

Volant nodded and brushed roughly past the rider. "Come on then, we'll see what this chaos is all about."

As they left the chamber, Tulak's shoulder brushed the door, which again slammed into the table, sending the flagon crashing to the floor a second time.

Volant turned so quickly that the young officer never saw his fist coming before it smashed into the side of his head. The Dragonleader stalked away from the rider's unconscious body, shaking the pain out of his hand. "By Lucia, I'm surrounded by an army of incompetent fools," he muttered, as he made his way down to the courtyard.

Everywhere he looked, there was chaos. All the cavern areas were in total upheaval. He saw many of his riders looking in much the same condition as himself. He had always allowed his riders to do as they pleased, so long as they could fly when the need arose. However, many of them kept their eyes averted as they hurried past. Volant could see by the pale, strained faces and matted hair that many of them were in no condition to fly. Many were falling in their tracks, trying to run and pull on boots at the same time. Volant made a mental note that this would be the last time his men would ever be unprepared for an emergency.

As he stepped from the dark cavern into the bright courtyard, the pounding in his head increased unbearably. He cursed the herbalist for not being able to come up with a more efficient remedy for a hangover.

"Ah, there you are, sir!" Sirtar yelled as he approached. Volant eyed him maliciously. "Keep your voice down, Sirtar, or I will have that foul tongue of yours ripped from your throat," he threatened softly.

Sirtar, not in the least intimidated, bowed slightly, and spoke just a trace more quietly. "As you wish, sir."

Volant took in the rampant disorder on all sides, watching in utter amazement, as rider after rider was rejected by their own beasts. He glanced at his Colonel, "What in the name of Lucia is the matter with them?"

Sirtar shrugged his shoulders, and leaned closer to Volant's ear, so that he could speak more softly, yet still be heard above the thunderous cacophony. "We don't know yet, sir. Not one of them will allow their riders to mount." He shook his head, "I'm stumped. They're either flying all over the place, roaring and trumpeting, or just sitting and wagging their heads back and forth and caterwauling like drunken sailors. We've heard nothing from the other outposts of uprisings anywhere, so they can't have sensed any trouble."

Volant pressed his eyes closed against the bright sunlight, wondering why he had ever considered this man to be capable of rational thought, much less given him the leadership of his troops. "Has it not occurred to you Colonel, that perhaps the dragons in the outposts are behaving in a similar manner?"

Sirtar had never been accused of being very quick minded, and so Volant, receiving only a blank look in response, continued. "Dhragh, Sirtar, there is a strong possibility that they have been unable to get a message through to us because their dragons won't allow them to fly, either."

Sirtar's face finally registered comprehension. "Yes, that could be an explanation." He spoke as though he had been responsible for the deduction. Volant merely shook his aching head in disbelief.

Beland had just arrived and stood beside them. "By the dark god, what is going on?" he shouted. Sirtar grinned maliciously, and stole a glance at his leader, as Volant grabbed his head, all color draining from his face. After a moment, he put his hand up to his old advisor, hoping to keep him silenced.

Beland knew immediately what was ailing Volant, and scowled his disapproval. He was from the old school, where leaders were expected to set the example for their troops. Even in his worst years of debauchery, he had always been capable of standing before his troops with military decorum. However, after observing the condition of many of Volant's troops on all sides, he decided that, indeed, Volant was a prime example *of* his troops.

Sirtar pointed to one of the riders as he attempted to climb atop his dragon. The beast sat, roaring in rage and anguish, writhing uncontrollably until he had pushed the man aside.

Beland brought his shaggy, gray eyebrows together. Looking at the other two men, he lowered his voice to accommodate the now gray-faced Volant. "Have either one of you tried to mount?"

Volant immediately followed the old man's thinking, "Of course. I'll see if Lok will allow me to fly him, and perhaps we can get the rest of these asinine beasts to follow his lead."

Beland glared at him for berating the dragons. "Begging your pardon, sir, but I don't take the same viewpoint as you."

"Give it a rest, old man," Sirtar mumbled just loud enough for the older man to hear. He knew Volant was in no mood for any of the old warrior's inane arguments today.

Beland shot him a withering glance, and continued belligerently, "These beasts are not unintelligent, and there has got to be a very good reason why they are behaving in this manner."

Both advisors watched as a red flush crept up Volant's neck and spread to cover his face. Beland braced himself for the blow he knew was coming. Instead, Volant clamped his jaws together, and jammed his hands into his riding gloves as he stalked away. His two advisors followed him at a prudent distance.

"You old fool," Sirtar said. "I don't know why he didn't have you cut up and used for dragon fodder long ago."

"Most likely because I'm the only one of his advisors with any brains, you witless mutation," he snapped back.

They followed Volant to Lok's lair, and found the dragon rocking back and forth, his golden eyes sparkling with an eerie brightness.

"What's the matter, Lok old boy?" Volant said quietly, attempting to soothe the huge beast by stroking its gigantic neck. "C'mon, old friend, why don't we go out and hunt down a few elves and dwarves today. That should lift your spirits, eh?"

The dragon instantly pulled away from the startled man, and increased the volume of his bellowing as his agitation increased.

Beland shook his head, "I don't understand this. I've never seen any dragon behave this way in my fifty years of experience with them."

Volant knew he would not fly Lok today or any time, as long as the dragon was in this state. He joined his advisors. "I don't like this. These dragons are the backbone of our military."

He lapsed into silence for a moment. "I think I should pay a visit to the Lucian priests. Perhaps they may be able to shed some light on this." He turned and stalked from the lair.

He strode across the courtyard, watching as every one of his troops was rebuffed by their dragons. His anger increased with the pounding of his head. What could possibly have caused the dragons' agitation and rebellion? They had always allowed men to fly them. He would get some answers soon, or heads would roll.

Movement in the sky above the mountain tops caught his attention. "What's this? Why has the morning patrol returned? They should have been well on their way by now." He spoke no one in particular. But then he saw that the dragons were without riders; some were weaving and rolling erratically, flapping their wings furiously in an attempt to stay aloft. The sound of their bellowing and shrieking sent bars of searing pain through Volant's head. Suddenly, several of the beasts began falling earthward. People began shouting and running in every direction so as not to be crushed by the dragons as they plummeted and crashed into houses and onto the courtyard near the caverns. Several of the dragons in the area were injured and dozens of people injured or killed. The dragons that didn't die while airborne landed in a careening, rolling, sliding mass of wings and talons, slashing and crashing to a halt before the poor beasts finally died. A few of the dragons, that moments before had bellowed in rejection, were now keening at their own imminent demise as their riders lay dead, crushed by the falling dragons.

Sirtar and Beland rushed up to the Dragon Leader. Beland was the first to find his tongue. "What sort of devilry is going on here? This is pure madness! We've got to find the cause of this, Volant."

Volant was in a fury as he approached the ebony temple. He noted the black smoke rising into the clear morning sky. *"Good,"* he thought, *"they have started their sacrifices early today. They obviously have had their morning prayers interrupted by all of this infernal uproar."*

Volant pulled the dagger from his belt and stepped onto the threshold of the temple. In his anger, he pricked the end of his finger rather more deeply than intended and re-sheathed the blade. Allowing a few drops of blood to fall upon the marble slab, a required precursory sacrifice, he entered the Lucian temple. He stepped through the doorway and into the semi-darkness of the huge altar room.

His nostrils were immediately assaulted with the odor of incense and burning flesh. He breathed deeply, savoring the stench with delight. He loved this place, and yet, as always, he felt a pang of sorrow that Lucia had not permitted him to become a priest. His ambition had always been three-fold: to become a Lucian priest, the Supreme Leader of the Dragonmasters, and Emperor of Kinthoria. He had prepared so eagerly for the priesthood, memorizing the hundreds of prayers and incantations, mutilating his body with the ritual cutting by blade and glass, and searing with hot irons. He had perversely enjoyed the pain of these rituals, but he loved the sacrifices more than any other function of the priesthood.

Galchobar, the ancient Lucian priest who had been his mentor, had recognized Volant as a future threat to his own authority and had convinced the young cadet that he could serve Lucia far more effectively by giving all of his energies to his military position, and to achieving his third goal. He had told him that it was Lucia's own word that he would become the greatest Dragonmaster of all time and Emperor of Kinthoria.

It was Lucia's will. Volant would not disappoint or disobey his god, but he had been loathe to set aside his ambition to the priesthood. Because he had already sacrificed this first ambition, he was rigorously determined to allow nothing to threaten his position as the Supreme Leader of the Dragonmasters. He must find out why

The Birth of a King

Lucia was allowing such rebellion among the dragons. *"I will get those beasts back into the air, or destroy every last one of them in the trying,"* he thought.

He walked toward the altar at the center of the temple. The priests, with their long, black robes, and heads shaved save for the single braid flowing down the back, were swaying to and fro under the watchful eyes of their god.

The hideous face of Lucia was smiling down at Volant, from amidst the haze of smoke above the fire pit. "My Master," Volant whispered reverently, basking in the presence of evil permeating the entire temple area. He began to feel the power of the dark god fill him anew, and he felt reborn. His crushing headache vanished.

He watched as the priests, chanting and moaning, offered various sacrifices, including their own blood; petitioning Lucia for more power in order to bring the whole of Kinthoria to its knees before his will. Out of the corner of his eye, Volant saw a dark shadow glide silently toward him. The priest spoke no word, but merely nodded for Volant to follow. He lingered just long enough to watch as another priest twisted the head off a pigeon and anointed the altar with the first few drops of its blood. Then he deftly cut out its heart and liver, laid them in a brazier of coals beside the altar, and then raised the offering toward the face of his god, chanting a blessing, before tossing its remains into the sacrificial flames.

Volant turned reluctantly to follow the priest through a side door and down a short corridor. The priest opened a huge door and stepped aside, allowing Volant to pass into the room beyond. The man bowed toward the cowled figure seated in the room, flitted a glance at Volant, and silently closed the door.

The only light in the small chamber came from two red candles set on a table littered with scrolls, parchments, and scraps of paper. A priest was bent over them, his face shadowed within his cowl. He seemed to be deep in thought, as he studied one of the manuscripts. He did not bother looking up, but gestured to a chair for the Dragonmaster.

"Sit down, Volant," he croaked in a raspy voice. "Too much carousing is going to be the death of you." He looked up at Volant with a face that resembled nothing so much as a living skeleton - its yellow, hollow eyes, set in pallid flesh draped like wrinkled parchment over the bones. His face split into a hideous grin. His mouth was crimson as blood, and his teeth yellow as ochre. "Do you wish so badly to meet with the Great Master?" he asked.

Volant twisted in his chair. *"Dhragh,"* he thought, *"will I never know peace when I'm with this priest?"*

The High Priest's eyes narrowed with intimidation, "You have more to concern you than peace, my ambitious Emperor."

Volant straightened nervously, struggling to control the thoughts he knew his Mentor could easily read.

Volant cleared his throat, "What has arisen, my Master? Has Lucia been offended in some way? Is he so angry with us that he will not even allow us to fly our dragons? Why is he allowing our dragons to die?"

The priest sat in silence for so long a time that Volant thought perhaps he had been abruptly dismissed. Finally, the ancient man whispered, "There is royal blood in the land, Volant, and it has the Power."

Volant leaped up knocking his chair aside with such force that the back of it splintered apart as it hit the stone floor. Fear gripped his heart so fiercely that he could not breathe, and he thought he would retch. He forced the bile back down his throat. He stood, trembling in rage at the unfamiliar emotion, able to force only a single word from his lips. "Where?"

The priest placed his hands on the parchment in front of him, arching the tips of his fingers together. "As yet we are not able to ascertain his location. We have just this morning been made aware of his existence."

This was clearly not the answer Volant wanted to hear. "You don't know?" he screamed at the High Priest. "Galchobar, you have scores of seers, crystals, and necromancers with which to gather information, and you can't locate someone with the Power? He should be as apparent as Solance," he raged.

The priest stared at Volant, the threatening gleam in his eyes growing with each of Volant's reckless demonstrations of disrespect. He was plainly considering retribution against the younger man for his daring familiarity in addressing him by his given name.

"You tread very close to obliteration, Volant," he said in a deadly quiet voice.

Volant forced himself to quietly pick up what remained of his chair, and sat before his Mentor once more. He let out a lengthy sigh, desperately pushing his own murderous thoughts away before the priest could sense them.

In the ominous silence that followed, and under Galchobar's steady, malignant gaze, Volant began perspiring freely, his face and neck splotching crimson. "Forgive my irreverence, my Master. I am somewhat overwrought by the events of this morning and by your news. But, surely, this is some impostor. There can be no Cathain blood left in Kinthoria," he replied.

Satisfied that his pupil was sufficiently abased, Galchobar continued. "As I stated before, the usurper has the Power. Therefore, he is truly of Cathain blood. The Power is shielding him from us, as it has ever done in times past."

Volant could feel his anger rising once again. He was rabidly zealous that Lucia's power should be supreme, and yet, once again the dark god seemed to be under some strange subjugation to this other Force. In frustration the Dragonleader asked, "Is there anything you can do to get the dragons flying again?"

The priest nodded, "We plan to arrange for some spell casting."

Volant's mind was whirling. "How long will it take? I need those beasts in the air no later than tomorrow morning. I'll tear this country apart looking for this one who dares to threaten my throne." He slammed his fist into his hand. He was so angry that he did not even notice the pain from his swollen fist, the result of his attack on Tulak.

Galchobar simply nodded. "It will be accomplished when our historians have found the components for a specific spell required for our purposes. There are hundreds of scrolls in the vaults. It may take some time. But be assured, they will search without rest until the answer is found."

He raised his hand in warning at the look of rising fury on Volant's face. "In the meantime, we must all prepare ourselves and pray most earnestly to Lucia, my Emperor. This threat to the power of our god and to the priesthood," he stopped and eyed Volant with a

The Birth of a King

reprimanding sneer, "and yes, your throne, which I notice was your primary concern, must be obliterated."

Volant turned toward the door, biting back words that could bring a painful and perhaps deadly response from Galchobar. However, as he stalked from the room, before slamming the door behind himself, his rage overcame caution and he shot a parting remark to his mentor. "We don't all live sequestered away deep inside a palatial temple. Prayer may be a difficult undertaking when accompanied by the deafening chaos of the present *real* world outside this place." This was an act that he immediately regretted, as he heard Galchobar's growl from behind the door. He took three steps and staggered as the blinding ache slammed back into his head with a vengeance.

He was only halfway to the cavern when Bendor raced up to him, out of breath. "Sir," he panted, "I've been looking all over for you," he leaned over, gasping for air.

Volant had never seen his Red Flight leader so agitated. "Well, speak up. What is it, man?" he demanded, wondering what more could possibly go wrong this day.

"It's Lok, sir, and some of the other dragons. They're taking the eggs from the chamber."

"What? Where are they taking them?" Volant screamed as he began running toward the egg chamber.

"We don't know, sir. No one can fly to follow them," Bendor panted as he tried to keep pace with his leader.

Volant thought immediately of the usurper who supposedly had the Power, and wondered if he had already learned how to make his will known to the dragons. Was he directing them steal the eggs? "Find Beland and Sirtar immediately. Have them meet me in my council chamber."

"Yes, sir," Bendor said, dashing away.

As Volant passed the feeding pits, he saw that the dragons would eat nothing offered to them. They merely sat rocking, and swaying their huge heads back and forth on their long necks as they kept up an eerie keening that made Volant's flesh crawl. He had never heard the beasts make such a bone chilling sound.

He cursed all the way to his council chamber. When he entered the room, he dropped onto a bench and rubbed his hand over his burning eyes.

"Would m'lord wish some wine?" the slave girl asked softly, fearfully standing just outside the entry to the chamber. Word of Volant's raging anger had spread quickly throughout the citadel.

He looked up to see Mavi standing in the doorway.

"I did not mean to intrude, m'lord," she dropped her eyes to the floor. "I saw you come in and thought you might wish refreshment."

Volant squinted his eyes and pressed the heels of his palms into his temples, as though trying to make sense of her words. "Yes," he snapped. "Bring three goblets and a pitcher of strong wine."

Mavi turned to obey, when Volant shouted, "Wait. On second thought, just bring three mugs of hot cafla."

Her face registered surprise, as she bowed silently and left the chamber.

Almost immediately, Sirtar and Beland rushed into the chamber, the strain of the morning's events written clearly on their faces. They both started to speak at once, when Volant held up his hand for silence.

"Sit down and hold your tongues. We have much to discuss, and for once, I'd like the two of you to try to come up with something that you can agree upon. I have neither the time nor the stomach for your quibbling and arguing this morning."

He looked at his oldest advisor, "Beland, what is the latest report on the dragons?"

Beland cleared his throat, "Well, sir, they have not eaten anything all morning. They seem to be calming down some, but they still won't abide even the simple touch of their riders. Some are still sitting out there by the feeding pits, rocking back and forth like they're anticipating something. But most of them have gathered near the egg chamber. Their necks are arched, and their nostrils are fuming, as though they are prepared for attack. They won't allow anyone into the chamber to stop the removal of the eggs." He looked across the table at his leader, and noted that the man had taken just

The Birth of a King

about all of the bad news he could handle in one day. However, he knew he must continue his report regardless of the consequence.

"Lok started taking the eggs out of the egg chamber about an hour ago. We sent out a rider on horse to follow him, but it was impossible for him to keep up with the dragon. Soon after that, a few of the other dragons," he paused and threw a glance at Sirtar, who shifted uncomfortably in his seat, "including Yturi and Usani, began carrying off more of the eggs."

At the mention of the queen dragon's name, Volant started in surprise. "Even Usani is removing the eggs?" he asked in disbelief.

"Yes, sir. We still don't know where they are being taken. I just can't understand it. The dragons have begun a crooning similar to when their eggs are about to hatch, but the hatching is still some time off. Although…the tone of their crooning *is* much deeper this time, so it may have nothing to do with the hatching. I just don't know, sir. I'm stumped." He threw up his hands in frustration.

Sirtar nodded his head in agreement. Volant looked at his stunned Force Commander. "Do you have anything to add?"

Before Sirtar could begin, Mavi walked into the chamber. She blushed as the three men stopped their conference and watched her lay the mugs of steaming cafla on the table.

Sirtar glared at the girl. "Cafla?" he roared. "Go and fetch us something decent to drink, you worthless wench. We need some strong port instead of this swill."

The young slave was motionless with fear, her eyes darting wildly from Sirtar to Volant. Sirtar rose from his bench and drew back his hand to slap the slave girl into action.

Volant smashed his hand down onto the tabletop, as Mavi flinched, expecting a blow from Sirtar's huge open hand.

"No!" he bellowed. "The girl has done exactly as I have instructed her." He glanced at Mavi. "Leave us," he said quietly. She bowed and fled from the chamber. Sirtar started to object, but saw that Volant was just waiting for the opportunity to vent his anger, so he kept his mouth closed.

"Now, you were about to add to Beland's story, were you not, Colonel?"

The Birth of a King

Sirtar cleared his throat, "Yes, sir. I was going to say that we received a message from Corbin only minutes ago. The boy he sent rode his horse to ground trying to get here from Chandor. The dragons to the north are behaving in the same manner as ours. The report also stated that they have detected no coastal landings, and their scouts have seen no trolls or gundroths moving from The Moors into the east." Sirtar hesitated just a moment before reporting the worst of his news. "So far, over a score of dragons who had been on patrol with their riders have returned both to the north and here in Keratha. They have returned riderless. We expect more of the same by the time the outer patrols are able to return."

Beland added quietly, "We believe it is probable that all of the posts are experiencing the same disaster."

Volant slowly stood and crossed the chamber to stand by the window. The salt air smelled clean and refreshing as he stood in silence, his dark eyes staring out at the Great Otten Sea. He sighed heavily as he turned to face the two men.

"There is an heir alive," he stated simply.

Sirtar choked on the cafla, and Beland jumped up, his stool spinning crazily into the wall behind him. "That's impossible," the older man raged, his face livid with rage and disbelief. "Who is fostering such ridiculous drivel? They must be stopped immediately."

"Galchobar just told me less than an hour ago. Are you volunteering to be the messenger I send to demand that he stop spreading such rumors?" he asked dryly.

Beland visibly shrank into himself, righted his chair, and collapsed into it.

"I was one of the company that raided the palace, sir," Sirtar said. "I saw to it that no one escaped alive."

Volant narrowed his eyes and shot back, "Well, it would seem that you once again did your usual thorough job, doesn't it, Sirtar."

"Where is this gutter rat?" Sirtar demanded. "It will give me great pleasure to rectify my mistake by slitting the traitor's throat." He started for the door, ready to leave the second Volant gave the miscreant's whereabouts. "I'll bring his head to you this very day, Volant."

The leader of the Dragonmasters glared at him, "Yes, and on foot, too. Idiot! Have you forgotten you are dragonless at the moment?"

The Colonel silently returned to his stool and sat as Volant followed suit. "The priests will be casting spells on the dragons tonight...hopefully."

Beland started to protest, but Volant stopped him, "I'll hear none of your preaching, old man. I need those dragons flying. I need every rider we have ready to go in the morning. I want every village searched from the Northern Regions to the Kroth Mountains. Am I making myself clear?" he asked, eyeing the two men dangerously.

Beland and Sirtar nodded. The older man was the first to speak. "Sir, I fear we are not strong enough to go south of the Shandra."

Volant slowly rose to his feet once again, and leaned across the table until his face was mere inches from Beland's. "Not strong enough? Not strong enough for what - fables and stories that we've been feeding the simpletons of Kinthoria? Have you heard your own fabrications so many times that you have come to believe them yourself?"

After several moments of facing down the older man, Volant backed away just enough to include Sirtar with his threat. "Both of you listen to me. You tell your riders anything you like, but as soon as we have the dragons airborne again, we will start searching, and I will hold each of you responsible for any rider who refuses to fly into the Southern Regions. Do we understand one another, gentlemen?"

The two men nodded their heads in acknowledgment.

Sirtar nervously cleared his throat again. Volant turned to stare at him. "You have something else, Sirtar?"

The gigantic man, second in rank and power only to Volant, was loathe to speak, especially with Volant in his present state of mind. His hatred increased for this man who had the ability to make him feel like a young cadet. "Yes, sir." He reluctantly pulled a stained and crumpled parchment from his tunic. "This message came by courier a couple of months ago. I found it in my gear trunk this morning. I planned to begin an investigation today, but, with the news you have just given us, I wonder if there could be any possibility that it might have something to do with all of this." He cautiously handed the missive to Volant, who quickly scanned the page, his eyes growing wider as he read.

He crushed the parchment and lunged at his Colonel, grabbing a fistful of his shirt. "You have had this for the past two months, and never saw fit to bring it to my attention until now?" he raged. He threw Sirtar backward over his stool.

Sirtar jumped to his feet and desperately tried to speak, but could only succeed in stammering "Sir...I...uh...I...."

"You fool, do you realize what this could mean?" Spittle shot from the corners of Volant's mouth, and the veins in his neck distended.

Sirtar's own rage increased and he said in accusation, "Sir, you didn't want to be disturbed the night this came in, so you ordered it delivered to me. After I'd read it, I assumed it was only two more boys dallying before the Day of Apprenticeship. It's an annual occurrence. I was going to look into it." He saw the glint of steel in Volant's hand and leaped backward.

Beland stepped between the two. "No, Volant! You need Sirtar too much to waste his life." The old man stared defiantly into his leader's eyes. "It was merely a routine judgment call two months ago. Even now, this is only one of many such missives from Halls all across Kinthoria. Sirtar's oversight of one report could be an extremely costly mistake, I agree, but it won't be undone through his death."

Volant was shaking uncontrollably. "Get out of my way, old man," he said menacingly.

Beland's old heart was racing under the strain of defying his leader, but he continued bravely, "I will not allow this, Volant!" he said with as much authority as his fear would allow. "Get hold of yourself, sir. There's every possibility that this is simply nothing more than just two truant boys. Are you willing to waste your Colonel's life on such a chance? Please...be reasonable."

Moments passed as the two wills pressed upon one another. Finally, Volant's scream of rage was savage as he hurled his dagger across the chamber. It lodged deeply into the frame of the door.

"Leave me!" he bellowed. "And make sure your men are ready to fly at a moment's notice." Both men scrambled for the door, thanking

Lucia that they were still alive and breathing, though Beland was coughing uncontrollably from his efforts to save Sirtar's life.

Retrieving the crumpled message he had flung away in his excitement, Volant walked to the table, and began slowly and deliberately smoothing it out with his hands. "Why didn't I take this foul message that night the courier knocked at my bedchamber?" He rued once again his unaccountable weakness for Vanessi's attraction. He very nearly hated his wife at that moment. Of all the women he had ever known, she alone could enslave his passion with a glance.

He whipped his head to the side and uttered a low, frustrated growl - then, willing his emotions to subside he began considering the present situation in a saner light. "We will begin looking in Reeban and the other scholars halls. Maybe...just maybe this is the key that will turn this debacle into nothing more than the easy elimination of one small lad."

Chapter Nineteen

BALGO

The four companions quickly headed in a southwest direction after leaving the camp by the Spring of Elyon.

Despite the danger of possible discovery, the spirits of the company were very high as they travelled, for Jaren's transformation at the Spring had included the gift of the Power of Elyon's Spirit: a power that most Dragonmasters, including Volant, feared above all else. They each found it difficult to suppress the laughter and gaiety in their spirits in order to remain vigilant and listening for signs of the enemy.

At the moment of Jaren's transformation, the false god, Lucia, had become aware of the existence of an heir, ensuring that Kinthoria would suffer severely a second time in their violent attempt to locate and destroy him. Therefore, it was vital that the small company should reach the Southern Passage in the Kroth Mountains as quickly as possible. The road that led through the gap in the mountain range would lead them directly to the dwarven city of Parth.

Hawk kept a constant watch on the sky overhead throughout the remainder of the morning and into the afternoon. The forests of pine and fir which had surrounded them since leaving the Spring of Elyon were becoming ever more dense the higher they ascended the foothills of the vast mountain range.

The trail along which Hawk led them was no more than a small animal path meandering through the forest. He did not want to leave a swath of newly trodden ground for any trackers to follow.

Tanner's eyes shot from one shadow to the next, alert for any attack. He rode, resting his hand on his leg within easy reach of his boot dagger, as he unconsciously clenched and unclenched his fist.

The forest canopy was both a blessing and a bane, for they knew that the dragon riders would have an impossible time discovering them under the thick boughs; yet, at the same time, they were unable to see any substantial part of the sky for ample warning of a dragon rider's approach. As a result, they lost precious time having to stop at the edge of each sunny meadow to scan the sky before dashing across to the safety of the forest beyond.

Eventually the forest became so deep that the sun was only occasionally able to filter down through green leaves, or to send small shafts of light upon the moss and fern covering the forest floor. The moist ground muffled the footfalls of their horses, so that the only sound to mark their passing was the creaking of the leather of their saddles, and the light jingle of their harness.

Jaren became increasingly aware of the occasional furtive glances of his riding companions throughout the afternoon. He patiently endured their scrutiny, understanding their need, as well as his own, to reconcile all of the implications of his physical and inward alterations.

Hawk felt a sense of gratitude and relief that he and his companions were by no means alone in this bold venture. His brethren had continually marked and guarded their progress since leaving Doddridge.

Korthak observed his friend as they rode along the trail. He could see in Hawk's face the longing to turn eastward and ever deeper into the eastern half of the Elven Forests. He had been away from his family and his people for more than two years, but Korthak knew that Hawk would not turn his mount in that direction, no matter how much his heart desired it. Everything must take second place to the completion of this quest. They must see Jaren placed upon the throne of Kinthoria, or all else would fail, including the relative peace and safety that the Southern Regions had enjoyed in the years since the war had ended. For some unknown reason, the Dragonmasters had seemed content with the conquest of all of Kinthoria north of the Shandra. The Southerners knew, however, that it was only a matter

The Birth of a King

of time before the Dragonmasters' insatiable desire for power, and their lust for battle, would overcome their fears and drive them southward.

The older man was surprised then, when Hawk pulled his horse to the side of the path and said, "I must leave you for a short time. Continue on this path until I return." He said nothing more as he turned his mount into the forest and quietly rode away east.

Tanner voiced his and Jaren's concern. "Where's he going, Korthak? Isn't it kind of dangerous for us to be splitting up?"

Korthak, not wanting to cause apprehension in the young men, replaced the frown on his face with a confident smile. "Don't worry, lads. Hawk is not going to do anything that will put us in danger. I don't know where he's going, but I do know there is a really good reason for his leaving. Let's be on our way. Maybe we can cover enough ground that Hawk will never be able to catch up with us and we'll lose the green-eyed oaf for good!"

The two young men stared at him in shock. Then seeing the smile on his face, they broke into laughter and continued down the path at a slightly faster pace.

As the uneventful afternoon wore on, and a premature dusk began to soften the features of the deep forest, Hawk rejoined the group. Korthak could see that whatever Hawk had been up to, he was not pleased with the results. The usually calm and amiable man was wearing a deeply concerned look, and was withdrawn and agitated.

Korthak, attempting to banish his friend's melancholy, reported that they still had not seen any sign of a dragon rider. However, this news only seemed to increase the man's agitation.

They came upon a small copse thickly overhung by the intertwining boughs of three massive oak trees. So complete was the covering of their canopy that sunlight never reached this glade, and there was no sign on the forest floor of undergrowth or young trees. A thick mat of years of fallen leaves lay slowly decaying on the ground beneath their enormous branches.

"We will rest here tonight," Hawk said as he slid from his horse and stretched his body to relieve saddle-weary bones and muscles.

The others quickly followed suit, grateful that Hawk did not intend to push them onward throughout the night. It had been a long day, full of tension.

Hawk gestured for Korthak to follow him several yards from the two young men. Korthak handed his reins over to Tanner and followed his tall friend.

The older man saw the concern written on his face. "What's wrong, Hawk?"

Hawk rubbed the back of his neck and sighed. "I don't know. I expected by now that Volant would be tearing Kinthoria apart looking for Jaren."

He turned back to watch the younger men tending to the horses and talking quietly together. Hawk had warned them ahead of time that there would be no fires between the Spring of Elyon and Parth. "It would be a beacon signal to any dragon riders in the area," he had explained.

"You didn't learn of any raids or anything, yet?" Korthak asked in astonishment.

Hawk shook his head, "That's what has me so uneasy. When I left you, I went out to speak to the scouts. I expected thorough reports on the dragon riders' activities. But there have been no sightings of even one dragon rider in the sky. Not even the usual scouts have been spotted." Hawk pulled off his riding gloves and sat on a moss-covered stump. "It just doesn't make any sense. Jaren confirmed the fact that the dragons knew about him as soon as the transformation took place. It wouldn't have taken long for the Dragonmasters to discover the fact, too."

He sat, rubbing his stubbled chin, his brow contracted in a deep frown. "So what are they waiting for? Why are they not amassing their armies and turning Kinthoria inside out in search of him? Something else very strange has happened. There have been reports that the bodies of several dragon riders have been found. Every one of them was crushed beyond recognition; some were even burst apart."

Korthak stood beside his friend, his thick arms crossed over his massive chest. This was extremely puzzling and troubling, and he wished he could offer Hawk some wise advice. An outrageous thought flicked at the edges of his mind, and he laughed at the absurdity of it. "Maybe the dragons somehow understand that Jaren is their true master. Maybe they won't let those bloodthirsty fools ride 'em anymore. Wouldn't that be a pretty trick on Volant?" He thought it was one of his better jokes, but Hawk's head shot up and he stared, open-mouthed at the older man for several seconds.

Suddenly, he jumped up and embraced Korthak, nearly knocking him to the ground. "Why you old duffer," he laughed, heartily slapping the huge man's back, "that's it!"

Korthak, completely confused, tried backing out of Hawk's bear hug. "What? What's it?"

Hawk looked into Korthak's astonished face, his emerald eyes shining brightly. "That's exactly why we haven't seen a sign of them, you old bear. The dragons won't fly because they *know* Jaren. They sense his authority and they will not submit to the will of Volant and his riffraff. Ha, ha!" he spun and capered in a small circle. "It would also explain the condition of the bodies. The dragon riders caught in flight when the dragons became aware of Jaren would have been thrown off in mid-air."

Korthak grimaced. "Ugh, I bet that hurt."

Jaren and Tanner watched Hawk's antics with rising concern. Tanner looked at Jaren and whispered out of the corner of his mouth, "Mind-plague?"

Jaren shrugged his shoulders, "I don't know. He seemed sane enough a few moments ago."

Jaren formed the words in his mind and sent them to Hawk. *"Um, Hawk, is everything all right? What's going on?"*

Hawk whirled around and saw his two young charges staring at him in wide-eyed wonder. He motioned for Korthak to join the younger men and paced back and forth in front of the trio, grinning from ear to ear. "This is great news. *Great* news! Our large friend here has just banished a lot of my worries."

He stopped in front of Jaren. "Young man, why do you suppose we have not seen a dragon all day?"

Jaren merely stared at him, non-plussed. Hawk smacked his own leg with his riding gloves. "Come on, lad, you're bright. Think about your birthmark."

The Birth of a King

Jaren, still unnerved by Hawk's boyish behavior, could not grasp the man's meaning. Tanner, however, offered the first thing that came to his mind. "It's the shape of a dragon, isn't it?"

Hawk laughed, "Keep going, you're doing great."

Tanner grinned and shot Jaren a withering, 'See-I-told-you-so' look, recalling the times Jaren had told him that his imagination and love for the dragons was muddling his mind.

Finally, out of sheer frustration, Jaren frowned and asked half angrily, "What are you talking about, Hawk?"

"The dragons, lad, the dragons! They won't fly because *you* are their Master, not Volant and his horde of hooligan cutthroats." Hawk could see that Jaren still did not comprehend the extent of their good fortune. He looked with mock sorrow at the two standing beside Jaren. He touched his finger to his forehead and said, "This is a dreadful, unforeseen setback, gentlemen. The poor lad must have left his brain at the Spring of Elyon. Do you suppose we should go back to retrieve it?"

Jaren clearly was ready to kill the green-eyed scout, so Hawk hurriedly continued. "The dragon riders could not begin searching for you because the dragons will not obey them. We've been given a short reprieve, gentlemen; at least until they figure out a way to fly, if that's even possible."

Jaren and Tanner finally understood the situation, and immediately joined in the celebration. Korthak's eyes brimmed with tears of joy, as he mentally pictured Volant raging at the beasts with frothing mouth. It was indeed a pleasant bit of daydreaming for the old warrior.

Hawk looked at his three weary friends and, still chuckling, said, "I think we can allow ourselves a warm fire, and something hot to eat. What do you think?"

His answer came quickly, as one young man immediately knelt to the ground and began scooping out a fire pit, while the other ran to gather wood. Korthak, still laughing and holding his aching belly, headed for his horse and the food sack.

Hawk stood smiling, hands on hips. "Dols, I guess I don't have to ask twice."

The Birth of a King

Once the fire was blazing, they settled about the fire pit to relax and thank Elyon for what He had done for them. They nibbled at hardbread, while Korthak roasted some meatsticks over the fire.

Jaren looked at Tanner, "Well, Tan, I wonder what they have been serving for food at the scholars hall since we've been gone."

Tanner smiled. "Your-guess-is-as-good-as-mine," he quoted and laughed.

Jaren explained the joke to the two older men. "The only times we really knew what we were eating were when Tanner and I would bring back our catch from hunting or fishing. Any other time eating was a scary risk, so it became a joke between us to guess what we were being fed. You should have heard some of the outrageous things we came up with." He laughed and glanced back at Tanner who was hungrily eyeing the roasting meatsticks sizzling over the fire.

"Well, we haven't had to worry about that since we left Reeban, have we, Tan?" He said slapping him soundly on the back, trying to break Tanner's mesmerized concentration on the meatsticks. Jaren swore he looked just like a wildcat ready to pounce on its prey. He fervently hoped that Korthak would hurry the meal.

The slap on the back did break Tanner's concentration, and he threw Jaren a conspiratorial look. "Oh, I don't know as I'd go so far as to say that. I have often wondered what this old man has slipped into his pot to serve up as food." He laughed and quickly shied away from Korthak's playful punch.

"Why, you ungrateful scullery brat," Korthak bellowed as he stabbed his finger toward the retreating youth, "we'll see who eats the largest portion of my meal tonight."

Hawk, Jaren, and Tanner laughed with the big man as he resumed tending the meat sticks. They caught snatches of his mumbling something about slaving over a hot fire for hours...ungrateful mongrels... dragon bait.

To no one's surprise, Tanner had, as usual, eaten more than the other three. Afterward, he savored the feeling of being completely sated while reclining against a log, a smug look of satisfaction on his face. He lay staring into the fire pit, while the others sipped cafla and chatted quietly.

The Birth of a King

He stole a look at the burly man sitting beside Hawk. He found himself experiencing emotions he had never felt before. He was embarrassed, yet exhilarated as he realized that Korthak was becoming like a father to him. He did not know if it would be proper to admit to the older man his growing affection.

Jaren had told him earlier that afternoon of the unimaginable sacrifice that Korthak had given in the death of his wife and his own son, in order to ensure Jaren's escape during the razing of the Cathain palace. He remembered the night in the camp outside Doddridge when he had asked if Korthak had ever lost anyone that he loved. Now that he knew the devastating truth, he felt incredibly selfish upon recalling his childish snit simply because Jaren was not paying enough attention to him.

Tanner took a sip of his cafla. He wished with all of his heart that he could become the son, for Korthak's sake, which had been lost to the older man. He wondered if there was any possibility that the huge, greathearted man might hold any fatherly affection for him, and if he would ever consider accepting him as a sort of substitute son. *"Wish I could ask Mum about it,"* he mused sadly.

His thoughts came to an abrupt halt. His Mum! He felt a deep pang of guilt as he realized that he had not consciously thought of her since leaving the scholars hall. He truly hoped that she was not desperately worried about him, for she surely would have been questioned by now as to his whereabouts. He hoped that she would someday be able to forgive him for leaving without a word. His thoughts drifted to his two brothers. He wondered if Brant and Colin were working in the fields now. He remembered them fondly, and was suddenly awash with homesickness. He vowed that when all of this was over he would return to Reeban and take care of his mum for the rest of her life. He longed for a family with which to share love and affection and memories, and he would show her how grateful he was for her having done the best she could through all of the tragic and dreadful years.

He sat up instantly, his ears straining to hear the sound again. His three companions were also hushed and alert now. He quickly grabbed his boot dagger, and saw Korthak silently slide his sword from its sheath. Hawk already had an arrow knocked.

The Birth of a King

"Dols, he's quick," he thought.

The unexpected noise sounded as though something was thrashing through the forest just off to the south of their camp.

Jaren and Korthak quickly kicked dirt into the fire pit to smother the flames. The horses stomped and pulled at their picket line. Whomever or whatever was coming toward their camp seemed to be deliberately making as much noise as possible.

"No one could make that much noise without wanting to," Tanner thought.

Korthak moved behind a tree and raised his sword. Hawk knelt behind a boulder aiming his arrow in the direction of the racket. Jaren and Tanner moved to the horses, trying to calm them, while crouching behind a fallen log.

"Durn fool of a donkey," a gruff voice scolded as the stranger burst into the clearing. "You are the a-onest, stubbornest, orneriest, most useless beastie I've ever seen!" he said yanking on the poor animal's lead rope. "Now haul your worthless hide out here or I'll strip it clean off your bones and sell it to one of them thieving hawkers in Doddridge. C'mon, now, move it!"

Hawk dropped his head, chuckling softly. Tanner watched as Korthak let his sword fall to his side. The huge man stepped out from behind the tree, scaring the poor donkey into a fit of kicking and braying. "Balgo, you lop-eared, hairy little stump, you were very nearly shorter by a head," he said as he shook his sword at the intruder.

The little man stopped dead in his tracks. "Bah! You'd have missed me by two arms' length, you overgrown tree trunk. I'm too short for you to reach, even with that ten foot blade you carry. I see you still haven't learned the proper way to handle that thing."

The grizzled little man dropped the axe from his shoulder, and pulled the struggling, frightened donkey over to a tree and tied him securely. "Where's that addle-brained half-elf?" he turned back to face Korthak. "I hear tell he has the Prince with him."

Korthak grinned broadly and shook his head. "He probably still has his arrow aimed at your black heart, debatin' on whether or not he should just go ahead and let 'er fly seeing as how it's only you."

The Birth of a King

Hawk laughed as he stood, putting his arrow back into his quiver. "Balgo, you noisy old coot, we almost had us a dwarf for breakfast." He leaned down and gave his old friend a hearty slap on the back.

"If I was noisy it was with coughing from the smoke of that forest fire you had blazing a moment ago. I smelled your camp three furlongs back!"

Tanner and Jaren remained crouched behind the log, staring in numb disbelief at the sight before them. The top of the little man's head reached mere inches above Hawk's waist. His gray hair was a tangled mat topped with a red cap that appeared to be a large, old stocking stretched over his head, the majority of it left hanging at the back to flop and wag every time he moved his head. Enormous eyebrows and a gray beard covered his face, until all that could be seen were two dark eyes and a rather large, bulbous nose. The young men could not even begin to guess his age. His features appeared ancient, yet he stood straight and proud with his feet apart and his thumbs tucked into his belt, as though he was a giant instead of a dwarf.

Jaren whispered to Tanner. "Did he just call Hawk a half-elf?" Tanner could only swallow and nod his head. They had been riding with an elf for close to three months and had not even realized it? Suddenly many things that had been nagging at the back of their minds began to come together, and they wondered how they could have been so blind. They recalled Hawk's strange clothes when they had first seen him, his tear-shaped green eyes, and his ability to disappear and appear so silently in the forest.

"And," Jaren thought, *"his age!"* He was stunned as he recalled seeing Hawk many times, as the history of his family had flashed into his mind at the Spring of Elyon. *"Hawk always looked the same each time I saw him in those memories."* He suddenly had an overwhelming curiosity to know just where Iain, the bruised combat pupil, fit into his family tree. And what of the beautifully strange words he had heard at the Spring? Had that been the language of the elves?

Hawk's voice interrupted their thoughts. "It's all right, you two," he called. "It's only a foolish old man who's lost his way in the woods."

Balgo kicked Hawk in the shin, causing him to grab his leg, howling in pain. "I'll show you who's lost, you green-eyed tree lover."

Korthak roared with laughter. Balgo was better than a traveling troupe of jesters for laughs, and the big bear of a man loved him dearly. Besides, Balgo was the only one he knew of who could get away with such shenanigans with Hawk and still have his brains left intact.

Hawk was laughing and howling and hobbling around on one leg, as the two young men stood and put away their weapons. They slowly left their hiding place and walked cautiously toward the trio.

Balgo winked at Hawk. "Armed to the teeth, aren't they?"

Korthak snickered, and then saw the look of embarrassment on Tanner's face. "Now just don't be underestimatin' these two, Balgo." He leaned over the fire pit and stirred it with a branch, trying to retrieve any live coals from under the dirt. "There's more to them than meets the eye."

"Hmph," grunted the little man, but when he looked at Jaren as the youth came closer, his eyes widened. He dropped to one knee, and bowed his head, striking his small fist over his heart. "M'lord, forgive my rude tongue. I did not believe that it could truly be Your Majesty."

Jaren's face flushed. He looked at Hawk with pleading eyes, but the tall elf merely frowned and shook his head. The young Prince took a deep breath and squared his shoulders. He closed his eyes for just seconds, as he searched through the memories given him at the Spring of Elyon. He touched Balgo's filthy red cap, and spoke with as much dignity as he could muster, "It was an honest mistake, good dwarf. You are forgiven. Now rise, and let us put the incident behind us."

Balgo rose to his feet and looked up at Jaren. The young Prince placed his hand on the shoulder of the proud, old dwarf. "I sense that you will serve me well and honorably, noble friend. We have far to go, through perils yet unknown. Therefore, let us put away formalities until such time as our quest is accomplished and we may speak freely and without danger. For the present, I am as one of you, an equal member of this band, and nothing more, in title at least."

The Birth of a King

Balgo stood in front of the lad, slack-jawed and staring. Finally he cleared his throat, "Yes, I s'pose that would probably be the wisest track to follow."

Tanner had watched the scene with a growing sense of awe and pride in his friend. He was delighted as he felt that, somehow, Jaren was being repaid for all of the years of self-restraint he had imposed upon himself when facing the badgering and torment he had endured from the boys at the scholars hall. He realized he would no longer need to step in to cow Jaren's adversaries into retreat. He knew that Jaren now had the powerful incentive of honor, and respect for the Cathain throne to urge him into defensive action. *"Dols,"* he thought, *"what I wouldn't give to be back at the scholars hall now, with this new Jaren, and watch all of those hooligans turn tail and run."*

Hawk and Korthak had also been astonished and impressed at the ease with which the young lad had just assumed the noble manner and speech of a monarch with a loyal subject. He had dealt with Balgo's error, and then graciously forgave him in a manner that had left the dwarf with his pride intact. He had asserted his sovereignty, and at the same time offered friendship and equality as a fellow human being. They became aware that they had just observed the birth of, quite possibly, Kinthoria's greatest King.

Jaren was very ill at ease, and still trembling from his first attempt at royal comportment. To relieve the awkwardness, he smiled and said, "Korthak, were you planning on rekindling that forest fire any time tonight? I certainly could use some more of that foul syrup that you pass off as cafla."

With the tension broken, everyone laughed at Korthak's discomfiture over Jaren's uncomplimentary words. He knelt over the fire pit once more and redoubled his efforts to rekindle the smothered embers.

Tanner, feeling somehow protective of his burly friend, quickly gathered tinder and extra kindling and brought them to the distracted man. "Here, Korthak, this should help," he said kindly. "Jaren was only kidding about the cafla; he truly likes it a lot."

Soon each of the company had a mug of the aromatic brew in his hands, and was seated comfortably around the fire. Balgo lit his pipe and proceeded to give Hawk and Korthak news of all that had happened in their absence.

"The abbey at the Great Mountain is completed," he said, eyes shining with excitement. "Everything will be ready for the coronation, providing things continue to go as planned."

Korthak and Hawk pressed the dwarf for detailed information on many topics, most importantly, the welfare of family and friends. Their talk went on deep into the night. Sometime during those hours, weariness got the better part of Jaren and Tanner. It was well onto midnight when Hawk woke them to turn into their bedrolls, and then returned to the homey companionship of his two old friends.

Tendrils of sweet scented smoke circled into the night air from Balgo's pipe. He looked at Jaren, already sleeping again, "It sure didn't take him long to catch onto this 'King' business, did it?" he murmured. "That was a nice piece of work, letting me off the hook in such a manner."

"He seems to have slid into the role with amazing alacrity," Hawk said with just a touch of pride.

Balgo puffed at his pipe again and furrowed his bushy eyebrows. "I wasn't certain how much the lad knows, or what you've told him, so I've kept some serious and confounding business until he wouldn't hear. We aren't certain what has happened, but there are reports that quite a few bodies of dragon riders have been found in pretty bad shape up north of the Shandra."

Hawk nodded his head in affirmation and told Balgo all he had learned from the adrastai and Korthak's plausible suspicion as to the cause of the demise of the dragon riders.

The dwarf sat straight up at Hawk's revelation. "Well I'll be. For once in your life you're probably right, my rotund friend," he said to Korthak with enthusiasm. "You see, I have not told you all of my news, yet. The bodies of over a score of dragons have been found as well. Now, if the riders die, we know that the dragons die soon after. We've been trying to determine the cause of their deaths. It would make perfect sense if the dragons finally found hope for deliverance and dumped their riders in flight the moment they knew that their true King was alive."

"Your assumption has the ring of truth, Balgo" Hawk said soberly.

"Yeah," murmured Korthak, "but what a horrifying way to die. I don't think I'd wish such an end even on a dragon rider." He shivered at the thought of the last moments of life for the dead riders."

After a few moments of solemn quiet, Balgo continued. "I came to find you before you turned down toward the Southern Passage. It was a hard winter up there, and I fear you'll not arrive in Parth earlier than three months hence if you travel that route. The deep cold and heavy ice cracked and blasted a lot of the boulders and trees up that way. There have been rockslides and avalanches in several places. It'll most likely take two summers before we have it opened back up completely. I can track a way up the northern face of the escarpment for you. It's not as accessible as the Southern Passage would be under normal circumstances, but even so, we'll reach Parth within a month by using the Glamorgan Mines."

Hawk glanced at Korthak. They were both familiar with the treacherous terrain of the Kroth Mountains. They were ahead of the Dragonmasters for the moment, and they understood all too well that they could not afford to lose any of the precious time that Elyon had given them. Balgo knew these mountains like the back of his hand, as did his entire race. They gratefully accepted his offer, hoping that the imposed detour would not give the dragon riders the upper hand.

"Right." The diminutive warrior smiled. "Then we'd better follow the good example of these two youngsters here, and turn in. We leave at first light."

Chapter Twenty

QUESTIONS AND ANSWERS

When the company set out once again, the mists of early morning were still lingering near the forest floor. The world was just faintly visible in the dim grayness of the pre-dawn, and dew dripped heavily from the trees with the sound of a soft rain. It was that time of day when every bird in the world tries to make itself heard above every other sound. The joy of heralding the new day with song infected the five travelers; each was in high spirits as Balgo led them ever higher into the ancient arms of the Kroth Mountains - far beyond, Hawk fervently hoped, the knowledge and probing eyes of the Dragonmasters.

For several days, their route wound its way past wide shale slides and boulders of granite as large as Tupper's cottage. The second week out from the Spring of Elyon found them high on a mountainside where oaks, maples, and birches slowly gave way to fir and pine. Hawk began to spot remnants of the vast bristlecone forests that had once crowned the highest peaks of mountain ranges across Kinthoria. The ancient trees were gnarled with long years of living, and twisted into grotesque and alien shapes by the winds that frequently raged through these high alpine canyons. Centuries of icy winters had maimed and blasted the tenacious trees. Yet, on cracked and broken limbs they persistently flaunted their sparse clusters of dark green needles and pinecones in varying stages of development, from bright rose and lime pollen sacks, to the steel blue compact cones of mid-life, to the brown, open cones of maturity.

The Birth of a King

Jaren stared at the stunted relics as he passed by, fascinated by their persistent participation in life, and wondering how old they truly were. The Master at the scholars hall had taught him that the trees were nearly half the age of the earth itself. Now, seeing the trees first hand, Jaren could actually believe what he had once considered a mere child's tale. He studied one particularly ancient looking tree and wished with all his heart that it could speak. Whom had this ancient and silent sentry seen pass by this very spot down through all of the ages of its life? Had this tree and its kin seen long forgotten kings with their retinues, or bands of thieves, or perhaps armies going to war and returning home either jubilant and blowing the victory note or silently bearing their wounded comrades and the memories of the lost in the wake of defeat? What treasures of knowledge this tree share, if only it could speak.

Balgo had promised as they set out this day that they would be in Parth within a fortnight, but he had also warned that the road ahead was more treacherous than any through which they had yet passed. The old dwarf was hoping the weather would hold throughout the next days, and that the mountains, well known to his race, would not extract a terrible toll for their passage. He pulled his cloak a little tighter around his shoulders. The cold air of the high mountains still clung to the north slopes, even in mid-summer, and he knew the chill would increase as their path took them higher into the mountains on their journey south.

Balgo turned in his saddle and studied the Prince. "Dols, boy, you do take after your father," he said in his husky voice, a wide grin on his face.

Sadness touched Jaren's eyes. "Yes...I know," he said quietly.

Balgo, seeing the boy's pain, stepped carefully into his next words. "Don't wish for things lost, lad. Your father and mother were very good people." He glanced up into the hazy sky, squinting into the fractured sunlight. "They are still with you in your heart, and I can imagine they are watching you even now as they sit with Yesha up there," he said nodding his head toward the heavens.

Jaren looked skyward. He knew that Balgo was right, but the knowledge did little to ease the intense longing of his heart. "Would

The Birth of a King

you excuse me, Balgo? You have just reminded me that I'm long overdue for a talk with Hawk," he said with a half-hearted smile.

"Of course, lad, and I'm truly sorry if I caused you any pain," Balgo said.

Jaren smiled and sighed. "No. You're right, Balgo. My parents are with me. In here," he touched his forehead, and then laid his hand over his heart, "and in here. Elyon has given me the gift of the knowledge of them, and I will be forever grateful to Him for that."

He pulled up and allowed Tanner and Korthak to pass him on the narrow stone trail. Hawk would give him the answers to all of his questions now. He need only ask.

As Jaren reined in beside him, Hawk was praying, as he had been during much of his ride at the rear of their small party. He could tell by the young man's expression that he was in for a long session of questioning. He greeted his student with his customary warm smile.

They rode in silence for a time, as Jaren collected his thoughts. There were so many questions, all of which seemed urgent, but Jaren wanted to start off easily, as a lighter mood seemed to strike him. He grinned to himself, as he asked, "Who was Iain?"

The muscles in Hawk's jaw immediately tightened, the only visible evidence of the effect of Jaren's question upon the half-elf. However, his reaction did not go unnoticed by the younger man, who smiled inwardly. "Gotcha!" he mused.

Quickly composing himself, Hawk stared with piercing eyes into the face of his young friend, and then replied as casually as possible. "Uh, Iain...his full name was Iain Chricton Brys Cathain." Hawk hesitated only briefly before continuing. "He was your grandfather."

Now it was Jaren's turn for shock, and the effect was far more evident upon his face than it had been on his friend's.

Hawk was thoroughly intrigued when he saw that the lad was so shaken by his reply that he could not find his tongue. "Jaren, why do you ask about him and how do you know of him?"

Jaren simply stared across at Hawk. He could see no trace of a wrinkle or line on Hawk's smooth face. Nor could he now, upon deliberate inspection, see any gray in his tawny mane. The young

The Birth of a King

Prince wondered if Hawk being half Elven had anything to do with his apparent agelessness. Then he felt extremely foolish, as he realized that Hawk must have been named after an ancestor whom he closely resembled.

Hawk shifted in his saddle and returned Jaren's gaze. "What is it, lad? What are you questioning?"

Jaren chuckled. "Oh, I thought I saw you training...I mean, I thought for a moment...." Jaren found himself reluctant to share with Hawk the wealth of memories he had been given at the Spring of Elyon. He wanted answers today, not questioning. Suddenly he recalled Korthak's tale of his youth, when he had met the man Hawk during the boar hunt. He decided to take a different tack. "Korthak said he met you when he was just a young lad, and he said you were a man. Or, were you named after your father, or your grandfather?"

Hawk laughed quietly, "So that's it. You're wondering how old I am."

Jaren nodded his head, unconsciously bracing himself for the answer.

"Well, if you must know, I'm ninety-six years old; still rather young for one of my race."

Jaren's jaw dropped in astonishment. It seemed that for every question he asked, five more were going to arise within the answers. He decided that perhaps his lessons today weren't going to be as easily understood, or as amusing as he had first anticipated.

"How can you be ninety-six and not be ancient looking?" he asked bluntly.

Hawk laughed again. "Well, it is the gift of the Elven race, Jaren. Most of my people live for two hundred and fifty years, more or less."

Jaren listened with growing wonder, as Hawk explained the longevity of his race.

They had ridden for perhaps a league, continuing their conversation, when Jaren posed another question. "Why does Balgo call you 'half-elf'?"

"He calls me that because I am only half Elven. My father, Braethorn, was human. My mother, Idril Felagund, was Elven. My father was a commander in King Chricton's army. The King was your great, great grandfather. I am told that Braethorn was an adventurous and very determined fellow. In any case, he saw my mother one afternoon as he was passing through the Elven forest. She was sitting in a 'patch of daisies and cornflowers,' as I recall the story, and the sun had transformed her hair to a 'cascade of liquid light.' Needless to say, my father was captured right there on the spot," Hawk smiled at his father's description of the elf maiden.

Jaren tried his hardest to picture in his mind an elf maiden of such rich beauty. Unfortunately every time he tried, the plain faces of the young girls he had known at the scholars hall kept interposing themselves upon this picture of perfection.

"Jaren, she was truly rare in beauty," Hawk was saying. "She had the heart of an angel. As it happened, she fell in love with my father the moment she saw him. I am told that she could instantly know the character of a person through reading their eyes, and she liked what she saw in Braethorn's eyes. They wanted to marry, but the Elven Council of Elders refused to even hear their petition, and your great, great grandfather was adamantly against the union as well."

A look of sadness crossed Hawk's face. "It was a time of extreme sorrow for my parents. They felt that they would never be able to obtain the blessing of their rulers. But, when Elyon has made a plan, no one can thwart His purposes, and it was His plan that they marry. So, after a few years of patient petitioning, and some concessions made by my father to the Elders, an agreement was reached. The concern of the elders was the simple fact that my father would age much faster than my mother, leaving her a widow at an early age by our standards. My father had to make arrangements with the elders for the provision of my mother and any children that might issue from their marriage. Part of those arrangements was that my mother and her children would live with the Elven people. This, of course, was absolutely unacceptable to King Chricton, as he would be losing one of his best knights, and so he continued to withhold his permission and blessing. Finally, the Council of Elders agreed to Chricton's demands, a bargain was struck, and consent was given. To make a long story short, the Elven Council and King Chricton's advisors spent months hashing out a final agreement, the end of which resulted in my father being made the Commander of a new post just within the boundary of the Elven forests.

So the marriage was a double blessing for my father, since he ended up with the best of both worlds. He married the woman he deeply loved, and through that marriage was allowed access to the Elven Council of Elders, a thing wholly unheard of with my independent race. He also became a highly valued member of King Chricton's advisory council. The King relied heavily upon him to promote mutual understanding and peace between the two races."

Jaren considered Hawk's story for a few moments and then said, "It seems to me that they went through an awful lot of time and work just because they wanted to get married. I would have thought that they would have given up the idea after a while. It seems impossible that they would have kept trying to get permission for years."

Hawk smiled. How little the lad understood of love, and of the will of Elyon. "Well, you see, Jaren, when two people, whom the Master has designed to be together, meet and fall in love, there is nothing on earth that can come between them. Although each is a person complete in oneself, Elyon has designed each to become the complimentary part of the other. He takes two complete people and makes one new entity by uniting them."

At Jaren's look of bewilderment, Hawk had to laugh. "I know it seems difficult to understand, Jaren. Sometimes it's hard to understand even after it's happened to you. But, believe me, when you meet your other half, you will know it, and you'll be surprised when you find out how incomplete you are without her."

They were silent for some time after that, as Jaren pondered the unknowable depths of love between a man and a woman, and Hawk recalled many of the memories of his childhood.

His reminiscing was interrupted by Jaren's next question. "You said that you were told that your father was adventurous. Didn't you know him?"

Hawk's look of sadness caused Jaren to immediately wish he could recall the question.

"No, Jaren. I never had the opportunity to know my father. He was killed by a renegade Lucian priest when he stumbled onto one of their illegal altar places. They were in the middle of a sacrifice

The Birth of a King

and could not allow my father to escape to tell others of their secret grove."

Jaren did not know how to respond, except to allow his eyes to speak the sorrow he felt for his friend.

In an effort to shake off the melancholy that had settled over the two friends, Hawk asked, "You have still not answered my question, Jaren. What do you know of Iain? I don't recall having mentioned his name to you."

"I'll tell you about the experience I had in the Spring of Elyon some other time, but that's how I found out about him. I'd really like for you to tell me about my father and mother, Hawk. What were they like? I have their memory...." He held up his hand as Hawk began to ask the obvious question. "That's for later, too. But tell me, what were they like? How did you view them?"

"Well, Jaren. Your father was the most good-hearted man I have ever met, very compassionate; very slow to anger in most cases, much like yourself. He treated his subjects with the same respect he wanted given to himself. The best way I know to describe Cadan is to tell you that he loved life. He loved Elyon, he loved his people." He glanced at the young man riding next to him. "You know, it's been a rare privilege getting to know you these last couple of months. You remind me so much of Cadan. Being in your company is almost like having the past years suddenly vanish. It's almost like being with your father when he was your age. There have been several times when I have had to stop myself from calling you Cadan," he laughed softly. "I remember watching Tanner working with you in the meadow that first day I saw you again after all those years." Hawk offered Jaren a drink from his waterskin.

Jaren drank freely then smiled and shook his head, remembering the soreness that seemed to fill his whole body after that lesson. That part of his life seemed as a distant past belonging to someone else.

"I used to work your father over like that, lad. I think I can say that I probably used to get as frustrated with Cadan as Tanner was with you that day. That man didn't have a mean bone in his body. He just did not have the heart to fight. That is not to say that he was weak or indecisive with his enemies. He had one of the most brilliant military minds I have ever known, and he brought his enemies firmly under his heel when his authority or the kingdom was threatened.

Cadan's love of life would not allow him to be a Warrior King. He wanted more than warfare for his people. He wanted to share knowledge and beauty, science and the arts with all of his subjects. That is why the scholars halls were so successful and flourishing during his time.

One of his and Alanna's great loves was botany. They used to fly his dragon all across Kinthoria to gather rare or unknown species of everything growing, bringing them back for the agronomists to study. He used to say, 'One day, we will find a way to triple our yields. Then not one person will ever go hungry again.' He was a fine, brilliant man, Jaren."

A gentle smile rested on Jaren's face as he paired Hawk's words with the memories he had been given of his father's excitement on those expeditionary flights. Finally, he asked. "What about my mother, Hawk? What was she like?"

"Ah, now she was a beauty, Jaren; the fairest lady in all of Kinthoria, and probably one of the most intelligent, too." Hawk said, as he replaced the cork in his water skin, hanging it once more from his saddle horn.

"She was the daughter of a very wealthy Duke." Hawk's eyes twinkled at the memory of his dear friend's bride. "It took your father almost a year of persistent courting to get Alanna to finally accept his proposal of marriage. You see, she was very strong-willed and opinionated. She would marry whom she would, when she would, and if she would, she told her father."

He chuckled, "I imagine that on the fateful day she finally announced her acceptance of Cadan's proposal, many other young maidens were swooning and weeping all over Kinthoria, as they saw their dreams for glory vanish into oblivion."

"Alanna was remarkably amusing. She was the perfect foil for your father's rather serious nature. She kept him balanced," he laughed, "and she knew how to keep him in line. Do you remember what I said earlier about each being the completing half of a whole?"

Jaren nodded, finally beginning to understand a little of what Hawk had said before.

"Sometimes your father could be awfully stubborn, but Alanna had the ability to sway him to her way of thinking when she could see that he was about to make a mistake. I think she could have easily resorted to playing it coy, but she was a unique queen. She disdained the use of such affectations, judging them far beneath the need or use of any woman of intelligence. She was also distinctive in that she sat with your father as he held court on any matter of state. She was always privy to state secrets and knew at all times what was transpiring in the kingdom. Much can be said for Cadan's good judgment, in that he recognized her intellectual worth and fostered it. He continued her already extensive education with the finest of tutors, and taught her himself as the opportunity and need presented itself. To accept Alanna's council was quite a bold step for Cadan, as it would be for any king. But she brought freshness and a woman's intuitive wisdom into his judgments, and the kingdom was blessed because of her partnership with your father."

Hawk smiled as he remembered the relationship between his two friends. He looked deeply into Jaren's eyes, "Their love and devotion to one another was very rare and spirited. I think that's what kept them so strong when the Great War began to rage."

Jaren was briefly silent as he continued to recall the infusion of memories from the Spring of Elyon. "Will you teach me how to properly pronounce the words of your language?" he asked.

Hawk laughed quietly, "Aye, would you like to start with the basics right now?" he offered. He pointed to a tree as he said, "orn." He slapped Deakin's rump and said, "roch." He pulled the stopper on his waterskin and poured some of the liquid into his hand. "alu." He continued in this manner until Jaren held up his hand and laughed.

"That's enough, my friend. You have begun an avalanche inside my head. The memories are now coming freely. You said, "Narwa" while everything was happening during my transformation, and I *have* remembered," he said with a smile. "Lle ume quell."

Hawk was astounded at the Father's generosity upon learning that Jaren had acquired this particular knowledge at the Spring of Elyon; for the Elven language was full of nuances and intricate complexities and would have taken months of daily instruction for the young man to have mastered. He was extremely pleased with the progress the young king had made during the afternoon, and was awed at Jaren's speed in assimilating the information bequeathed to him by Elyon. He knew that the Spirit of Elyon was accelerating Jaren's education, and realized that at this rate Jaren would be fully capable of taking on the mantle of monarchy in time for his coronation. Hawk sent up a silent and most heart-felt prayer of worship and thanksgiving to his Master.

Chapter Twenty-One

ELYON'S CHOICE

Tanner and Korthak had been conversing with Balgo about Parth for the last hour. Tanner was intrigued by the little dwarf, and he couldn't believe his naïveté at the deception of the Dragonmasters regarding Balgo's race. Even with his wild imagination, he could not picture this stocky little man wanting to cut up and eat a human being like so much venison. *"All the lies I've been told...all the lies I've believed,"* he shook his head, sick at heart that he had ever wanted to be a part of Volant's Dragon Army.

Tanner had been glancing at the sky from time to time, his military training causing him to be on the alert for the *"sky-borne scourges,"* a name he had given to the Dragonmasters since witnessing the devastation to Tupper's flock and to Stonehaven. He shaded his eyes with his hand as he peered up into the sky once again, and remarked, "That bird seems to be pretty interested in us."

Korthak followed Tanner's gaze. "Prob'ly vultures circling, knowing the wild goose chase this crazy old dwarf is leading us," he whispered.

Tanner laughed, as he chafed his hands to warm them, "Dols, its cold in these mountains."

Korthak nodded as he pulled his hand from under his arm and switched the reins to warm his other hand.

"Aye, but it will be nice and warm where your big friend is going to end up, if he keeps filling your young head with lies and foolishness," Balgo said indignantly, as he shot Korthak a stern look.

Korthak and Tanner stared at one another.

"Yes, I may look old, but the years haven't hurt my hearing a'tall. I know these mountains inside and out, sir, and I'll have you remember that when Balgo promises something, he keeps his word. I said we'd be in Parth within a month, and I didn't mean I'd be draggin' your picked bones with me."

He winked at Tanner. "I would hope, boy that your memory serves you better in the future than this old man's does him."

Tanner laughed, as he watched Korthak smile, and then quickly take on the demeanor of one insulted without warrant. The young man glanced skyward once more and found the bird still flying overhead. He watched as it circled upward, and then folded its wings to drop toward the earth at incredible speed. The little creature reached a certain point, unfolded his wings and hurtled over their heads.

Balgo, his eyes still on the trail, said, "That is a falcon, young man, and my gut is telling me that he is here as a sign to us that there is a great warrior among us; one whom Elyon Himself has chosen."

Korthak's chest puffed up slightly, and he squared his shoulders, sitting somewhat taller in the saddle.

The dwarf merely turned in his saddle to stare at the old man and rolled his eyes with a snort. "Cut the flap off that leather pouch and wrap it around the forepart of *Tanner's* arm," the dwarf instructed as he brought the company to a halt. "We need to eat and our mounts need water, so we might as well stop and give the bird a chance to get acquainted with the lad," he said, sliding off the back of his donkey.

Korthak meekly did as he was told, and as the other three went about watering the mounts, Korthak wrapped the thick but pliable leather around Tanner's arm and tied it off with a length of torn cloth. Balgo, surprisingly satisfied with Korthak's work, led the young man to a rock several paces away from the others. "Oompph," he mumbled, "be right back."

Tanner watched the little man as he rummaged through his saddle pack, and pulled out a small, cloth-bound package. "Caught this coney in a trap last night, so it should suit that little bird's appetite just fine," he said to no one in particular. "Give me your riding glove, half elf, and cut me up some of this meat," he ordered, tossing his package on a large, flat rock.

Hawk handed him one of his gloves, while Jaren began to cut a chunk of the rabbit into small pieces.

Balgo almost fell into a fit of apoplexy when he saw Jaren obeying the order he had just given. "I didn't mean for you to be doing that, Sire."

Jaren whirled around and shot an angry look at the dwarf. "Balgo, these men are all my closest friends. We have been through much hardship together in the past months. It would offend me deeply if you would treat any of them with any less respect than you treat me. I am more than capable of cutting a few bites of meat, and I am very willing and glad to do it. I refuse to be expected, indeed *required*, to sit idly by while others participate in life, simply because I happened to be born into a certain family. Now, if you'll excuse me, I think Tanner's winged friend is waiting."

Without observing the dumfounded faces of his friends, he picked up the dagger and continued cutting the meat.

Hawk turned his face, and raised his eyebrows, *"The King has spoken,"* he thought with amusement.

Korthak caught Hawk's gesture, and began whistling softly as he bent to fill his water skin. Balgo cleared his throat, as his eyes dropped to the ground. He was clearly abashed that he had drawn such a reprimand from Jaren, but his stubborn pride would not allow a straightforward apology. All he could say was, "I do not wish to find disfavor in your eyes, lad. I will try, as best I am able, to remember your words in the future."

Jaren would not look at the dwarf but merely nodded that he had heard him.

He dropped the little pieces of meat into the dwarf's small, calloused hand. Balgo turned, and walked back toward the rock upon which Tanner was sitting. "Now, let's see if I'm right about this bein' a warrior sign."

He told Tanner to put Hawk's glove on his right hand, and instructed him to feed the young bird some of the pieces of meat if he should land on his arm.

"Hold your arm out like this," he said, reaching up to pull Tanner's arm out to the side, "and don't try to touch him until you've fed him all he'll eat." Tanner nodded as Balgo stepped away to join the others.

Hawk sent a thought to Jaren. *"Are you all right, son?"*

Jaren looked at Hawk, and saw the sincerity on his face, and knew he was referring to his outburst with Balgo.

"Yes, I guess. I'm not at all comfortable talking to grown men in such a fashion. But, Dols, I don't want to be treated like a pampered fop."

Jaren paused momentarily, *"Was I too harsh with him?"*

Hawk shrugged, *"A bit. But you were honest and straight spoken and I will guarantee you've earned a very loyal friend in Balgo. He doesn't take too kindly to soft people."* He drank some water from his skin and handed it to Jaren. *"You're behaving more and more like your father, Jaren. I'm proud of you,"* he sent to the Prince. *"Just try to take a moment in situations like this, as Cadan did, to gather your emotions before you reprimand or instruct those who are loyal to you. It is possible and prudent to speak with* compassionate *authority."*

As the words entered his mind, Jaren's face flushed. *"Thank you, Hawk"* was his only reply, as he took a long pull at the water skin.

Tanner chewed on a meatstick Jaren had cut for him, waiting anxiously as the bird grew braver and braver. Each time he swooped down toward the lad, he got a little closer to Tanner's leather-clad arm. Just a short time had passed before the little creature landed on the offered perch. As soon as Tanner lifted his other arm to offer him food, he flew away. Tanner's heart sank as he looked to Balgo for help.

"It's all right, son. Put a piece of the meat on the leather for him to pick at. When he lands again you won't have to move your other hand. It frightens him too much. After he gets used to being so close, he won't be unsettled by your movements."

Tanner nodded, waiting nervously for his new little friend to return. The falcon flew back within minutes, and landed again squarely on Tanner's outstretched arm. The bird began to ravage the piece of meat. When that piece was gone, the little bird began a loud

The Birth of a King

scolding of the lad, stretching his neck to look Tanner squarely in the eye. Slowly he lifted his gloved hand to the bird, offering another morsel. The young falcon fluttered his wings as though to fly away, but instead grabbed at the meat and caught part of Tanner's finger in his sharp beak. It took all of Tanner's self control not to cry out, and Balgo winced, imagining the pain. Even through the riding glove, the little bird had pinched a blood blister on Tanner's finger.

Tanner blamed himself for being clumsy, and determined to be more careful in the future. The young man had already succumbed to that peculiar affection caused when another of Elyon's creatures willingly chooses to adopt a human.

He carefully set the meat between his thumb and forefinger, and turned his hand so the falcon would catch only the meat in his beak. Tanner continued feeding the greedy little beast until the feathers on its chest began to puff out and he thought that surely the bird's small craw would burst.

Only two pieces of meat remained, when the falcon suddenly looked him full in the face, winked one eye, and flew off.

Tanner watched in dismay as the bird soared upwards, spiraled back down, and then flew out of sight.

"He'll be back, lad. You'd better keep a small supply of fresh meat handy in your saddle pack from now on," Balgo said.

Jaren handed Tanner his water skin. "Here, you need to drink something before we get started. I'll hurry and cut some more meat for your new friend."

Tanner had not realized how thirsty he was after eating the salted meatstick. In no time at all he traded Jaren a half-empty water skin for the few pieces of meat.

After riding a short distance Korthak asked Tanner, "What are you going to name such a fine bird, lad?"

Tanner pinched his eyebrows together. He had been too excited about the bird's apparent adoption of him to give thought to naming it. "I don't know. I'll have to think about it a while."

Korthak laughed at him, "Well, don't hurt yourself."

Tanner laughed, and immediately started mulling over names in his mind.

The Birth of a King

They ascended a steep trail that hugged the face of the mountains on the left, and on the right fell sharply into a deep gorge. Jaren felt unusually warm for the coolness of the weather. He admitted to himself how nervous he was for fear of falling into the depths of the valley below. He shook his shoulders, as though to rid himself of the worry that had dogged him since beginning on this narrow track.

They rounded a bend in the trail and discovered that they had nearly reached the top of yet another mountain. Riding the escarpment that topped the northern wall of the Southern Passage was somewhat less strenuous than the ascent had been. They were at least able to ride abreast of one another. However, a stiff, cold wind chilled them to the bone. Their route had taken them high into the eastern arm of the Kroths. Balgo was loathe to spend the extra time making the loop to the northwest and having to backtrack to the east again, but because of the condition of the Southern Passage, there was no other alternative. He prayed to the Father that they would be able to make up the precious lost time in the final race to St. Ramsay's Abbey, away to the south.

Tanner had been watching the sky for hours, waiting for a glimpse of the falcon, and hoping that it would return for another meal.

As the afternoon wore on toward evening, Korthak could see how disheartened his young friend had become. "Don't worry, son, he'll come back to you." He laid his big hand on the young man's back. "He's probably just like you. Fill his belly and he wants to sleep all day." Tanner laughed at the truth in Korthak's barb.

Jaren turned in his saddle to glance at Tanner. "Have you come up with a name for him, yet?"

Tanner nodded his head and smiled, "Yep. I've been thinking about it all afternoon. I'm going to name him Kynon. It means intelligent or wise one...and since he chose me, I figure the name fits him perfectly." He looked at his friends for their reaction, daring them to dispute the reasoning behind his choice.

Korthak opened his mouth for a retort and then decided against it. Instead, he closed his eyes and rolled the name off his tongue, as though testing its merit. "Kynon. That's a perfect name. That little bird knew right away who Elyon's warrior was in this here travelin' circus. Very good, Tanner, I think you've made the perfect choice."

Jaren grinned, "I like it, Tan."

Korthak bellowed out to Balgo and Hawk, "The bird's name is Kynon!"

The old dwarf simply nodded and kept trudging along on his donkey. Hawk sat atop his mount, riding in silence. He was thinking how much Tanner had changed since he'd left the hall. He was highly impressed with the lad's strong character. He chuckled to himself as he considered how so many conflicting emotions and traits could live in one body. Tanner could be sullen one instant, and laughing his fool head off the next. He could be a pillar of strength and steadiness when need required, and then in a trice turn and become as skittish and excitable as a young colt.

Hawk bowed his head, and thanked Elyon for providing Jaren with a friend of Tanner's mettle. He knew that one day Jaren would have the need to draw upon the many qualities that made Tanner so unique. He asked the true God to prepare Tanner with the maturity to live up to such an obligation. Hawk felt assured that his prayer would be answered quickly in the coming months. Tanner was rapidly growing into manhood physically, and he would gain strength of character and wisdom through the harsh experiences that Hawk knew lay ahead for them. It was going to be remarkable to observe the metamorphosis of these two as they both emerged from such a fiery testing. There would be sadness too as they left behind boyhood dreams and fancies for more mature ideas, but Hawk was hoping there would not be any profound losses to endure. In his concern for the two young men, he forgot that Korthak and he would also be going through their own fiery refining - nor did he suspect how soon it would begin.

Chapter Twenty-Two

TOLL OF PASSAGE

A week later, they took a quick lunch and a short rest in the shelter of a small thicket beside a massive boulder. It offered some relief from the cold wind that had continued through the night and into the day. A thin rivulet of icy water fell over the face of the giant stone and was whipped into spray with each gust of wind. They refilled their water skins and allowed the horses to drink from the small pool at the stone's base.

Tanner had not seen Kynon for several days and despite assurances from Balgo, the lad was in a rather melancholy state of mind.

Hours later the constant wind had taken a physical toll on each of the travelers, bringing on an exhaustion increased as well by constant watchfulness, since their route had diminished to a nearly impassable trail cut into the sheer face of the mountainside. Their path was made even more treacherous for the loose shale and stones making it necessary for them to dismount and to cautiously lead their mounts. Solance sat just a hand span above the mountaintop. They had been walking in virtual silence, as each extended all of his concentration on keeping his mount on safe footing. Whenever Jaren lost his battle with self-control and ventured a look over the edge of the trail, his stomach immediately rose to his throat.

"Keep your eyes on the trail, Jaren," Hawk's voice whispered calmly in his mind.

Suddenly, Korthak's mare stumbled. She reared up, tearing the reins from Korthak's strong hands. The huge man tried in vain to grab the leather strips whipping from the horse's halter, but another misstep backward caused the mare's hind leg to go over the edge.

Korthak made several desperate and very dangerous attempts to grab her halter and heave her back onto the thin ledge. The other four stood in shock as the mare pawed at the slippery shale, trying to pull herself back onto the trail. Tanner stood frozen to the side of the mountain, only slightly aware of his own actions to keep his mount from following the mare. He saw her eyes white with fright; her nostrils flared in the exertion and foam dripped from her mouth as she champed at the bit in her frantic struggle for a firm footing. They watched, with sickening horror as the rocks and dirt slid from under the mare's hooves, sucking her over the edge and down the steep slope. She screamed in terror and pain as one of her hind legs snapped and she fell backward and plunged to her death far below.

As the dust settled in the depths of the chasm, silence and disbelief hung over the five companions. Slowly, tears welled in Korthak's eyes at the horror of the death of this close companion of many years.

Balgo was the first to speak. "Let her go, old bear. She didn't suffer long," he whispered.

Hawk could not move past the others on the narrow trail, and so could not come forward to comfort his friend. "Balgo's right, my friend, and the rest of the animals are close to bolting from fear."

Korthak wiped his eyes on the arm of his shirt and turned to slowly follow the dwarf in painful silence.

Jaren was heartbroken for his friend. *"How much more sorrow must he bear, Hawk? When will Yesha allow him to rest in happiness?"* he threw into Hawk's mind in frustration.

"Jaren, I don't know the answers to those questions. I only know that we will see more death. But we do not have to allow our sorrow and loss to turn into despair. Elyon is in complete control at all times, even when tragedy strikes so cruelly. It is not up to us to question His plan, since we can't see things from His long view; nor do we have the wisdom to work things out for the good of all. It is our responsibility in times like these, to trust His wisdom and to rely implicitly upon His unquestioning love for us," the half-elf replied.

Jaren glanced ahead at Korthak's huge back. The older man's steps were slow and cautious. He could see the sag in the broad shoulders, but amazingly, he could hear the older man talking with the Father about his sorrow.

Solance dipped below the mountain, sending a deep grey twilight into the depths of the canyons of the north face; however, as they crested the peak a quarter of an hour later, they were bathed in the blazing light still shining on the south slopes. They stood in awe at the perfect timing of this reminder of Elyon's power and constancy.

Chapter Twenty-Three

MEMORIES SHARED

As they quietly made camp that night, Hawk saw to the horses while Tanner and Jaren started a small, smokeless fire under a small, dense stand of fir trees. Balgo gathered food and pots from his pack, but Korthak would not hear of anyone else preparing their evening meal and went about busying himself with the mundane task.

There was very little conversation during their meal, after which Balgo, Tanner, and Korthak turned to their bedrolls and fell quickly asleep.

Hawk stood and tossed another log on the fire, causing a small cloud of sparks to shoot into the darkness. He refilled Jaren's mug and his own with the remains of the cafla, and stretched out his long legs toward the fire. They sat in thoughtful silence for some time, absently staring into the flames.

"I saw them, Hawk," Jaren spoke so softly that Hawk wasn't sure if he had actually spoken or sent one of his mental messages.

He looked at Jaren in the firelight and could easily see the emotions so plainly evident on the young man's face. "Who, son? Who did you see?"

"My parents...Iain...the others...hundreds," he replied softly.

Hawk looked away and tipped his head back slightly as he breathed deeply of the night air. "Tell me about the Spring of Elyon, Jaren. Tell me everything you can," he softly urged.

The memory of seeing his parents flashed through his mind once more: The beautifully carved features of his mother's face, the happy playfulness in her eyes, the warmth of her smile. He saw his father's ruggedly handsome face, his youthful yet serious eyes and his stubborn jaw, and that same warm smile that Hawk and Korthak shared.

Jaren spent the next hour and more recounting to Hawk many of the details and scenes that had raced before his eyes while he was submerged in the Spring of Elyon. Hawk sat in wonder as he listened to the young man's narrative. He had known what some of the effects of Jaren's transformation would be, but he had not imagined that Elyon would bestow a gift as priceless as the memories and knowledge of Jaren's predecessors.

Hawk beamed a smile at Jaren, "The Father is always so much more generous than we ever expect Him to be. I truly believe He delights in surprising us. What a treasure you have been given, my young friend."

Jaren nodded around a yawn. "Yes. I've been mentally fingering the wealth of this treasure ever since it was given to me. It's staggering."

Suddenly the fatigue and emotional stress of the day seemed to roll in upon him. He rose and headed for his bedroll. "I'm going to turn in. My eyes feel like they've been stuffed with sand. Good night, Hawk."

Hawk tossed the last of the cafla from his cold cup into the fire. He heard Jaren whisper, "Thank you for telling me about my parents last week."

Hawk smiled at the young man. "It was my pleasure, Jaren. It's your history, part of who you are. It is your right to know about them. They were extraordinary people. Thank you for telling me about the Spring of Elyon."

Chapter Twenty-Four

FALLEN FRIEND

The next morning, Jaren watched with pride and a deepening appreciation for his friend, as Tanner handed his tack to Korthak. He smiled as he overheard Tanner's excuse to the older man about the need to speak with Jaren privately, and asking him to saddle the stallion. With much thought for Korthak's pride, Tanner had just offered his "adopted father" the use of his only and most prized possession. Korthak, fully aware of the young man's intention, smiled his thanks and began saddling the proud stallion.

The old fears that Jaren had pondered back in Reeban, regarding the possibility of Tanner's need to feed his ego by intimidating others, disappeared entirely in that one quiet, generous deed. As Tanner approached him, Jaren feigned ignorance of the whole episode, leaning over the opposite side of his mount, ostensibly to check his stirrup.

"Jaren, would you mind hauling my hide around with you until we get to Parth?" he questioned softly.

Offering him a hand up, Jaren smiled broadly, "No, Tan, I would consider it an honor."

A quiet party set out from camp as Balgo led them deeper and deeper into the stark beauty of the Kroths. Balgo was eager to enter the Glamorgan Mines in order to find relief from the icy wind and blinding shafts of light reflecting off the tall peaks of obsidian as the mid-morning sun blasted their glassy crags.

Jaren called for a short halt, and said to Tanner, "I'll let you take the saddle for a while. Maybe you'll learn something useful by guiding a real horse for a while instead of that flea-bitten nag you usually have under you."

Tanner glared at his friend, barely concealing a smile. "Flea-bitten nag, huh? Me, learn something from a horse that's been used to your mishandling? Good joke, Jaren. But I think I'll take you up on it, anyway. Try to keep awake and just maybe we can continue the lessons that I've been trying to get through your thick skull for years."

Jaren smiled broadly as he remembered Tanner's awkward reticence toward him at the Spring of Elyon. Jaren had feared their friendship might not survive his transformation from an orphaned commoner to a prince with the ancient Power. He chuckled softly, thinking with grateful relief, *"Well, that was a short lived problem. Tan is back to treating me just like he always has."*

Near midday, as they rode through a narrow ribbon of a ravine, the company heard Kynon screeching loudly overhead. He dived at the party several times. The horses grew highly agitated and skittish, the whites of their eyes revealing their alarm. Balgo's donkey began kicking wildly and set up a loud braying that pierced the eerie silence of the ravine. There was no other bird sound, no rustling of unseen creatures scurrying through the dry brush. Several small rocks tumbled down the western wall of the ravine and onto the trail.

Balgo's forceful command reverberated off the walls of rock and stabbed into their minds. "Move it!" the dwarf roared.

He whipped his donkey on its haunches and the little animal bolted down the trail. The riders sped forward, following the dwarf. Increasing numbers of pebbles and rocks came sliding and bouncing down the sheer slope. A tremor shook the trail as the deafening cracking and shifting of stone echoed overhead; then huge slabs of earth moved, sending choking dust and boulders down around them.

Jaren cried out as he felt a searing pain tear down the length of his back. Tanner turned to see his friend's ashen, pain-filled face, but

The Birth of a King

could not give him aid, having to quickly turn his attention back to their panic-stricken mount.

As they raced forward, Jaren heard the command from Hawk in his mind. *"Go, son! Go!"* He could not see the trail over Tanner's shoulder. He prayed to Elyon that they would not have come this far just to die in the wilderness under a massive rockslide.

Tanner's voice was barely heard above the roar, "Look, a cave!" He pointed to a dark shadow in the dust just yards ahead.

Jaren could no longer see Korthak or Balgo, but he finally could just make out the dark patch in the side of the eastern wall. He painfully turned to see if Hawk was still following as they bolted for the cave. What he glimpsed through the choking dust filled him with alarm. Hawk's horse was heavily splattered with blood, and the foam flying from the beast's nostrils was dyed crimson. Hawk was slumped in the saddle.

It took mere seconds to reach the cave entrance, and Tanner reined in hard as he ducked into the darkness. The cave echoed and magnified the deafening rumble as the mountainside continued to give way. Time seemed suspended. Seconds became hours as they waited anxiously for Hawk to enter the cave. At last a shadow blocked the murky beam of light as both Jaren and Tanner jumped from their mount and raced to the inert figure slumped in the saddle.

"Hawk!" Jaren screamed as he and Tanner eased the half-elf's limp body gently from the horse.

Suddenly, two strong arms lifted Hawk from their hands as Korthak carried his friend away from the entrance and deeper into the cave.

"Bring the horses, lads, and follow me," Balgo directed tersely.

As the two young men obeyed, it became clear that this was not a cave, but the mouth of a tunnel. They had walked only a short distance before they heard Balgo striking flint to stone. In moments, the dwarf had a torch blazing. He led them further into the tunnel to a small chamber where he lit several more torches seating them into sconces on the stone walls.

"Tanner, gather some wood for a fire," Balgo said, nodding toward a wall with his head. "Take one of those torches with you.

There should be a nice stack of dry stuff just beyond the first bend down the corridor on the right."

Jaren was kneeling over Hawk, wholly absorbed in his concern for his friend. He was no longer aware of the pain of his own injury. Balgo, standing behind him, saw the large tear on the back of Jaren's shirt, and the deep crimson stain surrounding it. He surmised that a good-sized rock had scraped its way down Jaren's back, but he was not overly concerned about the lad, since he seemed to be in no pain. He would give it some attention later to avoid infection.

Balgo looked past Jaren and watched as Korthak ripped away the shredded and bloody sleeve of Hawk's shirt. The burly hands were tender as they dabbed at the bloody pulp that was the elf's muscular arm. He felt along the bone, looking for breaks, and gave Balgo a reassuring look after finding the arm whole.

Korthak moved to Hawk's head and found three small cuts on the top of as many lumps on the elf's scalp - no serious problems there. Hawk had a nasty cut at the outer edge of his left eyebrow. A few stitches would take care of that.

As Korthak tore away the blood-spattered tunic from Hawk's chest, Balgo saw the large, purplish-red splotch over the Elf's ribs. He heard Korthak suck in air between clenched teeth as he saw the unexpected seriousness of his friend's wounds. The dwarf shot a glance at the old warrior, warning him not to alert the young men to the elf's condition.

He immediately stepped around Jaren and knelt beside Hawk. His practiced fingers gingerly probed the quickly darkening area and Hawk groaned in pain, even in his unconsciousness. Balgo knew instantly that several of his ribs were broken. He quietly said to Korthak, "I'll need your help in binding him up, old bear." Korthak nodded stoically.

When Balgo returned from his pack with yards of binding cloths, he saw that the deep purple discoloration was spreading rapidly over Hawk's left side and was already creeping under his arm and toward his back.

Korthak had also seen, and had recognized it as a certain sign of internal bleeding. The old dwarf reluctantly acknowledged to himself that at least one of Hawk's broken ribs had pierced either a lung or a large blood vessel, or quite possibly his heart.

Balgo noted that Hawk's stomach was beginning to distend. He lightly pressed it with his fingertips, feeling the growing hardness under the skin, and knew with certainty that Hawk's abdomen was rapidly filling with blood. "We need to sit him up, Korthak," the dwarf said with quiet urgency.

Balgo and the old warrior gently raised their unconscious friend to a sitting position, trying to ease his struggle for breath as the blood gave less and less room for the lungs to expand. The half-elf's face turned deathly pale. That Hawk's death was imminent was without question. Balgo reached into his pack again and drew out a tiny earthenware bottle. He pulled out the cork and tipped the bottle slowly at the corner of Hawk's mouth, allowing only small amounts of the green fluid to drop into his throat at a time.

"That should ease his pain somewhat," Balgo said with a smile for the benefit of the two lads who had been watching with growing panic.

"The lads will know soon enough. No sense bringing them added alarm beforehand," the dwarf thought with grim resolve.

However, his efforts were for naught as Hawk coughed and bright red foam shot from between his lips.

Tanner stood, frozen in fear, his arms still clutching his load of firewood. The sight brought back memories of his father's painful death - memories of which he had never been aware, but that were at this moment so vivid as to be almost tangible. He held his breath, willing Hawk to continue breathing.

When Jaren saw the blood, he yelled, "What is it? He's going to be alright, isn't he? Balgo? Korthak?"

The two older men could not speak, being too overcome with sorrow and angry frustration at their inability to help their dying friend.

"No!" Jaren screamed, "He can't be dying!" He grabbed Korthak's shirt and shook the man with all of his strength. "You can't let him die, Korthak, he's your friend!" He turned to Balgo, "Do something!" he raged.

He turned his fevered eyes back to Hawk and saw the blood trickling from the side of his mouth. "Hawk! Hawk!" The words were torn from the very fabric of Jaren's soul, as he reached to wipe away the blood from the face of his friend.

Finally, Korthak found his voice and said with difficulty, "Jaren...son, Hawk is suffering terribly. You wouldn't want to prolong his pain when there is no hope, would you? The best any of us can do for him now is to pray to Elyon to let him go quickly to end his pain."

Jaren opened his mouth to rebel. Then, seeing the pain in Korthak's eyes, he relented and began with trance-like movements to once more wipe away the blood from Hawk's mouth before bowing his head to pray.

Tanner gently laid down his load of wood and came to join the others kneeling around their fallen friend and leader. They began praying silently, their throats too constricted with sorrow for speech. In the next few minutes, Hawk's shallow breathing came less often until his chest finally lay still.

A primal wail was heard far into the unlit reaches of the tunnel. "No-o-o!"

Chapter Twenty-Five

SCRYING AND FAILING

Scrying was one of the less demanding spells, as it required nothing more than clearing one's mind of distractions and focusing solely on the person or persons one wished to locate. Volant was exceptional at compartmentalizing his thoughts, so this was a relatively simple process for him. He smiled, recalling that the root meaning for scrying was "perceiving something which is concealed." He fully expected within the next few moments to know precisely where his enemy was and what he was doing. He fervently hoped that the would-be-king and his band of rebels were still in hiding. He shrank from the possibility that they could, at that moment, be amassing troops somewhere beyond sight of his dragonless, earth-bound watchers.

The dragons were still not allowing the riders to mount and fly, and the Lucian priests had not yet found the spell components needed to force the compliance of the beasts to get his troops back into the air. He was desperate for information from the reaches of Kinthoria beyond the present locations of the cavalry scouts dispatched the day the dragon rebellion began. He had even gone so far as to kill two of his riders, thereby causing the death of their dragons as well, in the hopes of frightening the remaining dragons into submission. This ill-conceived plan had achieved nothing but further chaos, the din of increased keening and wailing from the enormous beasts, and the widening of the chasm between the dragons and riders.

The Birth of a King

After taking several deep breaths and clearing his mind, Volant slowly released the air from his lungs. He had not eaten for the past twelve hours, and had imposed silence upon himself since sunset. He focused his thoughts as he gazed at the reflective surface of the oil in a large, polished obsidian bowl. The bowl sat upon a rich, black velvet cloth; a solitary candle completed his chosen implements, its occasional flickering, in some obscure sense, assisting his focus on the image in his mind.

As he stared at the dark, oily surface, a purple mist began to form and swirl along the edges of the bowl. He pressed his mind even more, coaxing his memories of King Cadan into sharp focus. He had no idea what image the Cathain heir would hold, but trusted that the Power that was now surging through the young upstart could be located by using the pronounced physical traits of the deposed royal family. Galchobar had assured him that several Lucian priests were performing this same ritual on an hourly basis with no luck in detecting the despicable and impudent whelp. More deep breaths, and Volant was now in control of the scrying channel; his eyes deeply focused on the images swirling about on the surface of the oil. Soon, he saw a crackling fire, and sensed confusion and then urgency rising within someone. He felt rather than saw a tremendously bright light. Exhilarated as he neared the edge of the ancient Power that had for centuries infused the Cathain line, he allowed himself to slip deeper into the realm between the material and spirit worlds.

Suddenly, he was slammed into the wall behind his stool. His hands flew to his temples as excruciating pain shot through his head. The air was knocked from his lungs and he could not breathe from the pressure on his body. There were bright dazzling lights swirling around his peripheral vision and he knew he was about to lose consciousness.

"Dragh! Begone, spirit!" he commanded in his mind, only to have the force increased. He quickly broke contact with the visions he had been casting and the pressure was removed. He forced himself to pull air into his lungs. He frantically fought against slipping into the blackness summoning him from all sides, but the battle was lost

The Birth of a King

nearly before it had begun. His eyelids dropped and he tumbled down into the dark abyss of unconsciousness.

While their Emperor lay insensible, Sirtar and Bendor were having a heated discussion just outside of the hatching chamber.

"Need I remind you Colonel, that *your* dragon was one of the ones carrying off the eggs?" Bendor hissed at his adversary.

"You watch your mouth, boy, or I won't care how much favor you have with the Emperor, I will relish tearing your heart out."

Bendor's face flushed. "Boy? Your mind must be withered from all the ale you soak yourself in every night, Sirtar." He was inches from the Colonel's face. "I am the Red Flight Leader, and my men and I have outclassed you and your flight in almost every single military exercise we have had in the past three years. So tell me; how does it feel to be whipped by a *boy*."

He was screaming at his superior officer and he knew he was treading a dangerous line; that it would not take much more to push the Colonel over the edge. But the past few weeks had taken their toll and he would stand no more of the insolent remarks and blatant lies Sirtar was spreading to anyone who would listen. He knew the Colonel was attempting to divert the anger and shame his dragon had caused by Yturi's involvement with removing the dragon eggs, even though Volant's own dragon had participated in the same episode.

Sirtar grabbed the young man's throat in a strangle hold. Bendor's hands quickly circled the older man's wrists, and he desperately tried to break Sirtar's vise-like grip.

The face that was inches from Bendor's appeared no longer human. Insanity had begun to extend its long fingers into Sirtar's mind and his flesh was mottled purple and red. The eyes that glared at him in fury were filled with a profound, wild hatred. Bendor was acutely aware of his failing senses, and realized he had precious few seconds to save himself before he blacked out.

He released Sirtar's wrists and with lightening speed, struck the muscles running along the sides of the Colonel's neck with the outside of his forearms. Bendor knew that the force of his blows would penetrate Sirtar's muscles, causing extreme pain and overloading his senses, temporarily stunning the crazed man. He knew his attempt was successful when Sirtar's hands slipped from his neck and the giant collapsed into a screaming heap on the ground.

Bendor slid down the corridor wall, too weak to stand. He gulped in great breaths of air as he felt for any damage to his throat. The young man inched away from his writhing opponent and fell into a fit of coughing. His throat was on fire, and his head was pounding so powerfully that a burst of light accompanied each heartbeat. He knew he must escape before Sirtar regained the ability to move. The Colonel was attempting to sit up, while cursing loudly with each failure to do so; spittle flew from his mouth at his exertion and the force of his tirade.

Bendor slowly pulled himself to a stand, and using the wall for support, moved down the corridor and out into the pre-dawn darkness of an overcast day. He went as quickly as possible to his quarters and gathered what belongings he could carry, knowing he would not return any day in the foreseeable future. He did not intend to purposely leave himself exposed to attempts of murder by Sirtar or his men.

He knew that Sirtar would not bring him up on charges for insubordination or for striking his superior officer. The Colonel always enjoyed meting out his own type of justice and punishment upon his juniors. No, Sirtar would definitely want any news of this incident kept completely off the records and certainly away from Volant. The outcome of this confrontation was a bitter and brutal blow to the Colonel's pride. Bendor was confident that he would never again be out of harm's way as long as the Blue Flight Leader lived.

Chapter Twenty-Six

A HEALER-KING

In his overwhelming sorrow, Jaren silently cried out to his new Father. He did not know anything more to do than to plead for help: Help for the friends Hawk was leaving behind and for his family as they learned of their loss. Help for himself, as he sensed that he would be responsible to take up the mantle of leadership without knowing even the first step to take. Finally, he prayed for his people, and healing for the very earth itself from the damage of the dragons. The more he prayed with such selflessness, the more he sensed a calm touching the outer edges of his mind. He felt the Presence that had filled the glade by the Spring of Elyon as it began once again to settle upon his spirit. Finally, it washed over him in a great tide of peace; an unaccountable confidence spread in his heart. Once more that indefinable energy of the glade infused his body. He began to feel the Power grow inside him until his body tingled, and the hairs on the back of his head stood on end. Once again, he could sense even the blood pulsing through his veins. He instinctively knew that the Spirit of Elyon was working in him.

The Presence of Yesha began to direct his formerly chaotic thoughts. Suddenly, and to his utter surprise, he leaned forward and placed his hands firmly on Hawk's still chest.

Korthak reached for his hands, thinking the lad was overwrought with sorrow. But Jaren's firm, steady voice stopped him short.

"No, my friend, it is not yet the time of your home going. You must return and walk with us a while longer. The purpose of your

The Birth of a King

life is not yet fulfilled." Jaren spoke the words with a strength and authority that would brook no argument or denial, even from the other side of death.

The others stared, open-mouthed at the young prince. His face seemed to shine from within. Then, they too began to sense the Power of the Presence.

"Hawk, Hawk, come back," he quietly commanded.

Hawk was following a brilliant light, relieved to be free of the piercing pain that had been his entire world just a heart beat before. His spirit was light and he was consumed with joy at the anticipation of seeing his Father and Yesha at last.

"Hawk!" He heard someone calling. *"Come back!"*

He hesitated. He did not want to go back. There was pain, and sorrow back there. He was glad to be rid of the weight of it. He wanted to let someone else take up the burden now that he had been able to lay it down.

"Hawk," the voice was insistent.

No. He wanted to follow the light to his Master. But the light ahead was suddenly diminishing, and sadly, he knew that the Master would not allow him to deny that call. "Master," he pleaded, reaching a hand forward.

"Do not fear, my son. You always have the strength for this burden in the Power of My Spirit within you. Go...return. We will have eternity together," Yesha said with tender authority.

In resignation, Hawk turned toward that commanding voice in the darkness behind.

Immediately he felt the pressure of his body surround his soul and spirit once more. Crushing pain seared through his consciousness, pushing aside all thought and sensibility. For Hawk the world became once again only darkness and pain.

The four startled companions watched as Hawk's body arched, gulping a deep breath into lungs that had been still for long minutes. He coughed deeply and repeatedly as the blood that had filled his lungs came bursting from his mouth.

Finally he moaned loudly, *"Shalafi."*

His companions looked on in wonder as new skin formed to cover the pulpy mass of raw flesh that was the lower portion of Hawk's arm. Not a sign of the wound remained. Korthak reached up, haltingly, and felt Hawk's scalp. No trace of lumps or cuts was found, nor was there any longer a gash above his left eye.

"Look," Balgo whispered, pointing to Hawk's chest. The blackish-purple that had spread across the elf's chest quickly faded to a mere reddish blush and then disappeared entirely.

Minutes later, to their complete astonishment, the elf's eyes opened and he looked at each one of his friends in turn, coming to rest at last upon Jaren. There was a look of wonder and awe in his eyes, mingled with profound regard.

"*Aaye, nan mankoi bru amin n alaquel, Aran?*" he whispered weakly.

Jaren smiled and took Hawk's hand in both of his own. "Yesha said it was not the time, my friend. I am not yet ready to do without my mentor. There is still much that I must learn from you. I need your wisdom and your friendship for many years yet to come." Jaren smiled broadly, "Apparently Elyon's Spirit expects me to be a slow learner."

"I am ever at your service, my Lord," Hawk said in resignation, as his eyes closed in sleep.

The three companions stared at Jaren as one. Amazement, awe, and apprehension touched each of their faces in rapid confusion.

Jaren's expression mirrored theirs. "Well, what are all of you looking at? The Father told me to call him back and that's what I did. That's *all* I did."

As the young prince looked at the fixed expressions on the faces of his friends, he knew he had a growing problem that needed immediate attention.

"Look. Don't get any strange ideas in your heads that I had anything to do with what happened here. I am just as stunned as you are. The will and the Presence of our Father are the reasons this happened. I'm telling you it was the one true God's Power that did this."

Finally, Korthak voiced what the others had been thinking, "But, Jaren...uh, Sire. Your face was glowing."

Jaren's hands shot up to his face. "It was? I thought I felt awfully warm. And quit calling me Sire. I'm just me."

It was Balgo who finally offered a solution to the riddle of Jaren's strange nimbus. "It is said that long ago, when people walked with Elyon more closely, the light from His Presence would sometimes reflect from their faces. It was a radiant light. There are records of such occurrences in the Word. The elves call it '*rolyn*.'"

"But Balgo, I've just become acquainted with Elyon. I really know very little about Him. Why would He decide to make me glow and give the gift of healing through my hands?"

"Because, Si...uh, Jaren, you are the chosen King. You are the one to whom He has *chosen* to give the Power. It's as simple as that. We knew you would receive the Power. We just didn't know how strong it was going to be or what direction it would take."

He smiled and poked Korthak in the ribs with his elbow. "Ha!" he croaked, jumping and capering all over the small cavern. "We've got a Healer King. A Healer! Isn't Elyon's wisdom incredible? At a time when Kinthoria most desperately needs healing, He sends a Healer King."

Korthak was beaming. He took another lingering look at his closest friend, making sure that the half-elf was sleeping soundly. "Yes, Balgo, Elyon is good. But I'm going to need some of that healing for myself if I don't get off these sore old knees of mine. Someone help me up," he said, greatly exaggerating his pain with much loud groaning and limping.

"Now, lads, let me take a look at you," Balgo said in a no-nonsense manner. He told Tanner to kneel and quickly examined him for any severe injuries. "A few scratches and such, but nothing serious, thanks be to Yesha."

The old dwarf patted him on the back. "We'll get some salve on those cuts in short order."

When he finished tending to Tanner, Balgo turned to Jaren, "And now I think it's time I saw to your back," Balgo said with the tone of Field Commander. The old dwarf pulled the lad closer to one of the torches and told him to remove his tunic. The cloth had dried in several places on the wound and he winced in pain as the tunic pulled away. He was quick enough only to hold back the end of a

The Birth of a King

sudden shout. The muscles in his back tightened in rebellion against this added pain to the torn skin.

Balgo took one look at the long, jagged gash and turned to Korthak. "Hand me that water skin and the salve and a strip of that linen, old bear," he ordered, his anger at his own negligence plainly heard in his tone.

Korthak caught the edge in Balgo's voice and looked at him. His eyes went to Jaren's back. He immediately berated himself for not having looked to the lad's safety, but Jaren had been standing and moving, while Hawk had been down and obviously dying.

Suddenly he realized that Jaren had not once complained about the pain that such a wound should be causing. Korthak wondered if Jaren had even been aware of his injury until Hawk was out of danger. It was then that Hawk's words echoed in his mind: "A part of Cadan's blessing in the ritual of the Dragon Stigmata was the bestowal of a strong love for the people, and a consuming desire to serve them." At that moment Korthak came to understand the full meaning of those words. Korthak had witnessed Elyon's supreme love as it had passed through Jaren to Hawk. He had seen tangible evidence of that love in the complete devotion offered selflessly by this Cathain heir to one of his subjects. Korthak was stunned by this revelation. To have such a King! Now he understood Hawk's refusal to hear any negative council when the time came to search for the hidden heir. The loss to Kinthoria would have been unthinkable.

Once he had regained his composure, he watched as Balgo poured water over the torn flesh; a crimson cascade spilled down the young man's muscular back. Jaren winced again and fought the urge to stand. "Dols, Balgo, it's just a scratch and you're making it feel as if some renegade dwarf has landed an axe in the middle of my back." He tried to laugh, but had to force down another cry of pain as Balgo scrubbed as gently as possible on the open wound.

In an attempt to divert Jaren's mind from the pain, Korthak said, "If a fool dwarf ever so much as put a scratch on you, I'd cleave him in two like a melon." Balgo, in need of some relief from the tension of causing Jaren so much pain, decided to take the bait and to defend his slandered race. "You'd have to catch him first, mighty oak."

They all chuckled at the good-natured bantering between the two old friends, unaware that Hawk had wakened just long enough to hear their remarks and to smile to himself. He sent a quick prayer of thankfulness to Elyon before slipping quietly back into a deep slumber.

Balgo took great care, gently smearing a numbing salve on Jaren's back.

"Tanner and Korthak, why don't we speed things up so we can eat and get some rest? The horses will need some inspection and attention to their wounds...especially Hawk's. Deakin had blood coming from his nostrils the last time I saw him. When you finish with them, look in my saddlebags for something we can eat," the dwarf directed.

As the two left the small chamber, Balgo quickly removed a needle with a long length of horsehair from his pouch. He deftly made multiple stitches at various places on Jaren's numbed back, and then, carefully pressing the flesh together on the less deep areas, he made just enough stitches to hold the skin together and bound it as tightly as possible. He smiled at his good timing, as Tanner and Korthak returned with the evening meal tucked under their arms.

"The horses took a pretty good pounding. They'll most likely be a little tender for a couple of days. Thank goodness Tanner's black "treasure" won't have any scars. It would be a shame to have to trade him off for another expensive piece of horseflesh," Korthak teased, looking at Tanner with a smile.

Tanner decided to let Korthak off the hook for once and came to inspect Jaren's back. "Looks like you got that 'little scratch' covered up pretty nicely, Balgo."

The dwarf smiled, "Well, it was a pretty routine patch job. I only had to sew him up from stem to stern," he said carelessly. Tanner laughed, never guessing the truth in the dwarf's words.

Balgo could see that the wound was still seeping, but at least it was clean and bound, and with care it would not cause Jaren too much discomfort. It would heal without complication, although he would always carry a couple of good-sized scars.

The little man scratched his head and smiled at the irony that Hawk, having died from his wounds, would bear no scars, while

Jaren, Yesha's instrument for his healing and renewed life, would bear his the rest of his life.

"Deakin took a pretty hard knock on his nose…has a pretty deep cut right on the bridge of it," Tanner reported. "He had some other cuts, too. That's where all the blood came from, but they weren't that deep. He has a nasty swelling on his right hindquarter again, but other than being stiff for a while, he should be fine. Pretty soon that poor beast is going to think that being lame is just a normal part of life. Of course, Balgo's donkey is too cantankerous already, so it looks like Elyon protected him from everything but fear," he chuckled.

"Aye, you're probably right, there. Thanks for taking care of the beasties," Balgo replied. "I think the young master here is patched up pretty well, too, but I have a sneaking suspicion that when Hawk wakes up he will be feeling a whole lot better than Jaren. The Spirit of Yesha is much better at this healing business than I am."

Jaren looked at Tanner sheepishly, "It's only a graze, but I think Balgo was trying to work through a whole year of Healers' academy on me."

Tanner laughed at Balgo's discomfiture, but upon glancing at Jaren's back a second time, he saw that the wound was already seeping through the dressing. He examined Jaren's discarded tunic with studied nonchalance. Suddenly, he wasn't so sure that Balgo had been joking about sewing his friend back together. He shot a glance at the little dwarf, and caught the fleeting warning in his steely eyes.

"Well, I think I spied some extra tunics in one of our illustrious leader's saddle packs," Tanner said with much more flippancy than he was feeling at the moment. He gestured for Jaren to follow him, "Let's see if we can find one that will drape decently over that skinny bag of bones you call a body."

Jaren laughed and picked up one of the sticks for the fire, threatening to use it on Tanner. The dark-haired youth dodged away and ran off toward the horses.

"You'd better hope I don't catch you, Tanner MacKechnie. I'll show you what this bag of bones can do to an overgrown child," Jaren shouted as he walked quickly, but gingerly after his friend.

The Birth of a King

Balgo placed a cookpot over the fire and started preparing a medicinal broth. It would ease their aching muscles and allow each of them a much needed, undisturbed sleep. He was careful not to touch the small cakes of bread that Korthak had placed on stones to bake at the edge of the fire.

Korthak glanced over his shoulder to make certain that neither Jaren nor Tanner could overhear and softly said to Balgo, "That was a wicked gash on the lad's back. Why didn't he say anything?"

Balgo shrugged. "I dunno. Could be Yesha was having him focus so much on the healing of Hawk that he took no notice of his own injuries."

Korthak stirred the fire a bit. "I'm feelin' a wee bit apprehensive over this whole thing, though. I mean, what if it had been more serious and he hadn't said anything and…" he stopped, unable to speak the words. "Hawk would have had my hide for not looking after that young man."

Balgo sprinkled some powder from a small packet into the cook pot and stirred it in. The dwarf hurried about his task, knowing that it would take him some time to get his stubborn half-elf friend to down a cup of the pottage.

"Shoosh with those thoughts, my friend. Elyon had the entire situation in His hands. You need not worry yourself over it."

When the young men returned, Jaren was wearing a tunic of Hawk's that, surprisingly, did very little "draping" over Jaren's rapidly maturing body.

The battered companions sat down to a meal of cheese, hot bread and Balgo's broth, much improved from Hawk's portion by Korthak's addition of several tasty ingredients. Jaren glanced across the fire at Korthak's haggard-looking face. "Were you able to get some of this broth down Hawk? I know he was already sleeping pretty soundly."

The older man gave no indication that he had even heard Jaren speak.

"Korthak?" Jaren spoke louder.

"Hmm? I'm sorry, Jaren, did you say something?"

"How is Hawk? Did you get any broth down him?" Jaren asked again.

The Birth of a King

Korthak smiled warmly. "He is doing just fine; probably better than all of the rest of us put together. Balgo threatened him with *certain* death this time if he didn't drink at least one cup. It was a nasty sight, and you wouldn't want to have seen it, but the green-eyed monster finally did down a cup of it."

Jaren chuckled, and then became serious once more. "Another question, then, my friend."

Korthak raised his eyes to the young man's. He could see in those eyes the reason that Elyon had chosen Jaren to be King, and he remembered the profound love he had witnessed only a short while ago.

"Are you all right?" The young man asked with quiet concern.

The question surprised Korthak. He had not expected Jaren to have even been mindful of the loss of his horse, after the near catastrophe of losing Hawk. He smiled and rubbed his eyes. "Yes, lad, I'm all right. I think it's just plain weariness that has all of us a little stoop-shouldered right now. Thank you for asking," he said softly, and then he rose to return to Hawk's side.

Jaren carefully rose and followed the huge man. He looked down at Hawk and smiled. He thanked Yesha for the thousandth time for giving him back to them. Then, satisfied that he was sleeping peacefully, he sat down beside him and prepared for Balgo's broth to lull him into a deep sleep.

"Are you well, son?" the words slipped softly into Jaren's mind. Jaren started just slightly at Hawk's unexpected presence. He closed his eyes. Tears of joy and exhaustion squeezed themselves from beneath his eyelids and trickled down the sides of his face.

The now-familiar touch and sound of Hawk's voice in his mind were such a welcome surprise that it wrenched his heart with unspeakable happiness. He drew in a deep breath and held it, trying to master his emotions. *"I'm fine, Hawk. I'm just a little tired. Balgo has tended the scratch on my back and I believe has added something into his broth to put us all to sleep."* He paused for a moment. *"Hawk,"* he sent with a son's love, *"It's good to have you back."*

A gentle smile crossed Hawk's face, as he understood in that moment that at least one reason the Master had sent him back was to be a mentor and father to a King.

"Hawk?" Jaren sent again.

"Yes...son."

"I was so scared for a while. I don't know what happened to my faith."

"We were all afraid, Jaren. When things like this happen, we don't have the opportunity for the normal, calm procedure of wading through the facts to gain the information we need to reinforce our faith. So we begin to question Elyon's thinking, and that frightens us. We just need to remember that He is always with us, working every detail out according to His will. Your faith was fine. Don't ever doubt it. Remember, Elyon always sees so much more in us than we do in ourselves."

Jaren fell silent and watched as Hawk finally succumbed to sleep. He glanced at Korthak and saw that he, too, had been unable to resist the effects of Balgo's broth. He thought he would say good night to Tanner and Balgo, but he blinked his eyes once and was suddenly sleeping.

Chapter Twenty-Seven

THE GLAMORGAN MINES

Two hours before the first rays of dawn would touch the peaks outside, the company awoke to stiff and aching muscles. Everyone, that is, except Hawk.

The four companions watched with growing envy as their industrious leader whistled and bounced from one task to another; building up the fire, squeezing his bedroll into a tiny, little package to be tied behind his saddle, making a pot of cafla.

It was obvious to the four observers that when Elyon does a miracle, He does it exceedingly well, and with infinite thoroughness.

Hawk looked at them with a large smile, then snapped his fingers and said, "Oh, I almost forgot." He quickly disappeared, returning shortly with his arms full of discarded winding cloth.

He scowled at the dwarf. "Really, Balgo, you're losing your touch. Is this *all* you were planning to bind around my chest? Or was this to shroud my body for burial?"

Balgo glared at Jaren. "Was it really necessary to bring him back? I mean, are you sure you didn't get your messages mixed?"

Jaren grinned, "Of course it was necessary. What would we do for comic relief on this journey if we didn't have the second half of Korthak's team?"

The company enjoyed a hearty laugh, each one feeling enormous comfort in having passed through the last two days with everyone alive and whole.

As Jaren rose from his bedroll, he winced and a gasp of pain escaped his lips. Balgo was immediately at his side, inspecting the bandage on the youth's back. "Hmmm. We're going to have to dress this again before we set out. Tanner, get some water boiling, and Hawk, since you're feeling so well this morning, you can begin tearing some strips of cloth for the bandage."

"How long will it take us to get through this tunnel?" Tanner asked Balgo as the dwarf attended to Jaren.

"This tunnel is one of the longest in the Norgrund Ehrak tunnel system that runs through these mountains. We won't see Solance again for about ten days," Balgo said absently as he inspected the stitches on some of Jaren's deeper wounds.

"I hope Kynon will be alright, and that he'll come back to me when we're outside again," Tanner worried.

"Tanner, that bird is still young, but he didn't hatch yesterday. He was caring for himself for several months before he spied you on the trail. He'll be just fine; and since it was Elyon who made Kynon choose you I doubt He'll let him forget you," Balgo responded.

In short order, Jaren's wound was cleaned, coated with the numbing salve, and rebound, much to the lad's relief. Hawk, on the other hand, was distressed at not having been told the extent of Jaren's injuries. He didn't say a word, but Balgo and Korthak saw the displeasure written on his face. However, minutes later the half-elf had decided to let the matter go, as he trusted Balgo's healing abilities implicitly and knew that Elyon would not allow anything to irreparably harm Jaren.

They were breaking their fast near the fire when Jaren shivered, rubbed his hand across his forehead and lightly moaned. He had sensed this intrusion into his awareness on several occasions since leaving the Spring of Elyon, but had been unable to identify the source. He had spoken of it to Hawk, wondering if it had something to do with the constant *presence* of the dragons in his mind. But he had become familiar enough with their nearness to know the dragons were not responsible.

Hawk noticed his apparent discomfort. "What's the matter, Jaren?" he said stepping toward the young prince. His eye caught

The Birth of a King

a glimmer in Jaren's cup and he saw its surface begin to alter. The half-elf immediately recognized the threat.

"Jaren, call upon Elyon for help! Someone is trying to scry you." He commanded.

The young man had obeyed at once and suddenly knew he was to cover the cup with his tingling hand. He felt the power of Elyon moving in him and wondered what his Master was doing. The true God had been watching Volant's defiant actions against His laws and, upon Jaren's request released but the slightest flicker of His power toward the Dragonmaster.

Jaren felt the power rush out of his body. He hoped the person had not been killed, but prayed that Elyon's action had been forceful enough to deter whoever it was from future attempts at using sorcery.

Jaren was so new in this close relationship with Elyon, and with the Power of His Spirit that he was still in the process of comprehending the scope of what was available to him and how Elyon would work in his life. Discerning his new sensitivities would be a long process as he learned from experience and from communicating with the one true God.

"Hawk, who else but Elyon and the dragons would be able to touch my mind without my permission?" he asked, still trembling from the power of Elyon that had coursed through him.

"Do you remember what I told you on the first day we met? The Dragonmasters know about you but don't really *know* you." Hawk asked.

Jaren's eyes widened with understanding, "Emperor Volant," he whispered.

"Yes," said Hawk, "but the Emperor is not acting alone, I fear. It is Lucia himself who is behind Volant's attempt, which means that the previous scrying attempts could have been performed by the Lucian priests."

Jaren shuddered that the reality of his lineage and his new life from Yesha had made him a prime target of the dark god's hatred and vengeance. Once again, gratefulness swelled within him at the knowledge of the one true God's power and superiority over the false god. He knew he was in the best possible position: right in the

The Birth of a King

middle of Elyon's hand. Jaren vowed to keep his thoughts closely guarded, and asked his Master to allow no one to extract any information of value from him.

Jaren looked at Hawk and said with grim resolve, "The Emperor has thrown down the gauntlet; the soon-to-be High King has chosen to take it up."

His four companions stared in wonder at the stern face of the young man. Each pondered with eager anticipation which signs of royal Cathain blood would be further revealed in the days to come.

As the hours wore on, during their first day under the mountain, the monotonous echo of the horses' hooves on the stone passageway, the physical and emotional strain of the previous afternoon, and the shock of the scrying attempt combined to lull Jaren into a half-sleep, where he touched his deepest consciousness. In the weeks since he had arisen from the waters of the Spring of Elyon, he had been aware of the hum of the dragons' thoughts in his mind. He was never quite able to grasp a specific concept, but instead was sensing a jumbled collection of their emotions and memories. He could decipher none of it, other than the impression of great hope and eagerness equally interwoven with anxiety and rebellion. Jaren assumed that the positive emotions were a result of the dragons' knowledge of his existence, but he could not identify a precise cause for their unease. He was at a loss as to how this gift of Elyon was in the least helpful, since he seemed powerless to respond to the mighty beasts with his mind. He had attempted on several occasions to converse with the dragons with the use of mind-speech, but had never received any indication that they had heard or understood. He had no idea if the dragons were not responding because Volant had interfered with their ability, or if speaking with the dragons was a thing either banned in the past or a function that simply was impossible to perform. He had spent many hours probing the memories of his ancestors to ascertain the answers to his questions, but had not as yet been successful in learning a thing.

When Jaren's horse stumbled slightly, he jerked awake. He considered what he had pieced together in his doze and decided to continue sifting through his memories; the solution had to be there somewhere. He just must try harder.

The Birth of a King

They traveled for what seemed an eternity through a wide, circuitous tunnel that ran through the heart of the mountain. The light from their torches jumped and flickered along the rough walls of the passage.

Tanner had begun on the second day of their journey to feel the weight of the mountain pressing in on him. In the constant semi-darkness, his mind became confused regarding day and night and he often felt a slight nausea from the disorientation. The light from the two torches was simply not enough to refresh the young man's soul. Even in the sizable passage, he felt as though he would suffocate, and he longed for the light of day and for a breath of air that was not ancient. To dispel his growing uneasiness he began a meticulous study of the tunnel. In the space of an hour, he counted seven smaller passages leading off this main tunnel before his curiosity got the better of him.

"Are these the Glamorgan Mines that you mentioned earlier, Balgo?" he asked.

"Yes, they are, lad," the dwarf replied.

Tanner was confused. "But why are all of the passages blocked with rocks? We must have passed at least a hundred of them since we began our ride. Certainly a mountain this big couldn't be completely mined out. Is it customary to close off a shaft when it's empty? Are the dwarves working in other areas of the mountain now? I haven't heard any noises...."

"Whoa there, son, let me answer one question before you ask ten more." Balgo chuckled. "At one time these mines were the major source of copper for my people, but they have lain unworked for two centuries now. You see, there was a strange, silvery-white stuff that was in the dross from refining the ore from these mines. Many of our folk became poisoned with the handling of it and died. Old Dak Glamorgan, the owner of the mines, went sort of daft after they found out what was killing everyone. He took the notion that somehow he had personally caused the calamity. No one blamed him, but he would not be talked out of thinkin' he was a murderer. He closed the mines down and ordered all of the passages that lead off this tunnel to be blasted shut, so as to keep travelers out of any danger. Now, it's just a tunnel to get from one side of the mountain to the other."

"Did he open mines somewhere else, then?" Jaren asked.

"No. After he watched the last of these passages blasted to smithereens, he went home and stood on his porch for a long time, just looking out at the village, and cryin' like the world was comin' to an end. Then he turned his back, walked into the house, and locked the door behind him. That's the last that anyone ever saw of old Dak."

"What do you mean?" asked Tanner. "Surely the people didn't let him starve to death in his own home?"

"Of course they didn't. His own children broke down the door the next morning and looked all through the house for him. He was nowhere to be found; just vanished without a trace. He left a note saying that his children were to sell the rich furniture, jewels, and works of art for their inheritance, and that they were to give the proceeds from the manse and land to the families of the dead workers."

On the fifth night of their monotonous ride, Balgo inspected Jaren's wound. "Ah, at last," he sighed and smiled, "The stitches can be removed tonight."

Jaren was not looking forward to the process and reluctantly turned his back to the fire so that the dwarf could see more easily. As it turned out, Balgo had dabbed the wound with a dark liquid that smelled like cloves and Jaren felt little pain as the stitches were removed.

"There you are, Sire," Balgo said with satisfaction after rebinding the wound. "You'll have a nice scar to remember this journey, and no doubt. It's red and mean-looking at the moment, but it will fade somewhat with time."

Hawk, riding in his usual place at the rear of the group, paid little attention to his surroundings or the conversation of his companions. He was eager to reach Parth, as he wanted very much to visit with Fernaig, one of the ancient Elders of the dwarven clans. He felt that the time gained with the dragon's rebellion would be far too short and he greatly desired Fernaig's wisdom and knowledge. His advice

The Birth of a King

would be invaluable to the company. He felt himself wishing this leg of their journey well behind them.

As if in answer to his thoughts, Balgo called out, "There's daylight ahead. And a very welcome sight it is, too. We'll be in Parth tonight, gentlemen," he announced. "We'll stop a few yards in from the cave entrance, and have a quick meal while we allow your eyes to adjust to the increased light. I don't want to be leading four blind men into Parth."

Even with this precaution, their eyes burned as they rode into the afternoon sunlight. The mountain air was more pleasant here, almost matching the temperature of the mines. Much to the relief of the road-weary group, the day proved to be pleasantly uneventful. The slopes on this southern face of the mountain were as beautiful in their lush verdancy as the northern face had been starkly barren.

They passed a beautiful tarn off to their right, and Balgo explained that it was continually filled with snowmelt from the mountains mirrored it is still surface. "It's a beauty, isn't it?" Balgo said fondly.

An hour before dusk they came upon a fast running brook, dismounted, and let their horses and Balgo's donkey drink from its icy waters.

Hawk used the short rest to apply another coating of salve to Deakin's swollen flank. "Let us hope this is the worst you will see, my friend," he said gently.

"It's not much farther now, and by the look and smell of all of you, I should probably allow you to bathe," Balgo grumbled.

He led the group upstream a few paces to a small tarn that was near to overflowing. The iciness of the crystal clear water bit cruelly at their toes. The thought of bathing in the frigid pond sent premature shivers through their bodies.

"This is Magewyn Glor, an ancient little body of water that has served our race for ages. I hope you will find its cleansing waters to your liking." He winked at all of them, and Tanner wasn't sure whether or not he had caught an evil twinkle in the dwarf's eye.

They almost envied Jaren, as Balgo had forbidden him to put his back into the icy water. "You can stand in the water up to your knees, but do not to let any water get on your wound," he had ordered after removing Jaren's bindings.

"Brrrrr," Korthak whined. He was standing knee-deep in the water, his arms wrapped tightly around his chest. Suddenly, Tanner jumped into the pool from the opposite shore, sending a sheet of melted snow crashing over him.

"Ahhh!" The big man bellowed, as his companions roared with laughter. Korthak thought of throwing caution to the wind by diving after the brazen jokester and drowning him. However, a more powerful urge sent him rushing for the warm grass at the edge of the pool. Balgo left the water and walked to his donkey, returning with his axe resting on his shoulder in mock threat.

"Perhaps you didn't hear my offer, old bear. I said I will *allow* you to bathe. Now haul yourself into that water or I'll do to you what Leonora will do to me if I bring your filthy hide into her home."

Hawk dived under the bone-chilling water and came up with a smile on his face. His teeth were chattering behind blue lips, as he blatantly lied to Korthak. "Come on, old man. It's not that cold." He laughed as Korthak stared at Balgo's axe. The man was clearly weighing the options of death by cleaving or death by freezing.

Korthak walked slowly into the water again and mumbled something about "no respect for an old man's health" before dunking his chest and head into the icy spring. He came up sputtering and coughing. "Dols, Balgo, this is torture."

Hawk laughed at him. "Quiet down, you old codger. If the Dragonmasters didn't know our whereabouts before, they surely will if you keep up your caterwauling."

Four shivering companions hurriedly bathed and rushed out of the pond, throwing themselves gratefully on the soft grass. Jaren had prudently rushed his bathing while enjoying the nonsense of the others, and was now gratefully dressed once again. Balgo carefully cleaned his wounds and applied more of the salve for Jaren's comfort.

Tanner rather reluctantly accepted one of Korthak's enormous shirts, as his only spare was as dirty as the one he had been wearing.

Tanner scowled as he scrutinized himself in the huge garment before mounting Jaren's horse. "Don't worry, boy. The way you eat, you'll have grown into that long before summer is passed," Korthak said, laughing at Tanner's obvious disapproval.

Tanner raised an eyebrow and stared at the man who was becoming more like a father with each passing day. "I guess that will be alright as long as my belly doesn't gain the girth of yours, *Slim*." he laughed and let out a yelp, as Korthak yanked him from the horse and mussed his hair with his knuckles.

Korthak put Tanner in a headlock and pretended to loose his belt from his waist. "I'll teach you yet to keep a civil tongue in that empty head of yours, boy."

Tanner was laughing so hard he could not defend himself. Korthak pulled him into a quick hug and pushed him away, kicking him lightly on the seat of his pants.

A screech of rage was all they heard, and a swish and ruffle of feathers near his face were all Korthak saw of the attack. He raised his arms, shielding his face and eyes from the raking talons of Kynon. The small falcon had heard Tanner's cry, while continuing his lofty search for his missing human, and had raced with all speed to save his young master from injury.

Tanner ran to his saddle for the leather arm protector, and hurriedly slid his forearm into it. "No, Kynon!" he shouted, as the falcon began another descent upon Korthak. "No!" He tied the leather thong and pulled it tight with his teeth.

He ran straight for Korthak, knocking the stunned giant to the ground. He shoved his arm in the air, squinted his eyes shut and waited for the birds' attack. The little falcon pulled up abruptly and landed heavily on Tanner's outstretched arm.

The youth blinked open his eyes, and saw Kynon jumping from one foot to the other and flapping his wings, while screeching furiously at Korthak.

Balgo was on the ground rolling in a fit of laughter. Hawk slid from his horse and offered Korthak a hand up.

"Well, it looks like you're going to have to take another bath, old man." he taunted and laughed.

Korthak glared at Hawk, and then rapidly glanced back at the still raving little bird. "Oh, no, I'll not set my little toe back in that liquid ice. Leonora will just have to put up with a clover-covered ruffian tonight." He was still in a daze as he climbed up onto Tanner's stallion. As he rode indignantly past the still laughing dwarf, he mumbled and snorted under his breath, "Someday I'm going to really ruffle that stupid bird's feathers. Hmpf."

It took Tanner the better part of the evening to soothe Kynon into silence, and to induce him to eat. During that time, Jaren saw his friend gaze frequently at Korthak with a curious expression on his face.

The gesture of paternal affection that Korthak had offered him with that brief hug before Kynon's attack had not gone unnoticed by Tanner. He felt strangely that, on this road, high in these treacherous mountains, hundreds of leagues from Reeban, he had somehow found home.

Chapter Twenty-Eight

TANNER'S DREAM

They arrived in Parth, as Balgo had promised, shortly after nightfall, to no fanfare or celebration. They had merely been five riders moving down the avenue in the soft glow of the starlight. Balgo was hallooed by a few passersby, but that was the extent of any acknowledgment as to the arrival in Parth of Prince Jaren Iain Renwyck Cathain, sole surviving heir to the throne of Kinthoria.

Hawk explained their quiet reception to Jaren, "Most Dwarves never leave their mountains, and so rarely, if ever, encounter the kings and queens who seem to take it for granted that they are ruling these people.

Don't misunderstand me; the Dwarves are fiercely loyal to the crown, but the Cathains have always highly respected the wisdom of the Hammerthanes and the Elders of this race, and so have allowed them to rule themselves for the most part," Hawk said.

Thus, Jaren's arrival had not caused so much as the raising of an eyebrow…that is, until he faced Leonora. As soon as they walked through the tiny wooden door of the Dwarven woman's cottage, she bowed as deeply as her small, round frame would allow, and then wrung her hands, fussing and fretting that her home was not fit for such a noble guest. She bustled about from hearth to the table, then on to disappear into the pantry, only to reappear, arms laden with bowls and platters.

She laid out so much food that Jaren quite literally did not know where to begin. The little woman had spent the better part of two days at her oven. She had prepared a large pork roast, lamb steaks, vegetables boiled in broth, stewed tomatoes, fresh bread, three delicious fruit pies, and a heaping tray of little spice cakes with poppy seeds sprinkled on top.

Jaren tried valiantly to eat at least some of all that had been placed on the board, but, like Tanner, his stomach had shrunk in the past two months of continuous travel. The boyish roundness of their faces had vanished, to be replaced with the chiseled features of manhood. Their bodies had turned leaner gaining in muscle what had been lost of the remnants of childhood. Even Korthak's belly was somewhat less round.

After an evening of pleasant conversation around the large hearth, the peacefulness in this place of safety began to lull Jaren into a languid half-sleep.

"Yes, I believe you're right, Korthak," Hawk's voice broke into Jaren's doze. He started and sat up straighter in the small chair.

The company was staring at Jaren, each with a large grin on his face.

"Korthak was just saying that perhaps the time has come to put the children to bed," Hawk said, laughing at the deep blush spreading over Jaren's face.

Not daring to touch Hawk, Leonora instead slapped Balgo with her dishcloth, "Och, don't you be teasing the poor lad; he's had a long and very trying journey from the sound of it." She held out her hand, showing the way to the room that Jaren and Tanner would share.

As they said goodnight to one another, Balgo slapped his forehead, "Ah, of all the durn' foolishness! I've completely forgotten Jaren's back. Leonora, my lovely, would you use your womanly know-how and see if I've botched up Jaren's wounds sufficiently to produce the greatest possible amount of scarring?"

The little woman was aghast. "What's that? Do you mean to tell me, *sir*, that he has been injured and in the hours since your return you have simply forgotten to mention it?"

Leonora looked at Jaren standing near the bedroom door. She hastily yanked out a chair and began rolling up her sleeves. "Sit, sit, sit!" she demanded in a high-pitched staccato. "Balgo, pour some hot water into a bowl, and then bring me a cloth for cleaning the wound and another for binding. You," she barked to Tanner, "fetch me that box of curatives." Soon the entire room was filled with men tripping over one another in obedience to the miniature tyrant.

As it turned out, she was happily impressed with her husband's handiwork. "Well, praise be," she smiled. "I see that I no longer need to repair your clothes in the future. You have missed your calling, my husband. You should have been a seamstress."

Balgo cringed and reddened at the barb while the others roared with laughter.

Leonora laid her hand on Jaren's shoulder, "I'll gently rub some compounds onto the scar each night. You'll be surprised how quickly the redness will fade, M'lord." When she had lightly bound Jaren's back once more, she assumed her former manner as hostess. "You and Tanner will find clean nightshirts on the end of the beds. They will be a wee might short, but they are Balgo's so you will have plenty of room to move in them."

Balgo frowned, trying to determine if he had just been maligned by his wife regarding his girth. She smiled at him innocently, "Now, I think we've had sufficient gaiety for one night, and I will bid you all a goodnight." She dipped a quick curtsy to Jaren and headed down the hall.

Late the following morning Jaren turned in his bed and rubbed the sleep from his eyes. He yawned, stretching broadly with a ridiculously satisfied grin on his face. He could not remember the last time he had slept so well. He could see Solance peeking through the wooden shutters of the little stone cottage as he lay, luxuriating in a real bed, with a real down counterpane. He turned and stretched again, immediately slamming his feet into the end of the small bed. He looked across at Tanner, who was sprawled with one leg hanging off the side of his bed and the other crooked and leaning against the wall. He chuckled softly as he tried to picture Hawk or Korthak trying to sleep on one of the miniature structures. He wondered what had become of the children whose room this must once have been. He would discover before they left Parth that they had died many years earlier, of a strange fever that sometimes afflicted Dwarven young. The contagion struck with lightning force, attacking only small children, and snuffing out their lives almost before the parents realized that their babes were in mortal danger. A home that one week had been a joyful place, filled with the noisy laughter and play of children, could the very next week be empty of one or all of the little ones. Hollow-eyed parents were left staring vacuously into the deafening quiet, in stunned disbelief and unimagined sorrow.

Jaren's thoughts were interrupted by raucous laughter coming from the next room. He listened as his three older companions attempted to outdo one another with the wildest tales.

He could hear Leonora bustling about the hearth, busying herself over the morning meal as the aroma of sweet muffins and salt pork and hot cafla drifted into his room.

He stretched his long frame one last time, taking care to shift his legs over the side of the bed. He threw back the quilt, climbed out of the bed, and yawned again as he picked up his worn breeches, inspecting them critically. *"Dols,"* he thought, *"I hope we can get some new clothes before too long. These things are getting pretty road worn."* He found that his saddle had just about worn the seat through, and noticed that the legs were riding a good three fingers higher above his feet than when he had fled Reeban. He scratched his head, puzzled. "Hmm, I've never heard of breeches shrinking before," he muttered to himself.

He quietly walked past Tanner's bed, and stooped through the little doorway to join the others.

"Ah, Master Jaren, you're still alive, I see," Balgo teased.

The old dwarf pulled a pipe from between his teeth and poked Hawk in the arm with the end of it. "That's the trouble with our young today," he winked at the half-elf. "Laziness," he slapped his hand to his knee, and Jaren spied the twinkle in his eye. "Yessir, laziness, pure and simple. They think they can sleep all day, and 'spect to be fed and cared for, but won't turn a hand to any work they aren't made to do."

The three old friends laughed, and Hawk pulled out a stool with the toe of his boot, motioning for Jaren to join them.

Leonora was instantly at the young man's side, dipping in a quick curtsy while offering a steaming cup of cafla, and some fresh squeezed juice. She turned to her husband and swatted at him. "Hush, old man. That's no way to speak to your Prince," she scolded.

Balgo made much of fearfully fending off her soft blows, and winked at Jaren. "Nay, lassie, this young lad and I had a nice little talk a few days ago. He knows that I mean no disrespect to him. And he's just new enough at this monarch business that he doesn't want people cow towing and calling him 'Sire.' So you see, my beautiful Leonora, we're safe as babes in a cradle from this young Prince's mighty wrath."

Jaren smiled and took a sip of his juice. He nodded to Leonora as she stared at him in wonder. "It's all right, Ma'am," he said softly. "I think Balgo and I have a proper understanding between us."

The little Dwarf woman shook her head, wiped her hands on her apron, turned on her heel, and returned to the fire and her meal with head held high and back ram-rod straight in disapproval at such a cavalier conduct toward royalty.

The four men were hard put to behave with decorum as they heard her speaking loudly to the fire. "No wonder we're in such a fine mess, if we don't even see the need to treat our betters with any respect a'tall. Hmpf," she snorted.

Korthak rose to go roust Tanner from his soft bed as Leonora was beginning to put the meal on the board. He felt sure that the little woman was already upset enough without having her huge meal go cold before she could get her guests to the table. He could after all, he told himself with pride, be a prudent man when the need arose.

The group once again filled themselves to the point of discomfort. Leonora plainly felt it her duty in life to overfeed anyone who put their feet under her table. She was thoroughly abashed at having her guests help clean up after breakfast, but Hawk had adamantly insisted, and eventually the old woman had relented, finding it quite amusing to discover the differences in a man's opinion of clean and her own.

After the little stone home was tidied, Balgo kissed his wife on the cheek and said, "We are going to see Fernaig. Hawk needs to talk with him, and to introduce him to our young Prince." Leonora smiled, and watched as the five men filed through the door. She sighed, and wondered what in the world she would do to keep occupied, now that the men had so *thoroughly* cleaned up after themselves. She chuckled and had just decided to surprise Jaren and Tanner by making them each a pair of much needed breeches, when Tanner burst back through the door.

"I'm sorry, Ma'am," he stammered, "but I forgot to get something to feed my bird."

"Oh, quite," she said sweetly, thinking to herself, *"How could I have forgotten that lice-infested, mange-ridden little beast he tried to bring into my house last night?"* She smiled broadly at Tanner as she found some fresh meat and cut it up for him. "We can't be having your precious little beauty starving now, can we?"

She placed the meat in Tanner's hands. "There you are, lad. That should keep him sated for a while."

Tanner beamed and thanked her as he rushed to the door. But in his haste to feed Kynon, he forgot that this was the home of a dwarf, and ran straight into the heavy oak lintel above the door, roughly striking his head against it. He fell backward, and landed flat on his back on the stone floor. Leonora screamed and ran to the unconscious youth. There was a deep cut on his forehead, which was bleeding quite freely.

Korthak and Jaren rushed inside at the old woman's scream. Korthak dropped to his knees and shook the young man. "Tanner! Tanner, are you all right?"

Tanner's head was spinning as he watched stars swirling before his eyes. "Korthak!" he yelled thickly, "We're under attack!"

Korthak lifted him from the floor and carried him into the bedchamber, "It's all right, lad. You've just had a wee bit of an accident."

Leonora was already busily concocting a tonic for the headache Tanner was sure to have. Korthak and Jaren stood back, as they could see that the little woman was in her element now, and would brook no interference. She gently dabbed at the blood on Tanner's forehead and pressed a damp, clean cloth over it.

Balgo and Hawk had picked up the pieces of meat and had laid them outside for Kynon to eat. But the falcon would have nothing to do with the food, for it had not been given with his master's hand. "I hope the lad feels up to feeding the poor beastie soon," Balgo said

The Birth of a King

with some concern as he re-closed the shutters to the bedchamber window. "That little one won't make it very long without something to eat, and I fear that he loves Tanner enough to starve to death before he'll eat from any one else's hand."

Leonora shooed Korthak and Jaren from the room and bent to check Tanner's cut more closely. It would not require stitches, she decided, but his head would be pounding like a dwarven smithy for a while and it would leave a scar at his hairline. She lifted his head gently, as she touched a wooden cup to his lips. "Here, laddie, drink this. It will make your head stop thumping quite so badly."

Tanner's face twisted in disgust at the taste of the medicine, but Leonora would not allow him to miss even one drop. As she was coaxing and threatening him to swallow the foul liquid, Tanner was wishing that Korthak or even Balgo had made the medicine instead, remembering, through the fog in his brain how surprisingly pleasant tasting their doses had been.

Leonora prayed silently for Yesha to ease the young man's pain, and after a short time, it seemed that the tonic and the true God had both worked perfectly, as Tanner's breathing slipped into an even rhythm and he fell asleep.

The tiny woman emerged from the bedchamber to face four men with the look of expectant fathers upon their faces. She noticed with some astonishment that Korthak's seemed to be the worst. *"So the old bear has found his lost son after all these years,"* she quietly noted to herself. She smiled at the bulky man, and patted his hairy hand. "Don't worry, my large friend. He's going to be just fine."

She could not help smiling at the relief that flooded Korthak's eyes as he tried to steal a glance into the dim bedchamber.

Balgo was the first to speak. "Well, if he's all right we may as well visit Fernaig as planned."

Hawk agreed, as he approached Korthak, whispering in his ear, "Come, my friend. Let him rest. He's in good hands."

Korthak looked at Hawk with just a trace of surprise behind his eyes, then quickly stooped and walked outside.

"What about Kynon?" Jaren asked, as he watched the little falcon pacing back and forth in front of Balgo's home. "Will he be all right?"

The Birth of a King

Hawk shrugged his shoulders. "There's nothing more we can do for him, Jaren. He has food, but he may not eat until he sees Tanner's hand offering it. Tanner is the one Kynon has chosen."

While his four companions were visiting Fernaig, another visitor was in Tanner's company, in his dreams.

Leonora saw only the young man sleeping quietly in the adjoining room as she sewed, with quick, skillful hands, at the new breeches for Jaren and Tanner. But Tanner's mind was very much aware. He knew that what he was experiencing was a dream, but everything was as real to him as though he were fully awake.

He was dressed in full Knight's armor. A sword was in his right hand, hanging down at his side, and his helmet was tucked under his left arm. Everywhere he looked, there was radiant light. He was standing in a beautiful, green meadow that seemed to go on forever. The sun, or whatever it was that was radiating the light, was warm and glared brightly off his polished breastplate and sword. He was surprised that, although it was warm, and he was in full armor, he was not in the least uncomfortable.

There was a light breeze blowing through his dark hair as he gazed at the scene before him. He was alone in this place, but for the abundant life filling the expansive meadow. Deer grazed and stood alert, watching the cattle and sheep, as their fawns romped through the tall grass alongside young lambs. At the edge of the meadow, a lion lay in the shadow of the trees watching his mate as she gave her two cubs a bath. Butterflies flitted by on the soft breeze. Sparrows and meadowlarks sailed through the sky overhead, and rabbits rapidly devoured the clover at his feet.

"*Where am I?*" he asked himself.

"*You are where you are supposed to be, Tanner aP MacKechnie.*" A deep, calm voice spoke to him, apparently from the breeze.

He whirled around, but could see no other person in the meadow. He chuckled at the absurd thought that Hawk and this unseen stranger should get together sometime. He'd like to be there to see who could find the other first.

"*Llenyddiaeth and I are already well acquainted, my son,*" the voice spoke again. "*But now I want* you *to come to know Me as well.*"

The Birth of a King

Tanner spun around again, still seeing no one, apprehension growing at the realization that, whoever this was, he had the ability to read his thoughts. *"Who are you? And where are you?"* he shouted into the breeze.

The gentle voice responded. *"I am."*

Tanner was confused, and became tenser with each passing moment. This *voice* knew his name, knew what he was thinking, and knew Hawk personally.

The young man did not know how to respond to the statement "I am," so he blurted out the first thing that came to mind. *"Why am I here?"* he asked.

"You are here, Tanner, because I have called you here," the voice said. *"I am giving you a task to perform, an extremely critical task."*

Tanner waited for just a moment, his confusion growing as the voice answered his questions. *"What is this task that I am to accomplish?"*

The voice answered, *"You are to protect, with your own life, the hope I have sent to your world, Tanner. I have made Jaren to become the example of My selfless love for your world during his lifetime. Others will look to him and see the promise for the future, and they will regain their hope. Jaren and you, as his champion, will be my tools to wrest Kinthoria from My enemies. When your quest is completed, I will restore once again the places of worship for those who call upon My name, and the people will live in the peace and prosperity which I have ever desired for them. Until then, you must watch over your friend, and see that no harm comes to him."*

Tanner sucked air into his lungs as he quickly realized to whom this disembodied voice belonged. No one in his right mind could refuse such a directive. He felt immediately humbled in the presence of Elyon. He dropped rather awkwardly in his armor to one knee and bowed his head. He had wanted to know this new Master of Jaren's, this one of whom Hawk and Korthak had spoken on so many occasions. But now that he was in His presence, he understood his unworthiness and was ashamed. How could he receive, in his rebellious condition, the wondrous gift being offered to him by the true God?

The voice swept in warmth over and through him once more, *"No, Tanner. Do not think of yourself any longer as unworthy to be My servant. I have called you. My Son's perfect sacrifice is more than able to save you from your rebellious self, more than able to wash you clean of evil, and more than enough for Me to forgive your rebellion. Do you believe this?"*

Tanner could not stop the tears from pouring down his face - tears of remorse mingled with joy, tears that had come from his very soul.

He shook his head, *"With all my heart, Master."*

The voice continued. *"Tanner ap MacKechnie, I will be with you and your companions now, and ever more, even as I have been with you in the past. I will help you stand against the many adversities and dangers that lie ahead. The road for each of you is long, and filled on every side with dangers and evils. The enemy will stop at nothing to cause the failure of your quest. But I will have you in the palm of My hand at all times. No matter how dark, no matter how powerful the evil around you may appear, you must always remember that I will never leave you alone or without aid."*

Tanner nodded, unable to speak, so full of awe and thanksgiving was he, for Elyon's promise. He vowed that he would be a faithful servant of this loving Master to the end of his days.

The voice was gone, and Tanner was back in Parth sound asleep on the little bed. But he would be forever changed from the young man he had been before his visitor had come to him in the dream.

Chapter Twenty-Nine

FERNAIG

The four men began the short walk to Fernaig's house as Jaren continued to glance over his shoulder at the frantic young falcon still pacing and scolding with his high-pitched screeches. He remembered something Balgo had taught him: that Yesha had said how the Father provides everything for the birds, and how He would look after people so much more.

Jaren smiled, squared his shoulders, and turned to hurry on with his companions. He knew in that moment that both Tanner and Kynon would be just fine, and that he need worry no further about either of them.

As the four walked down the street, Jaren's attention was finally drawn to his surroundings. He had been unable to see any details of the Dwarven village in the darkness when they had arrived in Parth the night before.

He noticed at once the perfect fit in the cut of the stones with which the road had been paved. He noticed how neatly and precisely the village had been designed. It would be virtually impossible to become lost in Parth, as the entire village was made up of uniform square sections. Jaren did not see one angling or crooked street. Every house, every stoop, every street was immaculately clean, as though the whole village had been recently scoured. The tiny cottages were no more than a few feet from one another, but each one had its own distinct character; some were whitewashed stone, with brightly colored shutters and doors, while others were built out of a dark brown brick or stone. Windows and paths were awash with colorful flowers of every kind. Chimneys and walls were covered with ivy and honeysuckle. Behind each house was a vegetable and herb garden. One entire square in the center of the village had been given over to a communal orchard, full of blossoming fruit trees. There were benches and paths throughout this fragrant park for the enjoyment of the citizens.

Jaren sensed that the beauty of this village, so obviously a product of careful planning and much hard and loving labor, perfectly reflected the great pride which these people had in their heritage and the dedication that was so rooted in their character.

The group came upon a rather long, low house on the far side of the village. Balgo asked them to wait at the front gate, while he disappeared round the back of the house. When he returned, he was being followed by a red-haired, jolly-faced youth.

"This is Graeth, gentlemen. He has come to help keep Fernaig's garden in order," said Balgo.

Graeth smiled widely and opened the front door of the house, bidding them to follow.

"I've been trying to get the old miser to hire a housekeeper. Since his wife died last year, he has let the place run to wrack and ruin," Balgo explained.

As Jaren stepped inside, he was surprised to see that the interior of the house was in fact for the most part neat and tidy, though the library was littered with books and scrolls scattered on tables and chairs, and even on the floor. *"Wrack and ruin?"* he mused. Granted, it lacked a woman's finishing touch but it certainly wasn't what he had expected from Balgo's remarks.

An ancient-looking dwarf sat bent over the largest book that Jaren had ever seen. He was pouring over its pages by the light of a nearly spent candle, clearly so intent upon his study that he was unaware of the presence of his guests. Thin wisps of purest white hair crowned his head, like tufts of soft down, and a thin, soft beard hung from round, pink cheeks. The hands that so lovingly touched the parchment pages were the thin, careful hands of a scholar.

Graeth cleared his throat rather loudly, and announced that the old man had guests who had come to call.

"Eh? What's that you say?" Fernaig grunted, not bothering to look up from the huge tome. "Rest 'til the sun falls, y'say? Come now, laddie, you'll never get the gardening done if you can't stand a bit of sunshine. Go and fetch my hat by the kitchen door, you can use it to keep the heat off your head."

"No sir! Begging your pardon, sir! I said you have *guests* that have come to *call*," he said more loudly.

This time the old dwarf looked up from his reading in surprise. He glanced over the top of his glasses, which, as with all true scholars, were sitting precariously on the tip of his nose.

"Eh? Oh, Balgo, lad, so, you finally came round for a visit, after half the day is gone. Does no one use the days that Elyon gives us, anymore? You laze in bed half the morning, and this soft lad here wants to quit weeding until after the sun goes down."

Graeth shrugged his shoulders, smiled good-naturedly and touched his closed hand to his forehead. Bowing slightly to the guests he said, "By your leave I'll just be off then to finish up the chores. If I may be of further service, you'll find me back of the house again."

Jaren, unable to control his curiosity, walked to the old dwarf's side and looked down at the massive book, which covered the entire top of the reading desk. "What is it that you are reading, sir?" he asked in awed tones. "It looks very old."

"Eh? What's that? Balgo, who is this impertinent young man? Why have you brought him into my house? And why does he *whisper* when he speaks? I don't hold to whispering...not *polite*...entirely disrespectful. Is this the one you went away for?"

Balgo chuckled and stepped forward. "Stop your teasing, you old fraud. We all know you can hear a pine needle drop to the forest floor a mile away. And yes, this is the one Hawk went to find. Fernaig, I have the great honor of presenting his majesty, Jaren Iain Renwyck Cathain, Prince of Kinthoria."

Fernaig bowed, while remaining seated. "Forgive me for not standing, Sire, but," he scowled darkly at Balgo, "*fraud* though I may be, I am still old by anyone's measure, and my bones rebel rather sharply when I move about too much."

"That's quite all right, sir, and please, just call me Jaren. 'Sire' makes me feel awfully strange, like I'm me, but not, if you understand my meaning, sir," Jaren replied rather sheepishly.

"I do understand, Jaren. And you may call me Fernaig, instead of 'sir.' Makes me feel too old, don't you know? But we both must face the truth, lad; our feelings are irrelevant to our responsibility to do what is right and fundamentally essential to any civilized realm. You are the Prince, and you must allow others the *right* to honor you as is your due. And I am old, and so I must allow others to venerate me, so that *honor* and *respect* are not lost among our peoples. Do you understand what I am saying, Sire?" he asked, purposely using the offending title.

Jaren smiled, "Yes, I do, Fernaig, *sir*. I had never really thought of it that way before, but I can see that you are right. Sometimes we have to settle for things that make us uncomfortable so that things worth saving are not lost," he ended, speaking more to himself than to Fernaig.

"I like this lad, Balgo. He's got a good head on those broad shoulders; picks up things real fast," the old dwarf said, a huge grin splitting his face.

"Speaking of learning, Fernaig, you still haven't answered my question. What is this book?" Jaren asked, leaning over the dwarf's hunched shoulders.

"This? Why, lad, haven't you ever seen the Word before?" Fernaig asked in astonishment.

Jaren's eyes bulged. "The Word?" he whispered in awe. He reached out his hand to gently touch the yellowed, brittle pages of the ancient manuscript. His eyes brimmed with tears. "The Word of the one true God?" He asked.

Fernaig dipped his head slightly, "Aye."

"May...may I read just a little of it, Fernaig? Just...just a couple sentences, maybe? Please," he pleaded, his heart plainly aching to read the words with his own eyes.

The ancient dwarf stared deeply into the young man's eyes, his own misting with tears. He cleared his throat, and said somewhat hoarsely, "You read as much as you like, Sire. Just take your time,

The Birth of a King

and enjoy it. Pull up a chair, boy," he said gently as he turned the book so that Jaren could read more easily.

Jaren immediately lost awareness of the people around him as he began to devour the words on the weathered pages, carefully turning each fragile leaf. His heart leapt as he read some of the actual words that Yesha had spoken when he walked in Kinthoria.

"These words," he thought, *"are alive and are coming straight to me from the mouth of the Master."* He was overwhelmed with joy.

After a short time, Fernaig interrupted Jaren's perusal. "I can see that you have a healthy thirst for knowledge of Elyon," he said with a smile. "It is unfortunate that we must include you in our council at the moment. There will be time for this," he said patting the pages of the tome, "before you must leave Parth."

Jaren eyed the book longingly. "You are right, sir. It's just that it is so amazing, isn't it?"

"Indeed it is, my young friend," the wizened dwarf agreed with enthusiasm as he again searched the young man's eyes for several moments.

He returned to the subject at hand, "I was just telling these gentlemen that you will have the support of all the dwarves in Parth and Dorath, Sire." He held up his hand to halt Jaren's complaint of his use of the title. "Tut, tut, tut, young man, we've already been through this once today. You will just have to get used to my lapses the same as I will have to get used to yours. What say we just give each other free rein here?"

Jaren smiled and nodded in agreement.

The old dwarf slapped the tabletop with his hand. "Excellent. Now, as I was saying, Parth and Dorath are pledged to you, but more importantly, all in Mag Caurak have pledged their support as well. That means that the entire Dwarven race is at your service. I have no doubt that when Hawk gets back to the Elven forests with you, the Elves will also swear allegiance to you."

Jaren's eager expression was suddenly shadowed with concern. "Have I no human allies besides Korthak, and Tanner?"

The Birth of a King

Fernaig took a long pull from his pipe, and let the sweet-smelling rings of smoke drift upward to disappear among the low-slung beams of the ceiling.

"Yes, Jaren," he said softly. "There are many humans scattered throughout Kinthoria; they have waited, and prepared and prayed many years for your rise to the throne, son."

Jaren could sense the sadness in the voice of the ancient little man sitting next to him. "Why is this a sad thing for you, Fernaig?"

The dwarf hesitated, and so Hawk answered for him. "Jaren, many of your race have been hunted down and martyred for their faith in the true God and for their steadfast belief that one day an heir would return to overthrow the Dragonmasters. As you may have guessed, faith and hope are not encouraged by Volant."

"You must understand that this is not some mere diversion for the Dragonmasters. They are deadly serious in their struggle to see evil triumph over good once and for all in Kinthoria," Fernaig added. "They would see the light of truth completely extinguished in the land, to be replaced by the suffocating darkness of unimagined evil. If you understand nothing else, understand that this is the driving force behind the Dragonmasters. It is the compelling force of their lives."

Balgo had been silent through most of the conversation. Now he stood before Jaren with the earnest eyes of a zealot. "We have spent close to twenty years of energy and planning and sacrifice for this, Jaren. Many have been in constant prayer for your safety, and for the thousands who are with you. Many new believers in our Master have joined with us as Elyon's truth has revealed to them the true character of the Dragonmasters. They have come to understand that this is no longer something that must be tolerated in order to survive, but that it is a fatal cancer which will kill our world and every living thing in it, if it isn't stopped and exposed to all for the lie it is. If we fail in this, everything will be lost." His voice was rising in urgency now. "This is the one chance that the Master has given us to see the races of Kinthoria free to live in obedience and devotion to Him; to live safely and in contentment."

Balgo stopped just long enough to take a deep breath. "I fear that if we fail to see you safely to your throne, the Southern Regions will not exist within a few years' span. Volant is building his Dragon Army even as we speak, and it's been rumored that he might even enlist the help of the Trolls and Gundroths, promising those foul, misbegotten creatures this entire region should they prove victorious." He shuddered at the thought of the filthy, drooling vermin stepping foot in his beloved mountains.

Korthak stepped in to give the little dwarf a chance to calm down. He put a steadying hand on Balgo's shoulder, and smiled reassuringly. "Everything they have said is true, Jaren. We each have our reasons for wanting to see our efforts come to a successful conclusion." He looked hesitantly at Hawk and the two dwarves. "Now don't take me wrong here, I'm not trying to slight anyone. But, Jaren, you and I have lost our entire families to those dragon-riding murderers. Now, I know I'm not supposed to be looking for revenge, but I can't help feeling mighty eager to see you sitting with a crown on your head, and with all of your enemies' necks under your authority."

To the amazement of the old warrior, not one of the others rebuked him for his hard words. Each knew the devastating loss Korthak had experienced, and each suspected that Jaren could possibly be feeling even more in need of retribution, since he had been deprived of any knowledge whatsoever of his family for all these years. He would never be able to physically share the love his parents had held in their hearts for him.

The meeting with Fernaig continued into the late afternoon. Much was discussed as to the strength of the Prince's armies and their present locations. Long planned strategies were prayed over and refined. They were all pleased with their accomplishments as the four friends bid farewell to Fernaig, with a promise to visit again soon.

As they were walking back through the village toward Balgo's home, Hawk put his arm across Jaren's shoulders. "Fernaig was impressed with you, lad. He told me that while we are here, you are more than welcome to come for a visit to read the Word whenever you wish. He offered to teach you what time and his abilities may permit. It is a very great honor and gift, Jaren, which he has offered you. Fernaig has been blessed with wisdom and understanding of Elyon's Word, which few enjoy today."

Jaren was ecstatic. He had wanted so badly to get the chance to read further in the ancient book, but the council this afternoon had been vital to their plans, and he had bowed to necessity and turned aside from those sacred words.

Jaren liked the old dwarf immensely, and he planned to spend as much time with him as time permitted.

The four men entered Balgo's cottage, passing by a forlorn looking falcon that had finally become hungry enough to eat a few morsels of meat.

As Korthak came through the door, Leonora grabbed his huge arm with both of her hands. "He's been calling for you for nigh onto an hour now," she whispered as her eyes flicked toward the bedchamber.

The old warrior patted her tiny hand gratefully and ducked through the doorway. Jaren stood silently leaning against the doorframe.

Korthak quietly sat on the bed. Tanner opened his eyes and turned his head toward the older man.

"Korthak," he mumbled. "Dream...voice...bright light...."

Korthak could make no sense of Tanner's ramblings and wondered if the lad was suffering some damage to his brain from the force of the blow to his head.

"Shush, boy," he patted Tanner's arm, "just rest."

Tanner frowned and sat up slowly, holding his head and trying to focus his eyes. He stared into Korthak's face. "No, Korthak...must tell you. I had a dream." At least he thought it had been a dream. *"Dols, what did that tyrannical dwarf woman put in that vile tonic?"* he asked himself once again.

"A dream? What was in this dream, Tanner?" Korthak probed tentatively, concerned that Tanner's eyes seemed to be shining rather too brightly in the shadowy room.

Tanner described his dream about the meadow, and the voice that had spoken to him out of the air, telling him how important their task was. His eyes began misting as he related to the older man the change in his heart.

The Birth of a King

Korthak beamed with joy at the young man as he finished his story. He understood, now, that the light shining in Tanner's eyes was not the fever he had feared. He knew in an instant that his prayers had been answered at last. Elyon had freed Tanner's soul.

He carefully folded Tanner into a bear hug, and gently patted his back. "Now you are truly a part of my family, son." He held Tanner at arm's length. "My son...my son," he whispered hoarsely.

He squeezed the tears from his eyes with his thumb and forefinger. "Would you mind adopting a lonely, old duffer for a father?" he asked softly, hope written across his face.

Tanner grinned from ear to ear. "You bet! Com'ere...Father," he said, clasping the man in as strong a hug as he could manage. Jaren smiled and turned quietly to join the others. He had not overheard the conversation, but he could plainly see that the "adoption" was final, and that these two orphans were no longer alone in the world.

Tanner wanted to rise and sit with the others before the fire, but Leonora would have none of it. The small despot set a tray of food down on the table next to Tanner's bed. "You will eat this, you young bull, then you will drink the rest of my lovely tonic and go back to sleep," she ordered, feet apart and hands on hips, ready to do war if necessary.

Tanner started to protest, especially at the word 'tonic,' but after a look from the eyes of the determined dwarf, he could only mouth the words, "Yes, ma'am."

With a nod and a smile of satisfaction, she scurried away to set the evening meal for the others.

He knew that Leonora was right. He would need to regain his strength and get his mind back in working order before he could ever think about being of any service to Jaren.

Jaren decided to hazard Leonora's wrath by spending a few quick minutes with his friend, while her attention lay elsewhere.

"How are you feeling, Tan?" he whispered as he sidled around the doorframe and into the bedchamber, looking over his shoulder to see the dwarf still bending over her cook pots. He slipped quickly behind the door.

Tanner's face brightened, even in the dim light of the single candle that Leonora had set beside his bed. "Lots better, Jaren. Dols,

I feel like such a bumbling idiot." He gingerly probed his tender forehead.

Jaren nodded. "Don't worry about it. You'll only make your thick head pound all the more," he teased.

Tanner balanced the tray of food on his legs. "How's Kynon doing?" he asked, merely picking at the stew in his bowl.

"He's fine; a little flustered, but fine."

Tanner merely nodded.

Jaren silently wondered if Tanner was indeed all right. He had never before seen him disinterested in food.

"Not very hungry, huh?" Jaren asked as he peeked around the door to see what their hostess was up to.

Tanner looked up at him and wrinkled his nose. "Not really. My stomach's still kind of queasy."

Jaren quickly crossed through the rectangle of light shining through the doorway, and sat at the other end of the tiny bed.

"Tan, I need to talk to you for a minute. We haven't done much talking just between the two of us since we left the Spring of Elyon."

Tanner sat the tray of uneaten food back on the table and picked up the mug of tonic, eyeing it with distaste.

"What is it?" he asked, taking a swig of the bitter liquid, as he held his nose. His body shivered at the acrid tang of the dosage. "Ugh, this has to be the worst tasting stuff I have ever had to put down my gullet," he shivered again.

Jaren laughed at him, but quickly turned serious again. "Tan, this journey is a lot more important than either one of us ever thought. This isn't just an adventure...it's deadly serious business."

Tanner rested the cup on his leg, and stared a Jaren with a look that clearly said, *"Oh, really? Nice of you to finally catch up with everyone else."*

Jaren ignored his friend's expression and continued. "You should have heard all the things Fernaig was telling us today. We've stumbled into something much bigger than I think we ever could have imagined."

Tanner sat for a moment, then shrugged his shoulders, and choked down more tonic. "You are the one who was always daydreaming, wanting to run away to do something different with your life. This is about as different as you could get. It's what you wanted, isn't it?"

Jaren nodded. "Yes. Well, yes and no; this is a whole lot more than I wanted. I could never have begun to imagine all of this in my future. But, Tan, you don't know all of the people who are involved in this."

Choking down the rest of his tonic, Tanner set the mug on the table. "Oh, but that's where you are wrong, my brother. I too, found out all about it today."

Jaren's face was a picture of confusion. "What do you mean?"

Tanner smiled at him, and Jaren saw for the first time, that warm, loving smile that was characteristic of all children of the true God.

"Tanner!" he said, laughing. "When? How?"

His brother grinned. "Today. I had a visitor in a dream. At least, I think it was a dream. I seemed so much awake though…I don't know. All I know is that the Master spoke to me."

"That's the best news I've heard since we left Reeban," Jaren slapped Tanner's leg. "Just a second, I've got to tell Hawk." He formed the words in his mind and sent them to Hawk, remembering at the last second to control the emotion behind his mind-voice.

"Thanks be to Elyon. Korthak just told me. Tell him I'm really happy for him. He's a part of our growing family now," Hawk flashed back to him.

Jaren relayed the message, and prodded Tanner for details about his talk with Elyon.

Tanner repeated the story he had just related to Korthak. When he had finished, he said, "That's how I know how important all of this is, even if I don't know all the details."

Jaren chuckled as he watched Tanner fight valiantly to keep his eyes opened. But the effort was useless. Leonora's tonic was quickly working its magic and Tanner was yawning widely.

"I'm going to let you sleep now. Dols, you don't know how happy I am for you."

Sleep was rapidly overtaking the youth, as Jaren slipped back into the other room, beaming from ear to ear.

The conversation around the supper table that night began as a joyous celebration of Tanner's newfound faith. Later it centered on Jaren's army. The young Prince was full of questions, and each one was answered patiently and in detail. Hawk made sure that Jaren thoroughly understood each bit of information, and he was very pleasantly surprised to find that the young man had the ability to understand military strategies, and the circumstances that sometimes drive sensible men into the insanity of war. Hawk knew that Jaren would need to begin using his own powers of deduction in order to make decisions on his own, and the half-elf was determined to make certain that every detail was given to Jaren to aid him in doing so with wisdom.

When Jaren's three friends began to voice their surprise and approval of his mental acumen, he stopped them short with a sheepish smile. "Whoa, let's get something straight before we go any further. A couple of months ago I may have laid claim to all of your praise. But I had a rather rude and humbling awakening at the Spring of Elyon."

He saw the puzzlement on Korthak's and Balgo's faces. "Oh, that's right...I didn't tell you yet. Part of my transformation was that I received many of the memories of my ancestors. I've 'seen' many wars fought by the capable and the inept, both kindred and foe. At the very least the last century is all up here," he said, touching his temple. "I just need to think about it and it's there, ready to use."

The dwarf and the old bear looked at one another, not knowing how to respond to such a revelation. Jaren spoke for them, "Sorry, friends, but I can't claim the praise for something that was given to me just because I happened to be born the son of a king."

Hawk's eyes glowed with approval at Jaren's humble honesty, and at the youth's grasp of the helplessness of men without the gifts of Elyon's Spirit to empower them.

Jaren lay awake that night mulling over everything he had been told that day: Which races of people were with him; whom he could trust, and whom he could not. He had been informed of the strengths and weaknesses of the Dragonmasters, and their dreaded cohorts, the Lucian priests.

His thoughts were interrupted by the distant, rumbling thunder of a mid-summer storm rolling across the mountaintops. He could see the lightning flash through the little wooden shutters closed tightly over the windows. He heard the faint spattering of raindrops falling outside, as the wind began to pick up, and suddenly the front edge of the storm was upon them.

He would learn even more tomorrow, as he had already planned to visit with Fernaig in the morning to read from the beautiful book once again. He hoped Tanner would be allowed to join him, now that his friend knew Elyon as Father, also.

He pulled the thick quilt up under his chin, and closed his eyes as the storm began to unleash its full fury on the mountain people and their serene, tranquil village.

Chapter Thirty

PRINCE OF THE AN'ILDEN

Jaren and Tanner quickly established a daily routine. Each morning they visited Fernaig to hear the old dwarf's readings from Elyon's Word, and for instruction in all of the ways that one may offer up worship of the true God. It was a quiet, reverent time in which their faith and understanding grew steadily, as Fernaig answered their many questions and continually commented on their quickness of mind in receiving and understanding so much information at such a rapid pace. These hours were the perfect way to start each day, and it was a time the young men would never forget, and for which they would be forever grateful to Elyon. Jaren vowed that when his kingdom had been established, every village and town would have a least one copy of this marvelous Book for everyone to share.

Once, when Jaren had commented on the orderly beauty and cleanliness of the village of Parth, Fernaig smiled and said, "Yes, it is even as you say. But our village is not unique. Every village and town which belongs to the Southern Regions, and the entire underground world where the vast majority of our race lives in Mag Caurak, is kept with the same loving care. You see, son, it is not just pride in our heritage that causes us to keep our homes in order. No, it is our way of thanking the Father and praising the Master for the things of which He has so generously made us stewards. Throughout the Southern Regions the people still hold fast to the teachings of the

Word, and they honor the true God by tending that which belongs to Him."

Later each morning the two young men rode out into the pristine glens and corries that were abundant in the mountains in which the village of Parth was nestled. There, in the open wilderness, they would work on training Kynon; and Tanner, hesitantly, and a bit reluctantly at first, continued with Jaren's training in horsemanship and swordplay. The young men had been amazed at Jaren's new aptitude toward things military since his transformation at the Spring of Elyon. Jaren understood now the details and objectives of the many techniques in Tanner's instruction, and much of his Weapons Master's teaching now made perfect sense to him.

"It sure makes a difference having memories stuck in your head of people who have actually fought battles. You're like a natural now," Tanner panted with a smile. His struggle against Jaren's newfound prowess was wearing at his energy.

"Hah, now you're getting just a small idea of what you've been putting me through for years. It's payback time, my friend," Jaren said as they both fell to the ground for a rest.

Often, they would catch sight of a red deer grazing a short distance from them, and they would simply sit and watch the majestic creature, in the still quietness of the meadow grass. Jaren planned for the rest of his life, to make it a life-long practice to set aside time for such "idylls of renewal," as he called them. He understood how vital it was to remind himself of Elyon's hand and power in creation, for in so doing, he sensed the inward strengthening so desperately needed in his life.

Evenings were given to Hawk, as he worked with Jaren, training him to use his new gifts from Elyon: healing, knowledge, the Spirit and His gifts, discernment, understanding. He learned the proper ranking within a monarchy, from a prince to a nobleman to a commoner. He learned the various cultural greetings for each of the races of Kinthoria, in preparation for his coronation at St. Ramsay's. To the wonder of both student and teacher, Jaren had no difficulty whatsoever with many of the exercises that Hawk required of him. The young Prince learned everything at such a rapid pace that Hawk was constantly smiling and commenting on Elyon's unlooked-for

The Birth of a King

gift to Jaren, in that he already "knew" his lessons from the knowledge and experiences of his ancestors. They both realized that these lessons were merely reminders that called up that knowledge from his memory, so he readily understood not just Hawk's words, but the meanings, nuances, and necessity of each lesson.

One evening Hawk picked up some pebbles and laid them out in the grass. "Now son, imagine this is a small company of soldiers. I want you to show me where they are the weakest in relation to the position of their enemy, say, over here, and here," he said, as he placed other stones at varying places on the ground.

Jaren studied the arrangement of the pebbles for some minutes before replying.

"I would say they are weakest to their left flank."

Hawk glanced back to the small stones. "And why is that, Jaren?"

Jaren sat down on his heels. "Well," he said, pointing to Hawk's original group of stones, "they are not in a position to cover an attack to this area."

Hawk nodded.

"See?" Jaren continued. "They are aligned in a diagonal more to the right side, so there is not enough strength to repel an attack on the left."

And so it went, until it was almost too dark to see Hawk's arrangements of the pebble armies. Hawk was highly pleased with Jaren's understanding of the correct military strategies for each new scenario.

Each night was a new lesson, and each night Jaren fell asleep with increasing gratefulness for the presence of Elyon's Spirit in his life, and for His willingness to use him to accomplish Elyon's will and plan.

During this imperative, albeit short respite from danger, Hawk was forever mindful that the reason they could take advantage of this peace was because Elyon was in control of every circumstance, and he knew that no matter what kind of apocalyptic chaos may be occurring elsewhere in Kinthoria, Elyon would keep His hands and His angels around this place for as long as there was a need for Jaren to learn, uninhibited by threat of danger. He knew that the true God was strengthening each of them for the tremendous burden of the days that lay before them.

Often that strange melancholy was seen around his green eyes, as he pondered the likelihood of the death of many of these small, brave people and the destruction of their homes by the dragon riders once Elyon's protection was lifted. His heart was nearly crushed with the burden of such knowledge. He could see that Jaren, too, was experiencing discomfort, but he had not yet discerned its source. Was the young man under the continual onslaught of the dragons' distress and rage through his mind link with them, or had he been given some unspoken, or perhaps as yet unknown, insight in the knowledge and memories imbued at the Spring of Elyon?

On one of their afternoon excursions, Jaren and Tanner visited their favorite meadow, taking the now scandalously spoiled Kynon with them. Leonora insisted that during the afternoons they should take him wherever they went, because when he was left behind he screeched and scolded continually, until the poor woman was near distraction.

The meadow, on this particular day, was full of delicious scents and exquisite sights. Colorful birds flew from tree to tree. White, green, and yellow moths flitted over the myriad blossoms of the wildflowers. The mountains on every side of the meadow still had traces of brilliant white snow tucked into their shadowy recesses. The air was clear and refreshing. Tanner felt that just being in this spot seemed to touch something inside with a strange cleansing and strengthening.

"Look, Tan," Jaren said in soft wonder, as they gazed all about them. "This, I swear on my heart, is what all of our homeland will be once again."

Tanner pulled the jesses down around his arm and tightened them to keep Kynon from flying off. "That will indeed be a sight to see, my friend. I, personally, just hope we can pull this whole thing off."

Jaren gently caressed the soft nose of his horse before replying. "I have the means now to change everything. I am positive that the Master has not given me His Power just to allow it rest idle within me. I don't know how He will chose to restore our earth, but I know that if our people are to survive after another war using the dragons for burning everything alive, the very soil itself will need to be cleansed, forests restored, and waters purified. The earth in the North barely yields enough for the people to live on now, even after all of these years of restoration. Now that ground, along with whole new regions, is being contaminated and destroyed by the dragons' fire. I believe that Elyon will have to step in and do miraculous things for our land if any living creatures are to survive."

Tanner stroked Kynon's breast feathers with the back of his finger. The little falcon had never had to be hooded, since he seemed to have been specially designed by Elyon for Tanner. Once the bird had chosen him, he was not fearful of any other human or animal. He looked into Tanner's eyes now, plainly adoring the youth. Tanner smiled and loosed the falcon to fly once more.

"At least everyone learned from the last war not to try to work the land without wearing masks and heavy clothing. The people will not die again of dust-plague," he said quietly, his voice full of sorrow. Then, straightening his shoulders, he said, "Still, there are many things to be considered, Jaren. Yes, you have the Power and resources of Elyon now, and the strength and heroic spirit of the many people who have pledged allegiance to you. I understand your consuming desire to help your people, but those desires, simply on their own merits, cannot protect the innocent ones who are going to die for you and for your throne. You must face up to the fact that hundreds will lose their lives, and Kinthoria *will* again be smoke and ruin, until this final war with the Dragonmasters is over. You will have to steel yourself to accept the fact that you will not be able to restore all the dead as you will the earth, if Elyon chooses to use you for such a miracle."

Jaren sat down on the grass, and watched Kynon as he spiraled upward on an invisible shaft of warm air.

"I know that, Tanner. A lot of noble, innocent people have died already. Not just for me, or my parents, but for the whole of Kinthoria. My mother and father were just the beginning of the massacre. Dols, Tanner, it tears me apart to think how much the Dragonmasters have already ravaged this land. You've seen the same things I have; heard the same lies. We sit here in peace and safety, enjoying all of this beauty, while others are dying in their tracks, either trying to stand

The Birth of a King

against the Dragonmasters, or fleeing from them." He paused to watch as Kynon made his incredibly swift dive, pulling up at the last moment to land softly on Tanner's leather covered arm.

"Look at Stonehaven," he continued. The thought of that desolate place sent a chill down his spine, despite the fact that Solance was shining brightly on this hot, summer afternoon. "And remember Tupper and his whole family, and his sheep. Dols, look at Reeban; there is no laughter, no singing...no hope anywhere north of the Shandra. The Dragonmasters haven't just destroyed physical things; they've destroyed the soul of Kinthoria."

Jaren shot Tanner a pleading look. "We must be determined in this, Tanner. We must not allow anything to stop us from freeing our land from the dragon riders and giving it back to the people. We must never allow fear of loss or death to stop us from reaching for victory, or the sacrifices that have already been given will have been for nothing, and Kinthoria will eventually become a dead world."

Tanner's dark eyes locked onto Jaren's. "I am not saying that we should quit, my friend. I have pledged my soul to see you to the throne." He patted Kynon's small, feathered head. "All I'm saying is that you need to be prepared for all that might be lost in the saving of Kinthoria. Otherwise, as you see the devastation and death occurring everywhere, you may become discouraged, and lose heart. You may begin to think that the price of freedom is too high. I'm merely saying that you need to steel yourself now, well ahead of time, for what we know is going to happen."

Tanner sat down beside his friend. "Your compassionate nature cannot be allowed to control you, until after this war is finished. You need to be reminded now, that this could mean the loss of Hawk, or Korthak, or myself. Jaren, you need to look at the worst possibilities and be ready to accept them and to determine in your heart to continue on even when you think that you and your people cannot bear to give any more."

Jaren turned anxious eyes toward him. "Do you think I am unaware of what the cost may be? After what happened in the Glamorgan Mines, my mind has been full of the possibility of great loss. But it doesn't mean I have to dwell on it. Dols, if I kept thinking on such things I would go mad. I would never have the courage to go forward with this! I just have to trust Elyon to give me whatever I need in the hard places...to take me through them with His own strong arm. Trusting Yesha with the lives of my friends and my people is the only way I can continue on with this terrible quest."

Tanner nodded his head in understanding, and they sat for some time in the silent comfort of their deep friendship. Finally, the time came to head back to the village.

They were unsaddling their horses when Hawk and Korthak came around the corner of Balgo's house.

"There you are!" Hawk said, his face beaming. "Fernaig sent word some time ago that he has visitors for you to meet. Let's not keep him waiting any longer."

They hurried to the old dwarf's home. There, in the front yard, walking about with a regal bearing which bespoke the pride and confidence of this ancient race was a group of broad shouldered men and women with glistening, chestnut-colored skin. The men, standing close to seven feet in height, wore their heads shaved, except for a curious black topknot which was cut a precise three fingers long, heavily waxed and made to stand straight on end. The two women stood around six feet tall, with shining blue-black hair braided as thick as Jaren's wrist, trailing to the back of their knees. They all wore crimson enameled breastplates and the jewel-encrusted hilts of their strangely curved swords glittered in the late afternoon sun. Their movements were marked with a graceful agility, which hinted at the remarkable athletic and military prowess for which this race was known.

"The An'ilden," Jaren mouthed to himself. His deep blue eyes were bright with awe and wonder.

Hawk turned to look at the lad. He softly cleared his throat and rushed a thought to Jaren. *"Um, Jaren...our lessons in protocol? It's impolite to keep such regal subjects waiting."*

Jaren flushed crimson at Hawk's use of the word *subjects*. It seemed beyond the absurd to consider these stately people of such ancient and noble heritage as subject to himself. He shook his head, squared his shoulders and sent up a silent plea to the true God for help. He was suddenly immensely grateful for Leonora's gift of new breeches for Tanner and himself. At least, he felt, he looked slightly more believable as the Prince of Kinthoria than he had upon arriving in Parth. He noticed with some amusement that Tanner had drawn in a huge breath and kept his chest out as far as possible, trying for all he was worth to look as much a warrior as possible. Jaren smiled slightly and continued on toward the strangers; at least he was not alone in his intimidation.

As they reached the group of An'ilden, Hawk, Korthak, and Tanner fell in behind Jaren.

The armed warriors each sank to one knee and saluted the young Prince by placing their huge fists against their chests.

Jaren bowed his head in acknowledgment of their fealty, even as Hawk had instructed him, and looked at Fernaig for the formal introductions.

"Ah, good afternoon, your Majesty," he said in his rough voice and stepping in front of the An'ilden. "I have someone here who is anxious to meet you."

As the An'ilden stood to their feet, Jaren noticed at once the keen, intelligent brown eyes set in the handsome young face towering behind the old dwarf. The young man wore on his right arm a wide golden band that encircled impossibly large biceps - a symbol to all of Kinthoria that he was Prince among the An'ilden. None were above him in status or authority, save Elyon, Jaren, and Ceara, the An'ilden queen, Seanachan's mother. He carried the responsibility of his position on massive, square shoulders.

"Your Majesty, I have the singular honor of presenting your most loyal subject, His Highness, Seanachan, Prince of the An'ilden." Jaren nodded as Fernaig continued. "My prince, I give you, Jaren Iain Renwyk Cathain, Prince of Kinthoria."

The nobleman bowed graciously to Jaren, once again saluting him with fist over heart. "Your humble servant is blessed and highly honored to meet Your Royal Majesty at last." Seanachan's deep voice resonated with eager sincerity. "It is truly a marvelous sight to behold one of royal blood in the land once again, Sire."

Jaren could feel that royal blood creeping into his neck and face. His ears were on fire. Someday he hoped he would be even a fraction as regal in bearing as this young warrior, standing so proudly before him. And yet, Jaren discerned no trace of arrogance in him.

He simply knew his own power, as he knew his own name. It was a part of who he was, but not the whole. He kept his power sealed away under the control of a heart full of compassion, to be used when necessary by an astonishingly agile mind.

Seanachan smiled and said, "I am your liege man, Sire. My life is yours to command."

Jaren smiled in return, "I am honored to accept the fealty of a man with such a true heart, and obvious valor and wisdom. My kingdom is highly blessed by your service." He grasped the man's forearm in the An'ilden greeting, "Seanachan, hmmm? You were perhaps named by a prophet of Elyon who was given knowledge of what you were to become?"

The huge man laughed good-naturedly, "Well, some have said that my mother is a prophetess, but I think in my case she was just hoping beyond hope that I would gain wisdom as I grew to manhood."

The entire company joined in his laughter as they entered Fernaig's cottage.

Hawk stepped past Jaren. "Forgive me, Sire, but I have not seen this young man in quite some time, and I have missed him terribly," he said as he embraced the young Prince in a bear hug.

"Dols, it's good to see you again," Hawk said, slapping him on the back, and grinning from ear to ear.

"And you also, my friend. I confess I feared you might be dead after all this time." Seanachan beamed.

Hawk stepped away from the Prince, holding him at arm's length. "Not yet, praise be to Elyon." He glanced over his shoulder to Jaren, the full meaning of his words passing between them. Then, turning his attention back to Seanachan, "I believe you have grown even more since last I saw you."

The young man looked down his frame. "Indeed, I have grown somewhat since last we met. Well, it serves you right for having been gone for two years. Now, who will win our wrestling matches, half-elf? I'm a full hand and a half taller than you now, and I'm certainly younger."

"Hah, I'm just coming into my prime, my Prince - just about your age in the elven race. So beware, I'm stronger than I look and I have experience on my side." Hawk laughed. "Besides, I've been taking care of some fairly important business, as you can see." They glanced once more at Jaren, who was thoroughly enjoying this reunion of two obviously close friends.

"Yes," Seanachan nodded. "Your business has been of the *utmost* importance."

"You remember Korthak?" Hawk stepped back and put his hand on the old bear's shoulder.

"Indeed I do," the An'ilden said, clasping Korthak's forearm. "Captain, you are still looking fit as ever."

Korthak laughed. "Yes and it's a pretty tight fit, too!" he said, tugging against the tightness of his belt. "Flattery will get you nowhere with me, young man."

Hawk glanced at Tanner and saw that the youth was trying desperately to become as inconspicuous as possible. Indeed, he was feeling very much out-of-place standing in such close proximity to all of this royal blood, and surrounded by the gigantic, battle-hardened warriors.

He had finally become accustomed to Jaren's royal status, because he knew that inside, Jaren was still the friend and brother with whom he had grown up. But Seanachan, in all of his strength and bearing was another matter. Tanner could actually sense, almost as a physical force, the power of this man's ancient An'ilden heritage.

Hawk winked at Korthak, and gave an almost imperceptible nod to his friend. The older man spun around to see the lad, and instantly knew what he was feeling. He turned back to the Prince.

"Forgive my rudeness, Seanachan. I, too, have an introduction to make."

Too late to flee, Tanner suddenly realized what Korthak was about to do, and took a step backward. Korthak put his huge hand behind his neck and gently pulled him to stand in front of the noble An'ilden.

"Your Highness, this is my adopted son, Tanner aP McKecknie, although it is as yet unofficial. Tanner, this is Seanachan, Prince of the An'ilden."

Tanner stood, dumbfounded. First because Korthak had just publicly acknowledged him as his son, and second because he was nothing more than a lowly commoner, and he was standing before an An'ilden prince, of all things, and he had not the slightest notion as to what to do.

He suddenly remembered what Hawk and Korthak had done when they first saw Jaren after his transformation at the Spring of Elyon, so he dropped to one knee and bowed his head.

"My Lord, I am honored," he stammered.

As the rest of the company looked on, Seanachan placed his hand on Tanner's shoulder. He had seen Tanner's discomfiture from the beginning, and would set the lad's mind at ease.

"No. It is I who am honored, warrior. For not only are you the son of a valiant Captain of the King's Army, you are also the Prince's brother, if I have read his Majesty's face aright. These are worthy titles to bear, my friend."

The Prince pulled Tanner up from his knee. He stared long into Tanner's eyes. "I also see that you wear the gear of a Falconer. So I surmise that you are the Warrior chosen by Elyon to champion the Prince and future King. You are Gil-Enrai," he nodded respectfully.

He smiled warmly at the speechless youth. "Do not look so surprised, Tanner. Can it be that you do not know that everyone in the village is talking about you? You are the envy of every youth in Parth."

Tanner's jaw dropped, and he looked questioningly at Jaren, and then to Hawk and finally back to Seanachan. "No, sir," he stammered. "I mean, your Highness. I didn't know. And yes, I do have a falcon. His name is Kynon. Jaren and I have just now returned from flying him this afternoon."

Korthak placed his hand on Tanner's shoulder, pride beaming on his face.

The Prince looked at Hawk. "A very formidable company you have formed here, my friend. Now, I will ask that we dispense with all of the formalities of titles and such, if that is agreeable with you, Sire." He bowed his head toward Jaren.

Jaren sighed and nodded an enthusiastic approval. "That would be a blessing, Seanachan, as I have not as yet grown accustomed to the speech and actions that are proper to my heritage. Thank you."

Fernaig once again popped his fluffy white head into the circle of friends, and snorted. "Now, if you are all quite finished with all of this blubbering and cow-towing, might it be possible for us to get down to business?" he scowled darkly.

Laughing at the ancient dwarf's audacity, they entered Fernaig's home and took seats around Fernaig's long, wooden table. The dwarf had them laughing uproariously when he asked if anyone noticed the increased heat in the small room from all of the hot air drifting about the place.

Seanachan's eyes glowed with good-natured menace, "Be careful, Dwarf. You tread dangerously close to contempt," he laughed.

Fernaig looked up at the proud young man, with wide eyes that bespoke infinite insult and long-suffering at such insolence. "Bah," he retorted.

It was long into the night when the company parted. As Hawk, Korthak, Balgo, Jaren, and Tanner headed back to Balgo's home. Seanachan slipped in behind their company.

"Jaren, may I please have a word with you?" he asked softly.

The young Prince suppressed a yawn, and told his friends to continue on to Balgo's. As soon as they were alone, Jaren gestured toward a boulder and directed the An'ilden to sit beside him.

"What is it, Seanachan?"

The young warrior looked up at Lunisk, shining full and bright, on this warm summer evening. He breathed in deeply of the night air.

"Some words of advice, if I may be so bold, my new friend," he paused and looked long into Jaren's eyes, "and a matter of some concern to myself?"

Jaren smiled with sincere humility at his new friend. "Any advice from a trustworthy friend will be a great boon to me, and you know that I will gladly help with any problem you may have, if I am able."

Seanachan relaxed somewhat, knowing he was free to speak his mind. "I want to advise you, first of all, not to judge yourself too harshly, Jaren. Today I sensed your embarrassment when we met." Jaren dropped his eyes and smiled weakly. "I understand your emotions, my friend, but trust me, I do not know of one person who is loyal to our cause who would expect your appearance and demeanor to be that of one who was reared in court. All of your people understand your loss and your former need for anonymity. The message has gone out from this quiet place, all over the land, that the true heir has been found after living a life of obscurity. Believe me when I say that everyone will be so filled with joy to see you standing before them that they will not care in the least if you bow correctly, or if you address them in the correct manner."

Jaren sat in silence, listening in earnest to Seanachan's words of encouragement.

"Jaren, it is very important that you know and understand that finally, after all these years of despair, there is a rising new hope in our land. There are whispers of freedom and joy. There are smiles, even in the midst of fear, because the people are prepared to rise up and follow you to freedom."

He took the time to carefully think through his next words, and their possible effect upon Jaren. "I think we may both be envious of one another, my Liege."

Jaren's eyes widened. "What do you mean? Why would you possibly envy me?" he asked incredulously.

Seanachan chuckled. "It surprises you...that I would be envious of you?"

Jaren nodded.

"You have been gifted by Elyon to have lived a simple life. You have seen and taken part in the ways of the common people. That is something I hope you will treasure for as long as you live. I, on the other hand, have been steeped in training for the position that I now hold. I have spent my entire life in preparation to become the leader of my people, without actually being given the chance to know them or their needs personally."

His voice broke slightly, "You envy me for all of my training, and I envy you for your lack of it." He smiled, "Incredible, isn't it? But what I am hoping for is that you and I will help one another to see that we have no reason to wish for that which we have not been given, but rather that we can share what each of us has learned, in order to improve both our capabilities. I want to be your friend, Jaren, besides being one of your many loyal subjects."

Jaren was speechless. He had no idea that anyone, especially the Prince of the most honored race in Kinthoria, would envy the lot of one who had lived as a commoner, and even more, wish to become his close friend. He took Seanachan's right hand and clasped his own hand around the forearm of the Prince in a firm handshake.

"Seanachan, I would be honored to have you as a friend. And I think you are right, we can learn much from one another."

The An'ilden returned Jaren's warm handshake and laughed. "Excellent! I was hoping you would be in accord."

Jaren's face sobered, "Now, you had a certain concern you wanted to discuss, and if I read your eyes correctly, it is weighing heavily upon you."

Seanachan sighed, "We must not delay overlong from entering this conflict."

Jaren looked at his new friend, "But, you just heard our plans; we leave tomorrow for the abbey at Coryn's Reach." He looked at the An'ilden's face. "Seanachan, what didn't you tell us in that council today?" he asked urgently.

The Prince's eyes were filled with pain as he softly said, "I did not wish to be seen as seeking revenge, or to be placing the plight of my people above any others, but there are not many of my race left in Kinthoria, Jaren. We relentlessly fight against the Dragonmasters whenever it is possible, but the skirmishes we win are far outnumbered by the defeats we suffer. We are only victorious when the dragon riders are not on dragon back, so they are extremely cautious when they must dismount.

We estimate that we are about forty thousand, at most. What good is all of my training if I have no people to lead? Those vile creatures are slaughtering my race by the thousands, and I cannot do anything but stand by and watch the carnage."

Scenes of Stonehaven rushed into Jaren's mind, and he felt sick to his stomach. Hawk had been right. Such evil destruction was not a thing of the past, but a continual reality to these people of strength and honor. Jaren began to speak, slowly choosing his words, searching for the best way to share his thoughts with Seanachan. "My friend, I have already made a vow to your race in my heart after seeing the truth revealed so forcefully at Stonehaven. The lives that have been

The Birth of a King

lost, the innocent blood that has been so viciously spilled will not be forgotten. Not ever. I give you my word that your people will once again flourish in Kinthoria." He looked deeply into this tall man's eyes, determination flashing from his own, as he continued. "You will indeed see your race thriving as it once was in its years of glory. Your women will increase in childbearing, birthing magnificent sons and daughters. You will be a great leader. Songs and tales about the glory of your reign will be sung in the banquet halls of kings and princes long after you are sitting beside Yesha in heaven. Your people will be happy and walk the land in honor and peace as they have in the past. You have my solemn promise of this, my friend." Jaren was shaken at these words spoken with such bold assurance, and wondered if his longing for avenging the An'ilden had overpowered his judgment.

"I have spoken these truths through you, Jaren," Elyon's words came in affirmation. *"I have created you to also be a prophet king, so that others may be strengthened in hope and courage in the knowledge of My will."* Jaren sighed in relief and smiled.

Seanachan sat in stunned silence before his Prince. Finally, his face beamed and he stood to his feet and bowed deeply. "I perceive that Elyon has made you a prophet as well as a King. I praise His wisdom and power, and I will forever be indebted to you, Majesty. My people are ready and waiting for your call, to aid and support you in any way possible. I just pray that we may come to their aid with all speed."

"Pray with me this night, that the Father will protect us all, and that He will encourage your soul," Jaren said as he rose.

"I will gladly do so. Thank you, Jaren. We are well met today," the Prince said warmly.

Jaren nodded and turned toward Balgo's cottage. "Thank you for your advice, and for your friendship."

As he walked down the quiet road, lit by Lunisk's bright fullness, Jaren acknowledged to himself before Elyon that it would be a long, and most certainly costly road ahead for each of them on many personal levels. But Elyon would keep His promise to the An'ilden prince and his people. That was one thing in his future of which he felt absolutely certain. As his excitement grew in this knowledge,

The Birth of a King

he could barely control the urge to begin the quest tonight, so eager was he to see how Elyon would accomplish this feat so crucial to his heart – the restoration of the An'ilden race.

Chapter Thirty-One

GIFTS

On their final morning in Parth, Jaren and his friends were breaking their fast around the bountiful board in Balgo and Leonora's cottage. He had been absently nibbling at one of Leonora's freshly baked fruit muffins, apparently deep in thought. Suddenly, he squared his shoulders, quickly finished his meal and rose from the table.

"Hawk, would you join me outside for a moment, please?" he said, in a tone which showed unmistakably that he expected nothing but compliance to his request.

Tanner was untroubled by the abrupt departure of his friend, but Korthak had caught the hint of a command and concern in Jaren's voice. He threw the barest glance at Hawk, knowing that eventually he would be informed, if need be, as to the cause of Jaren's behavior. He was pleased that Jaren seemed to be willing now, to take on the responsibilities of leadership when he was able. It was right that he should do so.

As they walked out of the tiny cottage, Jaren haltingly reached over to see if Kynon would allow a caress on his head, and was pleasantly surprised that the little bird seemed to welcome his touch.

Jaren motioned for Hawk to follow him across the wide lane which made up the main thoroughfare of the village. He sat down on the same granite boulder that he and Seanachan had occupied just hours before, and put his head in his hands.

"We must leave here at once, Hawk. The Father has been urgently calling me into immediate action ever since our council last night; something is happening that is causing a strong pressure at the back of my head. I think it has something to do with the dragons, but I am still so new at this that I am not certain of its meaning. I don't know what to expect, but I am sensing a sort of fearful anticipation from the dragons." He looked up at Hawk. "I'm not explaining this well at all."

Hawk laid his hand on his friend's shoulder. "You're doing fine, son. You are *Sanda Aran*, the dragons' master and will most likely sense much of their emotions. In the entire history of Kinthoria, we have never had to contend with this in an heir; the former male heirs grew up with the full knowledge of the dragons, and learned what to expect in their contact from the time they were born. That you must discover how to discern that interaction, is a temporary disadvantage. Unfortunately, we are walking blindly through some of this alongside you. We'll give you what training we can with, hopefully, a few generous doses of wisdom in the mix; but on this one I would suggest you continue sifting through the memories of your ancestors to find how they interacted with the dragons. Perhaps it would help if you zeroed in on their formative years, when they were being instructed in this matter," Hawk smiled. "I guess this daunting task will be your penance for trusting an elf."

Jaren laughed and stood, willing the tension from his body. "Yes, well I was always moaning to Tanner about not being able to have control of my own life. I guess that just goes to show you that you should be careful what you ask for."

Hawk grinned. "Ahh, but I will venture to guess that you never once had visions of this much change, eh?"

Jaren snorted. "No, not even close."

They headed back to Balgo's cottage. Jaren knew that Hawk could not help him decipher the implications of the dragons' discomfiture. However, he needed no help whatever in understanding the Father's clear imperative to leave immediately for Coryn's Reach.

Seanachan and his escort reigned in their horses at the gate. The Prince dismounted, and entered the cottage to a room full of concerned faces and chaotic movement, caused by Jaren's abrupt announcement of their immediate departure.

Seanachan noticed the tiny dwarf woman, hastily wrapping food in linen cloths and packing it into saddle bags, while roughly whisking away the tears running down her cheeks and sporting a brave smile as Hawk and Balgo tried in vain to comfort her.

He saw Korthak's face set with purpose, his eyes burning with anticipation as he gathered his gear and headed for the door.

Tanner had slipped on the heavy piece of leather that served as a perch for Kynon, and was just lifting his bedroll and saddle bag onto his shoulders.

Jaren, in the midst of all the chaos, had quietly entered the tiny bedroom which he had been sharing with Tanner. Seanachan found him on his knees, his head bowed, at the side of the bed, and so he waited at the bedroom door. The young prince was praying once again for the true God to be his courage to face a future filled with overwhelming responsibilities. He prayed that Elyon would take hold of his thoughts and emotions each time that he may start to lose control – to overlay them with His very own. He asked his Master to continually be the decisive calm and wisdom in action so essential to the stability of his kingdom. Jaren wanted very badly to be a good king; to never have any of his actions or decisions harm to even one of his countrymen. He knew this would be impossible to accomplish with his own strength. But he already knew enough of Elyon and His Power to know that being a good king was not only a probability, but a high certainty, if he would always keep in mind the fact that the one true God was also the one true King.

Seanachan watched in fascination as Jaren's shoulders slowly lost the bowed posture of his burden, and squared up into firm determination. He watched a calm settle over the young man, as Elyon's invisible force filled Jaren's entire body, until Seanachan could actually feel power radiating from him, even at such a distance. He could not be certain, but he seemed to see a thin aura of light clinging to the young prince.

Jaren lifted his head and stood; his clear blue eyes locked onto Seanachan. The An'ilden was irresistibly drawn to him, and he knelt before him, fist over heart, and said once more, "My Liege."

The Birth of a King

Jaren placed his hand upon the man's shoulder and smiled. "Come, my friend, ride with me to Coryn's Reach, and to the freeing of Kinthoria," he said softly, but firmly.

Seanachan looked into eyes that shone with confidence, even eagerness to engage the enemy that very second.

Jaren walked out of the bedroom to Leonora. He took her tiny hands in his own and smiled as he kissed them. "Thank you for everything, Leonora. Because of your gift of the new breeches, I'll not be entering St. Ramsay's looking like a vagabond, but like a true prince."

The little woman smiled bravely, and turned her head. Jaren followed her gaze and they both watched as Balgo, the giant of a man in a dwarf's body, strode purposefully out the door. He squeezed her hands gently, "Pray for us, my good woman, and remember we are all in Elyon's hands." He bent down, and to her infinite delight and embarrassment, gave her a huge hug.

As Jaren stepped out of the cottage, he overheard Seanachan speaking with Korthak. "My friend, you are in need of a strong and well-seasoned mount. I believe this one will serve you well," he said firmly, handing a stunned Korthak the reins to a stallion that was heavy in the neck and shoulders, and graced with powerfully muscled legs. Korthak hesitated only an instant before taking the reins from the An'ilden prince.

"Thank you, my giant friend. Once more you prove the eminence of your race with compassion and honor," he said, bowing deeply.

Hawk and Jaren smiled, and Tanner looked as though he would burst with joy for his adopted father.

At that moment, Fernaig arrived with two other dwarves in tow and bowed to Jaren. "Your majesty, I bring gifts for you and the *Gil-Enrai*. As I will not be accompanying you to your coronation, we have resolved to present to you these gifts as evidence that the Dwarven Elders have bestowed blessings upon you as you take up your royal name and titles, and as surety of our allegiance to you as the true Cathain heir."

Two dwarves stepped forward and Jaren saw the wide smile on Graeth's face. He presumed the young dwarf had been appointed an honor guard to the Elders on this occasion.

The Birth of a King

Graeth stepped in front of Tanner, and pulled the red velvet wrapping from a beautifully worked set of leather vambraces. Tanner's eyes widened and his jaw dropped. "They are magnificent," he whispered in awe. He yanked at the roughly cut leather he had been using and asked Graeth to clasp the new vambraces onto his arms. "What a splendid gift. Thank you, Fernaig. Please offer my thanks and deep appreciation to the Elders for the honor of such a rich gift," he said excitedly. Unable to contain his delight he gripped the old dwarf in a hug and patted him roughly on the back.

The beaming Graeth moved to stand in front of Jaren. "Your gift from the Elders, Sire." As he pulled back the wine-colored velvet of the gift, Jaren whispered, "Congratulations on your appointment!" When he looked down and saw Fernaig's gift, he sucked in his breath in astonishment. He reverently lifted a leather-bound volume of Elyon's Word from the young dwarf's hands and caressed the cover. "Fernaig, this is exquisite. I don't…" he swallowed the lump in his throat, "I can't.…" Jaren stepped up to the old dwarf and tightly embraced him. "This will be the truest treasure of my kingdom," he said softly. "I give you the charge to instruct your scribes to begin making the copies of this that will be spread throughout Kinthoria when our quest is completed."

A misty-eyed Fernaig smiled broadly, "You are too late, my Prince. We began that years ago and have hundreds of copies ready to distribute. People of all races who are faithful to Elyon have been employed in the task; it has been such a rich enhancement to our hope." He backed away from the travelers, relishing Jaren's stunned and delighted approval. "Godspeed, Your Highness, and to all of you, until we meet again," he shouted.

Jaren carefully stowed his treasure in his saddle bag, and mounted. He gazed at each of those who would be racing with him to St. Ramsey's Abbey. If ever a man looked like a sovereign, Jaren did in that moment. No imperial trappings for adornment, no glittering jewels, or trumpeting fanfare. But as the young prince looked around at his companions, there was an air of confidence, and a regal bearing about him, that caused every man in his company to sit taller in the saddle, and to vow to follow him to battle, freedom and glory.

"It is time to begin keeping the promises I have made to the memories of those I have met on this journey, both living and dead," Jaren shouted. "It is time to rid the land of the foul, reeking stench of our dark enemy and his hordes. It is time for the light of Truth to shine once again upon Kinthoria! Balgo," he shouted, "take us to Coryn's Reach!"

As one, the company dug their heels into the flanks of their horses, and quickly disappeared into the morning mists which softly blanketed the valleys and glens of the Kroth Mountains.

Chapter Thirty-Two

RIFTS IN COUNCIL

It had been seven intolerable weeks since Volant's dragon riders had been able to touch or mount their dragons. Every priceless dragon egg had been stolen by the dragons and presumably hidden somewhere in Kinthoria. The dragon's ear-splitting keening had died down in the first week, but they were still withdrawn and edgy as though gripped by some strange anticipation.

Upon observing the drunken, inept state of his troops on the day the dragon rebellion began, Volant had sent orders to the Cellarmaster that no ale or wine was to be served, beginning immediately and until further notice. He had further ordered his Flight Leaders and the officers of the cavalry and infantry units to instruct their troops that no one was to touch a drop of any private stock on penalty of death.

The Dragon Leader had spent much of the day in his war chamber with his Flight Leaders and Beland, discussing the disappointing reports from the infantry and cavalry scouts, and finalizing their strategy for locating the renegade heir whenever they got the dragons airborne again.

His gaze moved to Tomas. The man was thirty-three, less than average in height, and slender, but his size was deceptive of his strength and agility. He wore his long, brown hair pulled back and tied at the base of his neck. He was a quiet-spoken man, but that too, was misleading, for he could bark orders to his troops and be heard above the din of a parade ground full of confusion. The authority in

The Birth of a King

his voice could pierce through minds filled with either rebellion or fear and bring them back to the discipline of training. He was intelligent, levelheaded, and resolute. Volant had chosen him at an early age and placed him in charge of the training flight for just these reasons. He had needed a new leader for the Purple Flight, after a troll had savagely killed Pritan, the former Flight Leader, in a border skirmish. He would continue to observe him, *"He may just make a proper replacement for Beland when the time comes,"* he thought.

Volant turned next to Tulak, who shifted uncomfortably under the scrutiny of his leader. His wavy, black hair hung freely around his face and over his shoulders. The man, in his late thirties, bore the facial scars of his adolescence. Tulak was a stocky man, carrying some extra weight on his large frame. Volant considered him a clumsy oaf, as was evidenced the morning of the dragon rebellion. But Volant needed his uncanny knack for persuading frightened, homesick boys to do just about anything. His rapport with the dragons was amazing. There was not one dragon that did not adore the man. With these assets, he was the perfect choice for Green Flight leader, training the new cadets, and bringing each dragon and boy together with as little fear, and as much speed as possible. Many excellent dragon riders had come out of Tulak's flight, showing much promise, even to the cynical Sirtar. Tulak was highly proud of the fact that Volant had chosen his star pupil, Tomas, to lead the advanced training flight, instead of one of the older, seasoned veterans.

Volant looked at his Colonel. He was still so angry at Sirtar's mishandling of the Reeban message regarding two missing boys that he had to restrain himself from shaming him beyond recovery in front of his subordinates. However, the critical matter before them must take precedence at the moment.

Lastly, his eyes fell on Bendor, the man who would most likely be his heir, if Vanessi did not bear him a son. He thought of his several illegitimate children and could not for the life of him understand what was wrong with his wife. Her problem had dumfounded all the priests and so-called healers. But that was another matter. He knew his work would be carried on through Bendor. The young man was highly intelligent and believed with just as strong a conviction as his own, in the plan to subjugate all of Kinthoria once and for

The Birth of a King

all. Bendor had the strength to see the plan through, should Volant be disabled or killed. He would conquer and rule with sanity, while keeping a tight rein on Sirtar's savagery...or perhaps just killing him outright.

He cleared his throat, removing the smile from his face. "We are all agreed, then, that while we must move as quickly as possible, haste must not become the ruling factor. Our search must be comprehensive and meticulous; every possible hiding place must be searched thoroughly."

"Does anyone have anything further to add?" he asked.

"I would like to volunteer my flight for the mission into the Southern Regions, sir," said Bendor. "We could use the time to gain experience down there, and I know my troops would do a thorough job in searching that area for this impostor."

Without breaking contact with Bendor's gaze, Volant saw Sirtar slowly rise from his chair, every muscle taut.

Tulak and Tomas inched their seats away from the table, expecting Sirtar to send the massive board and all its contents flying.

Volant snapped his head toward Sirtar, a venomous grin twisting his mouth as he noted the rage in his Colonel's eyes. "Something wrong with that proposal, Colonel?" he asked matter-of-factly.

Sirtar's gaze bored through Bendor, hate flashing in his eyes. "Yes, Sir," he spat. "I would think you would see the error in sending a young, inexperienced, green *virgin* on a mission of this urgency, when most of my flight and I have scouted that region before." Sirtar's laugh was hideous with the tension of a barely controlled urge to kill the Red Flight leader. "Dhragh, Bendor was still a babe in dresses when I started flying patrols down there."

Bendor stood slowly, facing the huge man without fear, although remembering the stranglehold the Colonel had held him in the last time they had spoken to each other. His neck still bore the marks from Sirtar's hands, which he had hidden conspicuously with a tall riding shirt. "I am sorry to disagree, *sir*. My flight has many veteran troops who have done more than just scouting the Southern Regions. Many of them were stationed down there before the war. As for the rest of my troops, they have proved time and again that they are capable of such a task. Have you forgotten that I do not lead a training flight,

Colonel?" he threw back at Sirtar in anger. "Or has the weight of the age about which you have just boasted muddled your mind beyond the capability of recall?"

The Blue Flight leader lunged at the young man, the veins in his neck and on his forehead bulging with the intensity of his rage. Volant, Tomas, and Tulak grabbed the two enemies and wrestled them apart.

Volant was seething himself by now. "Enough!" he shrieked. "This is a military council, not a cat fight for jealous wenches. You will hold your petty bickering in abeyance for the present." He glared at both men. "Am I making myself clear enough for even the two of you to understand?"

Bendor broke free of Volant's grasp with a violent jerk, yanked his leather vest back into place and sat slowly back onto his stool.

Sirtar gave Tulak and Tomas a warning glare and the two men prudently released their grip on the Force Commander, stepping quickly out of reach of his massive fists.

Volant pierced him with his eyes. "Colonel, you are treading on very thin ice. I will ask you again to take a seat so we may continue."

Sirtar complied and the rest of the meeting passed without further incident, despite the unvented animosity of the two Flight Leaders.

Volant knew he could trust Bendor with the Southern Regions, but did he want to risk losing his only choice for an heir to an Elven arrow? Sirtar was a savage, and was familiar with the military methods of the Southern races, but would he set aside his insane hatred long enough to look for the traitor or would he simply go on a killing rampage to appease his lust for murder?

Long after the departure of the Flight Leaders, Volant considered the advice of his council, still uncertain which flight to send into the South. It was not until moments before he gave in to the need for sleep that he finally chose his man.

Chapter Thirty-Three

A Joke Reversed

As Jaren and his company rode through the high mountain reaches of the South, word of a Cathain heir was spreading like wildfire to the North. Many people of all races had been anxiously awaiting the news, and had been in a literal foot race to spread the spark of hope throughout the Northern Regions.

Hawk had spoken of these people briefly in Fernaig's chamber during their first council meeting. "We need the people behind us as quickly as possible. We will send couriers out from here to reach the scouts all along the Shandra River, and north from there."

Seanachan spoke next. "My people have more access to the North. If the word can get up to our territory, we will be able to spread it much more quickly through our underground channels, to every city and village up there. We have hundreds ready to go at any moment."

Korthak broke in, "Has anyone considered the possibility that people may not believe this news of an heir?"

Silence fell over the group sitting around the littered table.

Seanachan smiled triumphantly, "That is the best argument in the world for using my people to spread the news." He sat back and smiled with satisfaction. It was common knowledge that it was easier to hold back the tides of the Great Otten Sea than for an An'ilden to speak falsely. The giant prince looked at his friends. Jaren smiled along with the rest of the men around the table. "Then let it be so," he said with enthusiasm.

The Birth of a King

So it was that hundreds of Jaren's unknown, but loyal followers were flying north and east and west, whispering words of hope and inspiration to the disheartened people of Kinthoria. Word spread at the piers along the river, a helmsman to an oarsman; it spread in the inns, a scullery maid to a patron's valet; it spread on the roads, in the fields, in dairies, and tailor shops. The word was everywhere, "The King is alive! Long live the King!"

A tiny spark of hope had been ignited across the Shandra. Jaren and his companions could only hope that it would turn into a white hot blaze by the time they were ready to join with their countrymen to free the land from the Dragonmasters' reign of cruelty and terror.

Jaren's company rode hard all of the first day out of Parth. The pace which Balgo set for them left little time or opportunity for conversation. Each man's mind was centered entirely on the need for haste, and on the coming war with the Dragonmasters. Continual prayer went up to the Father, for guidance and protection, as each rider considered the utter hopelessness of fighting the dragons without the help of Elyon. They knew that their fight was doomed to failure if they tried to enter into it without the Power and the presence of the Master. They called for help to come from the Father's own army of mighty angels. They called for courage when facing the dragons, and asked for victory over them. They called for Elyon's Spirit to fill them full of the Father's strength, and to go before them and to bring chaos, confusion, and fear into the councils of the enemy, and into the ranks of the Dragonmaster Army.

As they rode and prayed and thought, the beauty and majesty of the countryside passed by unheeded. So intense was their concentration on the spiritual world that the natural world seemed but a misty dream to their eyes.

It was late in the afternoon when Balgo called for a halt. He turned in his saddle to speak to Jaren and Hawk. "This is Renfrew Beacon. There is a spring on the other side of that small thicket," he said pointing down the slope to a low line of gorse, "and there is plenty of grass for the horses."

Hawk gazed around the area, and up into the sky above the cliffs towering on all sides of this small mountain valley. He nodded his head. "We'll camp just inside that stand of trees beyond the spring."

As Jaren nodded in agreement, Balgo snorted with contempt. "I wouldn't be worrying about any dragons coming this far south of the Shandra. They haven't been that brave in over a decade," he spat, kicking his weary little pony into a fast jog down into the valley below.

After Jaren had watered and picketed his horse, he slowly made his way to a fallen log at the edge of the trees. It was the first time since they had set out that morning that he had been consciously aware of his surroundings. He was glad for this moment of solitude, as he drank in the breath-taking beauty of the ancient ruggedness of the mountains surrounding this valley. He saw the splendor of the deep azure sky stretching endlessly above the mountaintops, so high overhead. His gaze fell to the valley lying in serenity before him. The bright yellow and brown blanket flowers, coral columbine, orange and yellow day lilies, blue and white irises, saxifrage and poppies, and hundreds more blooming flowers in this summer landscape had clothed the valley in a myriad of colors. Jaren stood and slowly walked along the edge of the meadow, touching the flowers with his fingertips, and marveling at the perfection of each delicately shaped petal. The fragrance was pungent and heady. He was immediately awe-struck by the wonder of the mind of Elyon. "Father, You are the source of this beauty. All of this comes from You. How incredibly magnificent You are!" he whispered in praise.

Hawk, upon reaching the thicket, had slid from his mount, and was leading his horse to the spring rather stiff-legged, after a full day in the saddle, when Korthak fell into step beside him and slapped him heartily on the back.

"What's the matter, my friend? Is that nearly defunct old body tired of playing these games already?" the huge bear of a man asked, laughing heartily.

Hawk stopped dead in his tracks, placing a very muddled look on his face, and washing his features with a highly exaggerated weariness, he turned to face his teasing friend. "I...I don't know, Korthak," he said slowly, and with much effort, moving a trembling hand across his forehead. "Maybe if I could just sit here on this soft

The Birth of a King

grass for a few moments, I'd be all right." His voice and demeanor were now almost tragically comic. "Do you think, dear friend, that you could water my horse for me?" he asked with pleading eyes, and throwing in, for effect, just the hint of a gasp for air.

Korthak was completely shaken by this unexpected response from Hawk. He quickly took the reins from the half-elf, who was literally about to collapse, not from fatigue, but from holding in the laughter.

"Sure, Hawk," Korthak answered, putting his massive arm around Hawk's waist and helping him into the shade of the trees. As soon as Hawk was seated, Korthak quickly lifted a waterskin from his horse and pulled the stopper with his teeth. His face was etched with concern as he handed the skin to Hawk.

"Hawk, what is it? What's wrong?" a voice slipped into his mind. Jaren had seen him from the meadow and was beginning to run toward his friends.

"I'm fine, lad, and stay there! I'm just playing a little game with my mouthy friend here," Hawk sent. He watched as a flustered Korthak lumbered off to the spring with two horses in tow, and turned with an evil grin to look across the clearing at Jaren.

Jaren looked at Hawk, resting comfortably with his back against a tree, waterskin in hand. He stopped in his tracks and, grinning at the half-elf, shook his head. He beheld a very worried Korthak, standing knee deep in the spring, washing down the horses while trying to monitor Hawk at the same time.

"Psst!" Jaren hissed at Tanner, tapping his friend's saddle. He gestured toward the two men with his thumb.

Tanner looked up to see Jaren grinning from ear to ear. His gaze followed Jaren's. "What's going on?" he asked, as Jaren walked around the big stallion to join his friend.

"I don't know. I'm thinking it's another of Korthak's jokes being turned back on him."

"Not again," Tanner groaned, as Seanachan joined them.

"Is there a problem with Hawk?" he asked with concern.

Jaren shook his head. "No, at least not at the present moment. I'm not sure about the immediate future, though."

Seanachan nodded. "Oh. The two pranksters are at it again, are they?"

The three younger men watched as Korthak bathed the dust and sweat-covered horses, while repeatedly glancing at his friend.

"Maybe we shouldn't watch this," Tanner said out of the corner of his mouth.

Seanachan chuckled. "You're right. This could get ugly at any moment."

Jaren smiled and said, "Yes, but if we don't watch, we'll miss the look on Korthak's face when he realizes he's been made the fool! Then Hawk's suicide will have been for nothing."

The trio laughed quietly among themselves. They were not alone in their observations, however. Most of the other companions had seen Hawk's feigned collapse and had been immediately concerned, until they saw Jaren's sudden change in behavior. Then they knew that something amusing was afoot, and though seemingly busy with the mundane tasks of setting up camp, each was watching covertly, the little charade being played out by Hawk.

It wasn't long before a very soggy Korthak brought two clean and contented horses back to the picket rope. When he had them tied securely, and was just about to return to the tending of his fallen comrade, Hawk leaped up from his shady rest and bounded over to meet the astonished older man.

Seanachan leaned toward his two friends. "Should I go gather some of my men to keep Korthak off him?" All three broke into laughter once again.

Hawk was thanking Korthak profusely, with much energetic back slapping and gesturing, for washing his horse down so thoroughly. He said that amazingly he felt much better now that the dirty job was done.

Korthak's face went through several changes in the next few seconds, from disbelief to relief to a squinted look of anger as understanding finally broke upon his mind.

"Here it comes!" Tanner whispered to his companions.

Korthak looked down at his muddy, dripping breeches, and back up at Hawk with wide, wild eyes. "Why you no-good, faking, droopy-eyed, long-legged tree lover!" he screamed, lunging at Hawk. Try as he might, though, he never even came close to catching the now rested and faster half-elf.

The entire company was overtaken by fits of laughter as they gathered around the two men. Hawk was near tears with laughter, and poor Korthak was purple-faced with feigned rage and embarrassment.

No one ever found out how this stand-off might have ended, however, because Balgo, knowing that someone had to put a stop to the nonsense, marched his mountain pony between the two friends, barking sternly, "You two can help set up camp any time you're a mind to. We didn't accompany you on this little trip just so you two could play a jester's troupe!"

He then proceeded to stomp away to the spring as though he were a father completely fed up with two unruly sons. However, he betrayed his feigned disgust with the slightest trace of laughter around his eyes, and a merry little tune he began whistling.

With the tension broken, Korthak was finally able to see that Hawk had only reversed the joke on him, and he laughed heartily. However, he would not acknowledge that he forgave Hawk until he had promised to help him prepare the evening meal.

As the company gathered around the small fire, Balgo and Seanachan kept the conversation light, and they recounted more tales of the outrageous practical jokes which Korthak and Hawk had played on one another through the years of their friendship.

Balgo recalled, haltingly, through much laughter, the time that Korthak had smeared lard all over Hawk's saddle. When he described Hawk's ungraceful descent on the off side of his mount, the whole company roared with laughter.

As the sun disappeared early over the tops of the surrounding mountains, Balgo ordered the fire extinguished, and everyone to their bedrolls. That order was received gladly by an extremely weary group of men. They all were aware that, even with Balgo's shortcuts through tunnels and mines, the need for haste could over extend the strength of men and horses alike, for they must arrive at Coryn's Reach before two weeks had passed.

It had been decided to make as much haste as was humanly possible to get Jaren to the coronation and onto the road toward war

The Birth of a King

as the crowned King of Kinthoria. They knew that the vengeance of the Dragonmasters would be swift, brutal, and inconceivably vicious, and they wished to prevent as much carnage as possible.

Late into the night Hawk lay in his bedroll, staring up at the stars. He knew that all too soon the dragons would reach the Shandra River. He prayed earnestly that they would not cross that barrier, but somehow he knew that they would come. He fell asleep with a heavy heart, knowing what would become of the people and villages and forests, once the dragons breathed out their venomous flames.

Chapter Thirty-Four

CONTEMPLATION AND CONFRONTATION

Mavi kneaded the dough and brushed away the stray hair falling into her eyes with the back of her hand, leaving a smudge of flour on her forehead. A strange, volatile apprehension was very nearly palpable throughout the city and its surrounding areas. Something crucial was at hand, but Mavi could not put her finger on its cause. She had heard rumors that the dragons would be leaving soon on a mission of great importance, but she dismissed the idea from her mind. The dragon flights were still in disarray and were not even close to being functional. Beginning a massive undertaking of critical significance would be impossible if it involved the dragons. Besides, whenever Volant was seen walking about the city, he looked extremely irritated and distressed; not at all like someone preparing for a campaign in which he was confident of success.

She did not have the courage to question Bendor about it, as he had been especially troubled the last time she had encountered him. Besides, it would not be wise to expose the fact that servants and slaves were capable of intelligent thought; or that they would have interests and opinions regarding the governance of kingdoms. As Bendor spoke with her, she had noticed several deep bruises on his neck, but then quickly dropped her eyes as was proper for a slave. She was worried about him; his unusual distance and preoccupied manner only fueled her anxiety. Instinctively, she considered asking if she had somehow displeased him, but her common sense told her that, his behavior had been prompted by the current impending events churning about them.

Her agitation increased with her seeming helplessness to decipher the atmosphere roiling through the city. What could it be? What was happening? The Rebellion was in no manner ready to begin with any hope of success and so had not as yet thrown down the gauntlet before Volant. Had war come upon them from some unexpected quarter? She felt as though she was about to be caught up in a tidal wave of change in which everything she had known would somehow be transformed.

She rolled the dough again, and pinched off a chunk, placing it on the small wooden paddle she would use to slide it into the cook oven, nestling it near the glowing embers. She had also noticed several of the other slaves whispering among themselves with smiles on their faces, but she was too timid to inquire about the cause of their amusement. She was unaware that many of the slaves did not trust her because of the preference shown to her by the Red Flight Leader; they would never consider sharing any important gossip with her, whether she asked or not.

Mavi heard a group of riders enter the cookhall. They were noisily sliding benches around, bellowing loudly with each other. She could tell they were not faring well with the edict Volant had passed restricting the consumption of ale and wine. Everyone was on edge, especially those who were known to indulge in the kegs too deeply.

"He almost finished what he's been wantin' to do for years!" Mavi heard one of the riders say.

"Aye! I hears the Eunuch ran away like a whupped dog!" Another said with a rough laugh. "It's too bad Sirtar didn't finish it."

Mavi's ears perked up at that comment, since she had heard the rumors about Bendor's unflattering moniker. She finished working with the bread and moved closer to the Blue Flight riders, needlessly checking the wall sconces as she went. She desperately wanted to know any tidbit of information that might help her understand Bendor's dark mood of late, and maybe even the cause of tension in Keratha. But just as she was nearing the group of riders, men from the Red Flight entered the cookhall.

"Ahh…looky who we have here," one of the Blue Flight riders shouted as he nodded toward the new comers, "the Eunuch's harem has arrived."

His comrades roared with laughter.

Mavi prudently moved away from what was sure to be a rigorous brawl judging by the hostility crackling in the air. She recognized Rathak, the First Lieutenant in the Red Flight, directing his men to the other side of the hall. She busied herself with more needless tasks feeling her cheeks flush from the vulgar assertions being made about Bendor and his Red Flight troops. Mavi could see that Rathak was, for the most part successful in diverting his men's attention away from the remarks until one of the Blue Flight riders stood on a table and mimicked someone being hung from a noose. This caused another raucous outburst of laughter from the riders in the Blue Flight. One of the men next to Rathak stood up, glaring at the men across the cookhall. Rathak grabbed the man's tunic, but the man tore himself from his grasp.

"It's obvious that you men are nothing but a bunch of feeble-minded, adolescent, inept cretins to find amusement in such behavior when you should be focusing your attention on getting the dragons flying again – as any *real* men would do." He boldly strode toward the group of now incensed men who had leaped to their feet with such force that their benches were overturned. They closed in on the Red Flight rider as his comrades immediately rushed to join him.

Mavi fled back to the safety of the kitchen for fear of being caught up in the coming melee.

"Cretins?" One of the Blue Flight men shouted. "Adolescents? Let me teach you about being respectful to your betters, son." He lunged toward the man from the Red Flight, ramming him in the torso with his shoulder, causing a whoosh of air to burst from the man's lungs. The two fell to the stone floor, grappling with one other. Some of the Blue Flight riders had broken the legs from several stools and were now pummeling the Red Flight riders with them. Rathak was attempting to pull men off of one another, commanding them to cease and reminding them that they were bringing shame and dishonor to their flights in the eyes of those watching. But it was useless, as the cookhall had become a scene of raging, curse-filled pandemonium.

A very loud crash instantly froze each man in his place. They all turned to see that Bendor had dropped a large oaken table over the side of the stair case landing. The wooden board had splintered to pieces on impact with the stone floor.

"Have you men all gone mad?" The Red Flight leader shouted. "Why aren't you preparing for our mission instead of fighting each other? What in Lucia's name has come over the lot of you? If you have enough spare time on your hands to engage in senseless brawls, perhaps we can add extra duties to lengthen your daily service."

He knew this would be yet another strike against him for berating Sirtar's men in public, but he feared that when Volant got wind of this little escapade, one or two of these men would be condemned to become sacrifices on the temple's altars. He also knew that a part of their tension had been caused upon hearing of the fight between himself and Sirtar; their rivalry was understandable and there was nothing he could do about it. He wished they could get the dragons in the air again, and move forward with their plans; it would give the men something to focus on, and get them well apart.

"Get this mess cleaned up," he gestured to the broken table and stools, "and get back to making yourselves useful somewhere!" He watched as his orders were completed, then turned to glare at his men. "You, follow me."

Mavi poked her head out of the kitchen just in time to catch Bendor's eye. His gaze was stern and she could see the anger smoldering in his eyes. He nodded briefly, turned and left the hall, his men following nervously behind him.

Mavi leaned against the stone wall and breathed deeply. She said a quick prayer for Bendor, and for all of the men who were struggling with so many weighty concerns. She had not the slightest inkling of what was causing the crisis with the dragons and the riders, but she knew that at present the Dragonmaster Army was powerless.

After weeks of watching the dragons' dreadful state of rebellion, the inhabitants of Keratha had found much fodder for rampant conjecturing as to its cause. Rumors flew of a strange wasting sickness contracted by the dragons, causing Volant to ban the riders from contact with them; for fear that humans could also be infected. The creatures had starved themselves to mere skeletal remnants, but something had caused them to cease their near-deadly fast. They began ravaging their food and gorging themselves until once again they were fit, sleek and strong; their bodies muscular and shining. They seemed to be readying themselves for something, but as to what that might be, no answer had presented itself.

Volant was furious when he heard that witnesses to the dragons' removal of their eggs had spread the news throughout Keratha and the surrounding towns and villages. His anger was multiplied tenfold when people began whispering that the dragons had begun cannibalizing the eggs. Further news was spread by the families of the dead dragon riders who had been airborne when the dragon rebellion began; news that the dragons had thrown their riders, killing them purposely and without warrant. This began speculation that Volant's Dragon Army was now defunct and that the dragons had become a danger even to the riders with whom they were so closely bonded. It also served to incite even more fear of the gigantic creatures among the Kerathians, and many had begun suggesting in whispered conversations that, since the dragons were no longer useful, perhaps the dragon riders should just kill them all and be done with the destructive vermin.

The growing agitation of the citizenry and the continuing rebellion of the dragons served to increase Volant's anger to the point that he recklessly burst into Galchobar's study unannounced and accused the priesthood of weakness and impotency. He left the temple bloodied and barely walking, but he considered the effectiveness of his visit well worth the cost, as he knew that the Lucian High Priest would dispense even worse punishment upon the priests until they found a way to control the dragons.

In his quarters, Sirtar drank down the last gulp of his heavy, dark wine. He had no intention of obeying his "esteemed" leader's edict banning the use of fermented beverages, and had been enjoying his private cache since the order had been given. No one would dare to inventory his supply, but even if they did, everything would be found in order, since he always took the precaution of replenishing his own stock with duplicate bottles from the main cellar below the cookhall. He cared nothing for the slaves who would be accused of theft and cruelly put to death.

At the moment, his mind raced over the many preferred means to torture a human being slowly, postponing death until one's fury and hatred had been sufficiently gratified. He eagerly looked forward to the day he would begin the slow implementation of those means upon the loathsome, disrespectful, whelp who led the Red Flight. He rubbed the side of his neck remembering the shock and pain he had experienced when Bendor had struck and immobilized him, and how his rage had completely consumed his mind to the point that he could not remember anything that took place between then and the time he awakened in his bed late that same day. He no longer cared one dragon scale about the search for the young men from the scholar's hall. He was bent on revenge, and he intended to practice his torture techniques on as many rebels and innocents as he could lay his hands on. The elves, An'ilden and other fools who had not accepted the dominance of the Dragonmasters and who had refused to conform to absolute rule would rue the day that Sirtar the Invincible, had passed his shadow across their lands. He smiled, savoring the new descriptive of himself; he liked the sound of it. "Sirtar the Invincible," he rumbled ominously.

"Dragh!" He slammed his fist down on the table. "Those parasites would have been annihilated long ago had I been Emperor! I would have played with them like a cat with field mice." He smiled once again, closing his eyes to envision the means used in his career triumph at Stonehaven. Oh, how he had enjoyed prolonging their agony.

Sirtar had no awareness that his sanity was slowly receding from the back of his mind while his unbridled hatred and bitterness nourished a ravenous insanity. He only knew he hated Bendor with every fiber in his gigantic body. He quivered with delight as he imagined himself standing exultantly over the young man, watching Bendor's lifeblood pool on the ground beneath his body. He would make certain that the last thing Bendor ever saw before his death would be the look of utter triumph on the face of his worst enemy.

The Birth of a King

In the meantime, he would have fun "playing with the field mice" in the Southern Regions. He was certain Volant would not assign the southern quadrant of Kinthoria to Bendor, and would allow Sirtar the freedom to do as he wished with the inhabitants. Surely, Volant understood that Bendor did not have it in him to use the brutal and vile atrocities necessary to bring rebels to their knees and to demonstrate to all Kinthoria the consequences of disobedience. Only he, Sirtar, was capable of handling the elves and dwarves, and the abhorrent An'ilden. Those who bowed to any god other than Lucia would pay for their insolence.

Sirtar himself held belief in no god and he had no interest in promoting religion of any sort. Religion was for the mentally and constitutionally weak who could not think for themselves or control events to ensure one's own plan of destiny. Sirtar was his own master. He was his own god; to serve anyone else was unthinkable. Yes. He would annihilate the races in the south, leaving a trail of bloody carcasses and ravaged land; and if he could, he would find the upstart who dared claim, by birthright, the throne of the Cathain Dynasty. He had been in the royal nursery the night of the invasion and destruction of the palace, and he knew of a certainty that there was no "royal blood" left to press suit for the Cathain throne; for he had personally disposed of the dead child's body in the inferno that had been the queen's bed.

But for today, his mind relished most the thought of retribution through slaughtering one of his own kind, and his anticipation for that day grew with each passing moment.

He poured himself another goblet of wine, relaxing in contentment, while unaware that the false god, Lucia was exacting retribution of his own on this unbelieving piece of mortality; slowly stealing away his mind and plotting to leave behind a useless, mindless shell of a man.

Chapter Thirty-Five

CADAN'S LEGACY

For the past five weeks, they had been riding constantly with the speed born of the relentless determination of their Prince. Jaren's continual foreboding for the safety of his countrymen and the compelling urgency of the Spirit of his Master upon him drove the young monarch to demand ever-greater speed, longer hours upon the road, and shorter stops for much needed rest. Jaren knew that time was quickly racing away, and the presence of the dragons' rankling emotions chafed at his mind.

Traces of red and gold began touching the trees with the onset of autumn. By the time Jaren was crowned King and descended from the Kroths it would be near winter. Time to begin his campaign was three to four months past. There could be no waiting for spring to begin the war, because when the Dragonmasters were able to once again control their dragons, they would fly in winter in all but the harshest weather. No. Jaren must make all haste and hope for the miraculous intervention of the Master to aid his speed. Moment by moment the burden of all these facts impelled him to arrive at St. Ramsay's Abbey in Coryn's Reach, and to complete the necessary requirements, so that he could amass his armies and lead them to war and to freedom for their people.

He was once again awed and amazed at the apparently endless protection and mercy of the Master. Already His aid was plainly to be seen, as not one of the horses had pulled up lame on this reckless race through the treacherous ruggedness of the high reaches of the mountains. Each morning before breaking camp, an adrastai would appear with the latest news on the dragon riders. As yet, there were still no dragons flying the skies in the North, and each morning the band of riders would give thanks to Elyon for miraculously postponing the inevitable.

This morning the adrastai had given the same report. When he left, Hawk joined Jaren and Tanner by the fire. As he sipped his cafla and stared into the flames, he longed to know what was taking place on the other side of the continent. In frustration he said, "I wish we knew something - anything. I'm thankful that we're not hearing reports of razing and torture, but in another way I distrust that we are hearing naught of the dragons."

Balgo nodded his head. "Aye, it would ease our spirits a bit to know where our enemies lie, no doubt about it."

Jaren stood and was silent for a moment, then looked at Balgo and said gently, "Let us be off, my brave friends. If I remember my maps correctly, we should be only a half day's ride from the monastery."

As the Prince and his escort arrived at St. Ramsay's, they came upon a beautiful ironclad gate, hung from an immense granite monolith. The gate had been worked with much intricate detailing.

Hawk nudged his horse forward a few steps to stand beside Jaren. "Welcome to Saint Ramsay's Abbey, your Highness."

Jaren colored at Hawk's use of his title, but he never took his eyes from the beautiful metalwork. Everywhere he looked on the gate there was a newfound discovery of exquisite artistry and craftsmanship.

"What are these magnificent creatures here?" he asked, pointing to one of the images.

Hawk smiled at the young man, but his heart was saddened that a lad of eighteen years did not recognize an angel. "Those are some of Elyon's beloved servants. They are called angels." He paused to watch as Jaren and Tanner once again had the look of a child upon their faces. It was the look of wonder in a child's eyes upon seeing a butterfly for the first time.

"Beautiful, isn't it?" he said softly.

The Birth of a King

The Crown Prince of Kinthoria nodded. "They look more like warriors than servants; look at the muscles on their arms and the look of high vigilance on their faces. Are they truly this powerful, and are they warriors?"

"Yes, Jaren, they are all of that and more. Perhaps we'll have the opportunity to discuss it while we're here. Right now, though," he motioned toward the town with a smile, "duty calls."

Kynon chose that moment to return to his roost on Tanner's arm. He had disappeared two days earlier just as the band of riders set out for the day. He screeched good-naturedly to his human, looking him in the eye and then bending his head to accept Tanner's gentle head rub.

The porter, dressed in a coarse, brown habit, approached the gate. "I am Brother Derrick, Keeper of the Gate. You are welcome to Saint Ramsay's, if you enter in peace," he said with authority.

Hawk straightened his back and addressed the porter. "I am Llenyddiaeth aP Braethorn, Emrys aP Pendragon."

The poor monk gasped loudly as he realized to whom he had so casually spoken.

Hawk continued, amused at the brother's reaction. "I am escort to the Crown Prince Jaren Iain Renwyck Cathain, come for an audience with his Eminence the Archbishop."

By this time, Brother Derrick was near to tripping over himself, attempting to open the gate, his hands all thumbs as he awkwardly fumbled with the lock. Finally, the latch was free and he swung the enormous gate outward.

"P-please, your Highness...." Derrick motioned for them to enter. "Emrys..." he said, nodding to Hawk.

A number of other monks had gathered in the courtyard, curious of such a large company of visitors. Derrick grabbed one of the brothers, and whispered into his ear, causing the man's eyes to widen in wonder. The brother bowed deeply to the Prince and was quickly off to inform the Archbishop.

An older brother, perhaps in his late fifties, stepped toward Jaren. "Your Highness, I am Brother Eamon. May I have the honor of seeing to your horses?" he asked with quiet respect.

Jaren dismounted and handed the reins to the genteel looking man. He smiled and said, "Thank you, Brother Eamon, for your assistance. Please take care that they are treated gently and with honor. We've been riding the poor beasts very hard for weeks, and some are close to having their wind broken."

Brother Eamon smiled and nodded. "But of course, Sire. Such valiant steeds deserve the best of care. If it pleases my Lord, I will show your men to their dormitory, also, if you have no further need of their services for a time?"

Seanachan dismissed his retinue and watched as the horses were led toward the stables and the warriors were escorted to their quarters where they would be the grateful recipients of the gentle ministrations of the loyal brothers at St. Ramsay's.

The monk turned toward Tanner. "May I direct you to the falconer's area, sir?"

Tanner eyed Kynon critically, trying to decide if he would be less of a nuisance left free to fly or placed in the falconry. "Thank you, yes. I'll try lodging him there during our stay, though he is still half wild." He followed Brother Eamon down a side street that immediately curved behind a cluster of buildings.

A commotion behind the monks caught Jaren's eye, and he turned to see what was taking place. The brothers parted down the middle to make way for their Archbishop.

Stephen McLaren, His Eminence, the Archbishop of Kinthoria, looked anything but eminent as he ran through the gathered brothers, cassock gathered up over his knees, cincture fringes flying in the breeze behind him, and golden cross banging from the end of its heavy chain from one side of his chest to the other. He was grinning from ear to ear.

"Hawk!" he shouted as he came to a halt in front of the equally smiling half-elf, and hugged him roundly. "We are well met; it's been far too long since last we saw one another. I know I was supposed to wait up in yon ivory tower for you to come to me, but I just couldn't keep myself up there."

Hawk laughed at his old friend's continued disregard for propriety and protocol. "You'll get yourself into trouble one of these

The Birth of a King

days for holding the venerability of your high office with such light regard, my friend."

"I think not. Who is there to get into trouble with? Certainly not the Father; all of this bowing and sedateness is mere tradition by men and for men," he scowled with a rakish smile on his face. "We are all one and the same to the Father."

"Well, the crowning of a King is serious business. So if you will allow me to indulge in *tradition* for a moment or two...." Hawk said, kneeling in front of the Archbishop, and kissing the signet ring on his huge hand. Then he rose to his feet and turned to smile at Jaren. "Your Eminence, I present to you the Cathain heir."

Jaren had been astonished at the sight of the man standing before him. Archbishop McLaren was every bit as tall as Korthak, and though as broad in the shoulders, his body was much more trim than was the older man's. His hands were strong and very capable. His cassock was of soft wool, and the heavy cross resting on his chest was intricately tooled in gold, with one large ruby set in its middle. The man's flaxen-colored hair was cropped short and his beard, of the same color, was trimmed close to his face. His blue eyes were clear as the skies.

Jaren's perusal of the man was interrupted by Hawk's words in his mind. *"Close your mouth, son. Kneel down as I did, and kiss the man's ring. Then you may stand and speak with the Bishop."*

Jaren's mouth snapped shut, and he flushed crimson at his embarrassing discomfiture caused by this man's presence and affability. He slowly approached the tall cleric, and knelt down on one knee, kissing the signet ring, as Hawk had done, and wondering why he was doing so.

"Archbishop McLaren, this is the Crown Prince, Jaren Iain Renwyck Cathain, your nephew." Hawk said with infinite pleasure, watching Jaren's face register his shock at this last bit of information.

Stephen McLaren was a strong man, both physically and spiritually. But when he reached out his hand and placed it on top of Jaren's head, then brought the young Prince to his feet, his heart leaped in his chest, and tears spilled down his handsome face. He crushed the young man to his chest, holding him tightly. This was

The Birth of a King

indeed the Cathain heir. He could feel the incredible strength of the Power pulsating within Jaren.

"Oh, my sweet Yesha," the cleric prayed softly, "You are amazing and generous with Your grace. Don't ever let this weak heart doubt again."

Hawk knew why his old friend's emotions were running rampant, for this man had also been present when Jaren had been endued with his "birthmark," and he had agonized over sending the babe half a continent away to be kept in safety by strangers. It had nearly torn the heart from him when Hawk had spirited him away. The company was now complete once again. Jaren's father, Cadan, was vividly present in the memories of the young prince. Elyon was now the center of control in Jaren's life, and Hawk and Archbishop McLaren were again beside him. It was now their responsibility to go forward, using Elyon's Word and His Power to rid Kinthoria of Lucia and his corrupting influence.

Jaren was paralyzed with shock. The words "your nephew" sounded over and over again in his mind, confusing his thoughts like a deafening, off-key clarion call. He could not order his thoughts in any manner. His heart beat wildly and he found it difficult to breath. A whirlwind of emotions suddenly raged through his body: happiness, excitement, melancholy, irritation, wonder. He was actually in the embrace of his own flesh and blood. Never in his wildest imaginations had he ever thought to be able to touch or to see any member of his family. He looked to Hawk for help, but could see that none was forthcoming. The half-elf merely stood there with a huge grin on his face.

Archbishop McLaren wiped the tears from his eyes, releasing the young prince from his grip, but leaving his arm across Jaren's shoulders, "Come, you must all be very weary and hungry as wolves," he said. "We have prepared suitable apartments for you and your companions, Sire. I assume you would welcome a bath and a clean change of clothes?"

"Yes, but...what Hawk just said...I'm your nephew?" Jaren stammered. "Tell me...."

"All in good time, nephew, let's get you rested first and we'll discuss it when you dine with me later today. Hawk and I will give you all the details," the man smiled broadly.

Tanner rejoined their company and Jaren happily introduced his friend and his uncle to one another.

"Your uncle?" Tanner stammered. "I thought Hawk said you were the only Cathain still alive. Oh sure, you become King, get a little power, a few riches and family starts appearing out of the woodwor...."

"Enough, Tanner," Jaren broke in quickly, "don't say another word that you may live to regret. It would seem that there are at least two Cathains yet alive. I have been assured that we will be told all about it shortly."

Stephen laughed long and hard at this brash young man's lack of guile. "Well, Jaren, it looks as though you have one person in your company who will never back down from defending you." He slapped Tanner on the back. "I like you young man. I like you very much."

McLaren, once again disregarding his high office, took the responsibility of personally leading his visitors to find Brother Cuinn whose duty it was to see to the care and comfort of guests. He led them down a long, sheltered walkway paved with smooth, perfectly cut stones. On the right was a stone wall covered with ivy and deep blue morning glories; over their heads a roof was supported with intricately carved timbers adorned with more carefully tended ivy.

To their left lay the striking beauty of the courtyard of St. Ramsay's Abbey. The small group eyed the long garden with wonder as they breathed in the myriad delicious scents wafting to them from the beautiful scene. Jaren had never seen such a place of wonder designed by the hand of man. Golden and spotted fish moved slowly in small ponds that dotted the grounds throughout the immense garden; clusters of monks sat in quiet reflection beside a number of the pools. Others tended the enormous variety of trees, shrubs, and flowers that grew in abundance. Several marble sculptures of angels and mighty cherubim were placed in just the right locations so as to be very pleasing to the eye and encouraging to the spirit.

The Birth of a King

The meticulously manicured lawns in this ethereal place were as thick and lush as the carpeting of Borkau, and as deep a green as the priceless emeralds from An-Bhan. Jaren was intrigued by the use of so many different elements for the paths throughout the garden. Stones of many colors had been used, from gray, to white, to pale green and pink, and ranging in size from small peas to large flat stones bordered with springy moss. Some paths were thickly spread with sand in a variety of colors and textures.

Tanner's eyes went to a small, hunched figure of a man, who could not have reached five feet tall had he been standing erect and on his toes. He was carefully raking beautiful, flowing patterns into the sand around a cluster of short, compact trees in a corner of the garden. "Excuse me, your Eminence, sir, but I've never seen a human being that looks like that man. Where does he come from?" Tanner asked, pointing at the miniature gardener.

The Archbishop smiled, "Ah, that is Brother Jerome. I'm not surprised that you have not seen his like before. He is from the lesser branch of the Athdarag race. Somewhere in antiquity, that race was split in two. No one remembers the reason why. The greater branch stayed near the Kroth Mountains, where their beloved trees grow in abundance. The lesser branch migrated to the far west, to the edge of the Ra'aen Ocean, and they became fishermen. Brother Jerome was brought here as a small child, because his deformed back would not have allowed him to make a living on the sea. His kindred were hoping that he would find a useful, productive life here at the abbey. As you can see, he indeed has become indispensable to the beauty of this place. All of these paths were designed by him, and he personally has spent years separating mounds of stone into the separate colors and shapes that you see along our paths. It is work that he loves to do, making a place of quiet solitude for people to meditate and rest in our Master's love." He smiled once again. "Yes, Brother Jerome is a person of extraordinary beauty."

Most of the trees in the courtyard were fairly young; few were taller than the wall at the far end of the peaceful garden. But there was an amazing variety, many of which Jaren had never seen before. Under some of the taller trees, protected by ample shade, were small, ornately carved stone benches. Several were occupied by men in

The Birth of a King

clerical robes. But it was obvious that the abbey had other laic guests as well as Jaren and his company; for many of the benches were occupied by people of several of the Kinthorian races.

There was a massive fountain located in the center of the courtyard. It was filled with a life-sized bronze sculpture of a mighty warrior, who had seemingly just dismounted from his valiant steed. The noble beast's eyes were wide, and its nostrils distended with the thrill of the battle. The face of the man was stern, beautiful, and intelligent. He looked as though he was ready at any moment to call his troops to remount and re-engage the enemy. His mighty sword was drawn, clenched in a hand with an iron grip, and held high by a strong, powerfully muscled arm. Beneath his left heel was the crushed head of a snake, the body of which was a twisted, writhing mass of scales. Surrounding this magnificent piece was a wide, marble-edged, oblong pool. At each corner of the pool was a bronze, six-winged cherub blowing a ram's horn. Out of the horns, water shot into the air, forming a crystal-like canopy over the top of the horse and warrior. As Jaren looked at the sculpture, he immediately knew that it was the Master, the Conquering King, crushing the head of His age-old enemy, Lucia. Jaren's spirit was so moved by the power and undeniable victory emanating from the piece that he felt all the fatigue of his recent journey drain from his body, to be replaced with a confidence and an assurance of their own victory in the coming war. He felt nearly impelled to issue the challenge at that very moment.

At the pressure of a hand on his shoulder, he looked into the eyes of Stephen McLaren. The man looked long into the soul of the Prince, and then he smiled. "I see that the sculpture has already accomplished the purpose for which it was made." He shook his head with gratification.

"I...I'm afraid I don't understand, sir," Jaren confessed haltingly.

"That piece was commissioned by your father to be placed here for this very moment. You will notice that there are no other formal fountains in the courtyard. It is because there is no further message necessary for the believer than this one. Our Master has conquered and defeated our foe already. All we have to do is follow Him in and put out the fires that the enemy tries to start. Your father, Cadan, wanted you to know that even at this moment the Master is the Conqueror and the enemy is already vanquished," the Archbishop said solemnly.

Jaren reached out to touch the arm of the stone figure; he looked long into the eyes that so compellingly penetrated his very soul. He was amazed at the measure of Cadan's belief in Yesha, and he was physically shaken with the knowledge that the love of his father had spanned the years to touch him here in this quiet garden. Bittersweet tears brimmed his eyes and coursed down his cheeks. He could not speak, and mercifully, the cleric moved the others on around a corner in the gardens.

Soon, Jaren heard the Archbishop's booming voice, "Ah, Father Cuinn, there you are." Stephen turned as Jaren rejoined the group, "Your Highness, this is Father Cuinn. He is in charge of seeing to the comfort of our guests here at Saint Ramsay's. He will see you to your rooms, and provide you with anything you might need."

Jaren blotted his eyes a final time on the back of his sleeve and looked at the older monk, whose balding head was at the moment bowing to the Prince. Short, fuzzy tufts of gray hair sat above his ears, framing a serious face, with a long, pointed nose and a thin line of a mouth. But Jaren, upon looking into the man's eyes, saw quickly that here was a man of unusual good-heartedness and a jovial nature.

Archbishop McLaren squeezed Jaren's shoulder and gave the company a quick bow. "I must take leave of you for a while, but I trust that you will be dining with me shortly. There are many things to discuss."

Jaren nodded in agreement, and the man left them in Father Cuinn's care. The cleric motioned for them to follow as he led them to the southern end of the courtyard, and turned left onto the walk toward the east wing of the monastery.

"What are all of these buildings used for?" Tanner asked.

Judging the lad's age, despite his mature physique, and noting that Tanner would never have seen a church, much less an entire abbey, the guide explained, "Well, our only purpose for being in this place is to concentrate on our service to Elyon, lad. Part of that service is taking care of the needy, and, thanks to the Emperor," he looked at Jaren, "pardon the allusion to sovereignty, Sire, there are great numbers of the needy who make their way to our high reaches here. We must feed and clothe them all. The people of the Southern Regions are very generous and keep our storehouses well stocked. We have small farms in the lower valleys that provide meat and produce. Of course, at the backside of the Abbey, downwind," he smiled, "are the animal pens and barns. We have our own extensive gardens and orchards, and we have huntsmen, but to support such a large population, we simply do not have the land available up here for growing grain crops, or for pasturing very large herds."

He turned into a high archway on their right and led them down a cavernous hallway. "We have our own bakery and kitchens, and quite a large infirmary. We have many workshops, tanners, blacksmiths, glass and pottery crafters, basket weavers, candle makers, coopers, alchemists, fullers, vintners, and weavers of cloth. Most anything one may need is crafted right here at the Abbey.

Tanner asked many more questions, but his voice and Father Cuinn's were slowly lost to Jaren's consciousness as he studied their surroundings. He was intrigued with the ornate beauty of the stone floor; each stone had been cut to fit precisely with its neighbors, and then polished to a brilliant shine. Throughout the entire hallway, Jaren read words written out with different colored stones set in the floor. Some of the words were short passages taken from the Word, while others were simple praises to the Master. The intricately carved pillars that lined the hallway were easily two arm spans around. They were formed of the beautiful black and red mottled marble that was abundant in the Kroth Mountains. Thick granite walls were overlaid with oak and cherry, and carved with painstaking precision, with scenes of events from the Word. The rounded archways, under which they passed, were engraved with more quotes from the Word. Each door and frame was heavy oak, with elaborately worked wrought iron hinges.

Even in Jaren's memories of his father's castle, he had never seen anything as beautiful as the work of art through which they were passing at that moment.

"So you see, we are servants to Elyon, and that service is expressed as we serve those around us who are less fortunate, or

The Birth of a King

who are in need of spiritual care and knowledge," Father Cuinn's rich, baritone voice broke into Jaren's musings.

The older monk stopped. "Here we are," he said as he opened a door on his right and bowed. "This suite is yours for as long as you choose to stay with us, Sire." He smiled as he followed his guests into the large room. "This room is for receiving any guests to whom your Highness may wish to grant audience. The door on the far left leads to the apartments prepared for your companions." He stepped across the suite and opened a door. "This is your bedchamber, Sire. The door to the left opens into a small chapel for your convenience. The door on the right is the garderobe. Please," he said gently, "if you have any need at all, let me know." He bowed to Jaren and closed the door in silence, leaving the companions alone.

As soon as the monk had gone, everyone began speaking at once. "Did you see those floors?" Jaren exclaimed. "Did you notice the quality o' that metal work? They must have dwarves working here," Balgo beamed. "Can you imagine all of the stuff they have stored here?" came from an impressed Tanner. "This is an entire city stuck away in these mountains."

Korthak sank his weary body into a comfortable looking chair, and pulled off his battered boots. "Dols, this place has really changed since I was here last."

Balgo and Hawk nodded in agreement.

"Yup," the old dwarf shook his head, "I never thought they could come so far so fast."

Jaren and Tanner walked into Jaren's bedchamber. Across the huge four-poster bed, draped with heavy, deep green velvet, lay a newly tailored change of clothes. Tanner smiled. "I wonder if they have supplied all of us with new clothes or just the Prince."

Jaren gave him a punch in the arm and said, "Well, let's go find out," as he headed for the door leading to the other apartments. Sure enough, across each man's bed, lay a new suit of clothes. Tanner gathered up the ones obviously made for himself and for Korthak, one being much larger than the other, and took them back to Jaren's reception hall. He sauntered up to Korthak with a puzzled look on his face.

"Korthak, could you help me figure this out?" He held up the tunics, so clearly different in size. "They gave us these new clothes to wear and I can't tell which one is mine and which one's yours."

Jaren burst out laughing, while Hawk, Balgo, and Seanachan chuckled at the familiar bantering.

Korthak, too exhausted to pull his huge body back out of the chair to whip Tanner's young hide for such blatant disrespect, for once, merely sat there and rubbed his eyes with a huge hand. He finally looked mildly at Hawk and Balgo.

"Well, Dols, Hawk, don't just stand there. Go find the infirmarian," he said, tapping the side of his head with his finger. "It's obvious the boy has been riding in the saddle too long. All the grains in his hour-glass have sunk to the bottom. The poor lad's been sitting on his brains for weeks now."

Hawk knew that all too soon the bells would be tolling to announce Angelus, calling the brethren to their prayers before the mid-day meal and the Mass at Sext. He cleared his throat rather loudly, and walked toward the door to the adjoining apartments. "Well, I think we all need a good scrubbing, and I don't know about the rest of you, but I can't wait to get into the bathing pool." It was only a matter of moments before six sets of dirt-encrusted riding clothes lay in piles on the floor and six very weary travelers lay soaking in the enormous, steaming pool in the bathing chamber.

The relaxing herbs that had been added to the water quickly seeped into exhausted bodies and stiff, aching muscles. The aromatic spirits wafting in the steam were breathed in deeply and gratefully, and soon they began touching the edges of weary minds and causing them to submit to the insistent call to rest.

Hawk was thoroughly enjoying the soothing heat, and Jaren slowly slid himself further into the water up to his chin, lying back against the steps leading into the pool. He felt his fatigue ebbing away. "This must be what heaven feels like," he muttered under his breath, as he slowly drifted into a light slumber. Just before succumbing completely to sleep, he thought he heard Korthak's loud snoring, and he smiled lazily.

After what seemed only moments, a soft voice awoke the six bathers.

The Birth of a King

"I'm sorry to interrupt your rest, sirs, but the Angelus will chime in the next quarter hour. Brother Cuinn was sure that you had planned to dine with His Eminence after the reading," the young novice said.

Hawk was instantly alert. "Thank you. Yes, we will be dining with the Bishop."

The young man bowed and silently left the bathing chamber.

"It would be on the judicious side of wisdom not to keep the Archbishop waiting, my friends. There are many things to be discussed, one of which is the preparations for a coronation. Come, let us dress quickly and be off."

Hawk left the steaming water and the others followed with varying degrees of reluctance. However, all were surprised at how rested they felt, and it was not long before the companions were once again assembled in Jaren's reception chamber.

The Prince eyed each of his friends as they entered the room. Hawk wore fine tanned-leather breeches with soft suede boots that laced up the front. His torso was covered with a heavy two-piece garment made up of a long turquoise undershirt and a hunter's green quilted sleeveless gambeson. He looked every inch the former King's Champion.

Korthak had changed immensely. He had lost all similarity to a bear, and now appeared more the wealthy, landed gentleman. His hair was combed and his beard and mustache were clean and properly trimmed. His new deep brown suede breeches and alabaster hued tunic fit perfectly, showing that the older man had lost much of his girth on this journey. He was now very fit for a man of his age.

Jaren's eyes fell next on Tanner. He was still cinching up his leather belt as Jaren took in all of the changes that had so subtly taken place in his friend. He had turned from an older boy into a strong, young man, his athletic frame filling out a fresh linen tunic dyed indigo, and soft suede breeches the color of midnight. His face showed clearly the complexity of his nature, his jaw firm and set, revealing his courage and stubborn integrity, and his dark eyes dancing with the mischief of the playful boy still residing within. He was truly becoming the Gil-Enrai that Jaren would need by his side.

The Birth of a King

Balgo's dark brown wool breeches and bright red tunic were topped off by a new, beautifully knit emerald green stocking cap, with a golden tassel clasped to its end. Jaren could hear the old dwarf grumbling about having to break in another cap, but he noted with amusement the covert looks of childish delight in Balgo's eyes whenever that golden tassel flicked at his shoulders.

The An'ilden prince was by far the most striking member of their party. His sheer height alone was enough to make him the most noticeable, but he had been outfitted with an orange silk sleeveless tunic, and finely woven, wide-legged, linen trousers, dyed black and gathered at the ankles into golden bands that matched his arm band. His red lacquered breastplate had been re-fitted with new leather straps, and was highly polished. The topknot on his head had been meticulously cut and greased and gleamed blue-black in the sunlight streaming through the tall, narrow windows of the chamber.

While Jaren had been eyeing his friends, Tanner had been doing some examining of his own. Once they had all gathered in the reception chamber, he had chanced to look at his brother-friend. The last traces of his childhood friend had completely disappeared somewhere in the last hour, and a youthful man of kingly bearing had replaced him. Jaren stood tall, showing the beginning signs of what promised to be a magnificently built body in maturity. His golden hair was glistening with the dampness of his recent bath, and his skin was deeply tanned. His blue eyes were filled with the infused wisdom of his ancestors.

He had been provided with breeches and tunic of scarlet red, trimmed in black, and his black cloak was trimmed about the edges with sable. His soft, new black boots had been trimmed at toe and heel with small pieces of worked gold. His whole bearing spoke unmistakably of the health and strength of character of a Prince whose Master is in full control.

The others had become aware of Jaren's metamorphosis also, and as one, they knelt before him. The young man was embarrassed beyond words, but was at the same time deeply grateful for the loyalty of these companions and close friends with whom the Father had supplied him.

"Thank you, my friends," he said humbly, "but I wish you would stop doing that. If only you knew how uncomfortable it makes me. I don't think I shall ever get used to it."

They all rose, and Hawk approached Jaren, and putting his hands on the young man's shoulders, he looked deeply into his eyes. "You are the chosen King, Jaren. Elyon has made you worthy of honor. Whether you accept it or not, others will see your worth and will bow to you," he said quietly. Then smiling, he slapped him on the back and said in a husky voice, "Let's go eat! I'm famished!"

Brother Cuinn was waiting for them as they stepped from the chamber. His look was one of pleasant approval. He would thank Brother Marlin, the monastic chamberlain, for such a masterful job in the transformation of their guests. The old chamberlain was remarkably gifted, knowing just how to direct the tailor in making garments suitable to the wearer.

"Come, His Eminence will join you shortly in his private chambers." He turned and led them deeper into the abbey. As they walked, Brother Cuinn spoke to them over his shoulder. "I must confess that we are greatly overjoyed to have you lodging with us. The Archbishop has been very eager for this meeting and for the coronation ceremonies to come."

Jaren nodded with a slight smile on his face. "I think we are all feeling the same way, for a variety of reasons."

Brother Cuinn prayed yet one more time for this small group of people and their safety. For over two years, ever since Hawk had begun his mission to find the lost heir, the Archbishop had commissioned a non-stop prayer vigil for the young prince and any who would be traveling with him. Brother Cuinn knew in his heart that these guests were here only because of Elyon's able protection and endless mercy.

The monk led them down another hallway that was much smaller than the first, but which was no less ornate. He knocked lightly on a door at the end of the corridor. Another brother opened the door, bowing and bidding them enter. Jaren gasped, while it was all Tanner could do to keep from audibly voicing his astonishment.

Hawk and Korthak had to prod the two young men through the door.

In the center of the room was an enormous oak table adorned with a beautiful burgundy linen cloth, embroidered heavily on its corners with intricate designs in silver and gold threads. The table was surrounded by high-backed oak chairs, the seats and backs of which were amply padded and covered with the same linen. Each place was set with a large silver plate, the size of a small tray, and the knives were of silver with woven gold handles. An ornate brass goblet stood sentry at the head of each plate.

Tanner leaned toward Jaren and whispered, "That thing would fill my mother's entire house."

Jaren could only stare ahead blankly.

"Welcome, my friends. You look well rested," McLaren greeted them warmly as he rushed through the door at the far end of the room. "I became inspired during the Angelus and read over-long. It was a good passage considering the times in which we live. Please. Sit down. I hope you have brought tremendous appetites with you," McLaren said sheepishly. "I'm afraid our Cellarer is just as excited about your visit as I am. He kept bringing everything he could think of up to the cookhall to be prepared for you. I would say that he has about exhausted our poor kitchen and bakery staffs, but it seems that what he didn't think to order, they took upon themselves to prepare."

Jaren scanned the table in disbelief. There were entire trays of stuffed gaming hens, thick slabs of smoked ham, and racks of enormous beef ribs. There were bowls of steamed potatoes, beans and carrots and fresh baked rolls and pastries laid in linen covered baskets. Fruit and vegetable sauces and aspics laid in colorful profusion in every available space on the huge board. A bowl of delicious smelling soup sat steaming in front of each man.

When everyone was seated, McLaren looked at Hawk. "Would you offer our noon prayer today, my friend?" he asked nonchalantly.

Hawk looked at him with just a trace of askance in his green eyes, and then he smiled and shook his head. *"How did this rebel ever ascend to such a high position?"* he mused, knowing that when one was in the company of the Archbishop, it was unquestioned in the beliefs of this church, but that the Bishop, obviously being the

The Birth of a King

greater man of Elyon, should speak to Elyon on behalf of those with whom he was associating.

"Heavenly Father, thank You for giving us safe travel to this place. Thank You for the kind and thoughtful hearts with which You have blessed Archbishop McLaren and the rest of the brothers here at Saint Ramsay's. Thank You for the *abundance* of food which You have placed before us. Cause it to nourish and renew our bodies. I ask, as Your humble servant, that You uplift and strengthen our spirits during our time here. Be our spiritual eyes and ears to hear the speaking of Your Spirit in our midst. I beg Your guidance and wisdom in all of our counsels as we prepare ourselves to accomplish the tasks for which You have assembled us. In Your most high and holy Name I pray. Amen."

Stephen looked at Hawk with a knowing smile, and said mischievously, "Thank you, Hawk. It's not every day that we have someone speak with the Father on our behalf, who knows Him as intimately as do you, my friend."

Hawk, allowing his look of remonstrance to show a little more clearly this time, smiled and merely said, "My pleasure...Your Eminence."

McLaren looked at the half-elf closely and burst out laughing. "Eat up, gentlemen. We have much to accomplish and we will all need our strength."

Korthak had seen no necessity in waiting to be directed to eat by the Archbishop; after all, they had been asked to meet with him specifically for the purpose of dining, hadn't they? He had already transferred several of the large, dripping beef ribs to his plate and his knife had just skewered a potato he had been eyeing.

The cleric watched him for a moment, and then sent a message to Hawk. *"He hasn't changed a bit, has he?"*

Hawk shook his head, and smiled at the cleric. *"No, and I can't say that I would ever want him to."*

Discussion was purposely kept light during their lengthy meal. McLaren wanted his guests to thoroughly enjoy this short respite from the rigorous and dangerous times in which they all found themselves. He also wanted to take the time to get to know his brother's son, and his friend, Tanner, more closely, and to attempt to measure

The Birth of a King

the character of each. He was therefore particularly interested in the details of Tanner's attack on the demon in the cave, his vision/dream at Balgo's house, and of Hawk's healing at the Glamorgan Mines as the group related highlights of their journey from Reeban to Parth. He looked long and close at each of the young men as their stories were told, and was astonished at Elyon's close work in their young lives, and he gained new hope in his anticipation of their roles in the war to come. The hair on the nape of his neck stood up in excitement at the possibilities of what mighty works Elyon yet may do through these two unsuspecting friends.

When Jaren could no longer hold his curiosity in check he asked the Archbishop to explain their family connection.

"Well, *nephew*," Stephen spoke the word with obvious pleasure, "my father was Iain Chricton Brys. He had four sons; Cadan, Brann, Rinion and Eihlin. My name, before I took on another when I joined the brotherhood, was Rinion Ifan Cameron. So, I am Cadan's brother and your uncle from direct descent."

"So we are very closely related," Jaren said around a lump in his throat. "But, if you are in direct line from Iain, wouldn't you be the successor to my father's throne?" Jaren was hoping beyond hope that this would be the case and that there might yet be the possibility that he could live out his life free of the enormous burden of monarchy.

The Archbishop smiled, reading the hope in Jaren's eyes. "Jaren, let me ask you a question in return before I give you my answer. Think back on your life, and on everything that has happened to you since Hawk found you. Consider the events at the Spring of Elyon, and your dragon stigmata; indeed, consider the Glamorgan Mines." McLaren paused briefly to allow Jaren time to do as he had requested.

"Son, much as I would like to spare you the burden of sovereignty, surely you must see that the hand of Elyon has been upon you all your life long, preparing you for just such a time as this. Is it not clearly evident to you, as it is to us," he gestured toward Jaren's five companions, "that *you* are His chosen King, and the dragons' Sanda Aran? Elyon has called you to be King as surely as He has called me to lead this abbey. Neither of us can deny His call without stepping outside of His will."

Jaren felt his hope for a life of freedom take wings and disappear through the walls of the chamber. "Yes, sir, I can see that. I was just thinking…" he could not continue to voice his hope that he could avoid Elyon's call upon his life; for he could now see that he had unconsciously been chaffing against doing the will of the Father, and he was ashamed for his selfishness.

Chapter Thirty-Six

SAINT RAMSAY'S ABBEY

Jaren leaned back in his chair, and vowed to himself that he would never again eat to such excess. His new breeches had been generously cut by the abbey tailor, but for the past half hour, his gorged mid-section had been straining against even their ample girth. He thought about loosening his belt, but upon further speculation, felt that such an overt confession of gluttony would be even more embarrassing than a stomach swelling over the top of the confining piece of leather.

The Archbishop had been relating to them the story of the building of Saint Ramsay's.

"I must admit that I was somewhat of a doubting Thomas earlier on," he said at the end of his narrative. "But our Father kept me inspired, even though I have oftentimes pictured this beautiful place in ruins, ransacked and defiled by the Dragonmasters should they finally attack our region."

Jaren noticed Hawk smiling and nodding his head as Bishop McLaren stared at the half-elf with a mixture of affection and laughter in his deep blue eyes.

"It was only after we tried, in vain I might add, to stop this crazy elf from heading north to look for you, Jaren, that I came to the realization that Elyon was going to be working miracles for us."

A thought suddenly occurred to Jaren, and he pulled himself closer to the table, while deliberately pushing his plate away from easy reach. "Do the Dragonmasters know of this place, then?"

McLaren nodded. "Yes, I'm afraid they do."

Jaren's heart sank.

"Many people know of Saint Ramsay's, Jaren. I feel Elyon has allowed us to have the abbey as a kind of central hub from which to conduct His business; much the same as a King uses his castle from which to care for the kingdom matters. As I told you upon your arrival, many people have been fed, clothed, given a livelihood and a hope, and have been aided not only physically, but spiritually, as a result of this abbey."

He chuckled ruefully, and continued on. "When you have the harsh living conditions, so bountifully supplied by the Dragonmasters, any reprieve from those conditions will be talked about with enthusiasm in all quarters."

He was silent for a moment, and the sadness which Jaren had seen countless times in the eyes of his older companions, passed across the face of his uncle.

"I must say, with regret, that there are also some abroad in Kinthoria who have sold information about us to the Dragonmasters."

McLaren saw the anger immediately flare into the eyes of his guests and held up his hand. "Nay, my children. It is not for us to judge others. We do not know their circumstances," he spoke with the gentle rebuke of a loving father.

Three brown-robed brothers entered the room. Two began clearing the table as the third refilled glasses of water, and placed steaming cups of cafla in front of each of the men.

"I think a dram of red wine for our young Prince here, Jaime," the Bishop said, smiling at the confused look on Jaren's face. "It will help ease your overburdened stomach, my young friend."

Jaren colored crimson, as every other person at the table eyed his bulging abdomen.

Bishop McLaren rose. "I must leave you for now. The entire abbey is at your disposal, and I'm certain that you can find your way to the courtyard," he said. "I have found the gardens to be the perfect place for quiet conversations with our Father." He walked from the room, closing the door softly.

Jaren stood and stretched his legs. He could not believe that three hours had passed since first entering this chamber. "I don't know about the rest of you, but I think some fresh air would do me much good."

The companions retraced their steps, this time at a leisurely pace, taking the time to examine the details of the ornate works of art with which the abbey had been so abundantly built and decorated. The inlaid and carved woods, the marble sculptures and the vividly colored tapestries were each unique and finished with intricate excellence.

Jaren felt his tension lifting even before he stepped out into the warmth and brilliance of Solance. He, as well as the others, could easily sense the peaceful love and power radiating in this place. These became even more apparent once they stepped into the courtyard gardens. There was a serene tranquility that was beyond any description.

It only took moments for each of them to find his own quiet spot. Among the six companions much was in need of being given over to Elyon. Fear, anger, sadness, hatred and many other emotions must be released from each of them in order for Elyon to fill them with the spiritual weapons with which to fight this war and thus fulfill His purposes. The mightiest weapons ever conceived, Elyon's love, truth, will, and power, would provide them with extraordinary strength, bringing to each of them added confidence and courage.

Jaren lost track of time as he wrestled with so many conflicting thoughts. He was still trying to reconcile the fact that he had a living blood relative in which to confide. He was attempting to calm his anxiety caused by the dragon's apprehension of whatever phantoms were plaguing them. The mantle of his kingship weighed heavily upon his soul. He vaguely remembered hearing the bell sound for Vespers as he prayed for his friends, his people, and for himself.

He was startled by a voice that came from behind the tree against which he was leaning.

"Jaren, everyone is looking for you."

Jaren turned his head to see Tanner's crooked smile.

"C'mon," he said excitedly, offering a hand up to his friend. "I asked if we could eat with the monks. I'm telling you, Jaren, I'm completely intrigued by these men who live here," Tanner said enthusiastically.

The Birth of a King

Jaren stared at his friend to see if he was trying to pull another joke on him.

"No, Jaren," Tanner said, laughing and giving him a sideways glance. "I don't feel Elyon calling me into this way of life. I am merely interested to see what these people do each day, and to understand what draws them to live such a simple life."

Jaren knew he was being selfish, but he silently thanked Elyon for not taking Tanner away from him just yet.

They met the others at the door to the abbey. Father Cuinn escorted them to the evening meal with the brothers.

Having these distinguished guests interested in their daily life, and their quiet work for the Father thoroughly pleased Brother Cuinn. He was barely able to keep his enthusiasm under control.

"I am so glad you have asked to sup with us. I know it will fill all of our brethren with joy when they see that the Holy Warriors have come to dine with them."

Jaren looked at Tanner and mouthed the words, "Holy Warriors?" Tanner simply shook his head and shrugged.

Jaren felt the tingling sensation in his head, and instantly caught Hawk's gaze. *"That is how these people have come to perceive us, Jaren. We have taken up the sword of Yesha to do battle with the enemy. You see, the real battle is not with Volant, or the rest of the Dragonmasters. This war is against none other than Lucia and his hordes, and against the evil and darkness which surrounds them."*

Jaren nodded, and then had to almost grab Tanner to keep from stumbling into Brother Cuinn as he stopped abruptly before a huge archway.

"Before we enter, I want to tell you to feel free to ask the brothers any questions you may have. I am certain they would appreciate the opportunity to tell you about themselves and their service." This said, he turned and led them into the refectory.

The first thing Jaren noticed was the peacefulness radiating from the face of each man. There was lively conversation going on at all of the tables, though it was being carried on in hushed tones, as was proper for the monastic life.

As they sat down, Jaren and Tanner observed an older monk as he stood from his chair and the room became hushed.

"This came in a missive from my sister," he said in a voice surprisingly strong for one who looked so aged and frail. But as the white-haired monk read the beautiful and touching poem, the vibrancy of tone in his voice bespoke to the two younger men a much different story. This humble brother was a solid servant of Elyon. Inside that ancient body, his spiritual being was a powerful and intense cornerstone from which the rest of the brethren at the abbey could gain strength and wisdom.

When the old monk had finished reading, many "amens" were heard throughout the refectory.

During the meal, others stood in turn and recited from the Word, or from various sacred writings; each one offering a morsel to feed the soul and spirit, as they fed their bodies.

To Jaren, it was a unique and beautiful custom, and one which he would later use around his own table for family and guests alike.

It was not until after they had finished eating and the monks had begun filing out of the refectory that Brother Cuinn came bustling up to their table. "Excuse me for interrupting, Tanner, but you asked about getting a closer look at our lives here at Saint Ramsay's." He was beaming from ear to ear.

"This is Brother Chadwyck. He has graciously agreed to spend his brief leisure time before Compline with you, if you still wish."

Tanner stood and clasped the brother's hand. "I'm very pleased to meet you, Brother Chadwyck."

The young cleric smiled broadly.

Tanner turned to the rest of the group, "I'll be in the garden when you need me." He smiled and gave the monk's shoulder a hearty grip, and then they turned and hurried outside, chatting like old friends.

Korthak eyed Jaran with a nervous look, "He...he's not thinking..." he stammered, unable to finish the statement.

Jaren and Hawk both burst out laughing at the frightened expression on the face of their older friend.

"No," Jaren said, still chuckling. "I had the same reaction earlier. His curiosity about life in the abbey has been piqued, that's all."

The Birth of a King

Korthak let out a relieved sigh, while Hawk slapped him on the back. "Now, now, you old mother hen, just remember who Tanner really belongs to."

Korthak nodded imperceptibly, and muttered something under his breath about, "See who's a mother hen...egg and elf omelet."

"Would you mind if I went to get my falcon, Brother Chadwyck?" Tanner almost begged. "I haven't seen him since I left him with the falconer this morning, and he's probably driven Brother Fagan mad by now."

The young monk led Tanner back to the Falconry, and true to Tanner's words, they found the place in an upheaval of noise and drifting feathers. Kynon had spent the entire day sharing his rage with every other bird, exciting them into frenzy. The screeching din that assaulted the ears of the two young men was close to deafening. Brother Fagan had been so sorely tried by the spoiled little bird, that his face was purpled and his body drenched with perspiration. He was moments away from pulling the little beast's tail feathers out, one by one.

Tanner took Kynon on his arm, and apologized profusely to the falconer for the young bird's behavior. The poor brother collapsed onto a bench, dousing himself with a ladle of cool water. As they returned to the garden, Kynon continued his daylong tirade, scolding and berating his master for the abusive treatment he had endured that day.

"I'm truly sorry he is acting like this, Brother Chadwyck. He's usually better behaved," Tanner said, eyeing the young bird threateningly. However, Kynon knew that his master's looks were all show, especially since he continued to stroke the bird's head tenderly, and to feed him morsels of meat which the falconer had provided.

Brother Chadwyck watched, fascinated, as Tanner coaxed the beautiful creature into a quieter state, and smiled. "I guess we all feel more ourselves when we are in the presence of our Master, especially when He is also our provider and our friend." Tanner laughed, as he tied Kynon's tethers down around his arm. Having regained his master's presence, and having gorged his craw, the spoiled little bird began preening himself, almost as though to prove the truth of

The Birth of a King

Brother Chadwyck's words. Tanner knew that it would only be a matter of minutes before his little friend would be fast asleep in the quiet of the garden.

Tanner and Chad, as the young cleric had asked to be called, seated themselves comfortably under a small grape arbor on the western side of the garden. Chad was not much older than Tanner. He had come to Saint Ramsay's from Stornoway when his entire village had been razed in a raid by the dragon riders.

He spoke quietly, "When the elves found me, I was almost delirious from starvation. They said I looked like a wild animal. They brought me to this place, and I have to be honest with you..." he looked around sheepishly, "after hearing for years about the murderous elves and dwarves, I would have sworn they were going to put my bony body on the spit and eat what was left of me for dinner." He laughed at the memory of such foolishness.

"Don't worry, Chad. Your secret is safe with me. I've had to struggle with the lies of the Dragonmasters myself on many occasions."

As their conversation continued, Tanner was drawn increasingly deeper into the strength of this young man's convictions, and by his astounding faith.

"You see, Tanner, we want nothing but peace for our land and for its people." Chad was quiet for a few moments. Then he suddenly chuckled. "You know, Tanner, Elyon's peace is certainly unique," he said wryly.

"How do you mean, Chad?"

"Well, here at Saint Ramsay's we work extremely hard, and we hardly ever see the results of our labor. Each of us has his disappointments, his annoying interruptions, and misunderstandings, but the peace is always there, living inside each of us. Elyon's peace is something that is alive..." his voice trailed off as he pondered this last statement, and then, as the new revelation struck his mind, "I guess it's because it's a part Himself, so it would have to be alive, wouldn't it," he said softly, more to himself than to Tanner. "Hmmm, *'My own peace I give to you,'*" he quoted from the Word. *"Myself I give to you."*

The Birth of a King

Then, coloring slightly, he glanced at Tanner and said, "I'm sorry, Tanner. I'm afraid all this time spent in contemplation doesn't exactly promote the ability to converse with others too well. I'll try to do better, I promise."

Tanner had been astonished by this young man's faith and incredible understanding of the Word. He had vowed in his heart that someday he would be that strong spiritually. He hoped silently that it would be soon.

"No, no," Tanner said enthusiastically. "This is just what I was hoping for; to know what draws people to this sort of life; what makes you so strong in your faith. You've just given me a prime example of it. It was amazing being able to share a moment of revelation with you. I would imagine that moments like this make everything else pale in comparison."

Brother Chadwyck smiled broadly. "Yes. A lot of people think it would be the worst punishment on earth, to be sent to live in a monastery. I think that gradually coming to know the complexity and depth of love in Elyon's mind is one of the greatest ways one could ever spend his life. You're right, my friend, it is most exciting."

He reached up and plucked two large clusters of grapes from the vine, handed one to Tanner, and then continued.

He gazed long into Tanner's eyes, "Our Father continually supplies us with His peace. It's a part of the tremendous life with which He instills each one who belongs to Him. It is not dependent on circumstances like the peace the world offers to people. That is why we are trying to spread Elyon's kind of peace beyond the walls of this abbey. We want, more than anything, to teach others how to obtain this wonderful gift from the Father."

The bells in the abbey tolled once more. It was time for Compline, Chad explained. "After Compline is tolled, we observe the 'time of great silence' until the ringing of the bells for Matins at midnight. I must beg leave of you for now. It is time to retire to the dormitory for some of that contemplation I mentioned. Actually, I am looking forward to it. It will give me the chance to think more on the peace of Elyon being a living thing. Good evening, my new friend. I'm glad we have had this opportunity to begin what I hope to be a very long friendship. Elyon go with you through this night."

"Good night, Chad," Tanner said, as he turned to make his way back to the Falconry. "Thank you for sharing all of this with me. If you don't mind, I'd like to meet with you again before we leave."

Brother Chadwyck smiled and nodded, and then headed back into the abbey.

Tanner looked toward heaven and breathed a quiet and very sincere prayer. "Thank you, Father, for what You have taught me today through these brothers. Please take my body, my soul and my spirit and form me, by Your mighty hand, into the spiritual warrior you want me to be, for if I am not mistaken, You have made me Your chosen warrior for more than just the military arena."

Before he left the garden, he hooded Kynon, hoping that it would help the young falcon to behave himself. As he left him in Brother Fagan's clearly unwilling care, the little bird did indeed remain quiet. Satisfied that the poor bird keeper would not be driven to insanity during the coming hours, Tanner bid him good night and went to join his companions.

He found them sequestered in the apartments adjoining Jaren's suite.

Upon seeing his friend enter the room, Jaren smiled. "Ah, Tan. I trust your conversation with Brother Chadwyck went well?"

Tanner nodded, a crooked grin spread across his handsome face. "Yes. It was...how shall I put this...enlightening."

The rest of the friends noticed the peaceful aura surrounding the young man, and knew something special had passed between Brother Chadwyck and their spontaneous young friend.

"Join us, Tan," Jaren said, as Korthak pulled a stool up for him. "We are just discussing the events to take place tomorrow."

Tanner sat down, and leaning against the wall, propped his heel on the corner of Korthak's chair. "I'm all ears."

Korthak looked critically at the young man. "I hadn't noticed that before, but now that you mention it...."

"Ahem," Hawk interrupted, just as Tanner opened his mouth to throw a retort at his adopted father. "Now, as I was saying. Many people are going to begin arriving at Saint Ramsay's on the morrow. Indeed, many have already come and are either helping with the last of the preparations for the coronation, or are taking advantage of this short respite before the war begins.

Churyn D'Jdae, the Grand Elder of the Thigherns; Nan-Ging, High Clansman of the Athdarags; and Falkirk, King of the Murdocks are due to arrive before noon. Aberystwyth from Lleynhaven and Gwilym from Cairnhaven will also be arriving." He paused, checking his mental list once more. "Oh, and Yaggo, the Hammerthane of the dwarves will also attend. Seanachan, I understand that Ceara will bestow upon Jaren the distinct honor of her presence?" He looked at the An'ilden prince, who nodded.

"Yes, my mother said she would let nothing prevent her from witnessing the reclamation of the Cathain throne by its rightful heir," he said, smiling broadly.

"Thanks be to Elyon for keeping the rightful heir safe all these years in order to sit upon that throne," Hawk said with hearty enthusiasm.

"Here, here," the others spoke in unison.

Hawk looked at Jaren, who shifted uneasily in his chair; an action caused more by impatience than discomfiture these days. Hawk could sense the rising anticipation in the young prince.

"As I told you earlier, tomorrow will be taken up with the formal introductions of many great subjects to their Crown Prince..." he eyed everyone in the chamber, coming to rest at last upon Korthak. "So...*everyone* should be on their best behavior."

"Why are you looking at me like that?" Korthak protested.

Tanner and Balgo chuckled, as they watched the stern, serious look on Hawk's face melt away into a wry smile. He lifted one eyebrow, "Guilty conscience, old friend?"

Korthak turned his head away in disgust, and threw up his hands. "I can't for the life of me understand this," he barked.

Hawk's face became one of innocence and questioning, "What?"

Korthak stabbed his finger at Balgo, and then at Tanner. "This pint-sized, old, dirt-digging, stocking-capped, knee-knocker jests as much as this overgrown, still wet-behind-the-ears toddler, and yet I get all the blame. I just don't understand it!"

The Birth of a King

Everyone in the room burst into laughter as Korthak sat drumming his fingers on the arm of his chair and glared down at his feet stretched out in front of him.

Jaren stared at these two men whom he had come to love dearly. They were so vastly different from one another, and yet so very much alike as children of Elyon.

He stood and walked over to Korthak. Playfully squeezing the back of his friend's neck, Jaren said, "When are you ever going to quit swallowing Hawk's bait, my solid old friend?"

Korthak laughed good-naturedly, "If I did that, everyone would think I had taken ill. Besides, half the fun would be stripped from my life if I ignored him."

Jaren smiled around a yawn, "Well, I think a good night's sleep in comfortable beds will do us very well." He turned toward his own chamber and bid them all a good night.

As soon as he had closed the door, he sent a message to Hawk, *"There is one more thing I need to discuss with you; something that has been on my mind since Parth. Oh, and bring Korthak with you, please. This will involve him, also."*

Hawk waited patiently as the others headed to their own chambers, while insisting that he and Korthak needed to have a friendly chat.

The two older men went to Jaren's door, and knocked lightly. Jaren pulled the heavy oak door open, and bid them to enter.

"What's going on, Jaren?" He knew the lad was up to something, as soon as he saw the eagerness in Jaren's face, and the twinkle in his deep sapphire eyes.

"We need to do something, and if I understand my powers as sovereign, I have the right to do it."

Hawk and Korthak looked at one another again, and then watched as Jaren paced back and forth across the chamber floor.

"This is what I have in mind...."

Chapter Thirty-Seven

SECRETS REVEALED

Jaren rolled over and squinted into the bright sunlight streaming through the window of his bedchamber. He had fallen so deeply into a restful slumber that the bells tolling for Prime had not even broken into his dreams, nor had he heard the cleric enter his chamber to begin his service to the Prince.

Jaren stretched his tingling arm, trying to waken it. As he sat up, he noticed that whoever had been in the chamber had pulled open the velvety, golden draperies, and had placed a plate of fresh fruit on a table near the fire.

"Dols," he said as he yawned and reluctantly left his magnificent bed, "It's looking as though I won't be able to do anything for myself while we stay here."

He shrugged his shoulders in resignation as he remembered Fernaig's admonition that it was his duty as a Prince to allow people to honor him by giving him what service they could. He picked a few grapes from the inviting cluster which lay among fresh peaches, apples, and dates. He ate them slowly while pacing the floor and attempting to mentally arrange his day.

Almost in answer to his thoughts, a brown-robed monk stepped into the bedchamber. "I hope I'm not disturbing you, Sire, but your bath is prepared, and his Eminence has asked that you join him this morning to break your fast."

The Birth of a King

Jaren stopped pacing and popped another grape into his mouth. *"Well, a bath wasn't what I had in mind to do first today, but I guess it should have been,"* he mused.

He turned to the monk, who was standing at the door leading to the bathing room, his arms full of soft, thick towels. "Thank you," Jaren said, walking past him. "You can just lay the towels at the edge of the bathing pool," he said, dismissing the young man.

However, the monk remained in the bathing room, as though waiting for something further. Jaren eyed him questioningly.

Seeing the young Prince's confusion, the cleric cleared his throat and spoke quietly. "Your Highness, I have been assigned as your personal valet. I will be assisting you with your bath and with your attire."

Jaren was stunned and embarrassed. A scowl began to darken his brow. *"Since when is a grown man incapable of bathing and dressing himself? This is going too far!"* he seethed inwardly. Remembering his own duty just in time, he simply said, with just the merest trace of sarcasm, "Oh...yes... I'm sorry. I keep forgetting the *privileges* of my new station."

He allowed the monk to help remove his nightshirt, and quickly stepped into the steaming water. Just as it had the day before, the water began to soothe every part of him. It seemed mere minutes before the monk quietly told him it was time to dress.

Jaren lifted his eyes to study the man who stood waiting to attend him. The young monk looked to be in his late twenties. His black hair was cropped short, as required for the division of monks residing at Saint Ramsay's.

"What is your name, brother?"

The monk bowed his head. "I am called Ansel, Sire."

"Well, I know it's a little late to say this, but good morning, Ansel; and thank you for your service," he said, noting the brother's pleased smile.

When Jaren emerged from his suite, he was once again attired in royal finery. His silk tunic was purest white, with red satin brocades, stitched in gold around the neck and sleeves; his breeches were of soft, black leather. The crimson satin sash, which crossed his chest from shoulder to hip, was embroidered with the Cathain coat of arms; a cross of gold in the upper right corner, a royally crowned golden dragon rampant guardant, wings displayed, in the lower left corner, with a bend of sable dividing the two.

The young Prince was becoming accustomed to the attire of his station, and with it, unconsciously, came the regal bearing, as he walked about the abbey. This morning, as Jaren and his An'ilden bodyguard walked to the Archbishop's private quarters, he prayed a silent prayer for the Father to keep him humble in the overwhelming circumstances in which he found himself.

His escort knocked lightly on the door to the Archbishop's suite. It was opened immediately by yet another brother who bowed deeply to the Prince.

"Thank you," Jaren said warmly to his attendant, as the man bowed and took up his post beside the door.

"Ah, your Highness!" McLaren's voice roared. "I trust you slept well?"

Jaren nodded, still slightly uncomfortable in his uncle's presence. "Yes, I did, your Eminence. Thank you."

The Archbishop frowned, and shook his head sharply. "If you don't mind, titles are for people who feel a need for them." He led Jaren to a small table by a window. "I am your father's brother. I'd like for us to be friends, and friends should be able to speak freely with one another. Let's leave the titles for others to hear when it's necessary for us to be King and Archbishop instead of nephew and uncle." He seated himself across from Jaren with a rebellious twinkle in his eyes. "Would that be agreeable to you?" he asked, as a warm grin spread across his face.

Jaren's eyes shone with conspiracy, and he knew instantly that they would become fast and treasured friends.

"Yes, sir, I would like that very much."

"Good!" Stephen rubbed his hands together with delight. "You may start by calling me Uncle or Stephen." Then he glanced around the room, and cleared his throat. "Of course, this may be a little tricky, switching back and forth in front of the brothers whose ministry it is to be of service to the Archbishop."

Jaren adopted the most pompous pose he could muster, and said in mock self-importance, "Most assuredly, sir. We would not wish to be the cause of the lesser class developing a cavalier attitude toward persons of our obviously high distinction and office."

McLaren's eyes widened and he laughed heartily, "I can see that we are going to get along famously, my young nephew," he exclaimed.

"Uh..." Jaren stuttered, clearing his throat, "Uncle...where are the others this morning?"

The Archbishop lifted his hand, "Not to worry, lad. They are being *amply* cared for."

"Not again," Jaren groaned. The word 'amply' invoked in Jaren the memory of the over-ladened board at which they had dined the afternoon before. "If you keep this up, my friends and I won't be able to haul our bulky hides into the saddle when it's time to leave this amazing place."

During the meal, Jaren spoke at length of the plan he had shared with Hawk and Korthak the night before. He swallowed down some cafla and looked McLaren squarely in the face.

"You see, this is something of great importance to me. I've given it a lot of thought over the past couple of months. The sooner it's done, the better I'll feel," he pressed his case. "I'm sure that the coronation and all the ceremonies and what not will take up most of the time tomorrow, so we'll need to figure out a way to do it quickly. But I don't want anything left out. This has to be perfectly legal, so its validity can never be questioned."

The cleric sat thoughtfully for a few moments before replying. "I can see that you are a person who doesn't make such decisions rashly or in haste without weighing the consequences. Granted, it is unusual. It has been done once or twice before, but not during a coronation. I promise you, Jaren. It will be as you say, and I know just the perfect time for it to be done," he said with an impish smirk on his face.

Jaren thought, *"This man can be extremely serious when necessary, but he can also be downright mischievous. No wonder he and Hawk are such good friends; they're made of the same cloth."* Little did Jaren know how close he was to truth in using this familiar phrase.

"Would you tell me about angels? Hawk said that the images on the gates of the abbey are angels. I have never seen their like before; they are magnificent. Who are they and where do they live? We were never taught about their race at the scholars hall."

It seemed to Jaren that the Archbishop was so pleased to finally be asked an academic question that he immediately transformed into a different man. Suddenly, his eyes took on the look of a mentor, an academic and, to Jaren's immediate discomfort, an avid lecturer. The man pushed his plate aside and leaned forward on the table, folding his hands in anticipation. Jaren shuddered.

"Angels are created beings, just like everything and everyone else. They are the servants of Elyon, and they are immortal. Their existence is for the purpose of doing the will of the Father and praising Him continually. Angels are spiritual creations and so they cannot be seen by mortal eyes, *unless*, as sometimes happens, their business for Elyon necessitates taking on human form. At those times, they temporarily walk the earth as men. The Word tells us that mankind was formed just *'a little lower than the angels.'* We'll find out the full meaning of that phrase when we see Elyon face to face on the other side of death. In the meantime, we can know from the Word that He employs angels as warriors in the spiritual realm, and as ministers, messengers, and protectors to human beings. They are extremely powerful and full of beautiful majesty. Angels are incredible beings."

"Yes, the forms on the gates pictured them just as you have described," Jaren said in awe. "Have you ever seen one?"

"No, I haven't, but I certainly would like to," Stephen said, his eyes filled with excitement and hope.

"You said they are warriors in the spiritual realm. Are there wars then that we can't see?"

"Absolutely, angels are continually battling against demon creatures like the one that Tanner successfully attacked in the cave. Demons were at one time magnificent and pure angels. But they were contaminated with the evil and deception of Lucia and fell to their inherently evil condition with no hope of redemption. They are the antithesis of the undefiled angels. They are the servants of Lucia and must do his bidding at all times. He uses them for the purpose

The Birth of a King

of torturing and destroying humankind in the most excruciating manner possible. His design is to contaminate, distort, and eventually annihilate every part of creation in order to inflict unthinkable pain and dishonor upon his creator and archenemy, Elyon.

There is continual warfare as Lucia's attacks on creation must be thwarted and held in check to prevent the obliteration of our world and all it holds," the Archbishop stated with firm conviction.

Jaren was delighted with this *short* and very stimulating lesson. It was the first time he could recall being so excited by a lecture.

They continued their meal with conversation of personal interests, each sharing with the other bits and pieces of their lives and the story of their own discovery of the Father, and of Yesha, the Master. Jaren asked many questions about his family and was astonished yet again as Stephen related that his only sister, Catherine, had also escaped the massacre of the royal line. She was married to a Murdock nobleman who insisted that she flee to the safety of the Southern Regions when the war began. They had guarded the secret of her ancestry these many years. They had two daughters and lived in Maristhinil on the eastern edge of the Elven Forests. Jaren was elated to learn that more of his family was alive, hidden and kept by the grace of Elyon. Jaren vowed he would visit his family when this business with the Dragonmasters and the Lucian cult was accomplished. Perhaps they would know of others living in secrecy. He longed for the peace of the future, to safely draw his family together once again.

"Where does the ability to mind-speak come from? Do people just accidentally stumble upon this ability sometime in their lives? Hawk and you are the only ones I've heard use it," Jaren queried. *"I never thought of trying to use it with Tanner. I think I'll try it this afternoon. What a great joke it would be to throw a thought into his mind all of a sudden,"* he snickered at the thought.

"No, Jaren, it doesn't quite work that way. For some reason only male members of the actual ruling line have the ability to mind-speak. It fades out after the third or fourth generation of non-ruling branches of the family," Stephen blanched as he realized what he had just revealed. Most people who knew that bit of information had been murdered in the coup. When he looked into Jaren's

The Birth of a King

eyes, he knew that the young man had instantly made the obvious connection.

"But, Hawk can mind-speak," Jaren declared in a questioning tone.

"Yes, Hawk can mind-speak," his uncle sighed, wishing the lad was not quite so bright. "You are soon to be King, and you have the right to know. Hawk's father was the second son of Cameron Brys Arin Cathain, and brother to my grandfather, Chrichton. Hawk is my first cousin, and your cousin twice removed."

Jaren began to wonder if each day of his life as King would be marked with bits of news that would continually rock him to the core.

"There must be a very good reason that Hawk has not told you of his relationship to you. For years, he has jealously guarded this information and his family from the world outside the Elven Forests. I instantly recognized my possible mistake when explaining the mind-speech; not knowing whether or not Hawk had told you. But, unfortunately, there is no taking back my words. You must share this with no one without Hawk's permission, is that understood?" Stephen admonished.

"Yes, sir, but I wonder what could have prevented Hawk from telling me when he knew how much in need I was to have anyone living among my family." Jaren looked questioningly at his uncle, and then smiled brightly, "But suddenly I find my family is growing day by day."

Jaren rose from his chair. "I am very glad for your blunder, uncle. Thank you for all that you have told me. Would that I could spend an entire week locked away with you. There is no telling the secrets and knowledge I would learn. But I must go to find the others, and see what kind of mischief they've got themselves into already."

"You are quite welcome, lad. Thank you for breaking your fast with me. It's truly been a pleasure getting better acquainted. You are very much like your father."

Jaren embraced his uncle, smiling his thanks at the comparison and strode quickly down the hall whistling softly.

As Jaren passed through the halls of the abbey toward his apartments, a large band of riders entered through the gates of the abbey

The Birth of a King

so silently that many of the people strolling in the courtyard were unaware of their arrival. The entire company was cloaked and hooded in the strange cloth woven by the elves, causing each member of the group to blend into the autumnal colors surrounding St. Ramsay's. Many wore curious-looking long bows across their backs. Their features attested this to be the arrival of the Elvenkind: ears curved upward into graceful points; manes of long, straight or slightly waved hair golden as the sun and, for the most part worn pulled back from the crown and secured by an intricately worked leather hair glove. Their almond shaped eyes ranged in colors of green from hazel to bright emerald to deep forest shades. Their bearing was proud and impervious as they sat atop their pure white horses. One sensed an agelessness of dignity and honor in their ranks. Two elves rode in the center of the company, the marks of the longevity of their years written deeply on their faces. These wore circlets of gold about their heads, each with a single stone that shone softly from their foreheads; no one could have been unaware of the royal lineage of these two Elven kings.

It had not taken long for word of the arrival of the Elven contingency to reach Hawk, interrupting his visit with Yesha. Before he could leave his chamber, an urgent knocking began at his door. He opened it to find Brother Cuinn in a rather harried state.

"My apologies, sir, but your wife…"

At that moment, a cloaked figure burst through the door and into Hawk's arms, raining down kisses on his face, his lips, and his hands. The look of surprise and pleasure on Hawk's face was all Brother Cuinn needed for dismissal and he quietly closed the door to the suite, chuckling with joy for these two who had been so long parted.

As soon as the door closed, Celebriän whispered fervently between ardent kisses, "*Sh'mai, cormamin lindua ele lle*," clinging to him as though she would never release him.

Hawk buried his face in her mass of golden hair, breathing deeply of her scent, the scent of wild flowers, and deep forest glades. "My love, you do not know how my heart ached to come to you when we were passing through the forests. It was all I could do to keep from rushing to your side."

He held her at arm's length, and drank in the sight of her, looking deeply into her beautiful, tear-filled eyes. He thanked Elyon for the thousandth time for the gift of this priceless treasure. *"Lle naa vanima,"* he whispered as his lips touched hers.

Chapter Thirty-Eight

DUNCAN'S RENEWAL

Jaren was not long in finding his companions. They were seated on the lush grass at the south end of the courtyard, listening attentively to an older gentleman who was sitting on one of the polished granite benches under a small hickory tree. Tanner had gone to give Kynon some exercise.

Seeing Jaren emerge from the abbey, Hawk quickly rose and interrupted the elder man.

"Ah, Duncan, here is our prince."

The gray-haired man rose from the bench and turned toward Jaren.

"Duncan, I have the pleasure of introducing His Highness, Jaren Iain Renwyck Cathain. Your Highness, this is Duncan aP Iwan, one of the pastors who has come to pledge his allegiance to you."

The old man dropped to one knee. "Praise be to Elyon," he said with emotion. "You are a true miracle to behold, Sire!"

Jaren gently touched Duncan's head. "Thank you, Duncan aP Iwan. I am most pleased to make your acquaintance."

Korthak and Balgo helped the old pastor to his feet, as Jaren invited him to return to his seat.

Hawk's face was a paradigm of pleasure and pride as he took his wife's elbow and gently led her to stand before Jaren. "Your Highness, this is my beloved wife and soul treasure, Celebriän Súrion.

The Birth of a King

Jaren's face registered shock at suddenly meeting Hawk's "missing half", as the half-elf had often referred to his wife during their long months on the road. He smiled broadly, as he took her hand and kissed the back of it. Celebrïan was tall and lithe, with flawless skin, and hair of burnished gold. Her clear, honest eyes danced like sunlight on a wind-kissed mountain lake. She clearly adored her husband, and when she looked into his face, it was apparent that their love for Elyon served to amply enhance the love between them. Their marriage was a prime example of two lives entirely merged; the two were perfect compliments to one another.

Celebrïan curtsied deeply, *"Aaye, Sanda Aran, Mae govannen."*

Jaren nodded his head in acknowledgment. *"Il'er, herve aP pendragon. Mae govannen,"*

Now it was Celebrïan's turn to register surprise, "You speak the Elven tongue to perfection, Your Highness. Have I been laboring under a misconception that you were raised north of the Shandra? Or perhaps you were secretly tutored in your childhood?"

Jaren laughed and said, "No to both questions. It's a long story; one which I'm certain Hawk would love to relate to you as you share the amazing works that are accomplished in the wisdom of Elyon."

The elf woman turned to Hawk with a cunning smile and a raised eyebrow, "Husband, may we expect this coming reign to be characterized by evasiveness, or is this hopefully a momentary affliction?"

Laughter burst from the small company as they sat down on the lawn. Hawk remained standing and explained to Jaren the conversation in which they were engaged when the prince had approached.

"Duncan is just one of the many ministers we have serving Elyon among the people in the Southern Regions and even to the North," Hawk said as he seated himself on the grass. "You see, the abbey is not the only source of spiritual nourishment."

Jaren nodded his head, his eyes showing his eager interest to hear more, especially of this man's work in the North. He had thought that none knew of Elyon north of the Shandra.

Duncan smiled, and spoke with great animation. "Yes, your Highness, there are quite a few of us who travel about teaching Elyon's Word to those in need of hope and a life worth living in the midst of starvation and danger. This life of mine is truly most rewarding. I cannot find the words to relate my immense satisfaction when I travel north and see the hungry fed, the dying given life, the distressed given hope, those full of the poison of hatred cleansed and given peace instead. Here in the South, I am rejuvenated by the believers' strength of faith, love, and beneficence. There is nothing in this world I would rather be doing. I am so blessed that the Father has called me to this ministry of wandering the country."

Jaren smiled broadly at the enthusiastic evangelist. "Yes, it is more than apparent that you love the work you are doing for Yesha. It would appear that He has chosen exactly the right man for this purpose." Then his look sobered somewhat, "Are there enough people like you to feed the spiritually starving peoples in the North?"

Duncan's deep brown eyes burned with fire. "There has been a grievous shortage, to be sure. But that is only a temporary condition. Somehow, the more that people get fed, the more people there are to do the feeding. It's a true fact that there are many people in the North who are hungering for a reason to go on living, and we have sent many good people up there in the past few years to spread the Word of Life. But because the nature of our work is to share the light of truth with those who have never heard, and with those who walk in the dark night of Lucia's control, our trust in others has been sometimes rewarded with betrayal and death. Thus, the number of evangelists is constantly in a state of flux. But," the frail man's infectious smile spread once more across his face, "the true God is moving and working. The more of us who fall in the North, the more there are who are offering to cross the Shandra; so great is the need for people to know and share in the inexhaustible banquet found in the Word. Everyone who wishes to eat will find a banquet table that never diminishes in quantity or quality."

"Well, then," Jaren began, "I will ask that you and your fellow ministers begin recruiting as many of Yesha's followers as possible to go into the North when this war is over. You have my solemn promise that when we have taken back the lands of our ancestors, you and those who are willing to go with you will have all of the resources necessary to spend your entire time spreading the Word."

Duncan's old face glowed with delight. "Did you hear that, Hawk?" he said slapping his hand to his knee. "It will be just like the evangelists in the Word; going out to feed the flocks and bringing them back to the Shepherd. Oh, my precious Master, thank You for Your goodness," he prayed, tears misting his eyes.

Jaren laughed, infected with the old preacher's enthusiasm and delight.

Duncan picked up his wooden walking stick and rose with effort. "Excuse me, Sire, but I must speak with some of my fellow ministers right away. We have so many plans to make, so much to discuss, many preparations to...." his voice trailed away as he hobbled off as quickly as his old body would allow.

Hawk put his arm around the young Prince's shoulders and smiled at him. "Isn't it amazing to watch Elyon's Spirit transform people? That old man was really discouraged when we first met with him this morning. Now look at him."

Jaren laughed, "Yes, it's like watching creation happening before your eyes."

"Well," yawned Balgo, stretching his back. "You loafers can sit around here all day if you like, but I've got to be getting these hands to work before they turn to stone. I'm feeling a bit out of sorts with nothing to do. I'll join you later when your guests arrive," he said in his gruff old voice, walking off in the direction of the smithy's shop.

Korthak sat back down on the grass, and propped his head against a tree. "I kind of like being a loafer for once."

Hawk's eyebrow shot up. "I don't recall you having to overtax yourself with any hard labor for quite some time," he said as he turned and winked at Jaren.

The young Prince just shook his head and smiled. *"He's going to swallow the bait again,"* he thought to himself.

Korthak looked up at his friends with insult written on his face. "Excuse me? If my memory serves me well, I seem t'recall havin' trekked at break-neck speed into these high mountains...at great risk to my life, I might add. I seem t' also recall havin' hunted and fished for food to sustain all of us while you three did the loafin'. I had to stand watch, I cooked the meals," he paused, glaring at Hawk, "I washed horses..." he said heatedly, "and tended to runny-nosed boys when they were sick, besides numerous other tasks on our little jaunt from the North. But of course, I could have a touch of the mind-plague, and maybe I'm just imagining all of this."

Hawk and Jaren laughed as Korthak nestled himself deeper into the thick carpet of grass. "He'll never learn, will he," Jaren said, looking at Hawk.

The half-elf shook his head, smiling affectionately at his huge companion, "I doubt it...I don't think he wants to."

The two sat down a short distance from the apparently dozing Korthak.

"I have spoken to the Archbishop about our little plan. He seems very enthusiastic about it. In fact, he has already chosen what he says is the perfect time for it," Jaren whispered.

Hawk nodded. "Good. I'm sure he'll have everything prepared well in advance."

The two men did not see Korthak's reaction to these words, but if they would have turned to see their "dozing" friend lying peacefully under the tree, they would have caught the slightest glimpse of a smile, and one solitary tear slip from between his closed eyelids.

"Well, it shouldn't be too long now before our guests begin arriving." Hawk placed a hand on Jaren's shoulder. "You aren't getting nervous, are you?"

"No. No yet. But it might sneak up on me once I'm face to face with all those important people."

Hawk rested an arm on his knee while plucking at the grass with his other hand, his gaze turned from the young man. "I will take some of the blame for your uncertainty," he said quietly.

"What do you mean, Hawk?"

The half-elf sighed and leaned against the tree behind him. "I was hoping to find you well over a year earlier than we were able to. I wanted to prepare you, train you in court procedure and protocol, teach you much more than I have had the time to, so that you wouldn't feel such awkwardness," he paused. "I guess our Father had different plans for you than we did."

Jaren smiled. "Maybe He wants me to learn to rely on Him rather than on any teaching you could have given me."

The Birth of a King

Hawk nodded and smiled. "You may have something there. With the gift of all of your ancestors' memories, which we had no idea He would give you, He probably knows that you already have all the knowledge you need in order to do just fine with all of these 'important people,' as you call them. In fact, if I were you, I would not be the least bit concerned about how you will fare during the next couple of days. Just ask the Master to give you the memories you need and the words to say when the time comes." He sighed in satisfaction and relief, "Yep, come to think of it, I would much rather have the Father teaching you than myself. He is always so much more thorough. He thinks of everything."

The two friends spoke for over an hour, enjoying the beauty and serenity of the garden. Finally, Hawk stood and stretched broadly. "I think I'll go gather up everyone and make sure that they're presentable. It will probably be more impressive if you have a sizeable group of men standing with you when you greet your visiting dignitaries."

"I think that may be a wise move, since I'm sure that at this moment Tanner is probably covered from head to toe in falconry gear and feathers, and our small, stocking-capped friend is most likely coated with soot from the smithy."

Hawk smiled, walked over to the dozing Korthak, and kicking lightly on his foot, said, "Come on, old bear. I can see we're going to have to get you away from here as quickly as possible. You're becoming so idle I'll never get you back in a saddle."

Korthak sat up and rubbed his eyes. "Where are we going?"

"First, you are going down to the barracks to tell Seanachan's men to polish up their breastplates and wax their topknots, and do whatever else is necessary to stand honor guard for the Prince of Kinthoria while he greets his royal guests this afternoon. Then, you can meet the rest of us in the baths for another dip," he said as he began walking in the direction of their apartments.

Korthak was quickly on his feet. "I already had a bath this morning," he complained.

Hawk never looked back. "Another one is not going to take your hide off, old man. We have important guests coming, and we need to be at our best to honor our Prince."

Korthak threw a helpless look to Jaren, shrugged his shoulders, and lumbered off in the direction of the barracks.

Jaren was still chuckling to himself as he made his way back to his suite. He was hoping that his invisible valet had not laid out yet another change of clothes for him. He had never imagined that a monarch would spend so much time dressing and undressing, nor had he ever suspected the extent of a royal wardrobe.

As he approached his suite, the An'ilden guard smiled and opened the door for him to pass through. Jaren simply returned his smile; thanking him while considering how frail he would become for never again being allowed to use his muscles for anything. When he stepped through the door to his bedchamber his hopes were shattered. He stood in amazement, staring at yet another handsomely tailored ensemble awaiting him.

"Dols," he thought to himself, *"this is getting just a bit absurd if you ask me."* He walked over and fingered the white leather breeches, wondering how they ever managed to get them so soft. He ran his fingers over the scores of tiny dragons embroidered onto the deep sapphire satin tunic with silver thread, each with an eye of sparkling ruby. Jaren shook his head in wonder. He picked up the emerald green sash, and caressed the shield of red, emblazoned with the Cathain coat of arms. In his mind he saw a sparkling-eyed, ancient man with long, wispy white hair and beard, smiling and pointing to a sketch he had made, with the thin delicate fingers of an artisan. The sketch was the seed of the design for the coat of arms. *"Ah, very good, Hwindir. It's just what I had in mind,"* a strong voice reverberated in Jaren's mind. *"You have the dragon just right...strong, powerful, eyes bright with intelligence. There's something missing, though. Hmm. Yes, the Father has just reminded me that it is not the dragons, nor the Cathains who truly rule and keep peace across the land. It is Himself, and his Son. Yes, we must have a cross above the dragon, to remind ourselves and all who will come after us that the true God is the Maker and Ruler of all things, and without the sacrifice of His Son, our Master, there would never be peace in the world, because we would not be at peace with the Father."*

"Your Highness is pleased with his wardrobe?" a voice came from behind Jaren.

The Birth of a King

The Prince whirled around in surprise. He had been so caught up in his memories that he had not even heard the young man enter. "Yes!" he blurted out, as he tried to calm himself.

He walked over to the table and sat down, absently fingering the rods of sealing wax standing in a brass container.

The brother poured some fresh juice into a cup and offered it to his young master. "Sire, if you do not find the attire to your liking, I will remove it at once, and bring you something else to choose from," he said apologetically.

Jaren took a sip of his juice, nodded, and setting the cup on the table, retraced his steps to stand beside his new wardrobe. He laid his hand across the sash once more, standing in silence.

"Your Highness...truly, if you are the least bit displeased...."

Jaren held up his hand to silence the man. "Ansel, I am very pleased with the attire you have selected for me. I am only asking our Father to keep my feet firmly on the ground as I wear these magnificent garments," he said quietly.

He smiled, as he saw the anxiety in Ansel's eyes replaced with eager satisfaction. "You must understand that this is all very unfamiliar to me. Until a few months ago, I was just a nameless orphan, with just one set of tattered clothes to my name, and a future of slavery to look forward to. I'm just trying to stop my head from spinning at all that has happened in the past weeks. I don't want to misuse the advantage of everything that the Father has done for me."

Ansel nodded his head in understanding and smiled warmly at his Prince.

"Sire, if I may?" he asked hesitantly.

Jaren nodded for him to continue.

"With all due respect, Sire, I do not see that you are at all the kind of person who would become pompous or proud in any fashion."

Jaren smiled at the man. He walked to the window and stared out to the garden beyond. His gaze slowly rose, taking in the forest and the high peaks which disappeared into a mantle of clouds soaring far above. "I do not want to change so much that I lose touch with my fellow countrymen. I realize that some change is necessary. After all, I would be a poor representation for my people if I ruled with the manners with which I was raised. But I never want to lose sight of the fact that Elyon chose me, undeserving as I am, to become a King for the people."

Ansel shook his head. "Nay, my Lord. It is not so much for the people as for His glory that all of this is happening." Then he quickly bit off the rest of his words, realizing that he had just disputed the words of his Prince.

Jaren turned from the window to see the poor man standing crimson-faced, filled with apprehension, and wringing his hands. "I...I am sorry, your Highness. I have taken liberties, and have spoken rashly."

Jaren laughed. "No, Ansel. Trust me when I tell you that much harsher words than these have been spoken to me." He crossed the room and touched Ansel's shoulder. "Tell me what else you have to say, my brother."

Ansel lifted his eyes to Jaren's. He hesitated for only a moment before continuing. "I was just going to say that the Lord knew what His purpose was for you long before you were even born. I beg forgiveness for not agreeing with you, Sire, but the Father allowed you to experience all that you have for a reason. I don't believe He will allow all of your pain and misuse to go for naught by allowing you to forget it just by wearing magnificent clothes and keeping company with people who have titles in front of their names."

Jaren threw back his head and laughed, then he spread out his arms and spun around, "Ah," he sighed loudly, finally able to release his tension. "Ansel, you are a true gift from the Master. You have eased my spirit more than you'll ever know. I feel as though the weight of this entire abbey has just been lifted from my shoulders."

Ansel grinned sheepishly and glanced away. Then he quickly turned back to Jaren wide-eyed with anxiety. "Oh my!" he cried. "Father Cuinn will have my hide."

"What is it, Ansel?" Jaren asked, full of concern.

The poor man was bustling about the chamber. "Many of your guests had already assembled in the Reception Hall when I came to assist you. I was supposed to have you prepared to greet them as quickly as possible," he moaned.

The Birth of a King

"It's alright, I don't need another bath. Goodness knows I certainly haven't done anything to stir up a sweat, and I think that between the two of us, I can change into these clothes in no time."

Ansel began laughing with Jaren as the Prince quickly peeled off his sash and tunic, while the young monk carefully laid them aside and helped him dress.

"Besides," Jaren stated as an afterthought, "Father Cuinn certainly will understand when we tell him that I was delayed because I was gaining some spiritual guidance. We all have to wait on that once in a while, don't we?"

Ansel beamed and nodded his head in agreement.

Jaren unlaced the thongs of his boots, and kicked them off his feet with such gusto that they went sailing across the room and Ansel had to rush to retrieve them.

Jaren slipped out of his breeches, and was quickly handed the new pair, by a panting young monk with tears of laughter streaming down his face.

While Jaren was pulling on his boots, Ansel stepped quietly over to the table and picked up a box made of mahogany, and polished to a mirror shine.

"Uh, Sire. The Archbishop had this made for you. He said to present it to you before you left to meet with your guests."

Jaren finished lacing his boots, and looked up at the box. "What is it, Ansel?" he asked, taking it in his hands. Ansel turned to pick up the new sash, and then looked back at the young man to see his reaction.

Jaren was simply sitting in his chair, holding a thin coronet of gold in his hands.

The monk cleared his throat and walked back to stand in front of Jaren. "I know you will not be crowned until the morrow, but you are still the Prince today, and you must be presented as such."

Jaren lifted awe-filled eyes to him, as Ansel shook his head. "Come now, your Highness. I need to get this sash on you, and get you to your guests. I only hope we have not kept them waiting over long."

Jaren stood as Ansel draped the sash across his chest and tied it off.

The monk took just seconds to back away a few paces and inspect Jaren's appearance.

Just minutes after Jaren had entered his chamber, hoping against hope that he would not have to change clothes again, Ansel was putting the finishing brush strokes to Jaren's hair and they were rushing toward the door once more, the one pleased that they were finally taking steps toward the Reception Hall, and the other wishing he could take the same steps in any other direction.

As they rushed down the corridors, Jaren prayed silently to calm himself. When they reached the door to the Reception Hall he froze, as though in a trance.

"Your Highness, it is time to enter," Ansel pleaded with him.

Jaren jerked his eyes to Ansel as if suddenly being roused from sleep. "Oh. Yes. Am I ready?" he stammered nervously.

The monk cleared his throat and ever so faintly pointed to the golden circlet glittering in Jaren's shaking hands. Then he watched with satisfaction as the young Prince placed the circlet atop his head and pressed it down onto his forehead.

Jaren smiled at Ansel and placed a hand on his shoulder, giving it a squeeze. "Thank you for everything," he whispered as the monk hurried quickly from his side.

Chapter Thirty-Nine

FIRE AND ICE

Jaren stared in rising panic at the two clerics standing before the doors of the Reception Hall. The two men wore immaculate white linen surplices over black cassocks, red stoles hung over their shoulders. They smiled reassuringly at Jaren. He glanced at the two gigantic An'ilden warriors standing honor guard for him and could see on their proud, stern faces, the faintest hint of a smile about the edges of their eyes. He took a deep breath, pulled his sash down smoothly and nodded as the trumpets announcing his arrival, rang through the hall beyond.

As a majestic march filled the air, Jaren walked slowly down the aisle keeping his eyes fixed on Archbishop McLaren who was standing on the dais in front of the assembly.

"So glad you could join us, Sire," Hawk's voice came in gentle reproach at Jaren's tardiness.

The young Prince could not see his friend through the crowd of hundreds which were standing in excited anticipation throughout the hall.

Jaren did not allow any changes in his outward appearance, but sent a message back to Hawk. *"You have told me many times before that the Master has His own schedule. I was simply gaining some much needed spiritual guidance."*

Hawk smiled to himself with satisfaction, as he thanked Yesha for bringing Jaren so rapidly into his own, both as a monarch and as a child of Elyon.

The Birth of a King

It seemed to Jaren that the farther he walked the longer the distance became between himself and his uncle. However, eventually he came to stand beside the Archbishop, thankful to have made it through the crowd on legs that felt like mush.

As the music died away, McLaren announced, "To our dignified guests here assembled, brothers and sisters in Yesha, and fellow countrymen who have endured much and labored long for this moment, it is with the greatest pleasure and much thankfulness to our Father that I have the singular honor of presenting to you the next King of Kinthoria, Crown Prince Jaren Iain Renwyck Cathain," McLaren shouted.

The Great Hall erupted into shouts of "Hail Prince Jaren! Long live the King! Praise be to Elyon!" The applause was deafening. The An'ilden guardsmen drummed their spears on the marble floor; trumpets and cornets blasted peal upon peal. The din echoed from the vaulted ceilings, the countless pillars and marble walls of the hall. The jubilant outburst lasted for many long minutes, until the Archbishop held up his hands for silence. He motioned for Hawk to join them on the dais, and as the half-elf made his way up the stairs he saw a familiar twinkle in his cousin's eye and groaned inwardly, wondering what the mischievous cleric was up to now.

"My friends, many of you know this man personally. All of you have heard of him in whispers spoken in secret. But now, after fifteen years, it is time to speak his name aloud, and publicly, for all to hear. I present to you Llenyddiaeth aP Braethorn, Emrys aP Pendragon!"

Once more, the hall erupted into a cacophony of exuberant joy. "Emrys! Emrys!" began and continued for several minutes. Those who had been loyal to the Cathain line through all of the years of persecution, those who had whispered this name in clandestine meetings, behind locked doors, and only with absolutely trusted friends, were now shouting the loudest. Long had they waited for this moment; long had their heart's desire been to shout this name aloud, to bring hope and encouragement to their fellow countrymen. Their faces and voices radiated the victory in their souls.

Hawk looked at the Bishop with a crooked smile. *"You just couldn't do it, could you, McLaren?"* he sent to the cleric's mind, allowing a pleasantly surprised Jaren to overhear.

The Birth of a King

"What's that, my friend?" the Bishop sent back, all innocence written across his face, and taking Hawk's lead in allowing Jaren to overhear.

"You couldn't stand to behave yourself, even this once."

"Whatever do you mean?" he asked in feigned shock.

"I thought the plan was for me to come up here to escort Jaren through the assembly and to make the introductions."

"Oh, that! All in good time, my friend," McLaren chuckled as he looked at the flustered half-elf. "Really, Hawk. How many times have I told you that you must always be prepared for life's little surprises? Loosen up; it's going to be a long night. You're always much too tense."

Hawk rolled his eyes and shook his head in resignation. His "fool's mission" had turned into a triumph, with the return of the Cathain heir. He could now, finally, smile when he thought of his promise to his friend, King Cadan, instead of feeling the heaviness of that promise, which had been his burden for over sixteen years.

Finally, the Archbishop raised his hands once more for silence. "I know that every one of you wishes to meet the Crown Prince personally. It is only fitting that the Emrys, known more affectionately to all of us as Hawk, should make the introductions. He is the one whose constant trust in the true God supplied him with a never-ending assurance that the Prince was safe in the Father's keeping and that the Father would aid him in finding this young man," he said, smiling broadly at Jaren.

Hawk and Jaren descended the dais and began moving through the crowded hall. Tanner and Korthak fell in behind them. They went first to the Thighern delegation, and stood before a gigantic man who was beaming from ear to ear. He was garbed in the customary loose-fitting black breeches and leather vest of his countrymen. The deep magenta background of his knee high stockings and sash marked him as a man of supreme importance in his race.

"Your Highness, I would like to present Churyn D'Jdae, Grand Elder of the Thigherns," Hawk said formally, while returning the man's huge smile.

The Birth of a King

The massive man bowed respectfully to Jaren. "Sire, it gives my soul great pleasure to see a Cathain heir standing alive and well before my eyes."

Jaren smiled and nodded his head. "Grand Elder of the Thigherns, it is also a high honor to my soul that you have come to greet me as your Prince, and also as a fellow brother."

Churyn turned and held out his arm toward the small group of people standing behind him. A pair of equally enormous men stepped from behind the Grand Elder as he motioned them forward. As they bowed to Jaren, Churyn said, "Your Highness, this is my governor, Haroun D'Jinsok, and my regent, Andrej D'Jerbrin."

Jaren nodded respectfully as Churyn continued. "They have pledged their loyalty not only to my family but to the Cathain Crown as well.'"

Jaren searched the eyes of the two men for several moments and then smiled at them with confidence. "The Grand Elder has chosen his advisors wisely. Your presence is an honor to my court, gentlemen."

Churyn cleared his throat and said with hesitation, "Your Highness, I beg your permission to present my family to you on this historic and joyous occasion."

Jaren nodded his head. "Aye, Churyn. It will be my privilege to become acquainted with as many of your family and retinue as possible in the time left to us here at Saint Ramsay's."

The Grand Elder introduced his wife, Tynda, a slightly round, happy-faced woman, and his four small children. Senjau, the eldest son, even at a mere nine years of age, held himself with the proud confidence of the first-born and heir. Maladi was the next eldest son, and Melfi was the twin brother of Chara, the only daughter.

To the man's profound satisfaction, and to Jaren's astonishment, the two older boys came forward, bowed reverently and waited for Jaren to acknowledge them.

Jaren respectfully touched each of their heads. The proud and almost worshipful look on Senjau's face shook Jaren tremendously. He had been told by Hawk that the life of a monarch is filled with many demands and expectations. It had never occurred to him that his title would cause some people to look to him as a model of

The Birth of a King

impeccable living - someone to revere. He silently sent up a quick prayer. *"Father, You know me. There is no way I can live up to this boy's expectations in my own strength. You are the only one who can show the way to live. Please accept the sacrifice of all I am and use my body and actions to direct this child's reverence to Yourself, My Master, and to display for him the only true pattern for life."*

"Grand Elder," Jaren said aloud. "I am most grateful to have such strong support from your sons," he said with deep sincerity.

He turned his eyes to the boys. "Senjau, Maladi, you honor your father and your people, and I am deeply thankful for your friendship and loyalty."

As the Prince and Hawk moved away from the Thigherns, Jaren watched as a beautiful woman strode forward to greet him. Jaren had considered Seanachan a prime example of the nobility of his people. But the aura surrounding this striking woman, with jet-black, braided hair hanging to her ankles, proclaimed the ancient sovereignty of her line even in the manner with which she drew her breath.

Seanachan pulled himself up to his full seven foot height, and proudly struck his fist to his breastplate. "Prince Jaren Iain Renwyck Cathain, I, Prince Seanachan, do have the unparalleled honor to present to you my mother, Ceara, Queen of the An'ilden."

The woman bowed with stately grace, freely submitting her race to the authority of the Cathain throne, even though all present were fully aware that the royalty of her line reached back hundreds of years beyond that of the Cathains.

As she stood erect once more, she smiled proudly at her son, and then addressed Jaren. "I am honored, Prince Jaren. Elyon has answered our prayers and has raised up, at long last, a Warrior-King for our people. I thank Him for His kindness to us, for each day brings new reports of how our race is being ravaged and diminished by the enemy. It would seem that the emperor intends to wipe all memory of us from the face of the earth."

Jaren's eyes became dark and stern, as images of Stonehaven swept yet again across his mind. "Queen Ceara, as I have already promised your son, I will vow to you as well. I will do everything in my power and in the Power of the Father, to return your people to their former place of honor and peace. I pledge to you, dear Queen, that the noble An'ilden will once again flourish as in days past, and that they will be given once more the honorable title of The Aegis of the Seven Races."

Ceara's face radiated with hope and happiness, as Jaren bowed humbly and yet with no lessening of his own power and sovereignty.

The Prince and the Queen spoke for several minutes before Hawk led Jaren away to a group of people dressed in brown robes and curious-looking sandals. Jaren had thought, upon first seeing them from a distance, that they were visiting monks from another monastery. But then he recognized the diminutive people as the representation from the Athdarag race. Their full brown robes and small conical hats were unmistakable. Their clothing had looked rather drab in the kaleidoscope of colors swirling about them, but upon closer examination, Jaren could see that their robes were of heavy, rich silk, with multi-layered brocaded robes beneath. The blocks of their sandals were overlaid with gold, and the straps which held them were not of leather, but of velvet, heavily encrusted with gems. The conical hat of the Athdarag leader was adorned with a heavy gold chain from which hung a single, enormous topaz.

"Sire, it is with high honor I present to you Nan-Jing, High Clansman of the Athdarags."

Nan-Jing folded his hands together and bowed deeply to Jaren.

"Your Highness, I am greatly honored to be in your presence. Elyon is unceasingly gracious to have allowed this humble person to come to stand before His chosen King."

"It is also an honor and a privilege for me, Nan-Jing, to finally meet the man so renowned for his courage, and so highly respected among all the leaders of Kinthoria for his wisdom."

Nan-Jing's eyes shone at this high praise. He stood as tall as his diminutive frame would allow and, clapping his hands together once, waited momentarily.

A lad who looked to be three or four years younger than Jaren came forward to stand directly in front of him.

"Your Highness, this is my son and heir, Chenju. He is desiring that you will accept a small gift as token of the loyalty of the Jing Family."

The Birth of a King

The boy lifted his eyes to Jaren as he pulled from the sleeve of his robe an elaborately carved tiny, wooden dragon with shining eyes of gold-leaf, and highly lacquered to add depth to the unusual grain of the wood. He laid the exquisite piece on Jaren's palm, folded his hands and bowed deeply.

Jaren held the small, life-like creature up to inspect it more closely. Every scale, every tiny talon and tooth had been carved with precision and clarity. Small, dark whorls were scattered across the surface of the wood.

"Ask the lad if he is the one who carved it," Hawk's voice came into Jaren's mind.

"Chenju, is this the work of your own hand? What type of wood is this? I've never seen its like before."

The boy turned questioning eyes to his father, who nodded proudly.

"Yes, your Highness. Your insignificant servant has been honored to make this small gift for you. The wood is called 'the eye of the bird,' Sire. It is very rare."

Jaren was astonished at the gift. He looked deeply into the lad's eyes. "Chenju, my friend, no one is insignificant. We are all created by our Father, each for a specific purpose. We are all equal in His eyes, regardless of the station in which He has placed us upon this earth." He smiled and held up the dragon. "I am exceedingly thankful for such a kingly treasure. This creature needs only breath to give it life. Elyon has given you a marvelous talent. When we rebuild the palace at Rath Connacht I would ask that you promise to come to me, to aid me in giving life and beauty to the place."

The embarrassed, but highly pleased boy beamed with joy, bowed enthusiastically and retreated to the less conspicuous company of the rest of the Jing retinue.

Hawk steered Jaren toward a group of slender people of average height, dressed in soft leather breeches and green and azure tunics of the finest wool. Jaren immediately recognized Hawk's Elven race.

Hawk smiled and bowed deeply to the two elders who had come to Saint Ramsay's to represent these noble people. His heart was stirred as he felt the kinship of the elves surrounding him once more.

"Your Highness, long have I desired to present to you the most esteemed elders of our race, Aberystwth aP Ifander and Gwilym aP Awanil."

The two aged Kings were the eldest of the race of Elves. Jaren was nearly reeling from the Power of the Father emanating from these two men of such regal bearing.

"I am honored beyond words, your Majesties," he said in all truth. "I am most grateful to the Father for your loyalty to the Cathain House, for I know of a certainty that your wisdom and close communion with Elyon will be of invaluable help to us in our councils, as I am certain they have been in many councils through the long years. I truly believe that the time is right for the Elven and Human races to put aside past mistrust and alienation, and to come together in the unity of the true God whom we all serve. It is the time to rid Kinthoria of the enemy and his hordes."

The two Elders looked at one another and smiled faintly, each giving the other a slight nod. Then, turning to Jaren, Gwilym said, "We must admit that we attended this afternoon with much trepidation, but with equally as much hope in our hearts. Now that we see the Power of Elyon resting in you, we know that Llenyddiaeth has indeed found the true heir. Every resource which is ours now belongs to you, for you have judged rightly that our races will be as one in the love of the Father."

Aberystwth spoke softly to the Prince. "We regret, Your Highness, that our time at Saint Ramsay's Abbey will, of necessity, be very short. Our people are even now preparing for the coming war, and we must return to lead them."

The Elven entourage would be leaving Saint Ramsay's soon after the coronation, as would most of the other guests. The usual weeks-long festivities which followed such an auspicious and historic occasion were being postponed indefinitely. A brief period after the coronation would be taken up instead with hurried councils and meetings, finalizing plans for the imminent war with the Dragonmasters. "I will be forever in your debt, sirs. I covet your prayers on my behalf," Jaren said earnestly.

As Jaren spoke with the Elders, Hawk's eyes had been searching their entourage for a glimpse of his wife. As their eyes met, the half-

The Birth of a King

elf's heart was moved once more by her incredible beauty. He knew he would have only a few short hours in the coming days to hold Celebriän in his arms, and his heart already ached at the thought of parting from her once again. The only thing which sustained his resolve was his knowledge that he was doing Elyon's will. He quickly asked the Father to make their time together especially memorable for each of them.

Moving away from the elves, Hawk motioned for Balgo to step forward to introduce Jaren to the Dwarven contingent. The dwarf cleared his throat, and repositioned his stocking cap, making certain that the golden tassel was clearly visible, and then stepped beside an ancient dwarf, bent and grizzled with the weight of his years. His eyes shone with the stubborn strength and fire of the spirit which resided grudgingly within the nearly spent body.

"Your Highness, I have the extreme honor of presenting to you Yaggo, Hammerthane of the Dwarves," Balgo said, bowing deeply.

Yaggo slowly leaned forward into a bow, trying valiantly to conceal the pain which the effort caused him. But the stiffness in his extremely old bones would not allow him to pull himself up straight once more.

Jaren could sense the hurt pride and pain in the old man. "Hammerthane of the Dwarves, would you take great offense if I asked you to join me on this bench?" he said sheepishly. "I know I am young, and a prince, but I need to rest for a few minutes. It's been a most trying day for me."

Jaren had wanted to ease the old dwarf's uncomfortable situation, without being outwardly condescending, but by the scowl on Yaggo's face, the young Prince thought at first that he had made matters even worse.

Yaggo glared at him, and then turned to Balgo, speaking in what his near deaf ears considered a whisper. "They been pamperin' this lad too much already, I see. Can't even stand for a couple of hours through a small get-together like this."

Balgo's face burned with embarrassment, but inside he was proud to see the dwarven brashness was still alive in this ancient relative.

The Birth of a King

"Help me sit down with him, Balgo, so he can 'rest a few minutes,'" Yaggo said, mockingly attempting to imitate Jaren's voice.

Balgo and another dwarf helped the Hammerthane onto the bench beside Jaren, making sure he was comfortable before stepping away a bit to allow the two a private conversation.

After speaking with Yaggo for several minutes, Jaren excused himself and Balgo continued with the introductions of the Dwarf leaders, the Dwarknyri: Harerg of the Chalgrunalk; Nororil of the Gilraggak; Dimtil of the Ragdukr; Maain of the Klduuim; Gimmalk of the Calrunak. Jaren's head was spinning with the tongue-twisting names of the clan leaders. However, he had very much enjoyed their spontaneity and genuineness in speaking their minds to him.

Hawk stepped beside Jaren and they approached the final contingent. Jaren noted the colorful and varied plaids of the kilts which the men wore; plaids that perfectly matched the patterns of their knee-high stockings and their close fitting hats, each with a stiff bristle of horsehair standing at the front and held in place by a pewter brooch. The skirts of the women were of the same plaids, as were their shawls, which were held together in front by a single golden brooch. Their white cotton blouses, with wide, heavy lace collars, were spotless and crisply pressed. Red, green, and blue ribbands were clustered into coils of hair ranging in color from deep black to pale red.

"Sire, I am honored to present to you Falkirk Danageld, High King of all the Murdock clans," Hawk said with obvious warmth, as they came to stand before a large man, whose ruddy and weathered face sported a bright orange mustache of enormous proportions. His honest, hazel colored eyes were, at that moment, sparkling with delight. He smiled and bowed.

"Your Highness, I am very pleased and honored beyond measure t' be makin' your acquaintance. Your father and I were extremely good friends."

Jaren shot a surprised look at Hawk.

"It is true, Sire. You see, your father loved the sea, and on occasion, he would invent some ridiculous reason to visit the coast. He and Falkirk would then spend his entire visit sailing and fishing, as though neither of them had a kingdom to run."

"Aye, I'm afraid it was even as the Emrys speaks," the jolly man confessed.

"Chieftain of the Murdocks, I am very grateful that you have come to offer your friendship and your allegiance. It would be a great service if you would share your memories of my father with me sometime in the future, when there is time to enjoy a leisurely sail and some fishing. I have caught a few fish in my short years, and I highly enjoy the pull of a line," Jaren said with enthusiasm, while determining to revisit his father's memories.

"It would give me the greatest pleasure, your Highness," Falkirk said. He moved aside and beckoned for a group of men to step forward.

"Sire, it is my honor to present to you Duke Selwyn Mallaig, the highest ruling Clansman in the Ulaid Tuatha; Calum O'Felan, the Earl of the Midhe Tuatha; and Gavin MacLean, Baron of the Donnacht Tuatha."

The men bowed deeply to Jaren, each sensing the honor of being in the presence of the true heir to the Cathain throne.

Jaren nodded his head and, quickly searching each of their eyes, said simply, "I greatly welcome the support of men of such honor and renown."

Then Falkirk guided a solidly built, jolly faced woman to stand before the Prince. "Sire, this is my queen, Corunna."

The woman curtsied elegantly to Jaren, her face flushed crimson, but her eyes flashed and sparkled with delight. She stepped beside her husband, and looked into his eyes as she gave him the slightest nudge in the ribs with her elbow.

The Murdock King's face immediately lost its smile. He sighed with resignation and turned to scan the large company. It took him only seconds to spot the one for whom he was searching. He signaled for a young girl to come forward. When she hesitated, he scowled threateningly and signaled more forcefully a second time.

Jaren watched as the bright eyes of the young lady glinted defiantly with the same fire that burst forth from her deep auburn hair. Jaren was amused at the obvious clashing of wills between father and daughter.

The Chieftain turned and looked apologetically to Jaren.

The Birth of a King

Jaren, however, still had his eyes on the girl as she moved with grace and elegance through her kinfolk, and came to stand by her father's side.

The Prince saw that her face was not tanned as were most of the other Murdocks. On the contrary, her skin was smooth and fair, and delicate as a flower carved in alabaster. Its perfection was completed by the faintest trace of freckles sprinkled across her nose and onto her cheeks. He observed the intelligence and pride in her round green eyes. Her lips were full and perfectly shaped.

He noted all of this as casually and unaffectedly as he would have noted the beauty of a colorful bird or perhaps a perfectly formed flower.

Tanner, on the other hand, had noticed the very same things about the girl, but he had been overwhelmed by her attributes, as had almost every other man, young and old, with whom she had ever come into contact.

Korthak put his arm around Tanner's shoulders, and put his finger under the young man's jaw to close his mouth.

Falkirk cleared his throat, and said with trepidation, "Your Highness, my daughter, the Princess Kyriel."

The young princess flicked one last defiant look toward her father's stern face, and then executed an embarrassingly extravagant curtsy. She said in an icily mocking tone, "Your Highness."

Upon rising, she lifted her head slightly in a deliberate attempt to snub this young upstart. She had noted with rising anger that this young whelp was not the least bit moved by her beauty or her station, and she felt intensely insulted. She could see that she was going to have to teach this commoner in royal clothing a lesson or two in recognizing and esteeming his betters.

Seanachan had been watching the meeting of these two with extreme interest. He was beaming broadly, as he thought, "*I believe our young friend has found his soul-mate.*"

Jaren, whose mind at that moment was worlds apart from the An'ilden's, eyed the girl with barely masked anger. Her thoughts were clearly written upon her face, and had been spoken loudly, if not with her voice, then certainly with every movement of her body. Jaren knew that he had every right to publicly humiliate Kyriel. But

The Birth of a King

in so doing, he would also have tarnished the name of her honorable father, who had been his father's close friend.

Instead, he astounded everyone who had witnessed the shameful behavior of the girl. He even surprised himself. "Falkirk, King of the Murdocks, Chieftain of the Laigin Tuatha, I ask that you and your family would join me at my table for the festivities this evening. It would be a great pleasure to become better acquainted with each of you."

As the girl's face registered shock, and then belligerence, Jaren shot her a look of warning, as though to say, "Do not dare to disgrace your family further, as you have done just now."

A crimson Falkirk bowed deeply, as Jaren turned to walk back to the dais with Archbishop McLaren.

"Well done, lad. Your father would be proud of you!" came his uncle's thought. *"But tell me, how did you know that Falkirk was of the Laigin kingdom?"*

Jaren kept his pace steady, though his body was shaking with rage. He sent his thought back to McLaren. *"Part of my family's memories, I would think."* He cast a quick glance at the Archbishop, along with the words.

McLaren nodded, as they climbed the steps to the dais. As the crowd sensed the end of the solemnities, they began to approach the dais in an informal manner, to greet the Crown Prince once again and to eye the Emrys more closely.

Upon seeing that they were about to be overrun, McLaren stepped forward and held up his hands to halt the onslaught. He shouted above the din. "We have prepared a feast in honor of our Prince this evening. Please, everyone. Let us give Prince Jaren and his retinue what short time they have to rest and prepare for the festivities. You will be able to meet with them at leisure at that time. In the meantime, it is our hope that you will enjoy the peace and beauty of the abbey."

Much later that evening, Jaren sat at the banquet table, and was thoroughly enjoying Falkirk's tales of his father. As the older man finished relating a particularly outrageous fish tale, the young Prince felt a familiar tingling in his head.

"Why don't you offer to show the Princess Kyriel around the courtyard, lad?"

Jaren's head snapped around to stare directly at Hawk. The half-elf and Celebriän were sitting with Seanachan and Stephen McLaren. The men were leaning back in their seats, arms folded across their chests. All were smiling smugly in his direction.

"I had a somewhat better idea, I think," Jaren shot back to Hawk in anger. *"I had been considering something more along the lines of an extended tour of the cellars, and accidentally leaving her Haughtiness behind a locked door somewhere down there."*

McLaren had just sipped a mouthful of wine from his goblet, and was hard put to keep from spraying it across the table. Instead, he tried swallowing, and immediately choked. He coughed and laughed in turns. Rising crimson-faced at creating such a spectacle, he stepped away from the table and into a small alcove. Hawk and Seanachan had followed to see if they could assist him, while Celebriän concealed a soft burst of laughter behind her hand.

"I will repay you for this, my Prince!" McLaren sent good-naturedly to Jaren, who received the message with wide-eyed innocence.

"Serves you right for trying to think up ways to torture me," he said with a frown on his face.

"D' ye think he'll be all right, Sire?" Falkirk asked, his concern for the cleric obliterating his determination to keep his speech "civilized," as Corunna had put it, while he was at Court and in the presence of the Prince.

"I'm sure he'll be just fine. He just tried to drink and talk at the same time and choked on a little something...there, you see? He's waving and smiling to let us know everything is all right."

Falkirk laughed with relief. "Those three look like some wee joke is afoot! If you'll be excusin' me, Sire, I would dearly love t' investigate, and maybe catch up on some o' their escapades of late."

Jaren shook his head. "Please, go ahead. I have been selfish to keep you to myself for so long. Thank you very much for helping me to know my father better. I am forever grateful to you."

The Birth of a King

Falkirk stood and bowed to the Prince. "It really was all my pleasure, your Highness," he said, remembering his speech once again. "Being in your company has brought me a real sense of being with Cadan again. You and your father were cut from the same cloth. I am in your debt, Sire." He walked away and headed straight toward the source of Jaren's fit of pique.

"What makes any of you believe that I am the least interested in being the escort of that arrogant, disrespectful, spoiled piece of fluff? She's so full of fire and ice that the flowers would probably shrivel and die the moment she stepped foot out of doors," he shot to his friends.

Hawk lifted his eyes to Jaren, even as he was in the process of slapping the still coughing McLaren on the back. He lifted one eyebrow for effect, and sent to Jaren, "Tch, tch, your Highness. Is that any way for a man of noble birth to speak of a lady with bloodlines as impressive as yours? Pity. I thought you were a better man than that."

Jaren clenched his teeth and scowled once again. "Stop calling me 'your Highness.' It's making me dizzy having to keep my head up so high. And why should I have to be the one to try to smooth things over? She started it. She doesn't even know me; she's just decided to hate me out of contrariness."

This time McLaren spoke to him, in a rather loud and testy tone. "Because, nephew, tomorrow you will be crowned a King. It's high time you started behaving like one."

Jaren's shoulders sagged, as his anger all but obliterated by resignation. He knew he was beaten. Their logic and civility were, as usual, impeccable. He sat in brooding silence for several minutes, trying to gather every ounce of his will power to make his greatest sacrifice to date as the Prince of Kinthoria. Finally, he squared his shoulders and placing a look of martyred strength upon his face, he stood and walked toward a knot of young people where his pretentious little adversary was openly flaunting her charms with one of her distant relatives.

Jaren cleared his throat, to catch her attention, and then watched in disbelief as Kyriel's eyes flitted with disinterest in his direction, and then back to her cousin.

The Birth of a King

He lifted his head, and stared at the ceiling, thinking to himself, "*Dols, no one should have to endure such discourtesy, bloodlines or no.*"

He drew in a steady, deep breath. "Excuse me for interrupting, Princess Kyriel, but I was wondering if you would do me the honor of accompanying me on a turn through the courtyard," he said in a deceptively even tone.

Kyriel turned her head just enough to acknowledge his presence. Fixing a condescending smile on her face, she said in a voice which concealed her contempt just enough so as not to bring her father's wrath down upon her head, "Your Highness, my dear cousin and I are in the middle of a terribly interesting discussion on horticulture. If you wish to wait, I shall attend you the moment our discussion is completed." With the cutting remark issued, Kyriel turned her head away from Jaren, much as his scholars had done after giving him a lecture on proper behavior.

Jaren's blood was at the boiling point. He clenched his fists tightly, to regain control of his rage. He would not allow his actions to shame the Cathain name and heritage. With coldly calculated self-control, he once again gathered all his resolve, and, undaunted by the Princess' repugnant remark, took another deep breath.

He spoke with all of the gentility he could force through his constricted throat. "I find the study of flora a fascinating topic. Do you mind if I join your conversation?" He smiled gallantly.

Kyriel's fiery eyes turned to meet his in open shock. She had supposed that such a common creature would not even know the meaning of the word horticulture. She instantly composed herself, "You know about the science of flowers and trees, then?" she asked.

Jaren allowed himself just the smallest feeling of satisfaction that he had won this small battle. He sensed that the snobbish Princess probably would not have thought him capable of intelligence. He simply could not resist tossing out a double-edged barb. With as much naiveté as he could imitate, he said, "I know that when you put poison on them, they die."

Kyriel's emerald eyes flashed and her cheeks burned as the true understanding of Jaren's words were understood. She stared at him,

The Birth of a King

sizing up this new opponent, and considering that perhaps she had underestimated this brash young man.

"On second thought, I am feeling the need of some fresh air. I shall accompany you to the courtyard, Sire."

Jaren offered his hand to help her rise. She refused to touch it, saying, "I am strong and healthy, your Highness, and very much capable of standin' to my feet by myself." Then, thinking that maybe she had gone just a trace too far, she curtsied ever so slightly and said, "But thank you for your gentlemanly kindness."

Jaren merely turned his head and rolled his eyes heavenward. *"Dear Father, please don't make me suffer long with such a well-mannered woman. And help me to keep my hands at my sides instead of around her throat."*

He turned and smiled politely at the Princess.

As they began their stroll through the courtyard, Jaren raised his eyes once again. *"Couldn't you make it rain or something?"* he pleaded with the Father, knowing full well that such self-serving requests were not likely to be taken seriously.

As the two walked from the Banquet Hall escorted by a dozen An'ilden warriors, many eyes had followed their retreat.

Hawk and McLaren were curiously hopeful. Others were envious, Tanner being among them. Some, such as Falkirk and Corunna and many of the Princess' clan, who were well acquainted with the girl's mercurial temperament, were full of compassion for the young Prince.

Shortly after the departure of Jaren and Kyriel, Hawk and Celebriän exited the hall and made their way to his private apartment. Hawk felt he could certainly be spared these all too few hours with his wife.

Chapter Forty

THE CORONATION

Jaren found himself in a constant state of flux between his understandable uneasiness at becoming the King of all Kinthoria with all of the weight of responsibility in governing the seven races, and struggling with the urgency to be done with the coronation, and to be off to free his land from the deadly tyranny of the Dragonmasters.

Added to this was his disquiet over a flaming-haired princess with eyes the color of alder leaves in the sunshine, and with a freckled nose which turned up ever so slightly. Many times in his sleeplessness that night, Jaren had thought about their walk through the courtyard just hours before. He had tried to recall everything which had been said and done between them from the moment they had first met, and still he was at a loss as to any action or word which might have caused the lass to be so ardently set upon irritating him. He had considered that perhaps the girl had been jealous of his position, but then dismissed such an idea as absurd. After spending several hours pondering her strange, antagonistic behavior, he had finally given up the struggle and had fallen into a light, fitful sleep.

That sleep was interrupted by an early morning visit from Tanner. "Are you awake?" he heard Tanner whisper.

He sat up and rubbed his eyes, blinking at the distorted features of the face peering over a single candle; the only source of light in the deep shadows of his heavily draped bed.

He yawned, "I am now."

The Birth of a King

Tanner placed the candle on the bed table, and seated himself on the side of the enormous state bed. He remained silent for several moments.

"What is it, Tanner?" Jaren asked anxiously, sitting up among the pillows.

Tanner looked earnestly into Jaren's eyes, "I just want you to know that I won't let you down today like I did at the Spring of Elyon, no matter how many changes may occur when you are crowned. I want you to know that I will always consider you my brother." He stared into the candle flame, "I have to confess to you, Jaren that I have been jealous, at times, of your new life, with all of the power and respect it has brought you." He bitterly resented even the memory of such shameful thoughts. He lifted his dark eyes to the shadow of the young man sitting before him. "But Elyon has opened my eyes to the truth. I no longer envy your position in even the slightest way. The tasks that lay before you, my friend, would be impossible for me to perform. I know that your character and nature are much better suited for these things than mine. The Father has equipped each of us perfectly for the lives He has called us to."

He ran his hand through his dark, wavy hair. "I want you to know that I pledge with all of my heart to stand by you through all that Yesha asks you to do. Whatever you ask of me, I will do. I will never deserve the titles of Elyon's Chosen Warrior and the King's Champion, any more than anyone deserves the blessings given by the Creator; and I am more happy and content than I can say, for His goodness to me."

Jaren was moved beyond words by this selfless confession and confirmation of Tanner's deep love and loyalty. Finally, he nodded his head, and smiled warmly at his best friend. "Thank you, Tan," he said simply, and then added, "You know, it's a good thing that you have come to these decisions and the peace that they bring. According to the dream you had at Balgo's cottage our lives have been joined together for a very long time. It would be a pretty rough go if we were to continue to envy one another."

Jaren laughed at Tanner's stunned expression. "You are surprised that I envy you? Man, why wouldn't I? You have always excelled at everything. Who was always the best at archery, horsemanship, and

The Birth of a King

swordplay? Who always got a smile from the scholars and masters at the Hall - and who always got their scolding and frowns? Who had the mother, and the brothers - and who had no family at all? And now, who is it that still has freedom in his life - and who is the one bound by his ancestry to a lifetime of rules, responsibilities and service?"

He sighed and smiled, "You see, it's much different from my perspective, isn't it?" Jaren leaned over and clasped Tanner's shoulder. "You're right that we each have been given a life to live according to Elyon's plan. I was ready to merely be content, and obedient to His will, but thanks to you, I am now ready for so much more than that. You've helped me to see that my future isn't all about rules and responsibilities. It's a gift from the Father to give my life a meaning that will bring glory to Him." Jaren's eyes grew moist and he smiled as he remembered Ansel's council of the past morning, *"He was right,"* he thought. The young prince looked once again at his friend, "You have given me the happiness that was lacking in my perspective. I can't thank you enough, Tan."

Tanner smiled sheepishly, and then he looked at Jaren with a twinkle in his eye. "You really were envious of me?" he asked with genuine pleasure.

Jaren laughed and nodded his head.

Tanner lifted the candle from the table. "I'd better get out of here. The brother will probably be here soon," he said, heading for the door.

Jaren whispered, "I swear, he has become like my own shadow, always lurking about with another change of clothes."

Tanner laughed and opened the door. "Oomph," a muffled cry came from behind a stack of clothing blocking the doorway.

"Good morning, brother," Tanner laughed quietly as he made his way across the reception hall and entered his bedchamber.

Jaren leaped from his bed and hurried to help the startled monk as the load in his arms began a slow tilt to the side.

"Sorry, Brother Ansel," he said. "Tanner was sent by the Father this morning to give me a new perspective on life and to confirm the council you gave me yesterday."

The Birth of a King

The flustered cleric apologized profusely for his intrusion. "I had not expected that you would be awake yet, Sire."

"Well, were it not for Tanner your assumptions would have been correct," he smiled as he helped Ansel place the garments on the table.

The monk began pulling the drapes at the windows. "So then, you are ready for this, Sire?" he probed.

Jaren rubbed his forehead and shrugged his shoulders. "I am probably as ready as anyone ever could be who is just about to be crowned a High King." He poured himself a goblet of water. "Hawk spent the better part of two hours yesterday drilling me on all of the things he taught me about the coronation rites during our journey to Saint Ramsay's." Ansel nodded. "I think that was wise, Highness. Being well prepared seems to ease the mind so that the things which need to be recalled become second nature and the fear of making mistakes becomes minimal. That makes it possible to concentrate on the purpose and significance of our words and actions."

Jaren stared at the young cleric. "You know, Ansel, the Father has certainly given you an immense amount of wisdom for someone your age. Now I know why you were selected to be my valet. Elyon knew how badly I would need the encouragement of your insight."

Ansel bowed his head, hot with embarrassment at this high praise. "Elyon is good," he said simply.

Jaren poured himself another goblet of water and quickly drank it down. His stomach was loudly rebelling against the hours of fasting which Hawk had told him would be a physical and spiritual part of his preparation for the coronation.

Some time later, having shortened his time in the bathing chamber, Jaren donned a thick velvet, cowled robe and said to Ansel, "I feel the need to spend some time away from the eyes of others, Ansel. I will make use of the private chapel instead of going into the gardens this morning."

"As you wish, Sire, I will come for you when it is time to attend to your attire," the monk said.

Jaren had not been in the private chapel before, and so was awed by the beauty and stillness of the place. The stone floor was covered with a rich Borkau carpet. The tall window was a masterpiece of stained glass, portraying a risen Yesha showing the wounds of His sacrifice to the observer. The words, 'It was for you,' were painted on a glass panel beneath his feet. The rising sun shot through the window, creating bars of colored light that slanted horizontally through the haze from many candles burning in the tall chamber. Jaren absently wondered who kept these vigils of prayer burning all the time. The prie-dieu offered a leather covered cushion upon which to kneel for prayer. This had been placed before a rough-hewn rood hanging on the wall, with a candle sconce set in the wall at each side. Heavy velvet drapes hung from above the cross and were held back from the burning candles by golden ropes.

The young prince walked reverently to the prie-dieu and knelt. He felt somehow too awed for conversation with the Father just yet. He was content to rest in His holy presence. He sat back on his heels, raised his face to the sunlight and drank in the warmth of Elyon's love. That love seeped into Jaren's body and soul, quieting his mind and spirit, easing his tense muscles and bringing the refreshment which his body needed after a night of fighting for rest.

Finally, he began speaking with the Father, asking for guidance for himself and for all believers who would accomplish His will in Kinthoria. He asked Elyon to be the strength and courage within those who would come face to face with the enemy, both spiritually and physically. He asked the true God to be the wisdom within every person taking part in the councils which were continuing throughout the Southern Regions and in the clandestine councils within the rebellion in the North. He pleaded with the Father to show mercy on the innocent, by being their protection from the dragon riders and their barbarous vengeance and hatred. He began praising Elyon for His wondrous and miraculous ways, for His strength and power, for His righteousness and holiness, praising Him just for being the true God.

Jaren felt the need to pray earnestly for wisdom to bring the dragons back into their rightful place as the guardians of Kinthoria. He prayed for the safety of the dragons; for on the day before arriving at St. Ramsay's, his senses had been assaulted by deep rage, distress, betrayal, and alarm at some undefined helplessness in the dragons. Since that day there had been little contact with them other than a dull pain in his consciousness. Their ceaseless drone in his mind had become the welcome promise of a future strong friendship established on mutual trust and reliance. Now, it was barely discernable, and he found himself often tense from inwardly leaning toward its faintness in an attempt to hear and understand.

The young prince knew that in ages past, the royal heirs to the throne had been able to communicate freely with the ancient creatures. He had just this night past stumbled upon several instances locked away in his memory that had revealed this special gift. He prayed that Elyon would show him the way to re-establish communication, since their plans would be greatly hampered without Elyon's apparent intent to use the dragons.

"Father, I know that You eagerly wait to give full answer to my prayer. I am more grateful for this than I have the ability to express. Read my heart, mighty Elyon, and know how I long for You to place my feet upon the path to aid my fellow countrymen in understanding that the dragons have been forced against their very natures into the behavior of the past seventeen years, and so cannot be held accountable. I long for the day when all Kinthorians will once again shout in trust and joy at the sight of the dragons flying overhead. I long to rescue these noble beasts and to bring them comfort; to free them from the degradation imposed upon them by Volant. I confess to you, Master, my deep anger at my seeming helplessness to bring about what I know to be Your will concerning them."

At last, he was silent, and with bowed head, he laid his spirit before the Father, to minister to him in any way He would wish.

After a lengthy time of kneeling in silence in the companionship of the Father, he heard the true God's quiet voice speaking in his mind. *"My son, you give Me pleasure, in that you have not asked these things for yourself, but for others. Because you have so selflessly made your supplications, I will do all that you have asked of Me, and far more. Know that I am with you at all times, and that I will never, never,* never *leave you or abandon you. I will bring peace to Kinthoria through you and those who serve you. I will bless you greatly. Know that you are not helpless to bring about My will for the dragons. When the time is right, you will fully understand the extent of your power toward them. In the meantime, I am teaching you to perfectly trust in Me without the need of physical proofs."*

When Ansel came to call the prince, he found him leaning against the prie-dieu in a restful sleep, with cheeks still wet with tears, and a faint smile touching the corners of his mouth.

Ansel stood, looking down at the young man who would soon become his King. His heart was moved with love for him as he sensed what had been taking place in this little chapel. "So, you have been touched again by the heart of Yesha, my brother. You have been truly blessed," he whispered.

He leaned down and touched Jaren's shoulder. "Highness," he said, softly shaking him. "It is drawing near to the time when you must present yourself at the Cathedral."

A second pair of eyes had seen Jaren's descent into slumber, and the evil mind behind them had been filled with triumph, supposing his sleep to be death; the successful result of a powerful poison carefully applied to the Prince's breakfast tray. He had been unaware of the required twelve-hour fast traditionally imposed upon royal heirs the night before their ascension to the throne.

The assassin's hiding place had almost been revealed when Jaren awoke at Ansel's soft urging, but the scream of rage and disbelief had been choked off just in time.

As the prince and Ansel left the chapel for the bedchamber, another pair of feet flew down hidden stairs within the darkness of the abbey walls. Curses muttered in loud whispers, echoed like a myriad of demons flying after the shadowy figure, berating and threatening for the failed attempt to kill the upstart King.

The would-be assassin raced to the kitchens, there to lurk until the opportunity presented itself to undo the previous assassination attempt, so as not to reveal the presence of an enemy this far south, until the time was ripe to strike with absolute surety of success.

As Jaren was being fastidiously attired by the young monk, he became keenly aware of the dedication of the man, to himself, as Prince, and to the Father, and the abbey. "Ansel, before things get too hectic and I forget I want to thank you now, for your wonderful service to me. You have been very gracious. I can't tell you how much I have valued the wisdom you have shared with me. I hope that when the war is over, we may have the time to become better friends."

Ansel smiled broadly, "It is a great blessing, Sire, to know that you are the true heir to the throne, and that you walk with the Master. It has been a rare privilege to be the first one to serve you in this way."

He stood back to inspect his handiwork, and smiled with satisfaction. Jaren looked every inch a King. He stood tall and broad shouldered; his doublet and breeches, were of the finest white satin brocade. Golden satin inserts shone through several slits along the outer edges of his sleeves. His soft, white boots had been adorned with worked pieces of gold at heel and toe. A purple sash, free of any design, was draped across his broad chest; a short satin-lined, white brocade mantle hung from his right shoulder, secured with a heavy gold chain.

As Jaren looked at his image in the polished bronze mirror, he noticed the apparent oversight of the tailor, in not having embroidered the coat-of-arms upon his sash. He cleared his throat, and without saying a word, lowered his eyes to the empty space.

Ansel laughed. "It does seem to need something, doesn't it, Sire?" He picked up a box from the table, and opening it, held it out for Jaren.

Jaren stared in stunned amazement at the contents of the box. On red velvet cloth sat a palm-sized brooch. The Cathain coat-of-arms had been painstakingly worked in gold, diamonds, rubies, and onyx. This was laid on a background of white enamel, from which shot two layers of golden rays, each tipped with a diamond, an emerald, a ruby, or a sapphire.

"This has been in the Cathain family for many generations, Sire. It is used only for the highest state ceremonies. It's a very fine piece, don't you think?" Ansel said with admiration.

"Fine isn't the word for it, Ansel. In fact...I can't think of a word for it," Jaren exclaimed, as the monk pinned the exquisite brooch on the sash over his heart. "But how did this survive the razing of my father's palace?"

Ansel smiled, "Many of the royal jewels were stored away from the palace, and cared for by dwarven gem crafters. The dwarves

The Birth of a King

were also given the care of histories, books and ancient scrolls, art and other treasures that were used infrequently at the palace. It was a wise choice, do you not agree, Sire?"

"Indeed," Jaren responded, thankful for his father's careful attention to such details.

Ansel shook his head in satisfaction. "White is a very good color for you, Sire. It is chosen for coronations because it signifies the purity of the soul of the monarch. It is especially gratifying to know that, in your case, the color matches the work of Elyon in your life." He looked earnestly at Jaren, "I will keep you in my prayers...your Majesty," he said, smiling at the use of Jaren's new title, before his coronation. "I take my leave of you now, Sire. You will be escorted to the Cathedral by the An'ilden contingent and some of the brotherhood. I will take a somewhat faster route. I made Brother Chadwick promise to save a spot for me."

"Thank you once again, my friend," Jaren said with genuine warmth, as he clasped his hand tightly.

Ansel opened the door for the prince, and bowed as Jaren stepped between four An'ilden warriors. They saluted him by striking their breastplates and then proceeded to escort him down the corridor to the wide hall which led down the length of the abbey. Upon stepping into the hall, Jaren was surrounded by seven priests and seven pastors. Each priest wore a white alb, a dark green dalmatic with gold trim, and a gold satin stole with an embroidered cross at each end. The seven pastors were robed in soft, white wool. Each wore a heavy pewter chain with a simple pewter cross resting upon their chests. Seven of these clerics held a cushion of rich scarlet velvet, with golden tassels hanging from the corners. Upon each cushion lay a different item to be used during the coronation: the King's sword, the royal crown, the royal signet ring and scepter, the ancestral copy of the Word, a golden cross, and a fist-sized golden orb. The imperial purple mantle, weighing well over four stones, was carried by two of the clerics.

Twenty-four choirboys, dressed in black cassocks overlaid with white lace-trimmed surplices, preceded the clerics, singing praises to Elyon in their high, pure voices.

The Birth of a King

Hawk and Tanner stepped in behind Jaren, a solemn smile on their faces. Upon seeing Hawk, Jaren remembered Elyon's promise that the dragons would be kept safe and that he would be instructed in re-establishing the relationship between the Sanda Aran and his dragons. With the burden of the dragons made much lighter in that moment, Jaren squared his shoulders and breathed deeply of the morning air as they reached the doors of the abbey; he smiled broadly with anticipation.

The large company was escorted by a full cohort of An'ilden warriors with tall spears and shining breastplates and shields. The avenue along which the prince's procession passed was lined with hundreds of people who had come from all over Kinthoria to see their new King. Many knew that their lives would be at risk for having made the journey to pledge their allegiance to this Cathain heir. There were many spies in Kinthoria, all anxious to feel the weight of Dragonmaster coins in their purses.

But such thoughts were far from the minds of these loyal people, as they saw their Prince walking in such regal splendor. Shouts of "Hail! Long live the King!" and songs of praise were deafening as Jaren and his procession made their way up the short distance from the abbey to the Cathedral.

After climbing the twenty-four steps to the massive doors of the edifice, they entered into the cavernous nave, and began the long walk down the center aisle to the broad dais at the front of the sanctuary. As soon as Jaren entered the cathedral, the gigantic organ, which filled the gold gilt apse at the front of the nave, sounded the solemn notes of the regal procession.

Archbishop McLaren stood smiling at the top of the dais, awaiting Jaren's arrival. He was adorned in layers of magnificent clothing, completed by an amice of white brocade embroidered in golden thread, the wide collar and hem heavily encrusted with gold filigree and pearls. Atop his head sat a tall white and gold miter.

Pastor Duncan stood beside him in a new white robe of softest wool; a belt of twisted gold threads encircled his waist and hung to his knees; each end was adorned with a golden tassel. He trembled with joy and excitement.

The Birth of a King

The choir boys filed in to make four rows, two on each side of the lower steps of the dais. The priests and pastors ascended the dais to stand in a line across the middle of the dais. The seven clerics who held the scarlet pillows stood in the center of this group. The An'ilden warriors formed up in two rows on each side at the back wall of the nave. Hawk and Tanner took their places beside Korthak at the front row of the assembly.

When Jaren had ascended the steps of the dais, the Archbishop directed him to kneel on a large, scarlet cushion, and then lifted the cross which was hanging from its chain around his neck. Jaren kissed the cross reverently, thinking of its significance, and thanking Elyon for his salvation. As the Archbishop held his hand over Jaren's head to beseech the Father's daily cleansing of the young man's soul, and to sanctify him for the Father's use, a priest stepped forward and held forth the Book of the Word. The Archbishop lifted the book, held it for Jaren to kiss, and handed it back to the priest.

The priest opened the Word, and the Archbishop's resonant voice echoed through the vaulted ceiling of the nave as he read an ancient song urging all people everywhere to sing joyfully to Elyon, to serve Him gladly, and to know beyond doubt that He is the true God. "Praise Him, our Creator; be thankful to Him and bless His holy name. Know that He is good and that He gives mercy to all generations."

"*Sursum corda. Laudamus dominum Deum nostrun.*" "Lift up your hearts. Let us praise the Lord, the true God," the choir chanted in antiphonal response to this reading of the Word. The Archbishop held his hands over Jaren's head once again. "Our Holy Father, we ask that Your mercy and Your truth may dwell upon this Royal House through all its generations in the presence of Your Divine Spirit." The congregation responded, "Amen."

Pastor Duncan began to speak. "Jaren Iain Renwyck Cathain, do you hereby publicly profess your faith in the One True God, Elyon, the everlasting Father?"

Jaren lifted his eyes to both of the men standing before him. "I do."

The Birth of a King

"And do you also believe in His Holy Son, Yesha, the King and Lord, supreme above all others; the One Who's sacrifice redeems those who believe in Him?"

"I do."

"Finally, do you believe in Elyon's Spirit, the One Who protects, empowers, instructs, and keeps our souls in the Truth of our Father and Yesha, His Son?"

"I do," Jaren stated once more, in a voice full of quiet assurance.

The Archbishop lifted the golden cross from its crimson cushion and held it before Jaren to kiss in public confirmation of his faith in the salvation made available to him by Yesha's sacrifice.

The entire congregation began to sing, the choir joining in with antiphonal strains that wove in and out of the melody in a fashion which could only be described as heavenly. Jaren was deeply moved by the unearthly beauty of the sound. He felt as though he should know this song; he recognized, in its lilting melody, and in its masterful crescendos, faint traces of the song which he had heard the forest singing, on the very first day of their long journey. He thought he heard part of the haunting tune which Hawk had whistled on the road from Doddridge on that day which seemed long years in the past.

This reading of the Word with a choral response was repeated twice more, each time followed by a prayer by the Archbishop or by Duncan.

After the last of the beautiful strains had diminished and faded away for the final time, and Pastor Duncan had prayed over Jaren, McLaren helped the young man to his feet. He turned to Duncan and nodded his head slightly, and together they took the heavy, purple velvet imperial mantle from the priests and placed it around Jaren's shoulders. The Archbishop lifted Jaren's left hand and slipped onto his index finger the golden signet ring, its large ruby deeply engraved with the Cathain coat-of-arms. In doing so, McLaren noticed how badly the young man's hands were shaking, and he sent out a calming word to his mind. *"Take a couple of slow, deep breaths, lad. It will help to calm you. And don't worry; if this was not supposed to happen, you wouldn't be here. Remember the Father's*

Power and presence are sufficient for anything you will ever face as King. All things are in His hands."

Duncan placed the scepter into Jaren's right hand, and smiled his reassurance as he pressed the prince's hand between his own.

Then McLaren and one of the priests helped Jaren kneel once again. The young man bowed his head and the Archbishop placed his hands in the sign of the cross on top of Jaren's golden hair, and began to pray. "Father, we humbly ask that You would, by Your presence within, be the strength of Jaren Iain Renwyck Cathain; confer Thy wisdom upon him; grant him a long and prosperous life; keep in his right hand the scepter of salvation; sit on the throne of his heart and rule in righteousness; administer his earthly rule; and keep him safely unto Thyself. *In nomine Patris, et Filius, et Spiritus Sanctus.*"

Jaren swallowed back the urge to weep, as he thought how thankful he was that Elyon was fully capable of answering such weighty requests.

He opened moist eyes to watch as the Archbishop turned and lifted the royal crown from its cushion. He held it out for Pastor Duncan to place his hands upon and together they lifted it high, as McLaren intoned a blessing upon it. Then they lowered it onto the head of the young man who was feeling humbler and smaller with the conferring of each additional symbol of his royalty.

As Jaren closed his eyes and felt the weight of the crown press down upon his head, he saw once again, the face of his father, bent over him with that look of love in his eyes. *"My son, Jaren Iain Renwyck Cathain, receive the love for family, the love for your people and your kingdom. Receive the desire to rule with justice and compassion, and with all of the combined knowledge and wisdom of your forebears. I, Cadan Brys Renwyck Cathain, place this..."* "crown upon your head. *In nomine Patris, et Filius, et Spiritus Sanctus.*" Jaren once again became aware of the Archbishop's voice, but he would forever be grateful to the Heavenly Friend, Elyon's Spirit for allowing him this one special moment with his father during his coronation. It was such a sacred and treasured moment that he resolved never share it with another living soul.

The Birth of a King

The Archbishop stared down into Jaren's young face. "This prominent and visible adornment to the head shall forever be a sign of evidence that the King of Kings Himself hath crowned thee with unseen hands, the Head of the Throne of all Kinthoria."

Next, he took up the golden orb and placed it in Jaren's left hand. Once more, he made the sign of the cross over the young man's head and spoke, "*In nomine Patris, et Filius, et Spiritus Sanctus.*"

Then with a loud, booming voice he cried, "Jaren Iain Renwyck Cathain, thou hast been crowned by Elyon, given by Elyon, filled by Elyon, and adorned by Elyon. As it has been done throughout history, by thy father, and thy father's fathers, I urge thee to receive this orb and scepter, which are the discernible signs of the lands that are now subject to thee, and of the ruling power that has been bestowed upon thee, from the Most High, to wield over the peoples of Kinthoria, that thou mightest rule them, and offer to them imperial aid for which they implore."

The Archbishop turned toward the congregation and directed them to kneel in prayer before Elyon. He then held up his hands and beseeched, "Our most Holy Father, our beloved Master, our Divine Helper, we open our hearts to you. Search each one and fill us with Yourself. Bring Thy cleansing and Thy healing to us in our need. Be within us Love for our fellow man. Be our understanding and pour through us Your purifying forgiveness toward others. Rise up within us that we may long after You as the hart pants for the water brook, so that our days may be lived in Your presence until the Day of Redemption. In Thy Name we pray. Amen."

Jaren, now so familiar with the presence of Elyon's Spirit, immediately recognized the touch of his Friend. But never before had His Power come upon the young man with such strength. Jaren's legs felt weak and his heart was racing. The powerful Love of Elyon which he had first felt in the copse on the banks of the Shandra now encompassed him, washing over him in wave upon wave, reassuring him of his Father's never-ending presence, protection, and love. Jaren knew that from this moment forward, he would never again doubt his worth in the Father's eyes, nor would he ever forget the extent of Yesha's love for him - a love that had offered itself up and made the ultimate sacrifice centuries before Jaren was even born.

The Birth of a King

"Adsum Domine. Regere servum Tui." "Here am I, Lord. Guard Thy servant. Teach me in Thy way, upon which Thou hast placed my feet, and sent me forth." He continued praying earnestly, "Be my wisdom and lead me forward into this great ministry of governance over this realm."

Archbishop McLaren and a priest helped him to stand once more, and turned him to face the congregation for the first time since entering the Cathedral. The choir began a jubilant anthem of praise, and just at that moment, Solance burst through a large circular window set near the top of the eastern wall of the nave; its brilliant morning rays poured down upon the King of Kinthoria. Suddenly, it seemed Elyon's presence became nearly palpable throughout the nave, causing many to join their voices with those of the choir in praise to Him. Soon, the whole congregation was once again singing spontaneously with a vigor which could not have been suppressed, even were their new King to command it.

The notes of the anthem died away just as the bright ray of sunshine subsided. However, much to the astonishment of every person in the cathedral, the King's face continued to glow softly beneath his crown, as though lit by some quiet, inner light. As gasps and loud whispers began rippling through the congregation, the Archbishop cautiously reached out his hand to Jaren and led him to the edge of the dais. He bowed, and stepped back three paces. "I present to you, His Royal Majesty, Jaren Iain Renwyck Cathain, High King of all Kinthoria, Prince of all Regions, Lord of the Seven Races, the dragons' Sanda Aran!" he shouted as loudly as possible through a throat constricted with amazement.

The cathedral bells began peal upon peal, announcing the new king to the world. Everywhere trumpets and cornets declared this first victory over the Dragonmasters. The congregation burst forth once more into jubilant shouts. The applause and the cheering of the people were deafening, as they took the light in Jaren's face as a sign of absolute confirmation that this truly was the chosen King. Word of the King's aura quickly spread to the people massed outside the cathedral and shot through the crowds lining the streets.

Jaren stood looking out over his people, unaware of his nimbus. He rejoiced with them that this first step had been accomplished

The Birth of a King

toward the freeing of Kinthoria. His heart burst with love for them, and he longed to be a king worthy of such trust and loyalty.

The cheering and gaiety continued on for more than a quarter of an hour, as the aura slowly faded from the King's face. Finally, the Archbishop stepped forward, raising his hands for silence. Even at that, it took several more minutes before the congregation was quiet enough for him to be heard.

"Our new King wishes to exercise one of his rights as the Sovereign of Kinthoria."

Jaren glanced mischievously at Hawk and Korthak, who were each barely keeping a check on their delight.

The new King motioned two of the clerics to step forward, and laid his scepter and orb on the scarlet cushions.

"I now bid Tanner aP MacKechnie to stand before his King," the Archbishop commanded. Hushed whispers raced through the nave.

Tanner stared in disbelief as though he had not heard the man correctly. Korthak elbowed him. "Go on, son," he whispered. Tanner began what seemed to him the longest walk of his short life, hesitantly crossing the thirty feet of marbled floor between the lofty dais and the congregation. He climbed the stairs, covered with sumptuous crimson Borkau carpeting, to stand before his life-long friend.

The Archbishop's voice rang out once again. "Who will sponsor this young man, and bear witness for him?"

As Korthak moved to join Jaren and Tanner, he said with authority, "I will sponsor him, Your Eminence."

Tanner kept eying Jaren questioningly, but Jaren made a great vocation of purposely ignoring him.

"Your Majesty. Name your chosen witness," ordered the Archbishop.

"Llenyddiaeth aP Braethorn is to be my witness," Jaren responded.

Hawk strode with regal bearing to stand with Korthak on the top step of the dais.

Archbishop McLaren directed the two young men to kneel, facing one another. He bowed his head. "Father, we humbly thank You for the evidence of sending Your Spirit to this assembly today. Now, we ask Your blessing upon these two young men in evidence of Your approval of this most solemn rite in which they are about to participate. Amen."

The Archbishop took a tiny golden cup from the altar and dipping his finger into the oil, anointed Jaren and Tanner on the forehead. As he touched the oil to each of them, he said, "The sign of the gift of the Spirit of Elyon."

A priest came forward, carrying a velvet cushion upon which a white satin stole had been laid. A tiny dagger rested on top of the stole.

The Archbishop lifted the dagger and, taking Jaren's left hand, he ran the dagger lightly across the King's palm.

Tiny drops of blood began to form, as the Archbishop repeated the procedure with Tanner's left palm.

"You have been brothers in heart for as long as you both can remember. I now direct you to join your hands together," he said.

Jaren lifted his hand toward Tanner, smiling reassuringly to his friend. Tanner lifted his hand to Jaren's and clasped it firmly in his own.

The Archbishop wound the satin stole around their hands and tied the ends together. He placed a hand upon each of their heads and prayed, "Most Holy Father, in Thy presence we give outward evidence of an inward binding, by Your hand, of the hearts and souls of these two young men as though they had been born to the same father and mother. May their love and loyalty to one another be lifelong, and may their united efforts be a blessing to all the peoples of Kinthoria and a bane to Your enemies. With full assurance that You have made these two brothers in the truest sense, let no force dare question otherwise, both now and through the ages to come. In the power of Thy Name we pray. Amen."

As the Archbishop said his amen, Tanner suddenly sat back on his heels, placing his free hand on the dais to keep from toppling over. He reeled under the impact of the surge of Elyon's Spirit throughout his body. The young man was changed forever in that instant as the Father gifted him with a capacity for wisdom far beyond his years and education. Tanner knew that this gift was not for himself; but to make him a fit champion and counselor to Elyon's chosen King. He smiled, tears coursing down his cheeks, as he thanked the Father for the power of His wisdom and mercy.

It was apparent to the four men gathered with him, that Elyon desired the congregation to know that He was answering the Archbishop's request in binding them as true brothers, and for the sign of His approval. For a few brief seconds, the aura which had shown through Jaren now shone through his blood brother; evidence which the whole nation must accept in truth.

"From this time forward, you will not only be brothers in your hearts, but you will be forever bound in blood and spirit," the Archbishop's voice broke through Tanner's heady reaction to Elyon's nearness. The Archbishop removed the stole from around their hands as Hawk helped Jaren to his feet. Korthak restrained Tanner from rising by placing a firm hand upon his shoulder.

Archbishop McLaren lifted his face to the congregation once again. "There is yet one more matter of importance with which the King wishes to treat." He winked at Korthak, who then crossed to one of the priests, and received a sword wrapped in scarlet velvet. Hawk received, from another priest, a sword wrapped in purple velvet. Both men returned to present the swords for the Archbishop's blessing.

With a deep bow, Hawk handed Jaren Durgarndur, the ancient sword of his fathers. It was just slightly shorter than the length of Jaren's outstretched arm. The pommel and guard were of the rare "bryn" gold that the dwarves treasure above all other precious metals. The young King slowly pulled the sword from its scabbard and held it upright. It was simple, yet elegant. Its weight and balance were so perfectly suited to him that it felt as if the sword had become an extension of his arm. The blade was wide and the long handle had been fashioned from vruddroth, the ancient mountain oak. His voice rang through the nave, "Tanner aP MacKechnie, with this sword, we exercise the power granted to us through the bloodlines of our ancestors, the royal house of the Cathains. Therefore, hear us, and answer truthfully. Do you, in the presence of all here assembled, swear fealty to us, as rightful heir, and newly crowned King of Kinthoria, and to our heirs hereafter?"

Tanner looked up into the eyes of his King, and said with grave sincerity, "I do."

Jaren touched the flat of his blade to Tanner's left shoulder. "And do you, in the presence of all here assembled, swear fealty to the Knighthood of the true Dragon Army? Do you swear to keep yourself clean in spirit, mind, and body; to protect those who are unable to protect themselves; to keep alert to right any acts of wrong that are done in your presence, or of which you hear by trustworthy persons; to strive till you draw your last breath to serve those virtues which every true and noble knight has sworn to uphold?"

"I do," Tanner answered simply.

Jaren moved the sword to his brother's right shoulder. "And finally, do you, in the presence of all here assembled, swear fealty to Elyon, the one true God in Heaven? To lay hold of your rights as a child of the Father, to repel unrepentant evil lurking in the land, for the physical and spiritual safety of your countrymen; to adhere to the righteous laws of liberty which Yesha has laid down for all who believe in His Name?"

Tanner bowed his head, his throat so constricted with emotion that he could not speak the response running through his mind, *"I will do all this and more, until the day our Father dismisses me from this body."*

Jaren's eyes widened and he paused in surprise and uncertainty. *"Tanner, can you hear me?"* he sent softly...tentatively.

Tanner shook his bowed head, thinking that Jaren had spoken again as he waited for a reply. He raised his eyes to Jaren.

"You can hear my words in your head?" Jaren asked again.

When Tanner heard Jaren speaking without using his mouth, he looked into his friend's eyes in amazement, and nodded.

Jaren quickly suppressed his emotions and lifted the sword to Tanner's head. "As your Sovereign King and brother I command you to rise, Sir Tanner aP MacKechnie, first knight of the renewed Cathain throne."

"What's going on, Jaren? How is this happening?" Tanner asked as he stood rather unsteadily to his feet, shaken by yet another unexpected event.

"Truly, Elyon has made us brothers in every sense. We'll talk later, in the meantime we need to finish here," Jaren sent, smiling broadly and turning his new brother by blood to face the cheering congregation. *"In the meantime, let's keep this new ability of yours just between ourselves."*

After several minutes of celebration, Stephen McLaren held up his hand for silence and whispered for Tanner to face the King once again.

"Sir MacKechnie, take up the sword which was forged for the knighting of Captain Korthak's own son, Shayn, whose life was so foully cut short by our enemies," Jaren said, gesturing toward Korthak.

For a brief moment, sorrow for his son pierced Korthak's heart. He had dreamed of the day in which his own son would take the vows of knighthood, and had commissioned the forging of the beautiful sword the day the child was born. Looking now upon this young man whom he had recently adopted, he grinned broadly and held out the sword.

Tanner shot a look of surprise to the older man. He had never imagined that Korthak would so honor him. His emotions threatened to undo him; too much was changing too quickly.

Tanner stared at the handsome weapon in disbelief; his hand slowly rose and grasped the sword tightly. The weapon was battle ready with a long and wide fuller that would make it possible to deliver quick cuts and blows. The long guard would offer good protection from an opponent's shield or blade. Tanner held the leather wrapped grip, and felt the excellent balance, as though the sword had been forged to fit his hand and his alone. He fingered the dwarven runes along the blade, and said, "What do they mean?"

"*Drakorlak*," Korthak smiled, "In our tongue it would be interpreted "Foe Bane."

Tanner's eyes widened, and he began to tremble. "What did you say?" he whispered.

Korthak reached for Tanner's shoulders to steady him. "What is it, lad? What's wrong?"

Tanner breathed in deeply and said in awe, "Foe Bane is the name I was given for all of my victories at the Aonghas."

The Birth of a King

Korthak was shaken to his core. "What? How can such a thing be?" He gasped. Suddenly, he felt Elyon's Spirit come upon him; he stood quietly and listened to all that Elyon had to say, and then tightly gripped Tanner's forearm. The young man returned the gesture and then pulled him into a fierce embrace.

"Thank you, *father*," Tanner choked, "Thank you for this incredible honor."

"The honor is mine, *son*. We'll have a bit of a talk later. The Father has just given me some news." Korthak whispered.

Tanner beamed and placed the sword in its leather scabbard that was inscribed with the same runes. He belted the blade around his waist. "*Drakorlak* is a gift beyond words. I will wield it with Elyon's strength."

Korthak grinned broadly, *"You have no idea, my son,"* he thought. "May Elyon be with you, *Gil-Enrai*," he said aloud.

Jaren's voice rang out once more. "Safeguard this sword, made sacred by the sacrifice of our beloved Captain, as you would safeguard yourself. Learn its strengths and weaknesses, but place your trust in Elyon, and He will aid you in wielding it wisely and with victory."

Tanner turned to Jaren, understanding everything that his lifelong friend had done for him in the past minutes. He clasped Jaren's arm as tears of joy and gratitude ran unchecked down his cheeks. Jaren vigorously returned the gesture.

Archbishop McLaren stepped forward to address the congregation for a final time. "The majority of you have not yet been made aware that this young man standing with the King as his new Knight has been selected by Elyon as His Chosen Warrior. Therefore, King Jaren has also chosen him as *Gil-Enrai*."

At this declaration, the assemblage burst forth into loud cheers once more. The soldiers and men applauded and yelled loudly, filling the air with shrill whistles. The older women wiped tears from their eyes, the younger women smiled brazenly, clearly inviting Tanner's interest, and then lowered their eyes. Even the cold-hearted little princess of the Murdocks had been moved by the ceremonies. Truth be known, she had been profoundly shocked, and to some degree, fearful upon seeing the aura on Jaren's face after his coronation.

Even in her somewhat indifferent attitude toward Elyon, she knew that it had been His sign of approval upon the new heir, and she remembered with apprehension her disgraceful treatment of the young man the evening before.

"When you told me about the name Foe Bane given to you at the Aonghas, I was too shaken to speak," Korthak said, pouring himself and Tanner a goblet of water. They had slipped away to the privacy of Jaren's reception chamber late in the celebration feast following the coronation. "That turned out to be a good thing, because Elyon's Spirit needed to speak with me. He said Elyon knew before He founded the earth that my own son would die. He said that even then Elyon had determined to give me my 'truest son,' a spiritual son born from my testimony to you about Yesha and the Father. The sword feels like it was made for you because it was, by the will of the true God; and it was named for you by Him. You *are* my son, Tanner, in the truest sense." At that moment, the two men understood that the strong bond between them was a creation of the true God; a bond that could never be broken.

After a lengthy feast, marked by much gaiety and entertainment, the High King held his first court. The heads of the five races loyal to the crown each came before him, with their heirs, and with their ambassadors, and their highest government officials; this time pledging their fealty to the crown, in the precise verbiage required by their particular protocols. The hours wore away into mid-evening, until finally the last of the Murdock contingency had been presented before the weary King.

Jaren, Tanner, and Korthak slowly made their way back to the private apartments with the An'ilden escort. Upon entering the reception chamber, Jaren turned to the guards with a smile. "Well, that's over," he said with relief. "Thank you for your attendance to me through this long day. I would venture to say that no king before me could boast a more magnificent guard. You are dismissed for some much needed rest, gentlemen."

The Birth of a King

The smiling guards struck fists to breastplates, and bowed deeply to honor their King. "It has been our greatest honor, Highness. We bid you good evening, then," said their Lieutenant. Then he posted four of the men outside the door until their replacements should arrive.

Ansel rushed from Jaren's bedchamber; falling to one knee and laying his hand over his heart, he pledged his fealty to the new King.

Jaren laid his hand on the cleric's head and smiled wearily. "Thank you, Ansel. I will always remember that you were the first to address me as your King. Now rise. You may immediately prove your loyalty by pouring me a goblet of wine. I'm about ready to drop from thirst," he said with a laugh.

The monk returned with wine for the three men. Jaren lifted his goblet, "My first decree as King shall be that the King shall take a bath and relax for at least the better part of an hour," he said, and then immediately looked with consternation at Ansel. "That's all right, isn't it? I mean, I don't have any pressing appointments, do I?"

Ansel turned scarlet with embarrassment, at being spoken to in such a manner by his sovereign. It was doubly mortifying that he had done so in front of the Gil'Enrai and the Captain. The young cleric gaped at Jaren in disbelief. "My Liege, the entire world waits upon your pleasure now. You may soak until the world ends if you wish."

As Jaren's eyes lit up with delight, the monk said, barely above a whisper, "Of course, the kitchen staff may be a bit miffed, not to mention all of the ladies who will be spending the next two hours primping and preening to out shine one another at this evening's celebrations. Also, not to mention the husbands who have been put through torture by their wives, told what to wear, what to say...all of that sort of thing. You know the procedure, your Majesty."

Jaren's face grew distorted with horror. "No! I don't know! But it sounds like slow torture. Korthak! Is the treatment of husbands by their wives truly so?" he asked plaintively.

"Alas, I fear so, my Liege," Korthak said with greatly animated compassion.

"Well then, I'm never getting married," Jaren stated with finality.

The Birth of a King

"'Tis truly a bitter pill, but, as King one must have heirs if one desires for his line and his family name to continue," Korthak retorted.

"Is there any way I could maybe adopt an heir, so I wouldn't have to get married?" Jaren pleaded.

The old bear of a man put his arm across the King's shoulders, "I'm afraid that would be impossible under your circumstances, Jaren. It is a fairly well established tradition that the royal blood must run through the veins of the heir to a dynasty. People might get a little nervous if their monarchy started trying to fix a perfectly good system of perpetual governance."

Jaren plodded toward the bathing chamber, with sagging shoulders under a feigned pall of depression. His friends studiously ignored his martyred expression, to all appearances unaware of his hopeless state. He sighed heavily. "So much for a leisurely bath; we certainly wouldn't want the cooks to be unhappy...or the ladies... or all those poor...*unfortunate*, maligned husbands," he said with a shudder.

Despite Jaren's theatrics, he did spend enough time in the warm baths to be completely refreshed. As the companions lazed in the warmth of the bathing pool, Jaren spoke silently to Tanner. *"Tanner, let's have that little talk now."*

A slight splash in the water was the only evidence of Tanner's surprise at Jaren's mind voice. *"Okay. So what's going on? Why can I hear you speak in my head?"*

Jaren grinned, and closing his eyes he relaxed even deeper into the water, resting his head on the steps of the pool. *"You can hear me speak because you are now as real a brother to me as is humanly possible. As such, you have become a member of the ruling Cathain house, which entitles you to this ability. I don't believe even Hawk or my uncle suspected that such a thing would happen when I told them I wanted to publicly acknowledge you as my blood brother. I know I certainly was surprised."*

"Surprise is a little short of what I was feeling," Tanner said, giving Jaren a wry glance. *"So, you're telling me that an actual miracle took place today, making me a real Cathain?"*

"It would seem so...brother," Jaren sent with a feigned sigh and just a touch of nonchalance. He was relieved that his friend had not made the connection between the Cathain line and Hawk, and he wondered how long it would be before Tanner put the pieces together by recalling the events at the Spring of Elyon.

"Dols..." was Tanner's only reply. After considering what Jaren had said, he asked, *"Wait a minute. Have you been able to do this your whole life and never let me know? Who did you talk to with your mind? Why didn't you let me in on your secret?"*

Jaren choked down a chuckle. *"Whoa! The answers are no, no one and because I didn't have a secret to tell. I received my ability at the Spring of Elyon during my transformation."* Jaren fished about for a way to turn the conversation away from any further proximity to Hawk. *"I think it will be very amusing to talk to one another any place, any time and about anything we want."*

"Yeah," Tanner responded eagerly, already planning how to send Jaren little *surprises* from time to time...he would thoroughly enjoy watching Jaren's reactions to his mental ambushes.

A short time later, he and Tanner were taking advantage of the courtyard gardens and the cool evening twilight.

The Princess Kyriel joined them some time later, hoping to undo some of the damage she had done to Jaren's opinion of her the previous evening. True to Ansel's predictions, she had rushed to her apartment after Jaren had dismissed the court, and had been painstakingly doing and re-doing everything about her attire, from her hair to her fifth pair of dainty slippers.

The trio were being discreetly followed and guarded by a new contingent of An'ilden. They were enjoying the antics of Maladi, Senjau, and Chenju as they were engaged in mock swordplay.

Jaren had noted with relief that Kyriel was not nearly so cold and obnoxious as she had been the night before. He was entirely unaware that his kindly and generous gestures toward Tanner had deeply touched her. She had begun to rethink all of her previous, and obviously incorrect, judgments regarding him, and was gaining a profound interest in this strange young King. She could not deny that in every situation, he had conducted himself with high dignity, and an almost casual ease, as though a regal bearing was as natural

The Birth of a King

as breathing to him. She admitted to herself with chagrin that he had behaved much more like royalty than herself. *"Well, that is easily remedied,"* she thought, her former disdain for this would-be monarch being so automatic that the thought was there before she realized it. *"I can out shine this ragamuffin blindfolded. He's obviously putting on an act to make people think he belongs among his betters."*

Suddenly, she realized what had happened and she blushed with anger at herself. Even in a girl as fiery tempered, self-centered, and cynical as Kyriel, there was a side that wanted things to be what they truly seemed to be; a side that wanted more than anything to be swept off her feet by a knight in shining armor; a side that desired lifelong love.

Jaren saw her rosy cheeks and decided that the cold little princess was at least capable of enjoying the evening breeze.

"Maladi, you need to turn your sword out when you are attacked like that," Senjau offered to his little brother, trying valiantly to use the stern and authoritative voice which he had heard his father's own Weapons Master use while training his troops.

Maladi's small face contorted in a quizzical look, as he tried to put his brother's instruction into practice.

Tanner turned to Jaren, his face beaming. "Shall you and I give them a practical lesson in swordplay?"

Jaren shrugged his shoulders. "I don't know." He looked at the Princess. "Is that proper behavior for a King?" he asked teasingly.

Kyriel rolled her eyes and let out a sigh of exasperation, shooing both young men away with a toss of her hand.

Jaren cleared his throat and lifted his chin. "Well, I suppose I could look at it in the sense that we are training our future knights."

Tanner stood by Maladi, and showed him the proper way to hold his stick sword. He gestured for Jaren to attack, as Senjau had just done with the lad. When Jaren thrust with Senjau's twig sword, Tanner turned his wrist and easily flicked it out and away, rendering the attack harmless.

"There, you see, Maladi?" Tanner asked the beaming little boy. He moved the sword to Maladi's hand and wrapped his own hand

The Birth of a King

around the boy's. He flicked the child's wrist, so that Maladi could feel the result of the action upon his "sword."

Tanner looked up to smile at Jaren, remembering the lessons he had given his friend through the years. He noticed a monk standing several yards behind the new King. Something wasn't right about the man, and Tanner felt the hair stand up on the back of his neck. He glanced quickly to the An'ilden warriors, who had also taken a keen interest in the odd monk. Two of the men were already circling behind him, feigning casual talk, while others seemed to be thoroughly enjoying the lesson in swordplay as they moved to stand beside the Princess.

Tanner did not think it wise to alert Jaren to the situation and possibly cause the younger children to panic. He forced a laugh and picked up Maladi, bringing him closer to Jaren and Senjau. "Senjau, why don't you take Maladi to sit with the Princess Kyriel? The King and I will show you some real sword fighting, alright? Chenju, be careful to stay a good distance away."

The delighted boys ran off, laughing with excitement at the prospect of seeing their King and the Gil-Enrai put on a fight with real swords just for their amusement.

Tanner kept smiling, as he taunted Jaren into the swordplay. Looking past Jaren, he could just make out the sinister, half-crazed look in the monk's eyes, hidden within his cowl. The cheering and laughter of the Princess and the boys blurred into muffled sound as he steadied himself for the attack he knew was surely coming as the monk slowly advanced on the King.

His heightened senses saw the trace of movement, which even the An'ilden did not detect. With lightning speed, he reacted by tackling Jaren to the ground. He thrust his sword hilt into the lawn beside him, knowing as surely as did his enemy that the man could not stop quickly enough to keep himself from falling onto the blade.

Two An'ilden dived at him from behind, grabbing his feet and causing him to fall forward.

Tanner's blade pierced him square through the heart, and within seconds, the hooded figure lay still.

"Hawk! An assassin in the courtyard," Jaren had quickly sent the thought to Hawk.

The Birth of a King

Hawk jumped up and shouted the words "assassin in the courtyard" to Korthak and they raced to the other side of the gardens.

The An'ilden warriors had moved Tanner and Jaren away from the assassin, and over to the hysterical princess.

Little Maladi was screaming in terror, but the older Senjau was making the peculiar war clicks and high-pitched *whoots* to call his father's men to their aid.

The quiet Chenju stood like a stone sentinel between his King and the fallen assassin, he eyes searching for any trace of movement, ready to attack, should the man not be truly dead. His fingers deftly held a shining, thin dagger.

It took but moments for the entire courtyard to fill with people, causing confusion and chaos everywhere.

Hawk and Korthak pushed through the throng to reach Jaren and Tanner.

"Is everyone all right?" Hawk questioned, his eyes hurriedly taking in every inch of the King.

Tanner shook his head, and pointed to the still body of the monk, lying impaled on his sword. "He's not," he said in hot rage.

"Your Highness," Hawk took hold of Jaren's arm, pulling him away from the others. "Jaren, what you did for me back in the Glamorgan Mines after the rockslide...." he whispered.

Jaren paled and shot Hawk a look of horror.

"Do it now," he ordered the young man. "We need to know who this man is and if he was working alone or with others. We need to know why he attempted this."

"But, Hawk," Jaren whispered in shock, "that wasn't my doing in the cave! I was as surprised as the rest of you. The Master wanted you alive, so He brought you back."

"Just try it, Jaren; we really need information from him."

Jaren looked deeply into Hawk's eyes, wondering why his friend couldn't seem to understand that he had no power to choose whom he would help and whom he wouldn't. Finally, seeing that Hawk was adamant, Jaren walked slowly and reluctantly to the body of the dead man.

"Don't touch his dagger," Hawk warned. "It's probably been dipped in poison."

Hawk and Tanner lifted the body from the sword and rolled it over. Jaren was horrified to see the blood still pouring from the wound in the man's chest. He knelt down beside him, aware of the people as they began crowding around, speaking in hushed whispers.

He turned pleading eyes to Hawk. "What happened in the mines was based on love; both mine and Yesha's," he said softly, his voice breaking. "How can you ask me to even think of trying this with someone who has just attempted to kill me?"

Korthak laid a quieting hand on Jaren's shoulder, as Hawk pressed his will upon the King.

"I know this seems unthinkably cold and heartless to ask of you, lad," he whispered. "But I need information. The only way I can get it is if you bring him back to us."

Jaren, tears streaming down his face, laid his trembling hands on the still warm body. Bile rose in his throat at the touch of the lifeless form. He willed his eyes closed, and began to pray. "Father, please forgive this man for the wrong he has done…."

Then his resolve faltered. How could he pray such a prayer for this man who had come so close to killing him? Anger surged inside his mind. Why should he pray for Elyon to forgive an assassin? If the man's soul was in hell right now, it was no less than he deserved. Jaren wanted to beat and tear at the body of this traitor, instead of asking the Father to restore his life and forgive him.

Then, in his mind's eye, he saw Yesha, beaten beyond recognition, and suffering cruelly as He gave up His life. He heard his Master pray as He gasped for air against restricted lungs, "Father, forgive them…." Jaren's anger shattered in that instant and he asked for Elyon to forgive his hatred for this dead man, and asked Him once more, this time with sincerity, to forgive the man.

Those who were able to see the King's actions thought that Jaren was praying for the man's soul. It was beyond their imagination that he should be praying for the man's life to be restored. Only Jaren's close companions knew what was taking place in the silent King's mind.

Jaren prayed earnestly, truly willing life to return in the assassin's still body. After quite some time, Jaren sighed and opened his

The Birth of a King

eyes. He stared at Hawk apologetically. "Nothing more can be done for him," he said simply.

Hawk nodded, and bowed his head. He knelt beside the still figure, and began to slowly search the man's cassock, trying to avoid the blood soaked cloth. He found a small vial, tucked into the folds of the cloth, which he assumed held a potent poison. However, not yet satisfied with his search, he continued. Soon, he gave a slight yank with his hand, and lifted a chain upon which hung a small medallion. The image of the face which Volant had seen hanging from the ceiling of the forbidden Lucian temple, leered from the front of the silver piece. Hawk lifted it to Jaren, his face frozen with anger and resolve. "It's all right, Jaren. I have a pretty good idea where this man came from...and who sent him," he said with ominous quiet.

APPENDIX A

LIST OF CHARACTERS

ABERYSTWTH aP IFANDER - ancient Elven King who rules in Lleynhaven. Shares highest seat on Elven Council with King Gwilym.

ALANNA - murdered Queen of Kinthoria. Wife of Cadan, mother of Jaren.

ANDARIN RENWYCK ADUWIN CATHAIN – Prince. Second son of King Chricton. Married to Ghleanna.

ANDREJ D'JERBRIN - regent of the Thigherns under K'Jarem.

AN'ILDEN – proud and ancient warrior race of Kinthoria.

ANSEL, BROTHER - monk at Saint Ramsay's, personal valet to Jaren.

ATHDARAGS – woodworkers. People of the water and woods.

BALGO - dwarven friend of Hawk and Korthak. Sometime guide and companion to Jaren. Married to Leonora.

BELAND - former Flight Leader and General in Dragonmaster Army. Now old, but the trusted advisor to Volant.

BENDOR - Red Flight Leader in Dragonmaster Army. Volant's chosen successor.

BRAETHORN CAMERON IVRY CATHAIN – Prince. Brother of King Chricton and Queen Cadhal. Hawk's human father. A commander in King Chricton's Army. Became a liason to the elves, and post commander. Married to Idril.

BRANN IFAN ALWYN CATHAIN - Prince. Second son of Iain, brother of King Cadan. Uncle to Jaren. Murdered in Dragonmaster coup.

BRANT MacKECHNIE - second youngest son of Denham and Folanna. Brother of Tanner. Age 16.
BRYNNA - elven wife of Trevylan.
BRYTH - rider in the Red Flight.
CADAN BRYS RENWYCK CATHAIN - murdered King of Kinthoria. Eldest son of Iain. Married to Queen Alanna. Father of Jaren.
CADAWG – young courier for Volant.
CADHLA - Queen. Wife of Chricton Cathain. Great-Grandmother to Jaren.
CAECR – Beland's dragon.
CALUM O'FELAN - Earl of the Midhe Tuatha
CAMERON BRYS ARIN CATHAIN – former King of Kinthoria. Married to Gwyllenbrae.
CATHRYN ELLENBRAE - Princess of Kinthoria. Daughter of Iain. Sister of Cadan. Aunt to Jaren.
CAVAN MacAULEY - leader in resistance to Dragonmasters. Brutally murdered for his An'ilden bloodlines, and for his "treason" against the Dragonmasters under Volant.
CEARA - widowed Queen of the An'ilden. Mother of Seanachan
CELEBRIÄN SURION - elven wife of Hawk. Mother of Trevylan.
CHADWYCK, BROTHER - monk at Saint Ramsay's who befriended Tanner.
CHARA D'JDAE - daughter of Churyn. Twin sister of Melfi. Age 6.
CHENJU - son of Nan-Jing. Heir to position of High Clansman of the Athdarags. Age 14.
CHRICTON IFAN ARIN CATHAIN - previous King of Kinthoria. Great-Grandfather to Jaren. Married to Queen Cadhla.
CHURYN D'JDAE - Grand Elder of the Thigherns. Married to Tynda. Father of Senjau, Maladi, Melfi, and Chara.
COLIN MacKECHNIE - youngest son of Denham and Folanna. Brother of Tanner. Age 15.
CORUNNA DANAGELD - Queen of the Murdocks. Married to Falkirk. Mother of Jashon, Eadwin, and Kyriel.
CUINN, FATHER - Monk, and Guest Master at Saint Ramsay's.
DAK GLAMORGAN – dwarven owner of Glamorgan mines.

The Birth of a King

DENHAM MacKECHNIE - father of Rhondda, Tanner, Brant, and Colin. Husband of Folanna. Died of Dust Plague in third year of the war with the Dragonmasters.

DERICK, BROTHER - Monk and guardian of the gate at Saint Ramsay's

DEVYN BREWSTER - Proprietor, Golden Eagle Inn, Doddridge. Member of Kinthorian underground rebellion.

DIMTIL – dwarknyri of the Ragdukr

DREAG – Lucian priest

DUNCAN - Pastor, evangelist.

DWARVES – Miners and metalworkers. People of the mountains.

EADWIN DANAGELD- Prince of the Murdocks. Second oldest son of Falkirk. Brother of Jashon and Kyriel.

EAMON, BROTHER - Monk at Saint Ramsay's.

EIHLIN CHRICTON ARIN CATHAIN - Prince of Kinthoria. Youngest son of Iain. Murdered during Dragonmaster coup. Brother of Cadan. Uncle to Jaren.

ELVES – Historians, artisans, music masters. People of the deep woods.

ELYON – the One True God

FAGAN, BROTHER - falconer at Saint Ramsay's.

FALKIRK DANAGELD - High King of the Murdock Clans. Chieftain of the Laigin Tuatha. Married to Corunna. Father of Jashon, Eadwin, and Kyriel.

FERNAIG - wizened and ancient dwarf of Parth. One of the Elders of the Dwarves. Instructor in the Word to Jaren and Tanner.

FOLANNA MacKECHNIE - Wife of Denham. Mother of Rhondda, Tanner, Brant and Colin.

GALCHOBAR - most powerful high priest in the Lucian sect.

GAVIN MacLEAN - Baron of the Donnacht Tuatha.

GHLEANNA – Princess. Married to Prince Andarin.

GIMMALK – dwarknyri of the Calrunak

GRAETH - young dwarf who attends King Fernaig.

GWILYM aPAWANIL - ancient Elven King who rules in Cairnhaven. Shares highest seat on Elven Council with King Aberystwth.

GWYLLENBRAE – former Queen of Kinthoria.

HAROUN D'JINSOK - governor of the Thigherns under K'Jarem.

The Birth of a King

HARERG – dwarknyri of the Chalgrunalk

HWINDIR – artisan who sketched the Cathain coat-of-arms.

IAIN CHRICTON BRYS CATHAIN - previous King of Kinthoria. Married to Queen Aislyn. Father of Cadan, Brann, Rinion, Eihlin, and Cathryn. Grandfather to Jaren.

IDRIL FELAGUND - elven mother of Hawk. Married to Braethorn.

JASHON DANAGELD - Prince of the Murdocks. Eldest son of Falkirk. Heir to the Murdock throne.

JAREN IAIN RENWYCK CATHAIN - King of Kinthoria. Exiled son of Cadan and Alanna. Spent his childhood in the Scholars' Hall at Reeban until located by Hawk.

JEROME, BROTHER - Monk and deformed Athdarag gardener at Saint Ramsay's.

JICAE LINET– Princess. Married to Prince Brann. Murdered in Dragonmaster coup.

KEB – weapons master in Keratha

KEKN – Bendor's dragon.

KORTHAK McKONAR - Captain in King Cadan's Army. Wife Megen and infant son Shayn were murdered in Dragonmaster coup.

KYRIEL DANAGELD - Murdock Princess. Spoiled and high strung daughter of Falkirk and Corunna.

LEONORA - wife of Balgo. Hostess to Jaren and his company during their stay in Parth.

LLENYDDIAETH aP BRAETHORN - Emrys aP Pendragon of Kinthoria. War Chancellor to King Cadan. Half-elven, half-human. Under oath to return Cathain blood to the throne. Married to Celebrän. Father of Trevylan. Common name of Hawk.

LOK – Volant's dragon.

LUCIA – evil god of the Lucian religion. Enemy of the One True God

MAAIN – dwarknyri of the Klduuim

MALADI - second son of Churyn. Age 8.

MARLIN, BROTHER - monk and monastic chamberlain at Saint Ramsay's.

MAVI - slave girl in Keratha. Unknowing captor of Bendor's heart.

MEGEN McKONAR - murdered wife of Korthak. Mother of Shayn.

MELFI D'JDAE – son of Churyn. Twin brother of Chara. Age 6.
MERRICK - cousin of King Cadan. Hunting companion.
MURDOCKS – Seamen. People of the coasts and waterways.
NAN-JING - High Clansman of the Athdarags. Father of Chenju.
NIERIEL BRONWYN – Princess. Daughter of King Chricton and Queen Cadhla who died in infancy.
NORORIL – dwarknyri of the Gilraggak
PRITAN – former Purple Flight Leader.
RATHAK – First Lieutenant in the Red Flight.
RHONDDA MacKECHNIE - eldest child of Denham and Folanna. Succumbed to starvation and dust-plague shortly after her father.
ROSS McCAIG - trinket merchant in Doddridge.
SALAMUT D'JAMEN - Thighern merchant in Doddridge.
SEANACHAN - Prince and heir of the An'ilden. Son of Queen Ceara. His name means wisdom.
SELWYN MALLAIG - Duke of the Ulaid Tuatha.
SENJAU - eldest son of Churyn. Heir to position of Grand Elder of the Thigherns. Age 9.
SHAYN McKONAR - murdered infant son of Korthak.
SIRTAR - Colonel and Force Commander of Dragonmaster Army. Blue Flight Leader. Second in authority under Volant.
SORELY - slothful headmaster at Scholars' Hall in Reeban.
STEPHEN McLAREN (RINION IFAN CAMERON CATHAIN) - Archbishop residing at Saint Ramsay's.
TANNER MacKECHNIE - Eldest son of Denham and Folanna. Blood brother
of King Jaren. Duke of Errigal.
THIGHERNS – Horsebreeders. People of the plains.
TOMAS - Purple Flight Leader in Dragonmaster Army.
TREVYLAN - son of Hawk and Celebrän. Married to Brynna.
TULAK - Green Flight Leader in Dragonmaster Army.
TUPPER - shepherd who gave Jaren and his companions food and lodging for the night.
TYNDA D'JDAE - wife of Churyn. Mother of Senjau, Maladi, Melfi, and Chara.
VANESSI - wife of Volant. Empress of Kinthoria.

VOLANT - tyrrannical Emperor of Kinthoria who staged a successful coup over the royal Cathain family. Slave to the evil god Lucia.
YAGGO - Hammerthane of the dwarves.
YESHA – Son of the One True God.
YTURI – Sirtar's dragon.

APPENDIX B

LANGUAGE OF THE ELVES

Aaye - Hail!
Acheyla - Hello
Adrastai – scouts
Alu – water
Ashan'rai – my king
Aut - go
Caedaes - keeper
Corm - heart
Cormamin lindua ele lle - my heart sings to see thee
Dagor úr - battle heat
Dina - be silent
Gil-Enrai - Champion of the King
Il'er herve aP Pendragon – Greetings, wife of the Pendragon
Kaleaneaens - watchers
Kesol – guardian
Lle naa vanima – You are beautiful
Lle ume quell - You did well
Mae govannen – well met
Mahtars - warriors
Nan mankoi bru amin n ala quell, aran? - Why did you call me back, Sire?
Naur- fire
Narwa - remember
Pusta - stop
Ohta aha –-war rage

Ohtars - warriors
Oio naa ele alla alasse - ever is thy sight a joy
Orn - tree
Rauko - demon
Roch - horse
Rolyn - a radiating healing light
Sanda Aran - true King
Senta – spawn
Shalafi - master
Sh'mai - beloved of my soul
Unasae - Don't quit!

APPENDIX C

LANGUAGE OF THE DWARVES

Durgarndor – iron dragon
Drakorlak – foe bane
Dwarknyri – clan leader
Dwarmer – dwarf friend
Mag Caurak – black chasm
Magewyn Glor – a tarn in the Kroth Mountains
Norgrund Ehrak – ancient underground tunnel system under the Kroth mountains

The Birth of a King

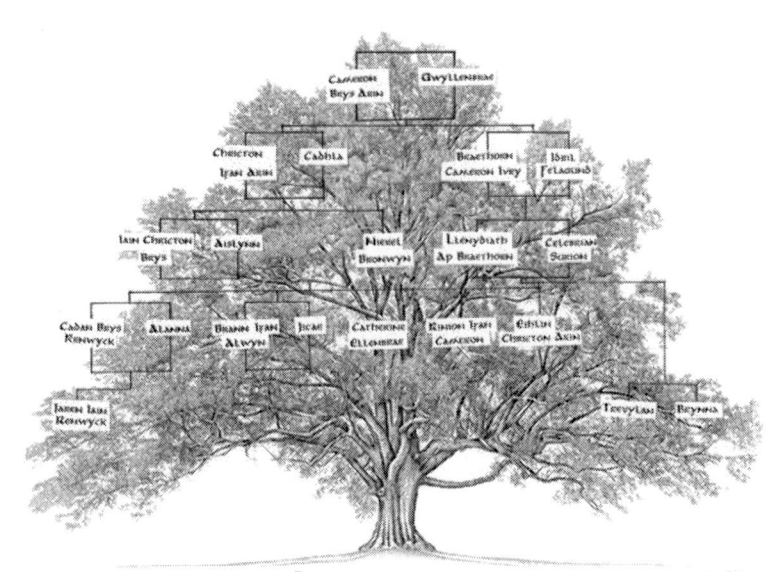

Royal Line of the Cathains

About the Authors

Deborah Marsh is the author of the new Legends of Kinthoria Christian fantasy series. Having long been captivated by numerous science fiction writers, she has developed a strong desire to create her own fantasy world suffused with her Christian faith and beliefs. Deborah is the storyteller and plot designer of this book. Her latest project is working to complete Volume Two of the Legends of Kinthoria series. This can sometimes be a challenge as she "shares her laptop" with four 'furballs' and a hundred and ten pound dog.

Carol Marsh is a detail person and is co-author only by having fleshed out this story while thoroughly enjoying a growing friendship with its characters and watching the plot develop in her daughter's wonderfully fertile mind. Carol is in the process of developing a series of children's books which she plans to publish in collaboration with her sister.

Cover layout design: Dominic Catalano and Deborah Marsh
Cover illustration: Carol Marsh
Map: Carol Marsh and Deborah Marsh
Authors' picture: Weston Marsh